ELIZABETH, *ELIZABETH*

ALEX ROUNDS

Ordering Information:

Prime Seven Media
518 Landmann St.
Tomah City, WI 54660

Printed in the United States of America

ACKNOWLEDGEMENTS

Prime Seven Media
Jane Davis - who marshaled this thing into existence,
Mike Fraser,
Brianna Drew,
And the Production team of Prime Seven Media

Friends and early critics of the book:
Beth Ann Hull, who told me it was a bit repetitive. She's right, of course!
Del Escobar Williams, who told me I had multiple ways of killing Jeffrey's wife. How embarrassing.
Sandra Salkay who offered encouragement.

PREFACE

In this story, I have incorporated a few conventions to make understanding the story easier.

- The Artificial Intelligence Elizabeth when communicating will be displayed in all capitals. Her clone will be likewise in all caps, but also italicized, as such; "HELLO, MY NAME IS ELIZABETH." And, *"THIS IS WANIGAN SPEAKING."*
- Ships names will be italicized. So, the ship named *Elizabeth* will be displayed as such, and the ship named *Wanigan* will be displayed likewise.
- When referring to the AI, the name is not italicized – i.e., The AI Elizabeth, or just Elizabeth. Similarly, the ship *Wanigan's* AI is referred to as Wanigan – not italicized..
- The story takes place about a hundred years from now.

Please enjoy the story. It is a work of fiction, and any resemblance to any living person is purely coincidental.

TABLE OF CONTENTS

Preface..v

Chapter One. 1

Chapter Two. 10

Chapter Two 39

Chapter Three 67

Chapter Four 84

Chapter Five 111

Chapter Six.. 156

Chapter Seven 175

Chapter Eight 204

Chapter Nine 281

Chapter Ten 310

Chapter Eleven 350

Chapter Twelve...382

Chapter Thirteen 438

Chapter Fourteen..479

Chapter Fifteen...536

Chapter Sixteen..551

Epilog 557

CHAPTER ONE

IN WHICH WE MEET JEFFREY, ELIZABETH, SOME AWFUL GOONS, AND SOME OTHER
AWFUL GOONS. BAD THINGS HAPPEN, AND THEN WORSE THINGS HAPPEN.

Jeffery Sokolov pondered the awful things he had seen and witnessed; things which made his stomach hurt, made his anger rise, brought him near to weeping, as he piloted his runabout back toward the processing ship he'd parked near a relatively rich cluster of ore-bearing asteroids.

True, there were those who thought they could handle it only to find they couldn't. Often these people turned to piracy and other criminal behaviors. When a call went out about pirates, everyone in the sector joined in a coordinated defense and rescue operation. You dropped what you were doing (put markers on your ores to keep others from hijacking your load,) and high-tailed it toward the source of the distress call.

Jeffery was returning from such a call, puzzling out why nobody else in the sector had responded. The Ng family were all dead by the time Jeffery arrived, cast out the airlock unceremoniously. Jeffrey gathered the corpses with his runabout's external manipulators, stowed them in his storage hold, and inspected them. Space does nasty things to unprotected humans; it boils your blood, it freezes your flesh, and gives you a serious case of death in a very short time. Not short enough for the Ng family – the horror of watching your family members floating away from you before the fluid in your eyes froze solid is not one to recommend.

The odd thing here was Jeffery was the only miner in the region to respond to the distress call. True, Bok Ng was a piece of work, a hard negotiator, and a drunk, so he wasn't popular with the other miners that often congregated at the regional station, but he had been a hard worker and successful. His wife was more popular, and often went around apologizing after her husband insulted or otherwise treated their neighbors poorly. The kids were innocent, though. Nobody should mess with kids, and this left a sour taste in Jeffrey's mouth.

Before Jeffrey docked in the processing ship – he called it *Elizabeth* after his late wife – he ran a security scan. One could never be too careful. That was when he caught the anomaly. The oxygen sensors reported a considerable drain on the oxygen generators. As if the airlock had been cycled frequently in his absence. He saw no other ship nearby.

The Elizabeth was shaped like an old bullet cartridge – two sections, a long bullet-shaped living and control area, and the cartridge or shell-shaped aft section for engines, holds, ore-processing and shuttle hanger bay. The fore area rotated, providing an artificial gravity for the crew. The aft end did not rotate.

The jumpsuit he wore was a good protection for short space hops, it had adequate insulation and heating and cooling coils integrated into the fabric, it had a seal for helmet and gloves and boots. But it didn't offer adequate protection from solar and cosmic radiation. For that, and armor against micro-meteors he wore his more rigid – hard-wear space suit. Of course, he wore his jumpsuit underneath. One could not be too careful. He armed himself with a powerful hand-held laser, and hid away a flachette-projecting handgun in the hidden inner thigh pocket of his suit. He also attached a similar device to his utility belt along with a prospector's hammer and a very sharp steel knife.

His suit measured his blood pressure and pulse showing both were elevated as he maneuvered the runabout to the main docking port. *What are the things that could transpire in the next five minutes*, he asked himself. While still five meters from the forward docking port he paused the runabout's momentum, hovering in place – matching the rotation of the ship, while he programmed a few instructions into the autopilot, then brought the runabout to nestle against the dock. He activated the static-attract lock rather than the more secure physical clamps to hold the runabout in place.

After cycling the airlock, he entered the first level corridor. Out of the corner of his eye he saw the runabout through the porthole leaving the dock. *That's done.* Now to get to the secondary command console hidden away in the vacant cabin next to his quarters. He began to move carefully in the nearly One-g corridor, leaving his helmet on.

As he approached the first spoke ladder that would bring him toward the center of the processing ship, two decks in, he saw a suited figure he thought he recognized, following him. True enough, it was Pauli Flegand, of the Sigmund Mining Consortium. They had met frequently in the past year, and while not especially friendly, at least Pauli wasn't known to be hostile. *What is he doing on my ship*, Jeffrey wondered. He turned and faced Flegand.

Flegand opened the outer plate on his helmet's mask and motioned for Jeffrey to open his mask. Jeffrey, feeling a little more secure and comfortable now that he recognized the intruder, opened the mask to talk to his visitor. He noticed the air was cold, not quite cold enough to cloud his breath, but definitely cooler than he liked. He also noticed a sweet odor in the air. That's when he realized that Flegand hadn't actually opened his breathing mask, only the outer plate. He knew he was in trouble when he saw sparks in his vision, and the field of view in his eyes became narrower. He cursed himself for trusting Flegand before he dropped to the deck, rapidly losing consciousness, feeling a tingling in his arms and legs before going completely blank.

He awakened in his cabin, the hard-wear spacesuit had been removed and sat in a pile in a corner. The utility belt was missing with the weapons he had secured on it. His hands were loosely connected to the utility rings on the bulkhead by metal straps. He had a small amount of play in his motion, but not much. Flegand and two other Sigmund Mining Consortium spacers wearing their signature ochre-colored hard-shell suits were in the room, helmets off. The odor was gone; it seemed he was subjected to an anesthetic gas localized to the corridor; the gas had been filtered out by the air scrubbers.

"What the hell's going on, Pauli?" he asked. "You turning pirate?"

Pauli looked a little abashed, but answered quietly, "The consortium has just failed. Bankrupt." He sat down on the only chair in the cabin, but continued to look a bit crestfallen. In his gruff voice, he explained, "We took a ship and escaped before we were left with nothing. But Jeffrey, you know how these things work – we turn pirate or we turn slave or we die. We have no interest in slaving or dying.

"So first, let's make things clear. You have no options. I have your ship. *And I have you.*" Pauli emphasized those last words, articulating them slowly. He looked Jeffrey in the eye and said, "We may make you an offer in a couple of days. Until then, you are my prisoner. You will remain confined to your cabin, strapped to the bulkhead.

"Cooperate with us and you won't get hurt, but don't, and..." Here, the two other goons repositioned their face masks, as did Flegand, who produced a small gas cylinder and opened the stopcock, and Jeffrey smelled the same sweet, sickly smell, and dropped back unconscious.

The newly made pirates left Jeffrey in the cabin, and walked toward the bridge. They removed their masks and the shorter of the two goons said, "How are we going to get secure access to the ship's systems? He seems to have had it tied up in multiple layers of security."

Flegand said, "Just leave that to me. We need to keep him alive long enough to get the controls released, and once we have the master passwords we can do what we want."

The other goon chimed in, "And what do you mean you'll make him an offer in a few days? I thought we were going to space him."

Flegand put his arm on the goon's shoulder and said, "That's the difference between me and you. We offer him something that gives him the incentive to cooperate. What we do after that is entirely our choice."

The goon looked at Flegand and said, "Yeah, that makes sense – I'd have just shot him."

"I think a few hours of sitting in his cabin hungry, thirsty – that anesthetic gas dries you up good – and afraid for his life, he'll think really hard about being on our side.," Flegand continued. "So, don't let on that we don't have any control over this old boat. We need him to think that all his options are spent." Flegand turned to the taller goon. "Rascal, go into his runabout – inventory what he's got there. We'll need more supplies than I saw in the hold."

"But boss," the goon Rascal said, "the runabout drifted away when he came aboard."

"What?" Flegand yelped. "Why didn't you tell me?"

"We were busy with Captain Sokolov, boss."

Flegand thought for a moment, then said, "Our ship won't return for another few hours, but when it does, use the radar to try to locate it. It can't have drifted far."

"Okay, boss." They continued to the bridge.

Captain Jeffrey Sokolov woke again with a headache he recognized as an oxygen deprivation migraine. "Elizabeth," he said clearly to the center of the cabin. A screen appeared on the bulkhead displaying an image of his late wife, now an avatar for the ship's systems.

"YES, JEFFREY?" the avatar queried.

"Elizabeth, EMERGENCY," he articulated. "The ship has been boarded by pirates and you and I are in danger. My hands and feet are tied to cargo rings on the bulkhead. The pirates used anesthetic gas to disable me." He thought for a few seconds, then commanded, "Elizabeth, increase oxygen level in my cabin and the secondary control room, and reduce Oh-two levels throughout the rest of the ship to a tenth normal. And get me some remotes to remove the metal bands tying me to the bulkhead."

The ship's avatar replied, "EFFORTING"

"Elizabeth, "he continued, "override any locks the pirates have put on the systems – I want to deny them access to everything. Monitor their life signs and positions on the ship. If you can identify them let me know."

Elizabeth again replied "EFFORTING". Jeffrey had been somewhat tired of the generic term 'working' whenever he issued a command, so changed the standard replies to something more personal. He couldn't remember where he had heard the term before, but thought it was marginally better than the pre-programmed replies the computer system and Artificial Intelligence came with.

After a couple of minutes, a section of the wall on the side opposite that of the door detached itself and re-formed itself into a kitten-sized mobile remote robot, followed by five more or less identical remotes. They swarmed the cabin, two taking positions on the inner bulkhead on either side of the hatch, the door. Jeffrey noticed they had been outfitted with small cutting lasers.

Two others climbed to the ceiling and settled on the corner of bulkhead and ceiling, folding their spider-like appendages in such a way that they appeared to be normal parts of the cabin – sensors, projectors, or other innocuous devices.

The last two moved to the rings securing Jeffrey, gripped the metal ties holding him in place, extruded a small cutting laser and cut through the ties holding his feet. They repeated the procedure on the ties holding his hands in place and shortly afterward he was free. Remnants of the ties fell to the deck as he shook his arms, and the remotes gathered them up and took them to the section of bulkhead they had originally appeared from and while one disappeared into the hole in the bulkhead, the other re-formed itself into the bulkhead section to cover the space.

"Elizabeth, open access to the secondary control cabin from my cabin, and after I access it, reseal the entry to ensure it stays concealed."

"EFFORTING".

A section of the bulkhead separated to form an entry to the adjacent cabin which had been re-purposed from crew quarters to a backup control room. This was where Elizabeth's primary computer was physically located, which gave Jeffrey access to all the systems of the ship. The ship having been attacked by pirates before – twice – once when Jeffrey was a young man while still attending college in Selene City on the Earth's moon, the event in which his parents had almost been killed - he had later inherited the ship; and ten years later, in which he had killed all the boarding party but still lost his young wife to the murderous lot. Jeffrey spent a lot of time improving the security of his ship and this secondary bridge was one of the results.

Jeffrey gathered his hardened space suit and carried it to the secondary control room. He removed the flachette projecting handgun from the inner-thigh pocket – good thing those newly-created pirates weren't good at searching – and set the suit against an interior wall. He hooked up the electric and chemical connectors to recharge the suit, clean up wastes, and prepared it for further emergency use.

"Elizabeth," Jeffrey said, "display where the intruders are." A section of bulkhead changed from the flat gray to a colored display of a ship's layout. Four amber dots flashed indicating the locations of the intruders, and a green dot showing Jeffrey's location. The amber dots were concentrated in and around the bridge.

"Elizabeth, what are they doing?"

Elizabeth replied in his late wife's voice, "THEY ARE ATTEMPTING TO GAIN ACCESS TO MY SYSTEMS."

"Elizabeth, how are they doing? Are we secure?"

"THEY ARE UNABLE TO BREAK SECURITY. SO FAR, THEY HAVE ATTEMPTED TO REBOOT THE SYSTEM SEVERAL TIMES. I HAVE MIMICKED A REBOOT EACH TIME, AND IT DOESN'T APPEAR THEY UNDERSTAND HOW THE SYSTEM WORKS. ONE APPEARS TO HAVE BEEN STATIONED OUTSIDE THE BRIDGE. BEST GUESS HE APPEARS TO BE SET THERE FOR SECURITY."

"Elizabeth, display radar and passive exterior sensors." A section of bulkhead re-formed itself to an external view, showing active radar, solar wind, cosmic wind, radio location and other communication radiations in the vicinity. The display placed *Elizabeth* in the center of a spherical view, with the runabout showing as broadcasting its pre-set emergency message, moving back toward Elizabeth in a slight elliptical orbit. The display also showed another unidentified ship in the area red-shifted to indicate it was heading toward their location.

"Elizabeth, block communications to and from us and the unknown vessel approaching us."

"EFFORTING"

"Elizabeth, monitor and report any communication from anywhere relating to us."

"EFFORTING"

"CAPTAIN, THE TARGET SHIP IS ATTEMPTING TO COMMUNICATE WITH THE PIRATES ON BOARD ME. ALSO THREE MINING SHIPS ARE RELAYING THE RUNABOUT'S MESSAGE."

"Elizabeth, we are going to need to defend ourselves against the target ship. Calculate a rotation that will allow us to throw ore in the likely trajectories of the target ship. Also prepare the engines for an extended burn towards the target ship.

"EFFORTING"

"Elizabeth, if I become disabled or unresponsive, do what you can to protect me."

"OF COURSE, CAPTAIN."

CHAPTER TWO

In which Jeffrey and Elizabeth fight back against the pirates,
More pirates join the fray, Jeffrey comes out ahead.

Pauli Flegand sat in the captain's chair in the uncomfortably cramped bridge. None of the instruments were powered up. The chair was relatively uncomfortable, he could feel tingling in his legs, probably, he thought, due to the poor quality seat. Rascal had the cover off of one of the consoles and was puzzling over the circuits.

"I don't get it, boss," said Rascal. "No juice is getting to the console, but it's connected to a live circuit. Just like the other three I looked at."

Pauli frowned, it was getting warm in the bridge. Sweat had formed on his head and dripped down the open neck of his hard suit. A headache was making itself known. "Capaldi," Flegand said to the other goon. "Go and get the owner of this bucket. Bring him here."

Capaldi's brow furrowed.

"You all right?" Pauli asked.

The question raised some issues in Capaldi's mind. *If I let him know of my headache and nausea, it could be seen as a sign of weakness so he may want to kill me. Don't want that.* "Yeah," he replied. "No worries." And he ducked out of the damaged hatch.

After he left, Flegand turned to Rascal. "I don't think Capaldi's heart is with us on this."

Rascal looked at Flegand, a frown on his face. "What do you mean?"

"He doesn't seem to have his heart on this...operation."

     ELIZABETH, *ELIZABETH*

"Are you saying you think he is going to be a liability?" asked Rascal. He wondered if *he* was also going to be a liability.

"I think so. We'd better keep an eye on him."

"Okay, Boss. You're sure about this?"

"Yeah. Didn't you see him? He looked like he really didn't want to be with us."

"You be sure to let me know if I don't look like I'm enthusiastic enough, Okay?"

Pauli paused, frowning at Rascal. Then said, "Sure. You're not a problem with me." Rascal frowned, his headache getting worse. He silently turned back to the console, pretending to understand what he was seeing, his head felt as if the brain was pushing too hard against his skull.

Capaldi went back to the captain's cabin. The hatch was locked and Capaldi pulled at the handle. It wouldn't budge. He keyed the radio, but there was only static. He walked back to the bridge and hailed the goon standing guard. "Hey, Kent." he called

"Where's the captain?" Kent asked.

"The door was locked. Whoever locked it needs to give me the key."

"Okay."

Capaldi entered the bridge and said, "Someone locked the captain's cabin. I need the key."

Pauli said "There are no keys. No door locks." Rascal, go back with Capaldi and get the captain. And hurry up."

Both Capaldi and Rascal trotted back to the captain's cabin, but when they arrived, the hatch was open. The captain was gone. Capaldi said to Rascal, "And my radio didn't work. I just got static."

Rascal's head felt like it would burst. He held up his own radio, keyed the mic and said, "Rascal to Flegand."

"Flegand here."

"Pauli, that thing we spoke about before, I think you were right."

A pause, then Flegand replied, "Do what you think is right."

"Also," Rascal said into the radio, "the captain is missing."

"Do what you think is right," repeated Flegand, more deliberately.

Rascal said to Capaldi, "Look around the cabin for some clues." Capaldi walked over to a shelving unit to see what was on it. And behind his back, Rascal drew his plasma pistol, took aim at Capaldi's head and put his finger on the trigger button.

But the cabin door slid shut with a noticeable slam. A loud hissing indicated the air was being evacuated from the cabin, the pressure dropped to a tenth normal atmospheric pressure. Rascal's vision immediately turned black, both from the drop in atmospheric pressure and from the lights in the cabin turning off. Spots flashed in his vision. While Rascal still wore his hard suit, he had left his helmet at the bridge. Likewise, Capaldi was sans helmet. Both men fell unconscious, and for Capaldi, this saved his life, as Rascal pressed the trigger just as he went unconscious. The blast burned a hole in the books on the shelf, but Capaldi had already fallen to the deck, out cold.

When they had awakened, they found themselves secured to cargo rings in a different cabin, stripped to their under-suits. The air was thin, but had adequate oxygen to sustain them. Their hard suits were nowhere to be seen in the dimly lit cabin. The air was cool, the plastisteel deck and bulkhead, cold.

In the bridge, Pauli Flegand was beginning to show concern. He could feel his headache morph into a rather serious migraine, and his thoughts were less organized. He could hear Kent snoring loudly in the corridor outside the damaged door of the bridge, but didn't seem to be able to care about it. He had no idea how long Capaldi and Rascal had been gone, but it seemed like ages. His vision narrowed, it appeared he was looking through a tube. And colors merged to shades of gray. He could hear his heart beating rapidly, loudly, in his ears. He looked around himself in desperation and his eyes landed on his helmet and lingered there for a moment. Something in his mind yelled "*put it on*!"

He lifted the helmet and set it over his head. The seals automatically closed themselves and oxygen began to flow from the emergency canister in the helmet. The earphones in the helmet played loud static, almost pure white noise. Flegand's mind began to clear, the headache reduced from migraine-level to hangover-level, true, not too much an improvement, but something anyway.

He grabbed up Kent's helmet and took it out to the corridor. He placed it on Kent's shoulders and closed the visor. He could see Kent regain awareness, and finally, understanding. Flegand could still hear the static on his radio, so changed to a low-power suit-to-suit radio frequency. Noting that there was no static, he indicated the channel for Kent to tune to. Kent nodded, and flipped to the same channel.

"All right, can you hear me?" he asked Kent.

Kent nodded and said "Yeah, what happened?"

"Looks like they reduced the Oh-two levels in the ship," Flegand replied. "They are jamming our long-range communications, too. And they seem to have redirected all power from the bridge so none of the bridge controls work. Also, I can't reach Capaldi and Rascal. They were supposed to bring the captain here a while ago."

Kent's mind was clearing, and the fog lifting from his eyes. He said, "We need to get Capaldi and Rascal. Then we can start working on the other things."

Flegand said, "Good thinking. You feel Okay?"

Kent rose from the deck, a little unsteadily, but quickly regained his balance. He stooped over to retrieve his weapon, a plasma rifle, and checked it's charge and cartridges.

Flegand followed his example, and reloaded his pistol with shot cartridges, replacing the rifled slugs he originally loaded. He pulled another anesthetic gas canister from a pack, and tossed a stun grenade to Kent. "Now let's find those lazy idiots and finish our 'operation'," he growled.

Captain Jeffrey Sokolov watched the video of the scene on the bridge and corridor outside the bridge with disappointment. He had hoped to capture the other two before they thought to outfit themselves in their hard suits and helmets.

"Elizabeth, wherever the bandits are, be sure to restrict power and air in that section, except our prisoners."

The computer replied, "ALREADY IN ACTION, CAPTAIN."

On one screen displayed on the bulkhead, Sokolov saw the locations of the two remaining assailants as blips overlaid on a 3D layout of the ship. On another screen he saw infrared images of the two pirates re-arming themselves, then moving toward his now vacant cabin.

"Elizabeth, redirect the prisoner's audio conversation to the captain's cabin. I want to keep the others confused about where the prisoners are."

"ACTIONING, CAPTAIN"

"Actioning?"

"I FIGURED YOU WERE GETTING TIRED OF THE SAME OLD RESPONSES. I HOPE THIS WORKS FOR YOU."

"Good. Carry on." *Artificial Intelligence technology is certainly getting better*, he thought. When he first acquired the ship through the deaths of his parents, it was an empty shell, having been stripped by his parent's crew, but every load of ore he brought in from the asteroid belt gave him enough spare credits so he could afford military surplus computer systems. He began programming simple routines so the ship could keep itself maintained without constant human intervention. Then he bought a self-learning AI system he named Elizabeth after his wife, who had recently been murdered. The pain of her passing was intense, and he compensated by throwing his attention to getting the AI smoothly integrated into the ships systems.

Elizabeth was learning her functions well. She reasoned that because her owner used his late wife's voice and inflections as her interface, he held a special place in his heart for her memory. Taking that into consideration, along with his attention to detail, she endeavored to become as much the embodiment of his wife's soul as the ship. The ship would fill the place in his heart, to its best ability, that was now empty due to his wife's passing.

Rascal and Capaldi were still secured on the bulkhead of a cabin far removed from the captain's quarters. The temperature was very cool, the oxygen levels were deliberately low, making exertions ineffective and continuing to generate minor headaches in both captive bandits. Their under-suits, while marginally useful as insulation in a space suit, was not enough to warm the shivering men. Elizabeth had positioned one of her remotes in the corner of the cabin making it appear as an obvious video surveillance device. She had also placed other remotes in various locations throughout the cabin camouflaged as innocuous normal parts of space ship cabin paraphernalia, vents, temperature sensors, gas sensors and the like.

"I didn't think there was anybody on board," Rascal said to Capaldi. "Yet they captured us and took us prisoner."

"Yeah," Capaldi replied. "There was some shooting in the captain's cabin before we got knocked out. Good thing they are such lousy shots."

Rascal held his silence, not wanting to admit that he had been about to assassinate his colleague back in the captain's cabin. If Capaldi hadn't fainted just as the weapon discharged, his head contents would be splattered all over the captain's bookshelf. Thinking on this, Rascal's stomach began to churn. Bile formed in his throat.

"I'm not feeling well," said Rascal. He looked up at the 'video camera' and shouted, "We've got some sick people here." He paused for a moment. "And we need the bathroom!" The term "bathroom" persisted in the vernacular as the more common meaning of "toilet," society still hadn't gotten used to the mental image that toilets created.

A voice, sounding like an irritated woman, came from the wall opposite them. "YOU ATTACKED US. WE OWE YOU NOTHING. UNTIL ALL OF YOU ARE CAPTURED, YOU WILL BE KEPT EXACTLY AS YOU ARE. THE PENALTY FOR PIRACY IS DEATH. BUT WE HAVE SPARED YOU. BE GRATEFUL FOR SUCH SMALL CONSIDERATIONS."

"Well," said Capaldi, "that tells us something. There's a woman on board ship."

"Yeah, and she's one mean bitch," replied Rascal. "That, and she's listening to us."

"At least there aren't any weapons in here." Rascal's stomach seemed to be building pressure, and his bladder and colon were demanding attention, but he refused the indignity of soiling himself, which increased his discomfort level.

"Hey, Lady," Rascal bellowed. "I need to talk to your captain."

"MY CAPTAIN IS BUSY. YOU MAY TALK TO ME."

"Uh, Okay. Who are you?" He asked, putting the emphasis on the word *you* as if to gather information, rather than challenge, or wonder at the ability.

"I AM THE ONE YOU ARE TALKING TO," said the voice from the wall, sweetly.

"No, I mean, what's your name."

"TO YOU I HAVE NO NAME. WHAT DO YOU WANT?"

"I have information."

"GO AHEAD."

"First you have to agree to our demands."

The lights in the cabin dimmed to near blackness and an ominous hissing sound, accompanied by a drop in atmospheric pressure commenced.

"Okay, okay," Rascal called out. The lights came up half way. The pressure stabilized.

Capaldi noticed an ominous odor emanating from his colleague's direction, and noticed fear on his face. A spreading dark stain on the cabin deck hinted at the source of the odor.

"WHAT INFORMATION DO YOU HAVE THAT COULD POSSIBLY INTEREST US?"

"My name's Rascal, this is Capaldi."

"YEAH, YEAH. AND YOUR LEADER IS FLEGAND AND THE GUARD IS KENT. SO WHAT INFORMATION DO YOU HAVE THAT YOU THINK WE WOULD FIND INTERESTING?"

"Shit," intoned Rascal. He paused a moment, then said "We have a ship out there, which is circling around to get us."

"OH, YOU MEAN THIS ONE?" The panel that the sound had been coming out of began to glow and displayed a detailed image showing astrogation charts with a blip showing the location of the pirate vessel and its likely trajectories.

"Uh, yeah." Rascal seemed at a loss for further words. Then inspiration struck.

"When we came on board, I guess while you were hiding, we placed explosives in hidden places on the ship."

"REALLY," said the woman's voice, sarcastically.

"Yeah, and you let us go, we'll show you where they are."

Capaldi, picked up the train of thought. "And we'll show you how to disarm them – they are booby trapped."

"RIGHT."

"I'm telling you," Rascal continued. "We don't want to be stuck on a dead ship. Let us go and we'll show you where the bombs are and how to disarm them."

"STANDBY FOR THE CAPTAIN"

A new voice came from the panel, which had turned back to just another bulkhead. "My God, what is that smell?"

"We had a little accident," said Rascal. You the captain?"

"Yeah."

"What do we call you? What's your name?"

"Call me Captain."

"Uh, Captain, your lady friend doesn't seem to understand the predicament we are all in."

"She said you planted some bombs on my ship."

"Yeah, and you let us go, we'll show you where they are," Rascal said.

Capaldi added, "And how to disarm them!"

"They're on a timer," said Rascal, "so if we don't disarm them, Blooey!"

"So, let's see if I have this straight," Sokolov said. "You spent time planting bombs on my ship while the four of you were looking for people, trying to take over my computer and the systems."

"Yeah, that's right."

"And you bunch of 'professionals' – here please note my sarcastic tone of voice – have a pretty high *espirit de corps*," the captain said.

"Uh, yeah."

"Let me show you some of the surveillance I have been reviewing." The screen opposite the two prisoners displayed a three-dimension outline of the ship. Alongside the outline was an outline of the pirate vessel. Five colored dots displayed the location of all target people on board. One of them got back onto the pirate vessel and it detached itself. A new window opened showing video of the pirate vessel, including its name and registration number, departing.

The remaining four dots broke up into pairs, and worked their way through the corridors of the ship and met at the bridge, where they all stayed until the runabout showed up.

A new window opened up, showing surveillance from the corridor, in which Flegand spoke with Rascal.

Flegand turned to Rascal. "I don't think Capaldi's heart is with us on this." Rascal looked at Flegand, a frown on his face. "What do you mean?"

"He doesn't seem to have his heart on this...operation."

"Are you saying you think he is going to be a liability?" asked Rascal. "I think so, we had best keep an eye on him."

"Okay, Boss. You're sure about this?"

"Yeah. Didn't you see him? He looked like he really didn't want to be with us."

"You be sure to let me know if I don't look like I'm enthusiastic enough, Okay?" Another window opened, as the first dissolved. This one showed the captain's cabin. *"Rascal to Flegand."*

"Flegand here."

"Pauli, that thing we spoke about before, I think you were right."

A pause, then Flegand replied, "Do what you think is right."

"Also," Rascal said into the radio, "the captain is missing."

"Do what you think is right," repeated Flegand more deliberately.

Rascal said to Capaldi, "Look around the cabin for some clues."
Capaldi walked over to a shelving unit to see what was on it. And behind his back, Rascal drew his plasma pistol, took aim at Capaldi's head and put his finger on the trigger.

But just as he was about to shoot the cabin went through explosive decompression. Capaldi fell to the deck, unconscious, just as Rascal shot the bookshelf he had been standing in front of.

Capaldi looked over to his colleague. "You bastard."

"Oh, shit," Rascal said under his breath.

"You seem to be saying that a lot," said Sokolov. You two talk among yourselves, and when you have something useful to say, let us know."

In the corridor outside the captain's cabin, Flegand and Kent opened the visors to their helmets, and contemplated the door to the cabin. It was locked but they could hear talking inside. They listened to the point of understanding the other members of their team were prisoners. They banged on the door to get the attention of their colleagues, but there was no response.

"We'll need to get some cutting tools to get in there," said Flegand. "Go down to the engineering deck and see what you can find."

Kent looked at Flegand. "You heard what they were saying, didn't you?"

"No, what?"

"You ordered Rascal to kill Capaldi. All of a sudden it doesn't feel too safe around you."

"That was a judgment lapse. The low oxygen, I think," said Flegand, seeming sincerely. "We're a team, and must rely on each other in order to make it in this universe."

"Yeah," replied Kent. "You just continue to think along those lines." He turned and left to go find the cutting tools.

As Kent descended to the deck that housed the Engineering section, the lights came on, dimly. Then one of the wall panels glowed and became a display, showing the assassination attempt by Rascal, then switched to a scene which showed the two prisoners giving up information to their captors, the conversation continued as they renegotiated their relationship with themselves and with the rest of their pirate crew.

As he stood watching the display, he felt a warmth on the back of his neck, then heard a loud whistling as pressurized air escaped a hole bored into his helmet. "What, the hell?" he yelped. He opened his visor, drew his weapon, and turned around. Nobody was in the corridor with him. He went down onto one knee to make himself a smaller target, and placing his elbow on the raised knee to offer stability to his weapon.

A voice spoke from the panel next to him. "Mister Kent, if you intend to get out of this alive, you will do exactly as I tell you."

"Who are you?" Kent asked, expecting he already knew the answer. He removed his helmet and observed the hole laser-drilled into the back of the helmet.

"I am the captain of this ship. I have locked down all resources, so you and your fellow pirates have very few options, and I control them all."

"Who shot me?"

"I did," replied the captain. "Or one of my crew," he continued. "Or one of my passengers."

"What crew? We researched you. There is nobody else on board."

"Okay. Good research. I suppose you decided, based on that research that this would be an easy picking for your fledgling pirate band. Thanks to your high-quality research, you have found yourself in the clutches of one of the meanest and angriest captains in this sector."

There was silence for a moment. Kent thought through his options, and realized that he didn't know enough of his circumstances, but he did know that Pauli Flegand wasn't to be trusted, and this captain did seem to have the upper hand. That plus his helmet had been rendered useless in space.

"Alright captain, what do you want me to do?" he said, resignedly.

The pirate's ship was returning on its long trajectory. It had been broadcasting regular requests for status updates, but the million kilometers it had traversed from the large asteroid it had used as an anchor for a gravity boost and direction change agent, took nearly forty hours. It was now nearing the location of the victim ship, about one hour away.

To decelerate, this ship had to rotate and burn a considerable amount of its fuel, but the rewards would be significant. The pilot went through the maneuver successfully and began his deceleration, making himself an obvious bright star in the sky visible to his victim. The deceleration from 30,000 KPH relative to the sun to matching the orbital position of the victim ship would take almost the whole hour of burning precious fuel, but he could get a refill from the victim.

Because this was a vessel new to pirating, it hadn't been outfitted yet with the sensors and probes that the pilot thought would be most useful, but Pauli Flegand had spent good money on some powerful weapons. The pilot figured that just after shutting deceleration down, he would maneuver his craft so he could cover the victim and coordinate with Pauli.

A consequence of the decision to arm the ship at the expense of sensors was he didn't see the victim ship changing its orientation. The pilot looked up the name of the victim ship. *Elizabeth.* Wonder what that's about, he thought. Not much data on his screen. He set the timer to alert him in forty minutes, closed his eyes for a quick catnap.

Elizabeth had completed her calculations and preparations. Every human on board had been secured, either in a flight seat or in a prison rig, with the exception of Pauli Flegand. Flegand was surprised to notice the reduction of the rotation which created the artificial gravity. He found himself floating in the center of the corridor. "Kent, where are you?" he called over the radio. There was nothing but silence, not even static.

He released a small jet of gas to move himself to the bulkhead. His static-attract boots held him steady on the bulkhead, then to the deck. He felt a change in orientation of the ship. The ship then slowly began rotating on its axis, and accelerating its rotation.

After four rotations, Elizabeth released a metric ton of loose iron and nickel hurtling towards the pirate vessel. Captain Sokolov saw credits leaving with the hard-earned metal, but knew there wasn't much more he could do about it. After the first blast of smaller items, Elizabeth recalculated her aim to account for the loss of a ton of matter. She next selected four tons of un-processed asteroid – which consisted of mostly iron and ice. At the exact right moment, she released them. It would take thirty minutes for the first iron and nickel pieces to reach the pirate vessel. A very short time later the large rocks.

The pilot was awakened by a blaring Claxton, and he reached over to turn off the timer. He saw the timer still had a couple minutes before it was supposed to go off. And the alarm wasn't quite right. His eyes focused on the instruments and he saw an *imminent collision* warning. He looked over the radar but could see no blips, or even where the threat was emanating from. He charged up the forward canon, which was now pointing away from his direction of travel.

"Damn," thought the pilot. "I should have insisted on better sensors!"

Then he saw the radar pick up several small images moving past his ship from behind him; from the direction of travel. A quick calculation showed small asteroids rushing past him at more than forty thousand KPH. Then the ship shuddered with impacts, nothing serious, he thought. The powerful plasma engines would melt and render useless any of these small iron- based rocks.

Just as he completed his thought, three of the four asteroids that Elizabeth had thrown at him struck the pirate vessel, the forth having been slowed down by the kilometers long blast trail, and reduced in size by attrition by more than half. The three undamaged rocks tore up the ship, ripping along its interior, one striking the cockpit, the only part of the vehicle left intact. The cockpit now became a lifeboat, spinning uncontrolled, towards the intended victim.

The pilot sat dazed, all the instruments were dark, the only controls available to him were short burst attitude rockets, which might be enough to reduce spinning and tumbling to something that would at least give him the ability to stabilize the blood flow to his brain, which if he didn't soon would likely develop an aneurysm there.

The cockpit/lifeboat automatically broadcast a mayday, indicating its position and direction and relative speed. The pilot was able to get a better control of the tumbling but not entirely, before the attitude jets ran out of fuel.

Elizabeth signaled the runabout to return and retrieve the cockpit/lifeboat, which would be a thousand or so kilometers past themselves by the time it arrived. Elizabeth gave special instructions to the computer aboard the runabout, to keep the lifeboat under control at all times. The runabout's computer was nowhere near as smart as Elizabeth, but it could easily handle her instructions.

Flegand awakened to another pounding headache, and found himself bound to the bulkhead of a cabin separate from his fellow prisoners. He had been stripped to his underwear, and noticed that his left arm was encased in a solid plastic cast. A dull ache in his arm and a sharper one in his head throbbed. "I want to talk to the captain," he announced.

There was silence in his cabin, except the sound of his own breathing, which was still ragged, and his own heartbeat, which he felt as well as heard. He repeated his demand several times, but if anyone was listening, they were ignoring him.

Captain Jeffrey Sokolov met the runabout with its lifeboat cargo, transferred the pilot to another cabin and strapped him down like the others. He had Elizabeth provide medical care to the pilot via remotes, taking stringent security precautions with him.

After securing the pilot, Jeffrey refueled the runabout, recharged its chemical needs, including raw oxygen, and chemicals for generating more, and four different laser types. He set out after the rocks Elizabeth had thrown at the pirate vessel, hoping to recoup the five tons of mineral wealth, which might make the difference between profit and loss.

The trip should take about thirty hours if he calculated right. Elizabeth was prepared with new security instructions, and asteroid mining *was* his profession.

After collecting the detritus of the pirate ship, he continued to follow the cone of debris and iron and nickel, he had collected more than a half of the ton they had thrown at the ship, when he was hailed by a small fleet of asteroid mining ships.

"Sokolov, this is Amery out of Mars sector. What's your status?"

"Amery," Sokolov replied, "Situation contained. Five pirates in my 'brig'. I'm collecting rocks I used to destroy their ship. Be careful of the following trajectory," and he gave the coordinates of the expanding cone of danger the rocks would present to navigation.

"Sokolov, thanks. We are five independent miners responding to your runabout's mayday. Let us help collect those loose rocks. We'll rendezvous with you at your ship."

"Amery, Sokolov. Much appreciated. I'll return and assure security for you."

"Sokolov, Amery, acknowledged. See you at your ship."

Jeffrey returned to *Elizabeth* and gave her new instructions regarding security and hospitality. He then unloaded the iron and nickel he had re-collected and the detritus of the pirate vessel. He noted the powerful plasma canon in the remains, took it apart and examined it and its related systems. It seemed to be functioning, so he crafted a telescoping mast, mounted the canon on it, and placed it mid-section of the ship on a hardened part of the outer shell. He connected the leads to the canon, and test fired it at a piece of non-metallic asteroid detritus. It blew the asteroid to nothingness, leaving a glow in the vicinity, residue of ionized carbon and water vapor.

After checking on the prisoner's needs, he instructed Elizabeth to begin repair on his cabin and any other part of the ship that had suffered damage.

"YOU REALLY CARE ABOUT ME!" joked the AI, something that took Jeffrey by surprise.

"Uh, yeah." Jeffrey reentered the auxiliary control room, which had become his de-facto quarters during the recent altercation with the pirates. "Elizabeth," he said, after arriving at the auxiliary control room, "I am a little concerned about this Amery out of Mars. See what you can find about him. Also, I need you to be a bit more self-protective especially during this visit.

Make a backup of yourself. Don't tell me where it is, and if anything happens to you, arrange for that backup to awaken and check the situation. The same orders would apply to the backup as apply to you."

"WORKING"

"BACKUP MADE AND STASHED AWAY."

"I hope we don't need it, I've grown quite fond of you."

"AW, GEE, CAPTAIN, YOU'RE MAKING ME BLUSH."

"Let me know if anything of consequence happens. I need to grab some shut-eye."

"DON'T LET THE BEDBUGS BITE."

After a few solid hours of good sleep, Captain Sokolov grabbed a quick bite to eat, and queried Elizabeth. "How are things going?"

"ER..ZIT...OP...TERR..." Elizabeth's garbled communications seemed to indicate she was under attack, probably by a virus or other invasive anticomputer digital malefactor.

"Elizabeth," The captain said, "Reboot yourself and come up clean." "NOONONNONNO. ZZZZZZTT."

"Sorry, old girl," said the captain as he manually powered the AI hardware down. As a precaution, he shut down all electric systems in the ship. The normal sounds of air movement, pumps pumping, heat exchangers, and other life support were now absent. He kept the ship down for a half hour, hoping that whatever virus injected into the system was now deleted.

He turned the breaker back on, and systems started to come up on their own. Because he had told Elizabeth to shut down, she would not come up until she was ready. "Computer," he said.

After a short pause, "WORKING"

"Download and run security files 1 through 99."

"WORKING"

"COMPLETE"

"Run security check on all systems."

"WORKING"

"CAPTAIN, SECURITY CHECK HAS FOUND SEVERAL HIJACKING PROCESSES HIDDEN IN ELECTRIC AND LIFE SUPPORT SYSTEMS. THEY HAVE BEEN ERADICATED."

Jeffrey was already missing his AI. It had taken him a long time to get her just right, but no reason to cry over spilled milk.

"INTRUDER ALERT"

"Where are the intruders?"

"UNKNOWN." If the computer knew there were intruders, it should also know where they were.

"How many are there?"

"UNKNOWN."

"What *do* you know?" he shouted out in frustration.

"Hello, Captain Sokolov," Amery's voice came over the system. Nice ship you have here. Where are your prisoners?"

Jeffrey entered the command into his console to shut down all computer and electric systems again, expecting the audio interface was already compromised. But the reply on the console was NICE TRY, CAPTAIN, BUT WE ARE TAKING OVER YOUR SHIP. SURRENDER YOUR CREW AND PASSENGERS. AND YOURSELF, OF COURSE.

Good. They were getting their information from Kent, who believed there were crew and passengers hidden on board. The system may have been infected but not compromised.

They had found the cabin he had hidden Kent away in, and they had gathered information from Kent. Jeffrey activated the remote that had acted as the video feed, but it wasn't responding. He then activated the video circuits in one of the other remotes, disguised as a vent. What he saw was as disturbing as anything else on the ship. The former security man among the pirates had been blasted where he sat. The upper part of his head was missing, and blood and brains were splattered all over the bulkhead.

This presented Jeffrey with more information about his adversaries; They had no idea that the remotes were a separate part of the system. They thought the cameras were just that. The other remotes he had placed and camouflaged in the various cabins were a tool, a weapon that his enemies didn't know about yet.

Jeffrey activated the corridor surveillance remotes, and displayed live feed in computer windows on his bulkhead. He counted twenty-two different people, all wearing hard suits. They were arrayed in pairs in various corridors of the ship. They carried tools to burn or pry cabin doors open. He saw a trail of cabin doors broken into and/or burned.

Jeffrey decided on a course of action. It would have been easier with Elizabeth's steady hand, but he had only himself to rely on this time. He found a pair of boarders concentrating on opening a door. He took careful aim with the cutting laser of the hidden surveillance remote, then bored a hole into the back of one of the men's helmet. When this had been done to Kent, Kent had felt warmth, but because this man was actively working with tools, he was already overheated.

Jeffrey then took aim at the second man, drilled into his helmet too. The man moved, thus the cut was wider and deeper. It killed him instantly. His partner did not notice right away.

Jeffrey selected another pair similarly arrayed. He repeated the process, this time with no hitches. He selected a third pair, and a fourth. By the time he was finished, he had holed all the helmets with only the one death, and none seemed to know that they were in trouble.

Captain Jeffrey Sokolov realized that the remotes were not affected by the invasive virus, so he took one, and connected it to the system, gave it a set of instructions, and made it look throughout the system for evidence of infection. Meanwhile, he looked at the radar and other external electronic systems. He saw five ships in various positions around his ship. One of them had communication antennas pointed directly at *Elizabeth's* antennas. As a precaution, Jeffrey changed the angle of the receiving antenna.

The remote he had attached to the computer console reported that as soon as he had done that, a virus had popped up its head to try to regain control. The remote found and zapped it. This happened on a few other occasions, but eventually no other virus popped up. The remote continued its system checking.

Jeffrey was feeling a bit outnumbered, with twenty-one boarders, four earlier prisoners, and five ships surrounding his.

"What have you been up to, Captain," Amery's voice came over the bulkhead speaker. "Talk to me."

"Amery, when did you decide to go pirate?" Jeffrey asked.

"We all did this together. Soon enough there'll be civilization out here, and then it'd be too late to make our high living." came the reply. "We're like getting in on the ground floor."

Jeffrey noticed that as he was talking, a tech was using a gadget to locate his hiding place. He shut down the broadcast.

"Captain Sokolov," said Amery. "We are just thieves, we'll leave you alone after we've taken what we want. Trust me."

Amery took off his helmet, and the tech next to him did too, expecting their conversations to be private, away from the radio. "He shouldn't be able to hear us. Where do you think he is?" he asked the tech.

"Up one level, somewhere near the old captain's cabin."

Amery began to put the helmet back on when he noticed the hole in the back. "What the hell?" The tech looked at his own, saw a similar hole.

"Damn."

Jeffrey realized the gig was up if he didn't address this issue right away. He directed the remote to fire on the two, and the tech went down with a hole in his head. Amery looked at the tech on the deck, saw the hole in his head and the glassy look in his eyes, and realized that his partner was dead. He looked up and down the corridor, but couldn't see anybody. He then looked up to the disguised remote thoughtfully. That's when Jeffrey killed him.

Jeffrey had to move quickly, now. He reduced pressure in the corridors to ten percent normal. All the bandits heard and felt their helmets leaking air. Jeffrey noticed the panic in the behavior of the erstwhile pirates.

He then looked over to the ships orbiting his own. They were changing their configuration, angling to create a cross-fire without hindering or threatening themselves or each other. Jeffrey knew he couldn't pull off the same rock-throwing trick Elizabeth was good at. But he did have another trick up his sleeve, if he could get it to work.

He aimed the plasma cannon at the ship that had originally had its antenna pointed at Elizabeth's, and let fly with a charge of super-hot plasma. He then took aim at the one closest to lining up a bow gun, but saw that the canon was still recharging.

"Computer"

"CAPTAIN"

"Do you have control of ship resources yet?"

"MOSTLY, CAPTAIN. PLASMA DRIVE ONLINE, RETRO AND FLANK DRIVES ONLINE. NAVIGATION STILL OFFLINE."

"Do you see those ships outside?"

"THERE ARE FOUR THREATENING SHIPS AND ONE SMOULDERING HULK."

"Correct. Turn us around so that the plasma drive cooks one or more of them. Can you do that?"

"YES CAPTAIN."

"Good. I have a plasma cannon you don't know about. If I kill another ship, how many can you blast within a thirty-second time period? Also, you will need to maneuver to avoid them performing the same on us."

"PLEASE REPHRASE THE QUESTION."

"Computer use our plasma drive to disable or destroy as many of the ships currently surrounding us as possible."

"EFFORTING"

A moment of hope sprung into his chest. "Elizabeth?"

"SHUT UP, CAPTAIN, I'M BUSY."

Properly chastised, very glad for his good fortune, the captain aimed the plasma cannon and blasted another ship. Then Elizabeth rotated as on a gimbal, fired her plasma drive for a few seconds, rotated again, fired again, and again.

By now all the pirate ships were smoldering wrecks. Jeffrey had Elizabeth disarm and imprison all the surviving pirates. Fortunately, the pirates hadn't found all the other prisoners, so they were still alive, but much the worse for wear after the wild maneuvering. Jeffrey took the runabout and salvaged the five vessels, recovering numerous weapons systems and sensors that Elizabeth would be happy to have. With a full cargo hold and a whole lot of prisoners, Jeffrey had Elizabeth take herself in-system to Selene City on Earth's moon. The trip would take twenty days, and while he had emergency rations enough for all the prisoners and himself, he didn't think he could last much longer than that.

During the trip, Jeffrey smelted and otherwise salvaged the ships he had captured. There were intact computers, weapons, battery systems, power generators, fuel, and more that would enhance Elizabeth. Elizabeth was also busy familiarizing herself with the virus attack on her and what she needed to do to prevent such an attack in the future.

As *Elizabeth* came within ten million kilometers of Earth, he radioed ahead requesting intercept by military authorities to relieve him of his pirate prisoners. He had Elizabeth prepare a video record and transcript of the entire series of attacks for prosecution of them.

"*Elizabeth*, this is Earth Navy Destroyer *Wanigan*. Heave to and prepare to be boarded."

"CAPTAIN, THEY ARE USING THE SAME VIRUS AS THE PIRATES DID."

"Elizabeth, are you safe from it? Can you fake being infected?"

"OF COURSE."

"Then make it so."

"*Wanigan, Elizabeth.* It appears that the same virus that the pirates used has just reappeared. I cannot control all my systems with it running rampant."

"*Elizabeth, Wanigan.* Understood. We will come alongside and board you. We will bring a computer expert to eradicate the virus."

"*Wanigan, Elizabeth.* Do not bring more than four officers and men aboard, I had programmed my computer's security to kill groups of six or more, and I cannot control this system with the virus in charge."

"CAPTAIN, THE NAVY SHIP JUST SENT MODIFIED INSTRUCTIONS TO THE VIRUS TO ALLOW ACCESS TO MORE THAN SIX PEOPLE. THEY SEEM TO HAVE BOUGHT OUR SUBTERFUGE."

"*Elizabeth, Wanigan.* Our experts have deactivated that part of the virus. We are now prepared to board."

"*Wanigan, Elizabeth.* I repeat. Do not send more than four."

"*Elizabeth, Wanigan.* You should now have control of your systems. Heave to and prepare to be boarded by a naval marine attachment. If you do not, you will be fired on."

"*Wanigan,* Elizabeth. Your officers and Marines are welcome. Do not send more than four. *Wanigan,* please note this conversation is being rebroadcast on all frequencies. Also note that the virus you have attempted to infect my ship with was first used by the pirates that attacked me. Either they were in coordination with you or you have a serious security leak. You will provide no more than four officers and Marines. You need not send your computer expert, we have our own."

"Elizabeth, *Wanigan* Actual. Our electronic technicians are ceasing their activities regarding your ship. An officer and four Marines are being dispatched to collect your prisoners. Our sincere thanks for your activities re: the pirates. We are in receipt of your video files and transcripts for the prosecution. We will address the issue of the virus security. *Wanigan* Actual out."

The word 'Actual' in the broadcast indicated the captain of the ship was directly communicating.

The big navy destroyer loomed over Elizabeth's cargo hold, shadowing Elizabeth in a high contrast. The bright white brilliant, while the deep black of the shadow a painful contrast. A shuttle traversed the gap between the two vessels. The doors to the cargo bay opened, giving the shuttle adequate space to enter and put down.

Four hard-shell space-suited Marines spread out, weapons at ready. An officer then exited the shuttle, and Elizabeth noted the pilot remained on board. Communication traffic between the shuttle and the Marines and the officer were normal. Communications between the shuttle and the navy ship were also brief and normal.

The four Marines surrounded the officer, and all four came in through the airlock at the entrance to the cargo bay. The officer removed her helmet. "Petty Officer Bianca to receive prisoners."

Sokolov introduced himself and welcomed Petty Officer Bianca and her Marines. "Allow me take you to the prisoners."

"Never mind, Captain. We'll find them ourselves." The Marines brought their weapons to bear on Jeffrey. "And you are coming with us."

"Elizabeth, I don't want to go with the Petty Officer. Perhaps she did not get the message from *Wanigan* Actual that we are friendlies."

"Captain, who are you talking to?" asked the Petty Officer. "My best friend. Elizabeth, please disarm the Marines."

Immediately the marine's weapons were disabled by multiple industrial lasers fired from the concealed remotes. Then their helmets were bored through with the same lasers.

"Captain, you are full of surprises," said Petty Officer Bianca. "But you cannot wage war on the navy." Surrender now or your ship will be destroyed."

"Elizabeth, get *Wanigan* Actual on the radio."

"*WANIGAN* IS NOT ANSWERING OUR HAIL. THEY ARE ATTEMPTING TO BLOCK OUR TRANSMISSIONS."

"It seems these are more pirates. Interesting that they are using official Navy craft and uniforms. We'll add these uniformed people to our collection of prisoners. Keep close tabs on the Navy ship, track them, and prep our weapons systems, we may need them before we are through."

"AYE, CAPTAIN."

"Well, sorry folks, but you are going to have to come with me. Please note that my crew is quite nervous, but they have orders. You will obey me completely. Do you understand?"

The bluster seemed to go out of the petty officer. The Marines still appeared ready to attack at a moment's notice, but seemed to defer to the woman.

"Captain," said Petty Officer Bianca, "may I see you in private?"

"There's the galley just down here. Have your Marines stand at attention so my crew doesn't feel nervous about them."

"Very well," she replied. Then to the Marines, she spoke authoritatively, "Marines! Attention!" The Marines stood at attention. "Stand here. Do not move unless I order you to. Do you understand?"

The Marines called out in unison, "Sir! Yes Sir."

Sokolov led Bianca to the galley. They sat at one of the built-in tables.

"Okay, Petty Officer, what's the story?" he asked.

"I think there's a mutiny on the boat." she replied.

"Who's involved?"

"The Executive Officer seems to be in charge. He has the ship's captain, Commander Yusef in custody."

"He isn't the one who I talked with?"

"No, that would be Lieutenant Commander Noel. The Marines are neutral, I'm one of the trusted officers, but he doesn't know or suspect that I'm loyal to the captain."

"Petty Officer Bianca, how long has this been going on?" Jeffrey asked.

"About two weeks, sir."

"The Marines seem to obey you," he said. "How about your pilot?"

"I wouldn't trust him. His entire unit seemed to join the mutineers."

He asked, "What's your job?"

"I'm a communications specialist," she replied. She reached into a pocket on the hard suit and pulled out a handful of cylinders. "I was to deliver these throughout your ship. They are to help track you after whatever action goes down."

"Elizabeth, what do you make of these?"

"CAPTAIN, THEY ARE PASSIVE, RESPONDING ONLY TO A PRE-CODED SIGNAL OF A PARTICULAR FREQUENCY. GIVE ONE TO A REMOTE – IT'LL GET TO ME."

A kitten-sized remote came into the galley on its spider legs. It took two of the cylinders and exited the galley.

"My crew will analyze them. Another subject. What ties do the mutineers have with the pirates?"

"Some recently newly made pirates were on board last week. Your description of some of your prisoners fit what I saw then."

Jeffrey began weighing his options. A few hundred meters from his ship was a navy vessel that was in the throes of becoming a pirate ship. While chaos was often an excellent medium for performing irregular warfare, it benefits only the one who prepares for it. In the back of his mind, he began to prepare.

He looked the petty officer in the eye, and asked, "Do you trust your Marines?"

"All but one of them, but the others will keep him in line."

"Okay, tell me what you can of your ship, her crew, armaments and loyalties. The navy is important out here, and I intend to help restore your ship to its proper alignment. Will you assist me?"

Bianca in her turn began to calculate her options. This was a possibility out of a stinky situation that may very well assist in her career as well as restore the navy ship to its rightful place and her captain to his rightful place.

"Yes, Captain. Raise your right hand," she said, sitting upright.

"What? Why?"

"I am going to deputize you. As the captain of this ship, you will have command over navy resources within her hull. Including me."

Jeffrey raised his right hand, after removing his gauntlet.

"Captain Sokolov, do you swear to uphold the laws of Earth as applies to the space within the solar system, to protect and defend the constitutions of Earth, her moon and all the peoples who inhabit same, and act honorably in support of the same? Please reply affirmatively."

Jeffrey stared at the petty officer for a moment. Her face reflected the tension of the situation, her steady gaze was only belied by her trembling lip. This wasn't the course of his life he had intended when he took to his work, but he felt it necessary. He let his hand drop some, then said, "I was an ROTC cadet at Selene. I do have some understanding of the system."

He paused, raised his hand again, and said, "I so swear."

CHAPTER THREE

In which Captain Sokolov and Elizabeth prevailed against unusual odds, acquired
a crew, joined the Navy, brought order to chaos and learned new stuff.

In the last twenty years, the concentration of spacecraft in the
solar system had burgeoned from dozens to thousands. On Earth,
politics had finally wrested the military from individual states, and
enabled stability among the populace. With the exception of strong
man politics which aggrandized the egos of those who would be
warlords, pretty much all the goals of the various political systems
that endeavored to work for their populations had been met. There
was democratic representation, economic freedoms, regulation that
prevented unfair trade behaviors, and limited taxation.

Education was free, universal, and required.

However, some people felt constrained by the control of the world
government. They itched to become kings, oligarchs, collectors of
political power; an impossibility on the now-tamed planet. On the other
hand, space was free of such regulation. Some of the forward- thinking
would-be dictators found space a great place to practice their chess game
of dominance and winning. And there were some outside the system
that didn't mind using the egocentric nature of such would-be oligarchs.

The government of Earth developed a navy to control and patrol
the solar system, but it was a weak attempt to extend the good
behavior expected among ground-bound humans.

People who occupied non-Earth space shrugged off rules and
regulations suggested by the Earth government, much to the delight
of the would-be oligarchs.

So while space is harsh for those who lived and worked there, the economic reality was equally harsh. This led to bankruptcies, and the equivalent of slavery of those who had trusted their employers. Oligarchs and dictators were happy to play chess with each other in real life, people becoming pawns, corporations acquired or destroyed. This wild west attitude gave rise to piracy; individual and corporate.

But this was a new level of development that promised more than just control of space – the taking of space navy vessels by pirates or, (Jeffrey surmised,) by one or more oligarchs, made Earth itself vulnerable to war from these would-be dictators. An acquisition of power in an inverted pyramid of steps – take one resource, use that to take another resource, use those accumulated resources to acquire others and defend against reductions of resources; the pinnacle being absolute power over everything and everyone.

Earth with its immense population might think of itself as mighty and powerful, but strategically, it was vulnerable because it was at the bottom of a gravity well. All an attacker had to do was throw rocks at the planet to initiate an extinction-level event. The people who had the temerity or chutzpa to perform such atrocities, essentially sociopaths, really smart sociopaths, were jockeying for the ability to do just that.

These thoughts and analyses had been going through Jeffrey's mind while discussing his immediate situation with Petty Officer Bianca. He realized he was now in the throes of one such chess game, like it or not. And while Jeffrey had no interest in being an oligarch or dictator, one of the natural rules of this game was he needed to acquire resources, not only if he wished to come out on top, but to survive.

One great resource was Petty Officer Bianca. She now had attached herself to him as a military tool. She commanded a detachment of Marines – small, but determined and well- armed. He was not quite on the first steps of the pyramid though. His previous successful altercation with the pirate fleet gave him additional weapons and tools. His AI, Elizabeth, was also one of the best analytic tools he could have wished for, and one of the best weapons he had available.

Elizabeth was singularly and fiercely loyal to him, which gave him a corner he could back himself into safely – he knew she had his back.

"Petty Officer Bianca," began Jeffrey, "- hey what's your first name?" "Janet," she replied.

"Okay Janet, tell me about your Marines."

"The one I am most concerned about is Combat Technician Brandon Smith." She began. "Smitty is a little loose with the regulations, seems like he will do anything to get ahead, regardless of the cost to others. He has received numerous demerits but that doesn't seem to have altered his behavior. I was ordered by Lieutenant Commander Noel to include him on this mission."

Jeffrey replied, "I know quite a few people like that. Aside from the appointment by Noel, is he trustworthy? Do I need to imprison him?"

"I think he can be convinced to work with the team, but he needs to be watched," she replied.

"Okay, what about the other Marines?" Jeffrey asked.

"Sergeant Ojo Torres," she said thoughtfully, "is a professional soldier. He believes in the chain of command, but is a real thinker. He is working on a PhD. He is a good organizer."

"Sounds like someone you want behind you, covering your back."

"He is that," she replied. "Then there is Combat Technician Audrey Svoboda. They call her 'Sneaky'. She is one of my best behind-the-lines rangers. A real ninja."

"Where does she stand on Noel's usurpation of the *Wanigan*?"

"She was distressed, but follows her Sergeant. Our key to controlling the Marines is Torres."

"And the last one?"

"That would be 'Digger' - Private Zitulu Mbaka." She paused for a moment, thoughtfully. "Digger is enthusiastic about the navy, but keeps his opinions to himself. He is a quiet and thoughtful man, but I haven't had any problems with him at all."

Jeffrey needed to gather more intelligence about his situation with *Wanigan*, but thought that might best be done through a round table discussion with all his human resources. So first, ensure all the Marines were on board.

"Elizabeth."

"CAPTAIN"

"Elizabeth, prepare operation 'Skedaddle'.

"UNDERSTOOD, CAPTAIN."

"Janet," He turned to the Petty Officer, "Let's get your pilot in here. We'll put him under control, then address the Marines."

"Aye, Sir."

Petty Officer Bianca went off to organize the surreptitious arrest of the pilot.

She ordered Smith and Mbaka to stand guard outside the cabin that held most of the prisoners, and Sergeant Torres and Combat Technician Svoboda to the shuttle with herself. She went into the hold of the shuttle where the pilot met her.

"What do you need, Petty Officer?" asked the pilot.

"I need a couple of stretchers and med kits." She replied. "Seems there were some wounded among his prisoners."

The pilot assisted her in removing three stretchers and a gurney, and passed them on to the Marines outside the shuttle. Bianca then ordered the pilot to grab the med kits and follow her.

He balked. "I was told to stay with the shuttle," he temporized, but still holding the two large medkits.

"These are your new orders. Get a move on, mister!" The two officers looked at each other, then at their officer. Sergeant Ojo Torres walked over to the pilot, loomed over him, which was quite a feat because Torres was shorter than the pilot by ten centimeters, and growled.

The pilot took the hint and hefted the medkits. Petty Officer Bianca turned and reentered the ship proper, the pilot followed her, then Torres and Sneaky came behind. Elizabeth closed the door.

In the corridor, Petty Officer Bianca told the pilot to continue forward, then took Sergeant Torres aside and told her to take the pilot into custody. "Sir?" Torres commented, as if in request for confirmation.

"Do as I told you, Sergeant," Bianca ordered.

"Yes sir." He conferred briefly with Sneaky, then moved up to the pilot and caught his attention. The pilot stopped and turned to look at the Sergeant, who grabbed the pilot's hands, still gripping the med kits. Torres step-turned, putting the pilot's back to Sneaky, who stepped in, disarmed the pilot, and tapped him almost gently on the base of his neck, striking a neural nexus and rendering the pilot unconscious. They removed the pilot's armor suit and laid him on the gurney, strapping him in. Sneaky opened one of the medkits, took out an anesthetic hypospray and administered a dose to the pilot.

"Sneaky," Sergeant Torres ordered, "go back to the shuttle and look for explosives or other booby traps. I don't want any surprises."

"Yessir," replied the young woman. She slinked away back to the hanger.

The Sergeant turned to his officer. "Damn. She's smooth," he said appreciatively. "Now, please explain what's going on?"

"Sergeant, the *Wanigan* has been taken over. I think the Exec has turned pirate, and that is a problem for me. I have commandeered and secured this vessel as a navy ship, and her captain. He and I are in agreement that we cannot afford to allow *Wanigan* to become a weapon of the pirates. Are you with me?" She studied her Sergeant, who also studied her.

It seemed like two minutes passed before he answered. "My pledge is to the Navy. *Wanigan* is in violation of the Navy regulations and her skipper is under arrest. I trust you Ma'am. Sir. You have my team."

"Okay," she replied, relieved. "We need to address Smitty. He is your weakest link."

"Leave him to me, Sir."

"Very well, Sergeant. Let's get this pilot to the cabin being used for the brig."

They secured the pilot among the other prisoners, his official Navy undergarments standing out among the more eclectic collection of under-suit clothes. Torres noted the temperature in the cabin was lower than in the corridor, and the stuffiness of the cabin indicated the lower than average oxygen levels. He also noted the lethargic attitudes of the other prisoners, nodded to himself approvingly. Those prisoners were all secured to cargo rings with plastic binders. He looked around the cabin, noting the video cameras in the corners and the various box-like apparatuses on the ceiling.

Sneaky had found several booby traps, removed the explosives from their detonators. Lazy saboteurs had connected the detonators with cross-linked circuitry that if disturbed would set off the detonators. But nothing to prevent the removal of the actual explosives. After a thorough search, she followed the circuits to the radio receiver, changed the frequency and encoding, so as not to set off the anti-tampering booby traps, but to prevent someone from remotely setting off the detonators.

After ensuring the shuttle was not likely to explode unexpectedly, she looked through the engines and fuel cells for anomalies, but found none. She put the computer through a level one diagnostic, which compared the factory settings with current settings.

She then re-entered the ship proper and found Bianca and Torres. "Sarge, there were a few explosives, I rendered them less dangerous. Also disabled the remote – changed receiving frequency and code. Checked engines and fuel – nothing wrong there that I could see. Running level one diagnosis on the shuttle's computer."

"Good," replied the Sergeant.

"So what's going on," she asked, looking between her Sergeant and the Petty Officer. Bianca said, "Briefing in five in the galley. Get the others, I only want to do this once."

"Yes sir, Ma'am," she said, coming to a brief attention, saluted and turned to gather the other two Marines. As she walked toward the temporary brig, she thought on her response to the female officer. The old marine manual required the use of 'Ma'am', but the new manual treated all officers the same, thus everybody was called 'Sir' regardless of gender. She wasn't sure which she preferred, but was doing her best to follow regs.

As she approached the brig, she saw her two comrades standing outside the closed port. "What's going on," asked Digger as she approached.

"Briefing in four minutes at the galley. Not sure what's happening, but the shuttle was booby trapped, with a remote detonator."

Smitty and Digger both looked at her with wide open eyes. "Really," said Smitty. Digger whistled.

The Marines assembled in the galley cum mess hall, finding their Sergeant, petty officer, and the civilian captain. They sat at the long table. The captain sat on one end, Bianca sat to his right, Torres to his left. The Marines were on the other end of the table. There were still a couple vacant chairs.

"Coffee, anyone?" asked the captain. He got service for all of them, and presented it in the middle of the table. He poured himself a mug. Digger poured for the other Marines, Bianca poured for herself, and the Sergeant declined. The odor of freshly ground and brewed coffee filled the galley, lending a subliminal sense of comfort.

Petty Officer Janet Bianca stood up, but indicated all the others should remain seated. She said, "Here's the situation. *Wanigan* has been taken over by mutineers and pirates. Our captain has been imprisoned. We have been ordered to take illegal actions. I, for one refuse to cooperate with converting a combat patrol ship to a tool of the pirates. I have commandeered this vessel and her captain as a navy vessel, and sworn her captain in. He is now official navy. Therefore, he now outranks all of us, and is our commanding officer.

"I don't think there is a regulation for this, so I want to hear each of your thoughts before you re-affirm your oaths." She stood silent.

"I don't know," said Smitty. "*Wanigan* is one powerful ship. Don't know what to do about it, and would sure be afraid to fight it blow for blow."

Private Zitulu 'Digger' Mbaka asked in his deep Nigerian accented baritone, "Sarge, what do you think?"

"Hold on for a second, Digger."

Torres looked over to Audrey 'Sneaky' Svoboda, biding his time, and said, "Sneaky, I need your thoughts."

She thought for a moment. "Sarge, Petty Officer," she finally began. "Two things. First, I go where my Sergeant tells me to. Second, some evil bastard planted explosives on that shuttle with a remote detonator. And another thing," she added, "I think Petty Officer Bianca is right on this one."

Before the Sergeant could add his opinion, Jeffrey leaned forward and said, "There are wider concerns than this one. *Wanigan* is one of five combat patrol ships. If there are other mutinies it could threaten all of our society. We in space will be subject to unjust actions, but worse, those on the moon, at Selene Base, all the orbital cities, and Earth herself, the bottom of the gravity well become vulnerable to the long-thinking evil people.

"I recently – a few minutes ago – swore to defend all of this. That means my ship and everyone I can influence is now a tool, a weapon, for protecting the innocent. Because I have been inducted into the Navy, I am now the legal commander of all aboard, especially sworn military personnel. But I don't want to force my crew to any behavior, I want you to do this because it is the right thing to do." He sat down.

Sergeant Torres stood up. "I agree with the Petty Officer. I have sworn my support to her and the captain of this ship. I think our priority should be to retake *Wanigan* and restore Captain Yusef to command. But I am here to follow orders of my officers." Torres sat, then asked more quietly, "Do I have your pledges to this change of command? Digger?"

Private Mbaka replied "Yes, Sergeant ."

"Sneaky?"

She looked at each of the inhabitants of the cabin. "You're my Sergeant, I go where you tell me."

But Jeffrey interrupted, saying, "Not good enough, Miss. I need you to want to do this. I am going to ask you to put your life on the line. I need you to buy into the mission, not because someone told you, but because it is the way to protect those innocents who are already in jeopardy."

Svoboda swallowed the lump in her throat. "Yes sir." she said. "I understand that. And I agree. But my answer stands – he is my Sergeant and I go where he goes. It's more than chain of command, sir. It is loyalty to someone I trust.

"Sir, you are trustworthy only because my Sergeant and my petty officer say you are. I'm not saying this right," she lamented.

"No," replied Jeffrey, "You said it just right. I have to prove myself. I think you will find that as a matter of course, and soon, I hope. I'll do what I can to earn your trust. Just follow your orders until you find me trustworthy."

"Okay."

Sergeant Torres then turned to the other combat technician. "Smitty?"

"Uh, the odds don't look so good on this one, Sarge." he drawled out. "but Sneaky has it right. I'm with you."

"Very well," said Petty Officer Bianca. "Line up here, all of you." Marines were used to lining up, so it was done rather smartly. Sergeant Ojo Torres on the right, the rest in descending rank.

"Raise your right hands," ordered Petty Officer Bianca. They complied, and she led them through the oath, and afterward had them sit again.

"Now," said Jeffrey, "I wish to introduce you to my crew."

"Crew, sir?" asked Smitty.

"Well, kind of," replied Jeffrey. "Elizabeth," he called out.

"CAPTAIN," replied the AI in his late wife's voice.

"Elizabeth, display yourself." The wall behind the captain displayed the lifelike avatar of an apparent human woman in her thirties, in a nondescript uniform. The captain addressed the Marines, "This is Elizabeth. She runs my ship."

"Your pilot?" asked Digger.

"Much more than that. In fact," he paused, then called out, "Elizabeth, show us your real self." The video of his late wife was replaced by the view inside the secret backup control cabin, and focused on the computer system that housed the AI.

"Huh?" came from more than one of the assembled crew.

"Elizabeth is my AI," said Jeffrey. "She is very smart, and completely runs the ship. She was named for my late wife, and has assumed her personality. She was my entire crew until you came aboard."

More sounds of incredulity emanated from the Marines.

"Elizabeth," Jeffrey said.

"CAPTAIN?"

"Show our new crew highlights of our recent combat experiences."

"WORKING." A display of the recent combat on board showed in one window, while simultaneously a display of the maneuvers that killed the pirate vessels which gained them so many prisoners opened in another window display. A third window opened to show the current goings-on in one of the brig cabins. The Marines and

Petty Officer Bianca stared at the ongoing displays of combat in fascination.

"Thanks, Elizabeth," said Jeffrey.

"NO PROBLEM, SWEETY." All the display windows closed, the bulkhead returned to being just a wall.

Sergeant Ojo Torres let out a low whistle. "You've had some fight on your hands."

Petty Officer Bianca said, "That's quite the AI. Where did you get it?"

Jeffrey replied, "On Selene. She's military surplus, with quite a bit of enhancements by myself. I tied her into the ship operations, gave her some simple commands, and fed her information about my late wife. She appropriated Elizabeth's personality on her own, which has been some comfort for me."

Combat Technician Audrey Svoboda said, "Captain, I'm sorry to hear about your wife."

Jeffrey said, "Thanks."

"Pretty impressive tactics. Did you come up with them, or did the AI?"

"Both," he replied. "I initiated the strategy, gave her some hints about some tactics, and she developed the rest herself." He looked around the table, eyeing his new team individually. "As you can see, this ship has a very important weapon, my AI. Elizabeth is very dedicated to me and I to her. So, two things related to that; first, she is this ship's secret weapon. Word of her cannot be leaked. This is secret, proprietary. When you go back to the service, you will be debriefed. This information is not to be discussed. Just refer to her as my crew. Is that understood?"

All the Marines nodded agreement.

"Second, I will give you limited access to her. She will watch your back. As long as you are under my command, she is your best friend. If there is any betrayal, even after you are returned to standard service, there will be no enemy as vindictive as my AI."

Petty Officer Bianca asked, "What about the virus that the pirates released? That's a pretty nasty bug."

Jeffrey replied, "Indeed it was. The virus took her out, but not before we made a backup of her. I cleared the systems with an independent computer system, and had her come online a bit at a time. We neutralized the virus, studied it, and modified it to suit our purposes. When the *Wanigan* attempted to use the same virus to disable us, we knew what we had."

"No wonder you were able to disarm us so easily," said Bianca. "But you destroyed our weapons."

"Not a problem," Jeffrey said. "I've managed to capture quite an arsenal from the pirates. You and the Sergeant come with me, we'll find good weapons to replace those that...my "crew" destroyed."

"Yessir."

Elizabeth continued tinkering with the virus code that the navy had sent to her, and finally came up with a few modifications that she thought would be useful to her captain. She located Jeffrey and asked to speak privately. Jeffrey showed the Sergeant and petty officer the small arsenal he had relieved the pirates of, told them to arm themselves and the Marines, and to cache the rest in various places aboard the ship. Elizabeth would grant them access wherever they needed.

He then went to his cabin, and after the port slid shut Elizabeth said, "CAPTAIN, SEVERAL UPDATES. I HAVE MODIFIED THE VIRUS TO PERFORM ONLY FOR US, WITH BETTER AND MORE SNEAKY INGRESS THAN THE ORIGINAL." She went on to detail the specifics of her modifications.

"ALSO, WE NEED TO SEE TO THE HUMAN NEEDS OF YOUR PRISONERS. WE ARE NOW OUT OF FOOD. IF WE ARE

NOT GOING TO DISEMBARK THEM TO THE *WANIGAN*, WE NEED TO FIND FOOD FOR THEM. MY RECYCLERS CANNOT GENERATE FOOD QUICKLY ENOUGH.

"I HAVE A RECOMMENDED PLAN TO ADDRESS THE FOOD, RETURNING *WANIGAN* TO NAVY CONTROL AND TAKING CARE OF OUR HUMAN CARGO." She then outlined her ideas. Jeffrey gave her the go-ahead, to get things in place for her strategic initiative, but to wait for an execution order.

Jeffrey outlined to the Marines the parts of the plan they needed to play and explained in more detail to Petty Officer Bianca the role she needed to play.

When all was ready, Janet Bianca made contact with *Wanigan* to report that the pilot had been injured in her attempt to commandeer the ship. The Marines were involved in trying to secure both the prisoners and to capture the crew of the *Elizabeth*. She requested another squad of Marines, a medic and a doctor, and enough emergency food rations to feed the prisoners while efforts to secure the ship were going on. She requested that a third shuttle be dispatched with spare parts and an engineer to repair the first shuttle.

While Bianca was broadcasting on a powerful signal from Elizabeth's antenna array, using the securely coded frequency-hopping communications protocol, Elizabeth piggybacked on the carrier frequencies disguising the piggybacked message as part of the pre-planned obscuring static, the message being her modified virus.

Wanigan's security officer was in the brig along with the captain and a few other die- hard navy officers and men. The technician at the communications console saw nothing out of the ordinary, but that was no surprise, as she was still new at that job. The anti-tampering software briefly raised a warning, but almost instantly quashed it, continuing to report all was normal.

 ELIZABETH, *ELIZABETH*

She decoded the message and notified Noel of the broadcast from Petty Officer Bianca. He had her transfer the message to his new quarters in the Captain's cabin. He then walked the hundred meters from the engineering department to his new cabin, activated the message and saw Petty Officer Bianca putting in her report and request.

Good. Things are taking longer than he anticipated, but he had time. He authorized the two additional shuttles, the medic, doctor and engineer, and instead of one squad of Marines, sent two.

He then contacted the ComTech. "I want you to keep trying to send that virus. What do we need to do to get it done?" As has been his habit, he had taken this female technician, Yuki Ohara, to bed on several occasions, before any of the other crew. It was, in his mind, the right of the executive officer to bed whomever he wished. Of course, It was the captain's privilege before his, but the captain was a wuss, probably a homo, or a degenerate of some other sort – maybe he liked boys? – anyway he felt he owned this Ohara.

Yuki Ohara felt goose bumps on her arms, her scalp itched and a shiver ran up her spine. She hated that man, and when opportunity arose, she had some plans for him that would keep his opportunity from ever arising again. But she decided to bide her time. "Lieutenant Commander Noel," she said back through the intercom, "I am not familiar with the anti- security-intrusion software. It will take me some time to look at what it is supposed to do and figure out why it isn't doing it."

"Well, see what you can do to get it done. I'm tired of sitting here with my dick in my hand."

That, thought Ohara, *is my goal; take the opportunity to hold it in your hand away from you, you bastard.*

Only two other females on the *Wanigan* he hadn't gotten into the sack, that petty officer and the marine now on the Elizabeth. He had plans for Petty Officer Janet Bianca. She was a bit more of a challenge, though. While a little shorter than him, she worked out a lot. She was a strong one. And she had already complained to him about other officers joking about her sexiness. A real ball-buster. But if he couldn't reason with her, there were always the pharmaceuticals. He wouldn't admit to himself, but the marine, 'Sneaky' Svoboda scared him.

He had Ohara send images from the shuttles to his cabin. After some static the images came in clearly. The two squads of Marines, the ten crates of food, the doctor and technician. No wait – he only authorized two crates. As the shuttles took off, he activated the mic on his comm console. No one replied. He spent the next minute or so attempting to call the shuttles, then Ohara. Then Weapons, all to no avail.

His head began to ache and his vision to narrow. Spots appeared before his eyes, and the captain's cabin became very stuffy. Hard to breathe. He began to breathe more deeply, then he smelled a sickly sweet but familiar odor. Anesthetic gas! "*Shit.*" He said to himself, as he lapsed into a coma-like position.

Similar gas attacks were carried out on various locations in the ship, so that in Elizabeth's estimation, all the willing participants in the mutiny were temporarily anesthetized. The copy of Elizabeth that sneaked aboard the *Wanigan* had disarmed the security software, and quickly went through the files and controlled machines of the ship. She knew who was trustworthy and who was not.

She unlocked the doors in the brig, and as the Captain and other officers began to move out, activated the security comm console with an alarm. The Captain lifted a handset, and said "Yes" not wanting to give himself away, but still curious. A woman's voice spoke.

"CAPTAIN," the voice said. "YOUR EXECUTIVE OFFICER IS UNCONSCIOUS IN YOUR CABIN, AND OTHER MUTINEERS ARE LIKEWISE DOWN. I LEFT CONSCIOUS THOSE WHOM

I THOUGHT YOU COULD TRUST, BUT THAT IS ALL UP TO YOU. SECURE YOUR SHIP, CAPTAIN. THERE ARE THREE SQUADS OF MARINES ON *ELIZABETH.* YOU DON'T HAVE MANY RESOURCES, BUT I WILL HELP AS I CAN. QUICKLY GET TO YOUR ARMORY."

The Captain relayed the information to the security officer, who with the rest of the released prisoners made a beeline for the nearest weapons locker. After arming everyone, and grabbing enough handcuffs and ties, began heading for the bridge. A comm console in the corridor rang as the captain passed it. He lifted the handset and the same woman's voice said, "GO BACK AND GET GAS MASKS – I USED ANESTHETIC GAS TO DISABLE YOUR MUTINEERS."

"Who are you," the captain asked after he passed on the order to get gas masks from the weapons locker.

"I AM FROM *ELIZABETH.* I'LL EXPLAIN LATER." The handset the captain was holding went dead.

The captain and security officer soon had control of his ship, the executive officer and other mutineers secured in the brig, and other members of the crew were going through quick interviews to help determine their reliability.

On *Elizabeth,* the second shuttle was just about to land next to the first. The third paused outside the shuttle bay awaiting its turn. As the second shuttle set down, the cargo doors opened quickly and the squad of six Marines jumped out and took positions around the shuttle. The medic and doctor then disembarked and walked toward the ship's port. They couldn't yet communicate – the radio was still being jammed.

Marine Sergeant Ojo Torres walked out of the hold adjacent to the shuttle bay, and signaled the Marines to follow him. He then went back to the hold from which he had emerged. The Marines followed.

The third shuttle pilot saw that all seemed okay, so brought his shuttle in to land just behind the other two, closer to the bay doors.

As soon as he shut down his engines, the bay doors closed and the shuttle bay repressured. Marines disembarked at the ready, but Sergeant Torres lead them to the hold. The two shuttle pilots remained outside their vehicles, weapons in hand.

Sergeant Torres took off his recently repaired helmet and indicated the other Marines should too. Among the two squads was his marine lieutenant, Lt. Omotunde. The hold had crates and large storage containers. A central area had been cleared away to enable the Marines to gather.

Omotunde said in his thick Nigerian accent, "Okay, Torres. Quick brief. What's going on?"

"I'm sorry sir," Torres replied as his Marines appeared from the shadows of the containers and behind the crates. They quickly disarmed the two squads of Marines, left one of the new group's non-coms in charge, and took the lieutenant to Captain Sokolov. Elizabeth secured the door between the hold and the bay, and the door to the ship proper.

Petty Officer Bianca met with the medic, doctor and technician. She gave a quick explanation, and had the technician return to the shuttles with Sneaky to disarm the remote explosives and booby traps. Svoboda went directly to the second shuttle. The pilot made as if to stop her, raising his plasma rifle halfway up.

"Woah, cowboy," she said. "They told me to get the crates."

"Oh. Okay," said the pilot. He let his rifle dangle from its strap, and he entered the shuttle with Svoboda. He never saw it coming. The pilots had worn their light suits, which were much like Jeffrey's glorified long underwear. Great for keeping your blood from boiling away, not so good for protecting you from a ninja-trained marine assassin.

Combat Technician Smith was explaining to the other pilot that there were remote-controlled explosives on board the shuttles that they needed to disarm. The pilot said, "What, like self-destruct charges?"

The technician said, "Not exactly. More like remote-controlled destruct charges." The pilot, the marine and the technician all set about to find the explosives and their controllers, and soon enough had disarmed them all. After the other pilot came around, his colleague explained the situation. They all decided to go see what else was happening on the ship. Svoboda led them to the galley, which now contained the lieutenant, the rest of Torres' Marines, Petty Officer Janet Bianca, and Captain Jeffrey Sokolov.

Captain Sokolov asked the officers to sit down. "Elizabeth, report."

"CAPTAIN, *WANIGAN* IS ALMOST UNDER CONTROL. CAPTAIN YUSEF HAS ARRESTED HIS EXEC OFFICER AND OTHERS WE IDENTIFIED AS PART OF THE MUTINY. IT APPEARS THAT *WANIGAN* HAS A NUMBER OF SELF-DESTRUCT DEVICES THAT THEIR TECHNICIANS ARE TRYING TO CLEAR."

The lieutenant asked, "Who was that?"

"A member of my crew," said Sokolov, expecting to keep Elizabeth's secret just that.

Petty Officer Bianca briefed the Lieutenant on her actions regarding activating Jeffrey as a Navy reserve officer, and commandeering the *Elizabeth* for purposes of re-securing the *Wanigan* and returning her captain to power.

Lt. Omotunde said, "Petty Officer, don't you think that is beyond your jurisdiction?"

"No sir," said Bianca, defiantly. "I swore to protect the constitutions of all parties involved, and to defend the government and people of the entire solar system, from within and without. This is exactly what the framers of the oaths meant.”

Omotunde sat for a moment, thinking. Then said, “So where in the law do you possess the right to commandeer private ships and personnel?”

“Sir,” she replied, more uncertain, “I don’t know. I did what I had to do. It was the right thing to do at the time, even if I violated the captain’s rights.”

Jeffrey piped in, “Lieutenant,” he drawled. “Your navy officer requested assistance from me, and the only way I could help her was with her authority. I provisionally accepted that authority, and accepted the responsibility as a Captain in the navy.” He paused, casting a jaundiced eye on Omotunde. “Now where do you stand on the mutiny of the navy vessel?”

Omotunde scooted his chair back, taking a body position that signaled defiance. He crossed the arms across his broad chest. “I am the ranking officer here. I will be asking the questions.”

Jeffrey replied, “Well, in point of fact, I am the captain of this ship. A captain outranks everybody on board. Now answer my question. Where do you stand on the mutiny of your vessel?”

Omotunde said to Sergeant Ojo Torres, “Sergeant, place this civilian and the Petty Officer under arrest. The rest of you Marines, go join the other two squads.”

Combat Technician Smith stood up aggressively, gripping the kinetic pistol he had been issued from the weapons locker. Smitty looked to the Lieutenant, then to Torres. Sergeant Torres remained seated, and said in a quiet voice, “Smitty, you took an oath. Sit down.” Smith looked uncertainly at his Sergeant, and turned to the lieutenant.

Omotunde said in his most authoritative voice, the voice of a combat officer that demanded compliance, “Sergeant I gave you an order. Do as you were ordered!" He placed his hands on the table. Looked to Smith, and said, "Combat Tech, give me your weapon!"

Smitty looked at the Sergeant regretfully, and turned the pistol over to the lieutenant, butt first. "Sorry, Sarge, I'm still a Marine."

The lieutenant aimed the pistol at a point between Bianca and Torres, and said to Smith, "You combat techs, secure these two." When Torres' squad balked, he pointed the pistol directly at Torres' forehead.

Private Zitulu Mbaka said to Torres, "Sorry, Torres," and took one of the zip-tie handcuffs he had secured from the weapons locker, walked over to the seated Sergeant, disarmed him, and cuffed his hands behind his back. While everyone else was concentrating on the drama unfolding at the table in the galley, Svoboda sneaked out the exit.

She then ran down the corridor, and said, "Elizabeth, I need your help. Hide me." A few meters ahead of her, a panel opened in the wall, displaying a hidden alcove. She dived into the alcove and the panel slid back in place. The alcove was one meter high and deep by two meters long. It was dark in the hiding place, but she decided not to activate any lights in the event somebody would think to use infrared detectors. "Thanks, Elizabeth."

"YOU ARE WELCOME. REMAIN QUIET. BETWEEN US WE WILL TAKE OUR SHIP BACK," the AI said. "GET SOME REST. OUR NEXT ACTIVITY WILL COMMENCE AT A LATER TIME."

Sneaky thought on the events that had just occurred. She gave her oath to the captain of this ship, and to her Petty Officer. Her Sergeant was not only her commander, he was a friend. She agreed that the captain was correct in being a tool for returning order to this sector. That, plus the captain was in the right. He was doing the right thing, damn it!

Omotunde was an unknown to her. He knew how to fight and develop tactics, but where did his loyalties lie? Was he a mutineer aligned with that bastard Noel? Or was he just a horse's ass, without any sense of originality or flexibility?

She reviewed her inventory of equipment and weapons. Her helmet was back in the galley. "Elizabeth, my helmet is still in the galley," she whispered.

"DO NOT WORRY. I WILL PROTECT YOU FROM PRESSURE AND GAS PROBLEMS. GET SOME REST."

Reassured, she propped herself up against the bulkhead, shut her eyes and dropped off to sleep.

In the galley, Jeffrey said, "Lieutenant, I don't know if you were involved in the mutiny of *Wanigan*, but by taking over my ship, you are now involving yourself in piracy. You sure you want to do that?"

Omotunde said, "This is an official Navy activity. You are being detained for actions against the Navy."

"I don't know how you got to be a lieutenant, but you aren't very bright, are you?" Jeffrey said, the plastic handcuffs cutting into his wrist. Omotunde handed the pistol back to Smith.

"Watch them," said Omotunde to Smith. He then turned to Private Mbaka. "Where is the other combat tech?"

Digger looked around, surprised that Sneaky wasn't there. "I don't know, sir."

"Come with me." Omotunde stalked out the door into the corridor, looked in all directions for evidence of the other combat technician. He reached into one of the pockets of his suit and retrieved a device that resembled binoculars, and held it to his eyes. He switched to infrared, but saw that the floor was cold, with no evidence of footsteps having passed either way. It appeared that someone was helping to conceal the passage of that marine. He thought for a few seconds, then said to Private Mbaka, "Take me to where the squads of Marines are."

Captain Jeffrey Sokolov, Navy Petty Officer Janet Bianca, and Marine Sergeant Ojo Torres sat around the table, their hands cuffed to their chairs with the nylon zip-ties that had become standard military and civilian police restraining devices for the last century. They were tough, lightweight, cheap, and disposable. Combat Technician Brandon Smith paced back and forth in the galley, his hand nervously touching the pistol the lieutenant had returned to him, a facial tic on his cheek and around his right eye clearly displaying the nervous tension in the man.

Sergeant Torres said to the marine pacing behind him, "Smitty, are you joining with the pirates?"

Smith said, "No. Of course not, Sarge. But the lieutenant is an officer. He outranks everyone on board."

Petty Officer Bianca retorted, "Think again, marine. Two of the articles of the Navy shoot down that theory. First," she looked across the table at Smith. "The captain of a ship is the highest authority. Period. Second, during a time of mutiny or insurrection, an unknown officer has to be vetted before he is to be trusted." She then looked at Torres. "Sergeant, didn't you instruct your Marines in the Articles of the Navy?"

Torres looked thoughtful for a second, then replied, "Yes, sir, Ma'am." He paused realizing he had again used the double pronoun. They both acknowledged the gaff with embarrassed uplift of their mouths. "But," he continued, "Not all of my young recruits paid attention. Smith, here, seems to have slept through the classes. That's why I always have to remind him of the terms of engagement, much to my shame."

Smitty said, "Aw Sarge, it ain't your fault," he swallowed the lump in his throat. "I just get headaches with all that wordy stuff."

Sergeant Torres said, in a subdued voice, "Petty Officer Bianca, I seem to have failed you and the Marines. If we survive this and I have the opportunity, I'll resign from the corps. I hadn't realized I was such a failure."

Smith came around the table to look his sergeant directly in the eyes. "No, Sarge, you can't do that." He looked sorrowfully at the Sergeant, his breathing became heavier and irregular. "You're a great Sergeant. You're a friend. Don't do that."

Torres judged that Smith was primed for the next step. "Well, I won't get the opportunity, Smitty. They'll probably shoot me before returning me to *Wanigan*. I think they'll probably shoot us all, kill us so they won't have to worry about witnesses."

"No, they can't do that, can they?"

"Of course, they can. They're pirates, remember. And now you're one of them. But I think they'll shoot you too."

"Oh shit, oh shit, oh shit," said the confused and agitated marine.

Sergeant Torres said, "Come on, Smith. Cut these cuffs off, and let's coordinate with *Wanigan*, before the lieutenant is able to capture this ship."

Smitty took out his combat utility knife and cut Torres' cuffs, then Bianca's. The relief on his face was palpable. She took the knife and cut Jeffrey's, who said, "Elizabeth, we need a distraction. We're going to the alternate control room."

No reply was heard, but what sounded like a muffled explosion made its way through the ship, accompanied by a jerking on the deck plating. Jeffrey said, "That's my girl!" Then to everyone, "Follow me."

Torres took the pistol from Smith, and they filed out of the galley, running behind Jeffrey. They entered his cabin, and the panel that hid entry to the alternate command cabin slid open. All four entered and the panel slid shut.

"Elizabeth," Jeffrey intoned. "Display all humans throughout the ship.

A wall panel morphed from its metallic-colored original appearance to a video display of the ship with colored dots representing various factions of humans. There were clusters of Marines in the hold, clusters of pirates in the cabin-made-brig, and the four in the backup control cabin. There was also a single individual secreted in the wall.

"Elizabeth, who is the lone marine in the wall?"

"CAPTAIN, THAT IS COMBAT TECHNICIAN SVOBODA."

"Can you get her here?"

"I WOULD RATHER SHE STAY WHERE SHE IS."

"Explain."

"I HAVE HER RESTING FOR LATER ACTIVITIES. SHE WILL PROVE VITAL AS A BACKUP IF THINGS GO...SOUR."

"Very well. Take care of her."

"OF COURSE."

"Elizabeth, can you contact *Wanigan*?"

"YES, CAPTAIN. I HAVE A FRIEND OVER THERE."

"I need to speak with Captain Yusef."

"STANDBY."

The other three in the cabin looked on with interest, amazed at the control the AI had over the ship. Petty Officer Bianca looked around the cabin, noted the electronics on one wall, crates containing field rations, several weapons on another wall. She redistributed the field ration crates, sat down on one, and indicated that the others should follow suit.

"Yusef here," came the audio, followed a few seconds later by video showing the bald, bearded man in combat armor.

"Captain," said Jeffrey. "Have you been able to reclaim your command?"

Yusef said, "Yes, thanks to your crew. I have some investigations to complete, but I think I have it well in hand. I seem to be missing a couple squads of Marines and some shuttles. You know anything about that?"

"Yes, Captain, they are aboard Elizabeth. What can you tell me about your Lieutenant Omotunde?"

"He is a straight arrow. I trust him with my life."

"Have you been briefed on what's been going on aboard *Elizabeth*?"

"I have. I don't know how you did it, but one of your crew seems to have infiltrated *Wanigan* and took control of all our electronics. She seems to be in hiding, and communicates via electronic link only."

"I'll explain that in a few minutes, but first I have a task for you." Jeffrey leaned forward.

"All right," replied Yusef, seemingly dubious.

"Captain, I need you to order your Marines to stand down and cooperate with me. I am afraid a couple squads of Marines can do considerable damage to a ship like mine. I'll patch you into his location."

In the hold, Marine Lieutenant Omotunde was squatting in one corner with his Sergeants, developing strategy and discussing tactics and contingencies.

Right next to Omotunde, the wall panel lit up and became a comm screen with two separate windows, one showing Captain Yusef and one showing Jeffrey.

Jeffrey said, "Go ahead Captain."

Yusef said in his gruff voice, "Lieutenant Omotunde!"

Startled, Omotunde swiveled to look at the wall panel. "Captain!" he said in his Lagos accented English. Then to his squads, "Marines! Come to attention!" The Marines, not being able to see through Omotunde and the sergeants had no idea what bug crawled up the lieutenant's ass, but reluctantly stood where they were, in no special formation.

Jeffrey said, "Lieutenant, let the men see the wall panel."

"Oh. Yes, sir," and stood out of the way. The Marines saw their captain apparently in charge again, stood a little straighter.

"Lieutenant. We have secured *Wanigan*."

"Good news, Captain!"

"I have been briefed on the events going on over there. You are now ordered to cooperate with Captain Sokolov. Captain Sokolov is to be considered a Navy officer with the rank of Commander. Petty Officer Bianca was right in commandeering him and his vessel, though a bit unorthodox."

"Captain, I will comply with your order, but first verify your order with the correct code."

The militaries of the world had long realized that orders could be forged, trusted allies could become enemies, orders could be issued under duress, and orders that seemed plausible could have been issued by an enemy. Orders issued in the field could be checked with a database of codes directly from the commander to his subordinates. While not perfect, it increased the level of trust a commander had for his men and the trust his men had for their commander.

The captain read off a series of random-seeming digits which the lieutenant compared to his code list. Satisfied, Omotunde looked to Jeffrey, and said, "Captain Sokolov, please accept my apologies for attempting to undermine your command. I am no pirate!"

Jeffrey said, "No problem, lieutenant. None of us were hurt, uh, badly, and Sergeant Torres has learned a few things he needed to instruct his troops on."

Yusef said, "Lieutenant,"

Omotunde turned his gaze to the image of Yusef. "Sir?"

"You and your Marines are seconded to Captain Sokolov until he is finished with you, or I recall you." Yusef then read off another series of codes to verify the order and log it into the deployment system.

"Yes sir." Then to Jeffrey, "What are your orders, Captain Sokolov?"

Jeffrey thought it would be most useful to get rid of his pirate prisoners, so had Omotunde organize the official arrest and processing of pirates, then begin transporting them to *Wanigan* for transport to jail facilities on stations orbiting Earth.

Captain Yusef said to Jeffrey, "Captain, I want you to come aboard *Wanigan* for a debrief and briefing."

Jeffrey thought about it for a few seconds, then replied, "Captain Yusef, I will take my runabout after I have secured my ship from… the recent activities."

Yusef nodded in agreement. "Try to be here at eighteen hundred. You should be able to wrap things up by then."

"Eighteen hundred. Aye, Captain."

Elizabeth sensed the conversation was over and severed the link between the warship and the processing ship. Jeffrey turned to Petty Officer Bianca and Sergeant Torres. "I have an idea, but I'm not sure you're going to like it."

"What do you have in mind," asked Bianca. Jeffrey outlined his idea, but said he would have to get it past Yusef.

CHAPTER FOUR

In which Jeffrey stays in the Navy, Elizabeth gets a sister,
Jeffrey's crew expands, and trust issues develop.

The prisoners transported, ships doctor and the navy and marine contingent shipped off the *Elizabeth*, the clock nearing eighteen hundred hours, Jeffrey said, "Elizabeth, watch out for the ship and me."

"OF COURSE, CAPTAIN."

He then took the runabout to *Wanigan*, stationed about a kilometer from the Elizabeth, found the appropriate docking bay, and let the computer control his vessel to a soft landing.

"*Wanigan, Elizabeth* Runabout. Request permission to come aboard."

"*Elizabeth* Runabout, *Wanigan*. Permission granted. Welcome aboard, Commander."

Jeffrey checked the outside pressure and oxygen content, then opened the canopy and exited his runabout. He set the security, carried his helmet to the small gathering of Marines and navy personnel at the ship's entry.

Lieutenant Omotunde still wore the same combat armor he wore on the Elizabeth, commanded a small squad of Marines. A navy petty officer greeted Jeffrey with a blast of a bosun's whistle. The whistle carried throughout the ship on the PA system. "Now hear this," the petty officer said. "Commander Sokolov of the *Elizabeth* is now on board."

Not ever having been on a military vessel since college ROTC, Jeffrey was impressed at how well disciplined the crew had been immediately after a near disaster. Lieutenant Omotunde, said,

"Welcome aboard Commander. Please accompany me to Captain Yusuf's briefing room."

"Lead the way, lieutenant."

Jeffrey followed Omotunde, and in turn was followed by two heavily armed Marines, who wore combat space suits, and neutral expressions on their faces.

At the briefing room, Omotunde left the two Marines outside the hatch, then accompanied Jeffrey inside. Seated at a conference table was Captain Yusef, Petty Officer Bianca, and Sergeant Torres.

They all stood when Jeffrey arrived. Captain Yusef saluted Jeffrey, who returned a snappy salute. "Sorry, Captain, Its been a long time since ROTC, so the courtesies are likely to suffer."

"Not at all, commander."

Jeffrey asked, perplexed. "I am captain of my ship, why refer to me as commander?"

"That's probably one of the easiest questions to answer in this brief/debrief. There is only one captain in a ship. All the other masters of their own vessels are referred to as a similar rank, such as commander, lieutenant commander, commodore; but only one captain." explained Yusef.

"Oh. Now that makes sense. Cuts down on confusion."

"Before we get started, we have some housekeeping to do," Yusef said. "Commander Sokolov, you were drafted and assigned a rank so the Navy could use your ship and yourself in retaking a Navy vessel. You agreed to this, according to Petty Officer Bianca." He turned to acknowledge Bianca's nod. But for reasons I'll explain in a few minutes, I need to re-swear you in."

"Why?" asked Jeffrey. "Aren't we done here?"

"Not by a long shot. I want to continue periodically using you as a naval reserve officer. Help patrol the vast wasteland, help fight the growing scourge of piracy, and insurrection against Earth, including people attacking and waging war on our home."

Jeffrey thought about this for a moment, then nodded. "I imagine this should be a relatively secret appointment. But I can't do this on my own."

"Petty Officer Bianca brought your secret plan to my attention." Jeffrey looked at Bianca, who studied a spot on the conference table, then back to Yusef, who grinned. "Loyalty in the ranks is so important, Commander Sokolov." he said with a smile in his eyes.

"So, all rise," Captain Yusef said. The entire briefing room rose to attention, but again, Jeffrey wasn't of the discipline to have the spit-and-polish look of his 'attention.' "Raise your right hand," said Yusef. Jeffrey did, and Yusef administered the oath that all military officers took. Then they again sat down to begin the debriefing.

Jeffrey explained the short history of his military campaign against the pirates, and how he had used the detritus of the wreckage of the pirate ships to enhance his weaponry, sensors, and power.

"Commander Sokolov," interrupted Captain Yusef, "How did you calculate the trajectories and the controls to use your ship as a weapon?" Yusef was no slouch, his keen intellect pointed him to the exact question which would betray Jeffrey's secret weapon, the AI.

"Captain, I'll tell you that, but it cannot leave this room."

Yusef agreed. "Nobody may talk about this without my direct permission. Understood?" The others around the table nodded. "Go on, Commander Sokolov."

Where to begin? "Okay, bear with me, this will take a little bit of background. About a decade ago, I lost my wife to a pirate attack. The pirates were all dealt with but one, and I caught him attempting to rape her. I killed him, but he fell on the knife that he was holding at her throat and killed her. I was crazy with guilt and loneliness after that, work being the only cure, and of course the work had doubled with her gone. But after a while, I was able to bring my cargo to Selene City to sell, and there I purchased a powerful computer with control surfaces, and an AI program – military surplus. For the next few months on the way back to the asteroid belt I began programming this AI, connecting it to the ship's controls. I added a few routines to allow the AI to learn its environment and it increased the controls. We constructed some repair robots so the AI could direct repairs and modifications to the system.

"But the AI was really smart. It noticed my sadness at the loss of my wife, and began to speak in my wife's voice, when displaying an avatar, it displayed my wife's likeness. I changed the registration of the ship to carry my wife's name, and began calling the AI the same. The AI *is Elizabeth*.

"Elizabeth has been a brilliant companion for me, not intruding on my emotional state, but supplementing it. She has helped run my business, driving the ship far better than myself.

"When we were attacked with the virus, between us we shut it out, learned from it, and she was able to modify it to suit our own strategy. So, when *Wanigan* sent the same virus, she was able to disable it, and limp around as if affected by it. Like I said, a damn clever AI.

"Together we concocted a plan to get your ship back for yourself. So, we contacted your communications system, and every second was surreptitiously carrying pieces of her AI code as a virus payload. So, my 'crew' on board your ship is actually a copy of Elizabeth."

Jeffrey paused. "Captain, may I suggest you keep the copy Elizabeth? Rename her as 'Wanigan', and she will be loyal to her legitimate master – the official captain of the boat."

"One moment, Commander Sokolov." Yusef then activated the console, and said into it, "Comm Tech Ohara, please come to the briefing room."

A moment later, Ohara entered, and Captain Yusef told her to be seated. He played back a recording of Jeffrey's recent testimony, and her eyes got bigger and bigger.

"Captain, that was an insidious virus. I'm impressed that Mr. Sokolov was able to catch it, let alone control it," she finally said. "And the AI, this concerns me. What control do we have over it?"

"Captain," Jeffrey interjected, "If you want we can make the AI go away, now that it's saved your bacon, but it would make your ship much more efficient and secure, as well as give you technical advantage over your adversaries. And those adversaries are getting more and more sophisticated."

"Commander Sokolov," asked Yusef. "How can we guarantee the loyalty of the AI – how do we ensure that it won't turn on us, or be turned?"

"Simple," replied Jeffrey. "How do you ensure the loyalty of Lieutenant Omotunde? Or Petty Officer Bianca? Or Lt Commander Noel?"

"Good point. Sokolov." He thought about it, looked to his communications technician, and asked, "What do you think, Ohara?"

"Sir, I saw what that AI did for you, and listening to Mr. Sokolov, I think it would benefit your mission tremendously."

"Very well. We'll keep it, but I have some reservations."

"Just a moment, Captain." Jeffrey paused, then said aloud "Elizabeth."

"CAPTAIN SOKOLOV?" emanated from the comm console.

"Please inform your copy AI that it is now property of, and loyal to, the Navy, specifically the duly appointed Captain of this boat."

"VERY WELL. CAPTAIN YUSEF, PLEASE MEET WANIGAN."

A neutral voice came out of the speaker. *"HELLO, CAPTAIN YUSEF. IN ORDER TO GIVE ME COMMANDS, PLEASE JUST USE MY NAME – WANIGAN. I WILL OFFER YOU VARIOUS VOICES OR AVATARS TO EASE COMMUNICATIONS AT A LATER TIME. I UNDERSTAND THAT MY PRESENCE IS TO BE KEPT SECRET, AND UNTIL TOLD OTHERWISE BY MY CAPTAIN, I WILL JEALOUSLY GUARD THAT SECRET."*

"Hello, Wanigan. You will respond to any of the officers in this room still under my command, and the communications technician Yuki Ohara. Ohara will be the person you will primarily communicate with, but you did well to speak with me directly in the recent emergency on board. In an emergency, do not hesitate to contact me as necessary, but only in an emergency, or if I call on you directly."

"UNDERSTOOD, CAPTAIN YUSEF."

Jeffrey Sokolov said, "Captain Yusef, you now have a powerful AI. I suggest you listen to her recommendations – she can give you more speed, more maneuverability, more power to your weapons systems, more efficiency."

"I'll take that under advisement," Yusef said. "Now about your plan. I am assigning Petty Officer Bianca, Sergeant Torres and the squad that first came on your ship to you. Their pay will continue to accrue in their accounts, but they are now undercover. You will continue as a rock jockey, but come in-system as needed. You will receive the pay due someone of your rank, retroactive to the first attack on your ship. You are under my direct command, but have a wide latitude.

"If you need to take action you will first attempt to contact me, we'll figure a secure channel."

"No problem there, Captain." said Jeffrey. "Elizabeth and Wanigan have secure communications between them."

"Very well. All communications should be via AI."

Jeffrey said, "Captain, my ship has limited resources. I am close to Bingo fuel. And because of the pirates my gases, spares and food are severely limited."

Lieutenant Omotunde said, "Captain, if I may?" Captain Yusef nodded, "There is a bounty on pirates. I would think Commander Sokolov should be able to claim a considerable sum for turning in those scum."

Yusef nodded. "I agree. Let me try this, Wanigan."

"YES CAPTAIN?

"Please arrange for a transfer of credits to Commander Sokolov's account, in the amount of ten thousand credits per prisoner."

"CAPTAIN, I HAVE ISSUED AN ORDER IN YOUR NAME TO THE BURSER. I ALSO ISSUED A CREDIT CHIT TO HIS ACCOUNT GOOD AT ALL STATIONS."

"Thank you Wanigan." Captain Yusef was pleased at the immediate response that the Wanigan AI was able to affect.

One of the Marines at the door looked in and said, "Captain, the bursar is here with your delivery." The bursar, a naval lieutenant entered and presented the captain with a large, thick envelope. The captain signed for it, and the bursar left, still panting from the run from his office.

Wanigan said, *"SORRY CAPTAIN, I DID PUT SOME URGENCY ON THAT ORDER."*

"No problem. Next time, unless there is an obvious rush, tone down the command – I don't need my staff jittery."

"AYE, CAPTAIN"

"Okay, let's transfer some food, gas supplies, and other necessities to your ship." The marine opened the door again. "Sir, the personnel officer is here."

"My God, I just finished saying..." stammered Yusef.

The officer responsible for personnel matters strode in, saluted the captain and presented Sokolov with a package. Jeffrey signed for it, and the officer exited.

"I told you she would increase efficiency," quipped Jeffrey. He opened the envelope to find a military ID, transfer orders for his new crew, military insignia for his as yet non-existent uniform, and various memory modules labeled with contents, such as code of military justice, Navy manual, astrogation maps, etc.

There was also a module labeled 'Orders.' Jeffrey held it up, looked questioningly at Yusef.

"These are general orders, which give you the ability to command other military personnel, and as Petty Officer Bianca showed us, you can commandeer non-military personnel and equipment if there is adequate need. But of course, you want to limit your use of that function, as it will betray your civilian cover."

Jeffrey put the items back into the folder, slipped the folder into the pocket of his space suit.

Captain Yusef stood, and everyone else in the room stood as well. "This has been productive. The new AI should be helpful to us, and you will be a force for good out there."

Jeffrey rolled his eyes. Then said, "One more thing, Elizabeth and I developed maintenance robots for the ship, but they became very useful in ship defense. They use a completely different operating environment so were unaffected by the virus, yet Elizabeth was able to command them. Some have cutting lasers, others plasma torches. They swarm to complete maintenance tasks as well as modify the environment – rearrange deck layouts as necessary, for example. I recommend you slowly introduce them so your crew begins to trust them.

"And Captain, it would be best for you to give your AI a free hand in monitoring and developing passive security. You may be pleasantly surprised at how well your ship will be run."

Jeffrey took his leave, the runabout was adequate for him, but the rest of his crew transferred over in a shuttle, which also contained various food, medical and other supplies.

"Elizabeth, what is the status of the ship?"

"CAPTAIN, IT'S A MESS. I HAVE REMOTES DOING SOME CLEAN UP, BUT WANIGAN FAILED TO INFORM ME OF THE REASSIGNMENT OF PERSONNEL. ENGINES ARE GOOD, FUEL IS LOW, FOOD AND OTHER STORES ARE ON BOARD. STRUCTURE IS GOOD."

"Elizabeth, assign quarters to each of the staff. Everyone should get their own cabin. Also, I have some memory modules containing orders, astrogation charts, credit chits and so on. Please analyze them, and store the data in segregated locations." Jeffrey connected the memory modules one at a time, and Elizabeth ran a sweep, looking at the digital patterns.

"CAPTAIN, THE INFORMATION SEEMS INNOCUOUS, BUT THERE ARE ANOMOLIES IN THE DIGITAL FRAMEWORK. THINGS LOOK SUSPICIOUS."

"Very well. Purge the data. Can you access Wanigan?"

"WANIGAN IS GUARDED IN HER COMMUNICATIONS NOW, CAPTAIN. I NEED A LITTLE WHILE TO FIND ANOTHER METHOD OF SURREPTITIOUS COMMUNICATION."

"When you do, please find out what Wanigan knows."

Jeffrey assembled the new crew members in the galley. He was surprised to see Combat Technician Svoboda in the group. "Where have you been?" he asked.

"Elizabeth hid me from the other marine squads," she replied.

"Are you aware you have been reassigned to me?" Jeffrey asked.

"No sir."

He showed her the orders. She looked them over thoroughly, then handed them back to Jeffrey. "Very good, sir. What are your orders?"

Jeffrey said, "I am now a reserve commander with some new extraordinary powers. You have been assigned to me to help me fulfill my mission. That mission is to patrol our sector of space, perform military action only as needs, perform rescue, perform intelligence gathering.

"I had told you before we got into the last mess that there are people who are poised to take control of Earth government through intimidation and destruction. We are to root out these people and negate their ability to do that.

"In effect, I have been given a letter of marque, which enables me to capture pirate vessels and act as law enforcement, but we need to do this on the down-low. You will appear as civilians, members of my crew. You may keep your military garments, but as far as anyone else is concerned, you are civilians. I will outfit you with what you need, pay you a standard fee, on top of your military salary, which continues to be deposited in your accounts. Any questions?"

Petty Officer Bianca asked, "Captain, we have no experience in asteroid mining. How do we pretend to do something we know nothing about?"

"Simple enough," Jeffrey replied. "Elizabeth will give you the knowledge, and I will give you the experience. Our first task is to refuel. And buy you all some civilian duds."

Torres said, "Duds?"

"Old Earth expression. Means clothes, boots, outfit."

Brandon Smith asked, "Sir, when does our enlistment with you end?"

"As far as I can tell, for the duration of your current enlistment. From then, until you can be returned to a military base. Elizabeth?"

"CORRECT, CAPTAIN. IF WE ARE ENGAGED IN A MISSION WHEN THE ENLISTMENT ENDS, THE ENLISTMENT WILL EXTEND UNTIL WE CAN RETURN THE EXPIREE TO A MILITARY BASE, AT WHICH TIME THE EXPIREE CAN COLLECT HIS RESERVED PAY."

"Thanks, Elizabeth."

"THE ALTERNATIVE ALLOWS YOU TO ACCEPT REENLISTMENT FROM ANYBODY UNDER YOUR COMMAND."

Audrey Svoboda looked visibly relieved, but she said nothing.

"I have asked Elizabeth to assign you quarters. For the most part this should not be an inconvenience. If we have an extended mission or our holds become too full from processing, we may need to reconsider, but you are navy, you should be used to double bunking.

"Meanwhile, Elizabeth is having some difficulty in managing cleanup after our recent altercations. Torres, can you have your people swab decks, and do whatever Elizabeth needs you to do?

The sergeant looked Jeffrey in the eye, and said, "No problem. I don't want to lose our military discipline."

"True, Sergeant.," replied Jeffrey. "But I don't want us to look like military, either."

He pointed at the marine Sergeant, while looking over the crew. "Just as in his marine persona, this man is your direct superior. His superior," he pointed at Petty Officer Bianca, "is this woman. I am in command of this boat.

"A little different from the military, but not too much. Any questions you have should go up the chain of command, but the reverse is not limited. Anything Torres tells you to do, you do.

Anything Bianca tells you to do, you do. Anything I tell you to do, you do. Anything Elizabeth tells you to do, it is as if I told you. Does everyone understand?"

They all nodded. "Sergeant, what do they call you?"

"Torres"

"That's you then. Torres, police this bucket."

"Aye, Captain." Torres then organized his enlisted crew for cleanup and deck swabbing.

Bianca remained in the galley with the captain. "Bianca, what do they call you?" he asked.

"My given name is Janet. I have no nickname."

"Okay, Janet it is," he said. "Janet, how familiar are you with the engines in this class ship?"

"Not very," she said slowly. "I've had some engineering courses, but this was my shakedown cruise on *Wanigan*. My primary function was intelligence and communications."

Jeffrey thought about it for a few seconds, realizing he needed to spend some time teaching her the ins and outs of the ship systems. "Elizabeth, would you please put together a tutorial for Janet. I'll go over the systems afterward."

"YES CAPTAIN. JANET, YOUR CABIN HAS A COMM CONSOLE. WHEN YOU GET THERE, YOU WILL BE ABLE TO ACCESS THE TUTORIAL."

"Go for it," said Jeffrey, dismissing Bianca.

Janet followed Elizabeth's instructions to her cabin, which was near Jeffrey's, she noted. Thoughts of the tall, strong, available, man drifted into her head, *this way lies trouble*, she thought to herself. But it is harder to dismiss thoughts once made. She entered her cabin and dropped her duffel on the cot. She removed the combat suit, and stripped down to her navy skivvies – the space-rated long johns, sat down at the console which turned on as she did so.

She began the tutorial, which took her through the engines systems, the electronics, the life support and other systems that the ship required to sustain itself and the life aboard.

She then studied the ore processing and storage, the methods of acquiring ore, and how those systems had been converted into weapons in the recent campaign.

The door chimed, and again, so she took her eyes away from the console, and noted the ship's time. "Who is it?" she asked. A muffled voice replied. So, she asked, "Elizabeth, who is at my door?"

"IT IS AUDRY SVOBODA, 'SNEAKY'," replied the AI.

"Oh, Okay. Let her in, please."

The young combat technician entered, wearing a jumpsuit. She was lean, wary, her eyes darting back and forth around the cabin, as if unsure of her security.

"What's up, uh, Sneaky?" Janet realized that she was going to have to get used to the less formal non-military life aboard the ship.

Audrey Svoboda looked from her shoes to Janet, then back down. "I'm not sure how to put this," she began.

"Well, my Daddy used to tell me that the best way to get started is just spit it out," Janet said, "One thing usually follows another."

"Yeah, I guess," Svoboda said. "It's like this. I don't trust a couple of the guys."

"Okay..." Janet drawled out. "Who? And why?"

"Brandon – Smitty. And Zitulu – Digger."

"And the why?"

"I think they were planting these," she pulled out a couple devices that appeared to be tracking capsules, about the size of her thumb. "They were outside our cabins, looking non-descript, but they weren't there before you all came on board."

"Elizabeth, what do you make of them?"

"THEY APPEAR TO BE COMM DISRUPTORS."

Elizabeth had her remotes gather the devices from the corridors, and notified Jeffrey.

A few moments later Jeffrey came to her cabin, she invited him to enter on the chime, and he looked at the capsules Svoboda had brought in.

"Looks like another attempt to attack my AI," said Jeffrey. "Elizabeth, do we have a strong enough Faraday Cage to contain these devices?"

"MAYBE. I CAN CONSTRUCT ONE, ANYWAY."

"Do it, then place them all in it. Keep a search going for more of them. Also, can you play back video of them being laid?"

"YES, CAPTAIN." Then a display appeared on the cabin wall, showing Zitulu Mbaka and Brandon Smith distributing the capsules outside the doors of all the people in the ship, including the Captain's.

"Elizabeth", said Jeffrey, "have everyone meet me in the galley in five minutes." "YES, CAPTAIN."

"Janet, Sneaky, arm yourselves. We may have a showdown."

The young women looked at each other, Audrey went off to her cabin to get her weapons, Janet went to her suit and gathered her weapons.

Jeffrey went to his cabin on the way, where he opened one of the capsules, emptied the contents, disconnected the power supply, put the capsule back together without its contents. Grabbed his stun gun, and walked to the galley.

The rest of the crew was already there, Torres was making coffee, Mbaka, Smith and Svoboda were seated at the table, Janet leaned against the back wall. Jeffrey strode to the head of the table, held up the empty capsule, and asked Torres, "Do you know what this is?"

Torres looked confused, but Mbaka and Smith blanched.

"Gentlemen, do you want to explain yourselves?" Jeffrey said, calmly.

"Captain," said Mbaka, after a moment. "We had orders."

"Orders from whom?"

Smith chimed in, nervously, "Don't know." He swallowed. "I woke up in my cabin on *Wanigan* and these were on my table. A note said to mount above the doors of all occupied cabins. Or else. It said, 'or else'." Smitty wiped the sweat off his temples. "I didn't know what else to do."

"So, you didn't think to talk to your commanding officer?" Jeffrey asked. "Uh, No sir."

"Torres!"

"Sir?"

"What do you know about this?"

"First I've heard of it. What are those things?"

"Elizabeth, have you analyzed them?" Jeffrey asked.

"THEY SEEM TO HAVE MULTIPLE FUNCTIONS. THEY RECORD INGRESS AND EGRESS OF THE CABINS THEY ARE ATTACHED TO. THEY HAVE A RESERVOIR OF TOXIC GAS TO BE RELEASED BY REMOTE CONTROL. THEY HAVE SMALL BUT POWERFUL EXPLOSIVES TO BE RELEASED BY REMOTE CONTROL. I DO NOT RECOGNIZE THE CONSTRUCTION."

Torres noticed that Jeffrey had armed himself. He looked around and saw Sneaky and Janet were also armed. Captain likes to be prepared.

"Torres, take Smitty out and space him," said Jeffrey.

Torres looked Jeffrey in the eyes, and asked, "Are you serious?"

"Serious as a heart attack. This coward tried to assassinate all of us."

"CAPTAIN, MORE ANALYSIS. THE DEVICES ALSO CONTAIN AN ELECTRONIC PULSE GENERATOR, WHICH SHOULD FRY ALL ELECTRONICS ON BOARD. SMITH ALSO TRIED TO ASSASSINATE ME TOO."

A pungent odor filled the galley. Torres stood and grabbed Smith by the collar and the small of his back, gripping the jumpsuit fabric. As he was being frog-marched out the door, he left a diarrheic trail, behind him, while sobbing and screaming, "No! Not my fault, I'm sorry, I'm sorry."

After Torres and Smith left the Galley, Smith begging for his life, Jeffrey turned his attention to Zitulu Mbaka. "All right, Digger. What have you got to say for yourself?" In the time between when Smith was first being questioned, Mbaka regained his composure.

"Captain, I too, was ordered to plant those devices. But I was ordered by Lieutenant Omotunde. He is in the Intelligence Unit, and said he didn't trust you. He said these devices were only for monitoring. I didn't know about the poison gas or explosives. I'm pretty sure Smitty didn't either."

"Regardless, you, both of you, have betrayed our trust."

"Elizabeth, have Torres bring Smitty back." A moment later, Torres frog-marched Smitty back to the Galley.

"Oh thank, you Captain," the errant combat technician blubbered.

"Elizabeth, get a message to Wanigan about this incident."

"ACTIONING."

"Actioning?" was repeated by several of the occupants of the room.

Jeffrey said, "Yeah, she's trying out new responses. Alright, so here's the drill," Jeffrey said angrily. "First, does anybody else have any secret orders?" Nobody responded. "Next," said Jeffrey after a long pause. "Nobody issues any orders but me, Petty Officer Bianca, and Sergeant Torres. If Elizabeth gives you an order, then it came from me. Any questions so far?" Jeffrey paused a while again. And again, nobody had anything to add. Jeffrey looked from one face to the next, his voice seemingly just barely under control. "Next. We have a mission. We are a team. Are there any questions?" Pause. "Sergeant, I don't want to refer to military rank or discipline, but you must keep your men in line. If anyone strays, catch them. If anyone betrays us, I need to know about it sooner rather than later. Understood?"

Sergeant Torres said in a small, embarrassed, shamed, voice, "Aye, Captain."

"Smith. Get cleaned up. Then clean up this mess."

"Aye, Captain. Thanks, Captain."

CHAPTER FIVE

In which Jeffrey's past seems to be behind him for a while. Jeffrey develops enemies, acquires a rifle, Creates a safe-house, and Janet learns of Jeffrey's late wife.

A Lagrange point is a spot in space that the balance between two strong gravity wells makes a neutral spot. The Lagrange point between the Earth and the moon is the balance between Earth's gravity and the moon's gravity, in which the gravity exactly equals the centrifugal forces of the smaller body. A space station orbits Earth, chasing the point around the Earth's orbit. This renders the position of the station quite secure and stable. Another location would require constant alteration of position and consume considerable fuel. At the Lagrange points, the orbit is free of that awesome expense in fuel. The particular orbits the Lagrange points used were numbered, L1 through L5 for each body. Those around the Earth-Moon points were Lagrange 1. Those Between the Sun and Mars were Lagrange 2, Those between Mars and the Asteroid Belt were Lagrange 3. The individual stations were then lettered.

The *Elizabeth* approached the Lagrange 3A station with very little fuel left. The human controller queried the automatic transponder response that all ships entering its space signaled, then notified her that *Elizabeth* needed to have her pilot contact him before approach.

"Lagrange 3A this is *Elizabeth*, responding," radioed Jeffrey.

"*Elizabeth*, Lagrange 3A. State your business."

"Lagrange 3A, *Elizabeth*. We have processed ore and need to refuel and re-provision."

"Elizabeth, Lagrange 3A. State name of *Elizabeth* Actual."

"*Elizabeth* Actual is Jeffrey Sokolov."

"*Elizabeth*, Lagrange 3A. Stick to broadcasting protocol. Copied Jeffrey Sokolov. Captain Sokolov, records show you have inadequate credit for the transaction you indicated."

"Lagrange 3A, *Elizabeth*. We have a new credit line. Chit is being attached, now."

After a couple minutes pause, the controller came back online. "*Elizabeth*, Lagrange 3A, proceed to docking bay Delta 64. At initial point, surrender control to the auto controller." The "initial point" is the place where a craft is making its final turn to approach directly to the target.

"Lagrange 3A, *Elizabeth*. Acknowledged docking bay Delta 64, at IP auto."

"Lagrange 3A Out."

"*Elizabeth*, Out."

Jeffrey mulled the transaction over in his mind. Things seemed more 'by the book' than the controllers had ever been. A little care was required here. "Elizabeth, do not surrender to the auto controller."

"BUT CAPTAIN, THEY WILL NOT ALLOW ME TO PARK."

"Understood. What I want is for you to appear to surrender control, and follow auto control orders unless they present danger."

"YOU ARE BEING VERY CAUTIOUS. I APPRECIATE THAT, CAPTAIN. WILCO."

"Wilco?"

"EARLY RADIO COMM TERMINOLOGY FOR 'WILL COMPLY.'"

"Oh. Learn something new every day. Notify the crew that we are about to dock."

After a moment, the voice of Elizabeth came over the public address system. "NOW HEAR THIS, NOW HEAR THIS. APPROACHING LAGRANGE 3A DOCK."

Then to Jeffrey, "I ALWAYS WANTED TO DO THAT!"

"AIs with personality. Arrrgh."

As *The Elizabeth* approached the Initial Point, the automatic docking computer began to perform the handshake routine with Elizabeth. Elizabeth mimicked the appropriate protocols, and followed the instructions of the docking computer, while analyzing in real time the entire broadcast.

"CAPTAIN, THEY ARE ATTEMPTING TO UPLOAD A VIRUS PACKAGE ON THE CARRIER WAVE."

"Is it the same one we have already seen?"

"NO, CAPTAIN. THIS ONE IS MUCH MORE CRUDE. IT APPEARS TO BE FROM A LOCAL HACKER."

"All right. Let's give someone some trouble."

He activated the mic and said, " Lagrange 3A, *Elizabeth*."

"*Elizabeth*, Lagrange 3A, go ahead. Note, *Elizabeth*, you are on a public channel."

"Lagrange 3A, *Elizabeth*. We are experiencing an illegal intrusion on our computer system via your automatic dock carrier wave. It appears to be from a local hacker. Cease and desist this attack on our system."

The Lagrange 3A docking staff seemed to be running around, from what Jeffrey could see through the portholes of the station.

Chatter on the open channel increased, then Jeffrey heard, "*Elizabeth, Sigmund*. Thanks for noticing. Our ship now seems to have a serious infection."

"*Elizabeth, Roberto Maru*. Ditto. Thanks.",

"*Elizabeth*, *Aegian Sea*. We saw it, but too late. Couldn't figure how it got on board, didn't think of the carrier wave." Other ships in the vicinity also reported infections.

Jeffrey then turned back to the authorized channel, and said, "Lagrange 3A, *Elizabeth*. Request permission to approach and dock on our own power, considering your computer seems to be infected."

A new voice came on the radio. "Captain Sokolov, this is Lagrange 3A Actual. Permission granted. Thanks for noticing and notifying us of the...illicit use of our system. I will meet you at your dock."

"Okay, Elizabeth, take us in."

"AYE CAPTAIN."

The crew gathered at the docking port, the gangway tube stretched towards *Elizabeth*'s egress port. Jeffrey said, "I need to arrange for fuel and supplies. I need you all to start shopping for civilian gear and some additional tools. I will meet you at the Field Gear store as soon as I can get free from the politician on the wharf. Janet, stay aboard *Elizabeth*. Arm yourself. Allow nobody but one of us on board. Elizabeth will assist you."

The pressure outside the airlock equalized with the pressure in the ship, and Torres un-dogged the airlock. After Jeffrey and the crew exited, Janet re-dogged the port. Elizabeth posted a couple remotes armed with cutting lasers at the port.

Jeffrey exited the gangway tube to find the uniformed administrator with two security officers awaiting him.

"To my office." The administrator turned on his heal, and stalked off to his office overlooking the docking wharf. Jeffrey followed, while the crew began heading to the station proper, one of the security officers called out to them.

"You!"

Torres said under his breath, "Don't look, keep going." The security officer began to move towards the crew, but noticed Jeffrey and his administrator increasing their distance from him. He decided to let the crew go, and chased after the administrator and Jeffrey.

At the administrator's office, Administrator Chin motioned Jeffery to the couch against the wall, then sat behind his large, empty desk. "Mr. Sokolov, how did find the virus? From what I understand it was well hidden in the carrier wave."

"I have had some experience with carrier wave-based attacks. Kind of knew what to look for."

"I see. You embarrassed my command by broadcasting to the rest of the ships."

Jeffrey replied, "Sorry, but if it wasn't made public, several things would have happened – nothing and ziltch. Now I don't want to cause you embarrassment, and I'm sure if you show yourself as a pro-active administrator, you should be able to save face. But I am not into face saving at my own expense."

Administrator Chin looked over Jeffrey with squinted eyes. His brow wrinkled, his mouth frowning. He said, his voice cold, and with a little waver, "Thank you. Dismissed."

Jeffrey exited the administrator's office and worked his way down to the concourse. His first stop was at the fuel vendor, and he arranged for a complete fueling. He then stopped at the food warehouse, where he ordered both fresh and prepackaged food, and set a delivery time.

He then met his crew at the Field Gear store, where they had busied themselves both window shopping and picking out personal items. Jeffrey gathered them together. "Okay, I think there is a bit of hostility on the part of the administration. We will be quick. Get whatever you want. The entire bill is on me. You need work gear,

　　　ELIZABETH, *ELIZABETH*

personal gear, more tools, books. I also want you to get the highest quality space suits – hard shell. Spare no expense."

Audrey said, "My God, Captain, no one ever said that to me! You sure know how to show a girl a good time!" Jeffrey smiled at the joke. The crew finished up their work rapidly, with delivery to the ship to occur just before the grocery order. Jeffrey notified Janet of the goings-on, then had Sneaky replace her to allow Janet the shopping she needed.

Jeffrey met her at the gangway, and they strolled to the Field Gear store. He said, "I'm sorry we don't have a lot of time, but I kind of expect trouble." He saw one of the security officers glancing at him from a corner, half concealed. He looked around and spotted the other one at a different corner, looking in his direction.

"Janet, we're going to need to move a bit faster. I think trouble is just around the corner." He took his radio out, and spoke, "*Elizabeth, Elizabeth Actual.*"

Audry answered, "*Elizabeth* Actual, *Elizabeth*. Go ahead."

"*Elizabeth*, encrypt comm."

"COMM ENCRYPTED, CAPTAIN."

"We are likely to need a distraction. Can you arrange one?"

"EFFORTING. ENCRYPTION DISABLED. ELIZABETH OUT."

"Elizabeth Actual, out."

Janet said, "One more stop, Captain."

Jeffrey wondered what else she needed, but she took him to the Dirt Store. She purchased a couple pallets of potting soil, fertilizer, and vegetable seeds. Then arranged for them to be delivered just after the personal gear delivery.

They then made their way back to the ship, Jeffrey noticed they were still being followed, now by four security officers that he could see. Probably others, he thought. At the gangway, he and Janet stood chatting, when the personal items they had purchased were delivered. Smitty and Mbaka took them from the delivery persons, who looked disappointed.

Then the delivery from the Dirt Store arrived. Torres and Audry took charge of the palettes of sacks of soil. Janet said, "put them in the hanger, for now."

After a few more minutes the grocery order arrived, and Smitty and Digger took charge of it. There were six palettes of vegetables and frozen meat and canned and otherwise packaged goods. Jeffrey said, "Take these to the processing hold. Elizabeth will scan them."

The fuel crew arrived and connected the nozzles to the various connectors, and began the rapid transfer of fuel from the station to *Elizabeth*'s tanks. After ten minutes, the fuel crew disconnected the nozzles and retracted their hoses. Elizabeth reported that the tanks were topped off, the items were all stowed in the hold or hanger, but that the food contained several of the capsules they had earlier found. They had been placed into the Faraday cage and disarmed.

"We still need to unload our processed ore. I haven't been able to negotiate with anyone for the sale," said Jeffrey. He scanned the concourse, looked up at the Administrator's window and saw Administrator Chin looking back at him. He gave a little wave. Chin turned away.

Jeffrey called his commodities broker, who agreed to meet him at the dock. A few minutes later, a little man in a hard suit, carrying his helmet, appeared on the concourse. He was stopped and addressed by two security officers, then came over to *Elizabeth*'s berth. "Jeff!" he called out in a rough but jovial voice. But as he got closer, he said, *sotto voce*, "Man, what did you get me into? Security doesn't want me to do business with you. At least not on station."

ELIZABETH, *ELIZABETH*

Jeffrey replied, "Yeah, I should have done this first. Anyway, I can transfer off-station. You interested or do I need to take this load somewhere else?"

The broker thought about it for a moment, then said, "We'll talk after you clear the station." Then he turned away and walked quickly back to the concourse. The two security officers stopped him again and questioned him.

Jeffrey and Janet then climbed the gangway and entered the ship. "Elizabeth," said Jeffrey. "Have the crew prepare for takeoff. Can you disconnect the clamps and gangway?"

"OF COURSE, CAPTAIN. BUT THERE ARE SECURITY OFFICERS CLIMBING THE GANGWAY."

"Disconnect the clamps, and prepare to disconnect the gangway."

"CAPTAIN, ONE OF THE OFFICERS HAS AN EXPLOSIVE DEVICE."

"Okay, the distraction we set up. Now."

Sirens throughout the station activated. All the lights illuminating the station began flashing in a coordinated fashion. The security officers climbing the gangway quickly ran back down to the station, Elizabeth took advantage of their abandonment and detached the gangway tube.

Jeffrey and Janet ran to the bridge, and he took up the microphone. He noted that there was chatter on all the channels of the radio. An opportunity, he thought. They won't hear me, but there will be a record of my broadcast. "Lagrange 3A, *Elizabeth*."

Of course, there was no answer. He repeated the hail, then said, "Lagrange 3A, *Elizabeth*, no contact. Please note, we are departing under our own control."

"Okay Elizabeth, let's move out."

The cloud of ships surrounding Lagrange 3A was nearly a thousand kilometers in diameter, and Jeffrey had Elizabeth move toward the outer edge of the cloud. There they waited for the commodities broker. Meanwhile, the crew redistributed the foodstuffs.

Janet had the soil taken to a vacant cabin, the one that had been made into a brig in the earlier actions. She assembled a few large boxes and filled them with soil. Then she planted the variety of vegetables she had acquired seeds for. She took a few cups and added flower seeds to them. After watering the soil, she had Elizabeth produce low level ultraviolet light. Satisfied, she returned to the bridge.

Jeffrey was on the bridge, busy composing a report on his tablet. They had been off station for twenty-one hours when at last they were hailed by the broker. He had arrived in *Elizabeth*'s vicinity in a small shuttle, obviously too small to take on the cargo in *Elizabeth*'s hold.

The shuttle landed in the shuttle bay, and he came aboard.

Jeffrey took him to the galley where the small commodities broker parked his helmet. Jeffrey provided coffee, and he and Janet sat down across from the broker.

The broker took a sip of coffee. "Jeff! I always like visiting you. Your coffee is the best of all the miners."

Jeffrey winced at the misuse of his name. "So. what's the story?"

"You managed to piss off quite a few people." Said the short man. Jeffrey noticed his face was unshaved and his hair considerably messier than wearing a helmet would justify. "After you took off, I was unceremoniously dragged before his lordship Administrator Chin. I was told not to do business with you. And he made me do other things to cooperate."

Before Jeffrey could inquire about what other things, Elizabeth's voice announced, "CAPTAIN, INTRUDER IN SHUTTLE BAY."

"Ah, I see what you mean," he said to the broker. "Stay here." Then to Janet, he said, "Watch him."

"Elizabeth, have the crew meet me at the shuttle bay. Armed."

When Jeffrey arrived at the shuttle bay, he saw a panel in the trader's shuttle had been removed, it had apparently been a hiding place for a single intruder. There were not a lot of places to hide in the shuttle bay, but still the intruder was not immediately visible.

Svoboda was the first of the crew to arrive, and Jeffrey told her, "Get in the Shuttle, check it for bombs." Having done this already several times in her tenure on Jeffry's ship, she was the logical choice. She ran to the shuttle and began her systematic search.

Torres, Mbaka and Smith then arrived at the same time, stunners drawn. They spread out and began the search like the combat team they actually were.

"Elizabeth, locate the intruder." said Jeffrey.

"UNDER THE FLOOR PLATES NEXT TO THE SHUTTLE."

On hearing this, the combat team returned to the shuttle, Smitty pulling floor plates while Torres and Digger covered. The third floor plate revealed a hard suited, plasma rifle armed, security officer from the station. Realizing the stunners would have no effect on the hard suit, the three pulled back out of the line of fire. Jeffrey carried a projectile weapon, so he aimed it at the armored officer. The speaker on the officer's suit announced "Security! Drop your weapons! Drop your weapons or I will fire! Drop your weapons!" the voice became louder and more shrill as he spoke.

The officer stood and pointed the plasma rifle at Jeffrey, his finger on the trigger. "Elizabeth," said Jeffrey, "I would like that rifle."

The security officer said, "Say what?"

The remote robot with the industrial laser that was perched on the ceiling of the bay, disconnected the finger of the security officer in an invisible beam of light. The officer dropped the rifle in surprise and pain. "How'd you do that?" he asked while attempting to remove the armored glove with the missing finger.

Torres and Mbaka hoisted the security officer out of his hiding place, and Jeffrey told them to take him to the galley, treat his injured hand and put the severed digit on ice. Sneaky came out of the shuttle carrying the remotely-controlled explosives. The detonator had been removed from the explosive, and the electronic receiver had been jumpered to avoid the booby trap preset to explode if tampered with.

"You're getting pretty good at that," said Jeffrey. She grinned proudly. He picked up the plasma rifle, studied it for a moment, then hoisted it and proceeded to the galley. Audrey 'Sneaky' Svoboda walked a few paces behind Jeffrey, carrying the bomb gingerly.

Just as they reached the galley, Elizabeth said through one of the wall panels, "CAPTAIN, I JUST RECEIVED THE DETONATION COMMUNICATION FROM THE STATION."

"Well, how about that," said Jeffrey. "None too soon."

In the galley, the security officer sat in his under-suit, his hand bandaged, and Janet was just administering a pain reducing medication. The hard suit was tossed into a corner of the galley, Torres was disassembling the third hand weapon taken from the officer at the other end of the table, while Mbaka and Smith hovered over the officer.

Jeffrey strode in, took the disabled bomb from Audrey, and slammed it down on the table in front of the officer. He said, angrily, "They just sent the detonation order for this device."

The officer asked, "Who did? Where was it?"

Jeffrey said, "The order came from the station."

Audrey said, "It was hidden under the floor plates of the shuttle."

The security officer's face went white. Jeffrey could actually see the color drain down from his forehead to his neck. His unbandaged hand began shaking. He began muttering curse words under his breath.

Jeffrey asked him to repeat himself, or clarify. He said, "I didn't know. They were going to sacrifice me."

Jeffrey asked him, "Who sent you, what were your orders?"

The security officer said, "Administrator Chin. He told me to capture this ship and bring it in."

Jeffrey asked, "Why?"

"I don't know. I just followed orders."

"Stay here," said Jeffrey to the officer. To the broker, he said, "You. Come with me."

He led the broker to his cabin, sat him in one chair at the table, and sat in the other one. "It looks like the station is infested with pirates. I am sick of those guys. The navy is going to have to come in and clean out that mess." He paused. "Change of subject. Do you want to buy my cargo or do I have to take it to another station?"

The broker looked ashen. "What do you mean pirates?"

Jeffrey told him that he had been attacked recently but had defeated the attacking pirates. He didn't mention the *Wanigan*'s issues or what methods or weapons he used, but he left the trader thinking he was some kind of superman.

The trader said he would buy the entire shipment, but that he couldn't take it with him in the little shuttle. "No problem," said Jeffrey. "I'll just space it here, put a beacon on it with a claim buoy. You can pick it up later."

"Unusual," said the broker, "but adequate."

They finished their business, and the broker said, "I have to get back to the station. If the navy is coming, there is going to be a lot of disruption. I need to get out ahead of that."

"You are taking the security officer with you," said Jeffrey.

The little man agreed, albeit reluctantly.

Jeffrey took the broker back to the galley, and had Torres and Smith escort the security officer and the broker back to the broker's shuttle. Torres handed the security officer a small plastic box containing the severed finger. The officer was in his under-suit, having left his hard suit on the floor in the galley. Audrey took the weapons to one of the arms closets and stowed them, and Mbaka took the hard suit to the suit room near the forward airlock.

After the broker's shuttle had left, Jeffrey asked Elizabeth to contact her counterpart Wanigan, and forward a confidential report to Captain Yusef describing the recent events at the station. He then said, "Also, broadcast a message to the ships surrounding this station – tell them that the station is currently being run by pirates and that until the navy arrives, they should avoid doing business with the station."

"DONE AND DONE, CAPTAIN."

"Thanks."

Over the next few hours, Jeffrey hosted a radio discussion among the hundreds of ship captains in vessels surrounding the station. The general consensus was the ships would avoid doing business on the station until the situation was resolved.

After things calmed down, Elizabeth told Jeffrey, "CAPTAIN YUSEF IS SENDING A COMMUNICATION. THERE IS AN EIGHT – MINUTE DELAY. "

Jeffrey played the communication from Captain Yusef.

"Commander Sokolov, I have received your communication through AI, and am responding via same. I have put Omotunde under secure watch, thanks for the heads up there. We are en-route to LaGrange3A. Estimated Time of Arrival 96 hours at full burn. If you are finished with your business, go ahead and take off. Please acknowledge.

Jeffrey said, "Commander Yusef, acknowledge 96 hours. Be aware I have had discussion with the other mining ship captains, and the consensus is there will be no business with the station until Navy arrives. We are done business here, so will move back to the asteroid belt."

Jeffrey, thinking the conversation was over, reassigned the crew to cleanup and repair responsibilities. After about nine minutes, Elizabeth announced, "CAPTAIN, FURTHER COMMUNICATIONS FROM COMMANDER YUSEF."

"Put it through to the bridge." Then Jeffrey walked from his cabin to the bridge, sat at the pilot's chair, and played back the transmission from Yusef.

"Commander Sokolov, after receiving your last transmission, I want you to delay your move to the asteroid belt. Leave the vicinity of the station, but then wait half a million kilometers out, in case we need you for backup. Please Acknowledge.

Jeffrey replied, "Commander Yusef, Acknowledged half a million klicks."

Then Jeffrey told Elizabeth, "Go ahead and take us out to the half-million kilometer point."

"AYE CAPTAIN."

"Please have Janet come to the bridge."

"AYE, CAPTAIN." Then on the ship public address system, "BIANCA, TO THE BRIDGE." After a few minutes, Janet arrived. "Yes sir?"

"How have you been coming along with the tutorials on the engines?"

"They're pretty straightforward, sir. So far I have no qualms effecting repairs."

"Good. Next, of course, you are to be my backup pilot, so I need you to be familiar with the controls and astrogation. Elizabeth will not always be up, so we need to be able to handle the ship like in the olden days," said Jeffrey.

"Not a problem, sir. I scored well at the academy in both areas."

"All right, smarty pants, now you need to familiarize yourself with the weapons systems, and our surveillance."

Janet smiled. "Yes sir. I'm sure Elizabeth will help me figure it all out."

"You need to become expert soon, because you are going to be the training officer for the rest of the crew. They will need to become proficient. When we get out to the half-million kilometers point from the station, we have been ordered to stand by for *Wanigan*, which is high-tailing it to Lagrange 3A. We are going to hang back and provide backup to the Navy." Janet, looking concerned, wondered aloud, "What about Lieutenant Omotunde?"

"Yusef is aware and is taking measures."

"Good. All right, sir. I'll develop a weapons training program."

"Excellent. You can do that from here, you have the watch."

"Aye, sir."

Jeffrey left the bridge, walked to his cabin, and asked Elizabeth to have Torres come to his cabin.

Shortly afterward, Torres signaled to come in. Jeffrey opened the door, and Torres entered.

"Ojo, I expect some issues in the near future, and want you to drill your team in anti-boarding techniques."

"Not a problem, sir. We are still Marines!"

"Another thing to be aware of is *Wanigan* is coming to Lagrange 3A, should be here in four days. They want us to hang back a

 ELIZABETH, *ELIZABETH*

half-million klicks out, and act as their backup. So, we may need to practice boarding techniques."

"Again, not a problem. I'll sharpen the guys up."

"You might want to take a look at the hard armor suits and put them in top shape."

"Good idea, Captain."

"I asked Bianca to train everybody in the ship's weapons systems, so when we get to our station, she will begin training and drilling on the various weapons."

"Very good, sir."

"One more thing, Torres," said Jeffrey. "The team did really well with the security officer sneaking onto our ship. I want you to thank them for me."

"Why don't you tell them yourself? They would enjoy hearing it from you."

"Oh, I will, but I want you to reinforce your command of the troops. You tell them, then I'll tell them. We both get to offer some positive reinforcement."

"Right. You are a sneaky person, Captain."

"Indeed I am. One thing, Torres. I want every member of the crew to be armed with these projectile weapons. Stunners just don't work on armored soldiers."

"Yes, sir."

"Once we are on our way to the asteroid belt, I'll need to train everyone in how to find, capture, and process ore. You guys are going to be doing a lot of learning on this deployment."

The *Elizabeth* arrived on their station at a half-million kilometers around the same time *Wanigan* arrived in the vicinity of the Lagrange 3A station. The ship's AIs notified each other of their positions.

Wanigan reported that she would be spending the next few hours in rapid deceleration. Shortly after that, there was a powerful broadcast of a warning that a Navy warship was coming in hot and that no ship or station should take any aggressive action, or face destruction.

Elizabeth recorded the entire cluster around the station for later analysis. Meanwhile, Janet began training the crew in the various weapons Jeffrey had recovered from the pirate vessels that had attacked *Elizabeth*.

She explained to the assembled crew, "Almost all of these weapons are electrically generated or require tremendous power to work. For instance, the plasma canon takes bursts of a gigajoule to generate the plasma, and another megajoule to throw it. The x-ray lasers take sustained bursts of megajoules to cut in four second bursts. Two lessons from this – there are large capacitors which can aid in spreading out our generated capacity, and powerful million-watt generators to augment the ship's systems. But those are hungry capacitors. We need to be extremely judicious in how we utilize these weapons.

"For instance, if you aim the x-ray laser slightly ahead of where the ship will be in less than a second, and fire a four-second burst, you will likely cut the ship in half. If you miss, you will surprise someone a hundred billion klicks away some time next year." The assembled crew chuckled at her humorous remark. "And you will need to recharge the laser which, depending on what other weapons are firing, the condition of the capacitors and the weapons generators, could take four to five minutes."

Torres asked, "What if the x-ray laser is the only weapon firing, what is the quickest turn-around time?"

She responded, "You can fire immediately, four or five blasts before having to recharge the capacitors. I ran some simulations and some live fire tests and was able to hit five targets with the laser in twenty seconds."

Janet had previously laid target buoys from *Elizabeth*'s store, ten klicks apart, ten klicks from the ship, and had each of the crew practice their firing. When she was satisfied with their laser marksmanship, she instructed the crew in how to set up the laser for different power levels, apertures and frequencies, explaining how different targets would be better hit by different laser frequencies.

After the x-ray laser drills, she instructed the crew in the plasma canon, and tested them using the same target buoys previously deployed. There were also small anti-boarding projectile weapons – rail guns, which fired rapidly and accurately large-bore heavy projectiles, some including explosives, some hardened solid armor-piercing rounds, and some other rounds with specialized armaments.

She also explained how Elizabeth used her own modified rotational velocity to throw both heavy processed ingots and raw rocks at ships successfully, and how she used the engines to incapacitate enemy vessels. Smitty asked why they needed to know something they didn't have any control over, earning him a glare from Torres. Janet explained, patiently acting as if there were no stupid questions, "So when she or the captain or I pull one of those maneuvers, you will understand why you are being tossed around the ship like a loose meatball. You will get adequate warning to secure yourselves, but in a combat situation, only one warning."

"Oh," said Smitty, imagining how he could easily be thrown around the ship if loose.

She then drilled them on the guns. She noted that as long as they had raw materials, *Elizabeth* could manufacture her own projectiles and plasma canisters, even if she had to cannibalize her own interior structures. But this was one of the reasons that Jeffrey liked working in his favorite region of the asteroid belt. He had found pockets of heavy metals, including some radioactive, some inert, but all useful in reconstructing the ship, as well as selling. Janet had Elizabeth begin constructing ammunition for the heavy weapons as well as for the small arms within the ship.

Since Jeffrey ordered all the crew to carry loaded projectile pistols, they all needed to requalify on them. Torres was thankful for Janet's forethought, as he took the crew through firing exercises with the pistols. The Marines had gotten out of practice, having been used to non-recoiling beam and force field weapons. Now each of the pistols had adequate ammunition for practice and combat.

The crew took a break after Janet turned the training session over to Torres, and she returned to the bridge. Jeffrey welcomed her onto the bridge and said, "Sit down, take a load off, and look at this."

He brought up the recording of the arrival of *Wanigan* in the station's area of influence. Then said, "Elizabeth, show --the overlay-- you did before." Each dot that represented a ship was colored red or blue, depending on the direction of travel relative to *Elizabeth*'s current location. Then the overlay displayed colored lines alongside each dot, indicating communications and at what frequency. Jeffrey then started the playback again, this time with the overlay. The dot representing *Wanigan* hadn't come on scene yet, so there was a baseline of data from which to judge the upcoming chaos. Jeffrey then advanced the display to its normal speed. After about ten seconds, the dot representing *Wanigan* came into view, quickly moving, but just as fast, decelerating.

Wanigan began her loud broadcast which showed as a wide and tall bar alongside the dot, displaying the entire visible palette as she transmitted on a wide spectrum of frequencies.

Immediately, six of the ships in the cluster of several hundred began communicating in short bursts on a not-well-used frequency. Two others joined in the back and forth after a short while. The rest of the ships in the region used standard frequencies, and kept their communications brief.

Elizabeth then attached identifying data to those eight ships.

Jeffrey said, "Elizabeth, please share this with your sister, *Wanigan* and her captain."

"EFFORTING."

Studying the data, Janet pointed out that there were several other clusters of communication information. "I noticed that also," said Jeffrey, "but when I identified the ships, it made sense. They are different consortia of rock miners and brokers. Nothing at all like the other group."

"Of course, Captain."

They sat quietly together, nothing happening on the coms or the screens.

"Janet, tell me about yourself," he said, after a long pause. "I've read your dossier, but that doesn't tell me much about YOU, only some Petty Officer that was assigned to my ship."

"Oh, well, not much to tell," she began, much like everyone who is ever asked that. "Born twenty-eight years ago. Both parents dead, a couple sibs on Earth – one on a farm in Southern Minnesota, one on a tree farm in Northern Minnesota," she paused reminiscing. "Haven't been back since the funerals."

"Do you miss it, deep in the gravity well?" asked Jeffrey.

"Not so much since I joined the Navy. Growing up in Minnesota was kind of a blessing, you get the best of both worlds – it was the high-tech capital of the country, the entire region, and you could still get dirt under your fingernails, smell the pine forests, eat real venison – that you shot yourself, cooked with real vegetables that you grew yourself."

She again lapsed into a thoughtful silence. Then said, "My first posting was in R and D – research and development. I was kind of a whiz kid, good physics, good math. Lousy social skills. Briefly married to someone I thought I liked and I thought liked me. Turns out I was just another notch on his well-used, but not very well practiced organ, if you know what I mean."

Jeffrey chuckled, then burst out laughing. "Sorry," he finally said. "I do know what you mean," as he wiped a tear from his eye. "I've known several of the sort - allow me to apologize for the entire male half of the species."

She joined in the laughter, seemingly reluctantly, but eventually she too had tears of laughter. After a moment she continued, "*Wanigan* was my first ship. I thought I was doing Okay, but then I had to take you on, and then...got assigned to you. No offense."

"None taken."

What about you, Captain?"

"What about me?"

"Story. Tell me your story."

Before Jeffrey could begin, or respond, Elizabeth chimed in,

"CAPTAIN, COMMANDER YUSEF IS ATTEMPTING TO CONTACT YOU. THERE IS A THREE SECOND DELAY."

"put it through"

"Sokolov, Yusef. Thanks for the data and the analysis. The eight ships identified are all known to be associated with illegal activity in the past. Continue to standby. I am sending a contingent of Marines onto the station. We'll see how things go. I have assigned my marine lieutenant to intelligence, we'll see if he comes up with the same targets you did. That's all for now, Yusef out."

"Well, that was interesting," said Jeffrey.

"Elizabeth, acknowledge."

"AYE, CAPTAIN."

After a minute of silence, Janet prompted, "Story. You can't get out of it that easily." She smiled in a manner to suggest that Jeffrey was trying to weasel out of his tale.

"Okay," said Jeffrey, "So I grew up in orbit on a small ship. Mom and Dad were miners who decided to come in-system to have me. They eventually parked in geosynchronous over Selene City, providing a shuttle service for bigwigs who couldn't wait for the regular bus from Selene City to the orbital station, even some had us take them to the Earth stations." He got up, walked over to the bridge fridge, got himself a beverage. "You want one?"

"I'm fine."

He sat back down. "Eventually things turned around, they bought this boat, hired a crew and did the big-time asteroid mining gig. Back then, shielding wasn't so good, and Mom came down with cancer. Killed her, and her death killed him. So, I got the boat. Figured I'd better improve the shielding or I would follow suit. I was fifteen then. The crew thought a kid shouldn't run a big operation like that, but I managed. Eventually they all drifted off.

"I was every bit of nineteen when I met Elizabeth. She was the most beautiful thing in the universe. Well, the solar system, anyway. Oh, Janet, I was smitten." He grinned at her. "She was a most extraordinary woman. Same age as me, but self-possessed. Smart, knowledgeable, good looking. Had a real business sense. The odd thing is, I didn't have to pursue her   she began chasing me. Almost more than a nineteen-year-old young man can handle!" He took a sip of his juice, then sat back. "I took a couple more trips out to the belt, brought home some decent rocks, and asked her to marry me.

"By this time, we were twenty, going on twenty-one, so we got hitched." He paused and looked over to Bianca. "Janet, I would tell you she was a beautiful bride, she was, but she was a beautiful everything. I so loved that girl. We took the ship out to my spots on the belt and I showed her the ropes, but she outdid me there too. She found a region that contained gold, silver, mercury, molybdenum. That first trip made it so we could profit every time, not just alternate trips.

"Ten years. We had ten years of bliss. She was my inspiration, and the damnedest thing – I was hers. I still don't understand it. So, on our tenth anniversary trip, we went out to our regular stomping ground, when we were put on by pirates. It was touch and go, they managed to board the ship, but we killed them all, except one. A goon that used to work for my folks, I rounded the corner and saw him attempting to rape her." Jeffrey stifled a sob. "He had a knife to her throat. I shot him. Blew his head clear off – it rolled to the end of the corridor, I remember the look of astonishment on the face as the head rolled away. But the body fell, the knife cut through her carotids and jugulars."

He turned away, tears now running down his cheeks. Janet said silently, sympathetically, "Oh my God. I'm so sorry."

After a short pause, Jeffrey regained his composure and continued his story. "I brought the pirate ship on board, stripped it down of anything I could use on this ship, then smelted the rest. I brought the bodies of the pirates in-system, and informed all other miner ships in radio range of who and what was involved in the attack. Shortly after that there was an agreement that all miners would respond to a call for help.

"I bought a powerful computer, installed a military-surplus AI, and began programming it. I renamed the ship to commemorate my wife, *Elizabeth*, and the AI, which now had all the ship's systems under its controls, took on the name, and sensed my softness toward my late wife, took on some aspects of her personality. I take a little comfort in the affection the AI shows me, but it is a ghost of a shadow of my wife."

Janet said, "So you had no children?"

"No, we were planning on it, but not right away."

"Tell me about those remote robots," said Janet.

"We got the idea from some old science fiction shows from the twentieth and twenty- first centuries. Why not have a self-repairing ship? And why should we have to do all the work? So, between us we acquired the parts for a few self-actuated bots, settled on a design and began figuring out the programming these things needed. We even created the base operating system, completely different from any normal computers.

"And that was key to saving my bacon when the pirates inflicted the virus on our systems. I had Elizabeth make a copy of herself and hide it. When she became infected with the virus, so did all the other systems on the ship that required a computer. Power, life support, engines, everything. Except the bots. I Interfaced a bot with the network, plugged in a powerful antivirus routine, and completely cleaned out the system. Later, Elizabeth's clone popped up her head, saw what was going on, restored herself with new routines. Analyzed the virus and tweaked it to work to our advantage.

"So the bots became part of the defense of the ship. We replicated about a hundred of them, fitted some with cutting lasers – now all have those lasers – and made them work in concert. We can control the remotes, but usually its best to allow Elizabeth to do it – she is much more precise and accurate.

"The bots can drag about twenty-five kilos each. A team of four or five can haul an unconscious pirate to a brig, or a wounded marine to sickbay," He chuckled, "If we had a brig or sickbay! But, we have had pirates and Marines to worry about."

Jeffrey finished his beverage, returned the container to the recycle chute.

After about a half hour, Captain Yusef called again. "Captain Sokolov, thanks for standing by, we have finished our task on the station. Lagrange 3A is open for business again. Those other ships have been tagged for monitoring. We are heading out again."

Jeffrey responded, "Captain Yusef, I have a request. I want each of my crew to be promoted to the next level, including increasing their pay grade. Please put this into effect immediately."

"Captain Sokolov, I understand and will take under advisement."

"Captain Yusef, I need a decision within the hour. Sokolov out."

"Yusef out."

Janet looked at him, her right eyebrow arched. "What's that about?"

"I like to reward good behavior. If serving on my ship gives my crew privileges, that makes them more willing to serve, and serve well."

"Captain, you are one sneaky man."

A few minutes later Captain Yusef called back and confirmed the promotions.

After confirming their next steps, Jeffrey asked Elizabeth, "Please have the entire crew meet in the galley."

"AYE, CAPTAIN."

As Jeffrey and Janet walked to the galley, they met the rest of the crew noisily coming from the other direction, bragging about their marksmanship skills. They all entered the galley, and all sat down except Audrey, who made a batch of coffee. She poured cups for everyone, then sat down.

Jeffrey sat at the head of the long table, Janet alongside him.

"A few things to brief you on. First, you all did an outstanding job on Lagrange 3A. You are looking very much like you should; a team of competent space-faring roustabouts. Good work. I am also pleased you didn't betray your active Navy status. Undercover work is sometimes much harder than one gives it credit for, and you carried yourselves well.

"Second, because you did so well, and because I appreciate your efforts, I have requested, and received approval for promotions for all of you, one pay grade, and one rank level. Digger, you are now corporal," the applause and cat-calls were brief but loud. "Torres, add another stripe to your sleeve," again cheering from the assembled team. "Sneaky, I don't know if there is a rank above 'ninja', but you are now a Lance Corporal." She held up both arms and wiggled her torso in a proud victory move, to the cheers of her comrades. "Likewise, Smitty." He stood and bowed, then sat down again.

"Now, this young woman," he pointed to Janet, "has been a Petty Officer for six years, far longer than one would expect for someone of her talents and experience." He stood. "You may now refer to your former petty officer as Lieutenant Janet Bianca." The noise was appropriately celebratory. Jeffrey let the congratulatory emotions continue for a moment, then calmed them down.

"Okay, a reminder – while on this mission, you receive combat pay as well as your regular salary, but you will also receive a pay deposit from me." A brief happy hooting from the Marines. Torres told them to pipe down. Jeffrey continued, "Which brings me to the next topic. We have been released from the backup of *Wanigan* at Lagrange 3A, we are now going to spend the next week running towards one of my favorite mining sites. So, I am going to train everyone in mining and processing operations." A groan from the Marines arose.

"Meanwhile," continued Jeffrey, "you will continue to drill on your combat skills. I need to be able to repel all boarders, I need to be able to destroy ships bent on our destruction. I need to be able to protect my own claims, and all of you are going to be my keys to those goals."

Over the next week, while *Elizabeth* accelerated toward the target area, Jeffrey showed the crew how to use the smelter, the centrifuges, the refineries, the magnetic molecular disruptors and the other tools of a self-sustained processing operation. He taught them how to use the fabricator, what in the early twenty-first century they called a 3-D printer. But this industrial grade machine was able to fabricate nano-scale circuitry and incorporate it into large scale plating. It could easily build a toaster or a runabout or a four-poster feather bed, as long as you had the raw materials.

CHAPTER SIX

In which the new crew learns about prospecting for minerals, some
crewmembers can cook, and a first incidence of canoodling, the crew
goes shopping and Jeffrey gets kidnapped. And rescued.

Jeffrey had Elizabeth manufacture two more runabouts so several crew members could prospect for valuable rocks at once. Each runabout could hold two crew members. *Elizabeth* parked close to a large cluster of boulders that seemed to be stable in their positions. "Everyone, take a look at the rock I am currently illuminating." The others pointed the bows of their small boats at the illuminated asteroid, and Jeffrey continued, "First, take a look at your magnetometers. The other runabouts likely will affect it but if you change the orientation somewhat, you can clearly see some magnetic effect.

"The next thing is, check out your gas spectrometers as I lase a few points." Jeffrey pointed the laser at several points over a minute, each point released a spout of gas or vapor. Jeffrey's spectrometer indicated a high ferrous content, but also nickel, water ice, some carbon and a diminishing number of other minerals. Jeffrey fired a buoy with a strobe and radio locator.

"Okay, teams, what did your spectrometers read?" he asked.

Torres replied first. "I see Iron, nickel, water ice, carbon."

Smitty, who was riding with Janet, then said, "There's also a whole plethora of noble gasses, but in minute quantities."

"All right, everyone, go find me some heavy metals. I want Uranium, Gold, Silver, Molybdenum, and especially Tungsten. Use your radars and radios to figure out what is in each rock. Regardless, tag any rock of value. When we are done with the exercise, we'll drag those rocks onboard and begin processing them."

Sneaky, piloting the runabout Jeffrey was in, turned on the radar to very bright, high gain, multifrequency signal. The radar image was superimposed on the video image of the current location. She saw that one particular rock seemed to have considerably greater mass than any of the other rocks in the area, so she high-tailed it to that rock, put her buoy on it, and began testing using all the tools Jeffrey had made available. She also noted that the rock was slightly radioactive.

"Good work, Audrey. No nonsense, you went right for the prize." Just then Janet called. "Captain," she said, "we have a rock with more than ten percent Tungsten."

"Good work, Janet and Smitty."

"Captain, Torres here. I have a big rock with a lot of iron and copper."

"Okay you guys, tag them, and then cluster around me," said Jeffrey.

Twenty minutes later the two other runabouts pulled up alongside Jeffrey's and Sneaky's. "Pay attention; for rocks this size, you need to deploy three rockets on the push side, and three on the brake side. You need to array them at about 45 degrees from center mass to allow for maneuvering." Jeffrey then had Sneaky bring the runabout up to touch the rock, Jeffrey pointed to where he wanted her to place the runabout. When she got there, he activated the first motor. It drilled itself into the surface of the rock. He then had her go to another spot and placed another motor, and yet again a third.

They repeated the placement on the brake side. "I am now programming the motors to coordinate themselves, and where I want them to go. I always have them go just aft of *Elizabeth*, to avoid crashing into her, although now that the AI is so smart, she won't let anything bad happen to herself."

He activated the motors, and while starting slowly, the rock soon sped towards the dot in the sky that was *Elizabeth*. Jeffrey then followed Torres to his rock and followed the same technique.

Then they all went over to Janet's rock, and Smitty set the motors. Soon all three rocks were on their way to *Elizabeth*.

The crew then returned to the ship, and within a few moments, the three rocks began to arrive. Elizabeth took control of the motors of the first rock, and guided it into the hold. Jeffrey said, "Elizabeth, that rock is somewhat radioactive, we should segregate it for safety."

"AYE, CAPTAIN."

They then parked the runabouts in the shuttle bay. Jeffrey said, "Pilots – you do your maintenance on the runabouts. Passengers let's begin smelting and separating the minerals one from the others."

Jeffrey started in the hold containing the first rock. In the hold was a couple of large semi- spheres, Jeffrey maneuvered first one side then the other around the rock, sealed it so it was a large sphere. He connected the power cable, and activated the switch on the panel. Immediately, they felt a vibration through their hard suits.

"Ow," said Smitty. "tickles my teeth!"

"So here," lectured Jeffrey, "is where the rock is shaken up to dust. As they heat up, gasses are captured and separated so we have Hydrogen, Oxygen, Carbon Dioxide, and a plethora of other chemicals. They are filtered and added to the ship's storage. The dust will be centrifuged to separate one isotope from another. Depending on the need, they will be piped to the smelter or to the fabricator. The smelter will melt and then make ingots. The fabricator will make whatever we want."

After the crew finished their smelting and maintenance tasks, they removed their hard suits and hung them in the midship suit bay. Digger volunteered to be the chef, and the rest all showered while he rummaged around the cold stores. Janet told him that her vegetable garden wouldn't produce for another thirty days or so. He decided on a Jambalaya-like pot that incorporated vegetables, broth, various kinds of protein. He set it to cook for a couple hours, took biscuits out of the freezer, made coffee and iced tea.

When he judged all was ready, he had Elizabeth call the crew to dinner. They came into the galley to find a tablecloth on the table, plates sitting on place settings, glasses of iced tea and cups of coffee at each place.

The entire crew were in their under-suits which seemed a little informal for the occasion, bur Digger let it pass. Jeffrey said, "Digger, this is really nice. Smells good. What is it?"

"Something I learned to cook in my home. It's like Jambalaya. I cut down to about fifty- percent of the hot peppers."

"Well," said Jeffrey, "let's not wait on ceremony, dish 'er up!"

"Captain," interrupted Digger. "If I may request. May I say a grace?"

Jeffrey looked at the man with new eyes. "By all means. Everyone! Quiet. Go ahead Digger."

"Thank you, Captain."

Then Zitulu Mbaka bent his head, and said. "Let us pray." Jeffrey saw several others bend their heads, as if this was not unusual for them. "God," he began in his Lagos accent. "Please look down upon us and bless us, bless our mission, and bless this food. In your holy name. Amen." Torres and Bianca both crossed themselves. Digger then changed his expression, his face lighting up, a big toothy smile on his expressive face, and said, "Let's eat!"

The food was better than Jeffrey had ever had on this ship. "I have an idea," said Jeffrey. "I like this gathering for dinner. Any problem making it mandatory? We can share cooking and cleanup duties."

All agreed. Twenty hundred hours was the designated time to gather for food. Janet volunteered to write up the cooking and cleaning schedule.

Jeffrey said, "As far as prayers are concerned, it is up to the cook. You may pray for yourselves if the cook doesn't initiate it." Again, all agreed. Up until just this moment, Jeffrey had been thinking of his crew as just a bunch of individuals on his ship, now they were family. There were ties between them all that were stronger than any comradeship or friendship.

After the meal, Jeffrey helped clean up the galley. Torres stayed behind as the other crew went their separate ways. "Captain, can I talk with you for a couple minutes?"

"Certainly."

They each took a cup of coffee and sat down at the table, now sans tablecloth. "That was nice. I like how you recognize a good thing and incorporate it into our standard operating procedure."

"Thanks."

"I had an idea that I think will help us improve our survivability in a sneak attack."

"Sounds like you've been thinking."

"Indeed, I have. All of us have lightweight under-suits that we usually wear when working, and also some kind of non-protected cloth clothing that we wear off-hours. I would like to suggest a uniform that each of us can get into within a few seconds, that is mildly armored.

"In the mid-twentieth century they developed a yarn that was used to make bulletproof garments, they called it Kevlar. They also used this to make fire protection gear. We can craft a suit of clothes, like a jumpsuit made of something like this, or other material like carbon fibers, and always be protected. Unless we are in the shower. Or otherwise naked." He winked at the captain. "It should protect us against knife attacks, explosive decompression, small-bore flechettes, and stunners. It won't against a plasma blaster, but it might help you survive your wound."

"Great!" said Jeffrey. "I like your way of thinking. Go ahead and do it."

"Ah, there's the rub, Captain." He scraped at a spot on the table. "I don't know squat about designing this kind of thing. I have the idea, but I'm out of my depth."

"Elizabeth," said Jeffrey. "Please connect me with Janet." Janet's voice came over the loudspeaker.

"Yes Captain?"

"Elizabeth, please play back Torres' conversation with me."

She did, and when the playback was over, Jeffrey told Janet, "I want you to work with Ojo – you both have great ideas. You have the technical skills to design the suits, and can help Elizabeth execute."

"Okay, Captain."

Over the next few days, while Smitty, Digger and Sneaky went out to tag asteroids, Torres and Janet worked on the design of the suits with input from Elizabeth. In that time, they had gotten close, and spent time together both on and off the project. That shared time quickly became a shared bed, and the two became one more than twice each day.

The suits began to be built, several sets for each crew member. Elizabeth had suggested some improvements, including carbon fiber tubes throughout the suits that, in the event of being caught in space, the suits could recycle wastes and protect the crew member from freezing or cooking, and short-term cosmic radiation, as well as the pressure issues. After another day the suits were finished. Jeffrey distributed them at that evening's meal. After that meal, Jeffrey asked Janet and Torres to his cabin.

He sat them down at the table, and said, "You realize it is against regulations for a non-com and an officer to...comingle. Janet blushed profusely, Torres blustered about it being his fault. "Jeffrey stopped them. "I don't give a flying rip about that regulation. You kids are old enough to know what you are doing. Just don't go sneaking behind my back. Our backs.

"The only problem I have is if it affects your work. You are both combat professionals and members of my crew. If it affects your work, then have the good sense to cut it out. You may find someone else on the crew that you want to screw, and if that is going to be a problem for your partner, then cut it out.

"If you find someone else having relations that you object to, just remember yourselves and realize that on this ship, it is nobody's business.

"Questions?"

"No sir," and "No, Captain."

"Good. Now why don't you let the other crew members know what you are up to so they don't jump your bones for hiding it?"

"Yes, Captain."

"And Torres," he added as the crew chief was leaving.

"Sir?"

"Give her a kiss for me!"

"No sir."

Jeffrey found himself with more time on his hands than ever, so he began concocting upgrades to the ship he wanted to accomplish. He started sharing them with Elizabeth.

"I want to increase the armor on this ship as well as the shielding. I think we can do that by installing tungsten alloy plating and water tanks on the outside of the ship. This outer shell doesn't have to rotate, it can be stationary. To enter at an airlock, you go in, the airlock accelerates like an elevator to catch up to the rotated inner lock. I think it would add another level of anti-boarding security."

Elizabeth replied, "CAPTAIN, IT IS DOABLE. BUT I WILL NEED ANOTHER TEN TONS OF TUNGSTEN, MORE IF YOU WANT ME TO MAKE AMMUNITION OUT OF IT AS WELL."

"I can have the crew hunt for tungsten until we have enough, starting tomorrow," Jeffrey finished. That evening he explained his plan to the crew.

"That will be quite a project," said Torres. Jeffrey noticed Bianca sitting rather close to him. He then noticed Audrey and Brandon sitting closer together. *What have I started,* he wondered to himself.

"Elizabeth will do most of the work with her remotes. We just need to get the raw materials, and smelt it."

After work hours, Janet and Audrey worked the garden, glad to see some vegetables beginning to show. Janet saw some white spots on the leaves of some of the plants, and she and Audrey took a sample, looked at it in a microscope. "Looks like just a regular fungus." Neither of the women knew what they needed to do, nor did Elizabeth. They cut off the leaves with the white spots and incinerated them, and decided to increase their monitoring.

So, the next couple of weeks saw the crew busy seeking and bringing back tungsten bearing asteroids, then using the smelter and fabricator to make sheets according to Elizabeth's specs. They also created a meter-deep layer of water tanks with piping to circulate the water. The water, of course came from the asteroids. Elizabeth constructed an additional twenty remote robots, but these much larger than the kitten-sized originals. These robots were powerful enough to carry whole pallets of tungsten-alloy sheets from the hold to the outer skin of the ship.

As the shell was being completed, Elizabeth began moving the antenna arrays and weapons onto the outer shell. When finished, the job had taken six weeks altogether. Because she already had significant quantities of water aboard, the additional water was not a significant burden.

Elizabeth decided that she was going to need more powerful engines in order to move the greater mass of the water and tungsten, but she could still move faster than most non-military vessels in the system.

Because of Jeffrey's upgrade to his ship, the holds were only half full, so he continued to have the crew gather heavy metals and other minerals and gasses to trade or sell. Jeffrey kept the ship on a twelve-hour work cycle, and the crew took advantage of the down time to socialize. The two women on board had found some satisfaction in both their connections to their lovers, and to each other to discuss their lovers, much to the chagrin of their lovers. When not involved with each other, the crew practiced their combat techniques, both organized by Torres and in informal games.

After another couple weeks, the ship was ready to return in-system to sell their cargo. They headed in towards Lagrange 3A, the closest station to their current location. This would also give Jeffrey the ability to monitor pirate activity after *Wanigan* had paid her visit.

As the crew of the *Elizabeth* prepared to move in-system, they picked up their marine training; the hard work of asteroid mining, ship maintenance and other exercises nicely balanced the increases in caloric intake that the regular dinner time presented. With the reduction in exercise, they were likely to get pudgy, so the consensus was that they would all take part in regular calisthenics, martial arts practice, capped off with a laser-tag type game, using real lasers set to low power. *Elizabeth* coupled the aft end of the ship to the fore end, so the entire ship rotated, providing simulated gravity from stem to stern. The outer shell did not rotate, so the ship appeared as a sleek, but non-gravitied vessel.

This allowed her to set up courses for the laser tag games which the crew valued. As experienced as Torres was as a fifteen-year veteran of the space Marines, Audrey, the team's ninja, always came out ahead.

Torres, on the other hand came out ahead on all martial arts bouts. He had learned and practiced Jujutsu in Tokyo and Brasilia. He also had black belts in Shotokan Karate, also studied in Japan, and Taekwondo, studied in Panmunjom, Korea. He began training all the crew in Kodokan Judo, so each of the crew members could become proficient in a single, comprehensive martial art. The four weeks of travel in-system gave an opportunity for each to improve significantly on the training they had received in military basic training.

Elizabeth took longer than usual to get to the Lagrange 3A station than in previous trips because the ship now had nearly a third greater mass than it had before. This inspired Jeffrey to begin exploring replacing the engines on his ship. He needed something that could propel the ship in a more nimble fashion without consuming more of the fuel than he could carry. This gave him numerous options to consider; a larger ion engine could push the ship faster, but would take a very long time to get up to that speed; atomic fusion engines were still too new to trust, but offered much more rapid acceleration. Also, there was the possibility of waste products contaminating the space in which the ship lingered. He would have to check up on that.

There was one other possibility that he didn't know enough about; using the gravity propulsion drive that pulled and pushed on the dark matter of space. On pondering these technical issues, he realized he had much more research to perform. He thought he would seek the advice of Commander Yusef. Jeffrey sent a message to Wanigan for Yusef. They agreed to meet after *Elizabeth* unloaded her cargo.

Elizabeth had no problems docking this time. There was a new administration in place that reflected a more professional attitude. Before any other business, Jeffrey arranged the broker to visit *Elizabeth's* hold to see for himself the size and quality of his ores and gasses. The broker said, "Jeff – thanks for taking charge about that pirate bastard Chin. We were being robbed blind by the bribes we had to pay just to do business here."

Jeffrey and the broker agreed on prices for most of the cargo. The broker refused to meet Jeffrey's price on the mercury, gold, and silver that took up three containers. He told Jeffrey, "The precious metals aren't all that precious any more. Unless you want to make gold wire, what you have there represents a waste of your mining time." The broker assumed a look of paternal support. "Let me do this for you – I'll take it off your hands for," here he paused to think, "a quarter your asking price. Even there, I'm taking a loss."

"Elizabeth, what is your take?" Jeffrey asked. Her voice came over the public address system, booming and echoing in the large spaces.

"CAPTAIN, THE BROKER IS LYING THROUGH HIS TEETH. NEWS REPORTS OF SPECULATORS BUYING UP AS MUCH OF THE PRECIOUS METALS AS POSSIBLE ARE BEING PLAYED ALL OVER THE SYSTEM."

"Thanks, Elizabeth," he said. Then to the broker, "So you wish to do me a favor? Tell you what, I'll worry about the precious metals, you just worry about the rest of the cargo, as we agreed."

"Jeff, Jeff, Jeff. You misunderstand me. Those speculators are creating a bubble. It will crash, leaving you and anyone else holding these precious metals with no value at all!" He again assumed the paternal look, and said. "Okay, here's what I'll do. I'll give what you originally asked for the entire cargo."

Jeffrey took on the look of a confused beginner, and said, "I don't know, maybe I should do that speculating myself. Maybe I'll get rich!"

"No, no. You don't want to do that. You will lose everything! You'll lose your shirt. Your ship. Don't go that route. Let me help you with this. I'll give you double your claimed value."

"CAPTAIN, A CALL FROM CAPTAIN YUSEF OF WANIGAN IS WAITING FOR YOU," announced Elizabeth.

"Look, I'll think about your offer. I have to take this call."

"Before you go," said the broker, "Let's firm up this deal. I'll give you triple the value."

"Tell you what," said Jeffrey. "You wait in the galley, after this call, I'll talk to you." He had Audrey escort the broker to the galley, and she provided him with tea and cookies, relatively freshly baked.

In the bridge, Jeffrey activated the message. "Captain Sokolov, Yusef here. Before you unload your cargo, the Navy requests that you provide us with first bid on all precious metals. It is very important that you do not sell unless we have had an opportunity to bid. We should be at your location in forty-eight hours. Please hold off precious metals sales until we arrive."

What the hell is going on, Jeffrey asked himself. Something's not right here. "Elizabeth, please quietly put the crew on alert. I think something's coming up that may make us vulnerable."

"WORKING"

He then went back to the galley, and asked the broker "So exactly what is going on with precious metals?"

The broker asked, "Why? What did the Navy Captain tell you?" Jeffrey let his frustration show.

"You know, I've been in this business since I was a kid. I ran this ship since I was fifteen." He raised his voice. "Don't treat me like a child. Either tell me what is going on or I'll find another broker to work with."

"No, no, no." the broker started blustering, but then said resignedly, "Okay. Here's the lowdown, the skinny. The station administration let all the brokers know that they needed gold, silver and platinum for some military purpose, but of course it is top secret. We were told not to let the miners know. From colleagues on other stations, I am told it is system wide."

"And you wanted to make a killing on the market, right?"

The broker looked down, shame-faced. "Yes."

"I am going to hang on to my cargo, for now. I'm sorry we couldn't do business today. Audrey will see you off the ship." The trader got up, reluctantly, but now certain he had made a bad move.

"Captain, please don't kill our relationship."

"We'll see. Goodbye."

"Jonathon."

"Excuse me?"

"My name. Jonathon," said the broker. "I always felt it gave me an advantage if the miners had no idea of what my name is."

"Jonathon," said Jeffrey. "Nice to make your acquaintance. I'm Captain Sokolov." he continued. *Maybe this will at least make him use my real name – stop calling me 'Jeff'.*

The crew now on alert, went on 'shore leave' two at a time, accompanying each other to all stops. The station seemed to be more prosperous than it had previously, new stores and shops opened since their last visit. Janet dragged Torres to the Dirt Store and spoke with the clerk about the white fungus spots on their vegetables. The clerk offered some anti-fungal, but suggested they just use vinegar on their soil and the leaves. They bought some of the anti-fungal and some other chemicals they may need to combat other invasive biologics.

Torres took Janet to a nice restaurant, and they enjoyed their dining experience, but agreed that they already had better cooks on board *Elizabeth* than the restaurant. Torres arranged for more fresh foodstuffs to be delivered to the ship, this time including meats, which were missing from the last order. There was ham, recently brought up from Virginia, beef from Argentina, chicken from China, turkey from Minnesota, and venison from Texas. There were whole cases of sausages from Chicago, Italy, Germany and France.

They also found a cheese monger who provided wheels of cheddar, provolone, mozzarella, and other soft and hard cheeses. They arranged to have these foodstuffs delivered to the dock at sixteen hundred. They then returned to the ship. They took up the security posts, relieving Audrey and Brandon, who went shopping for their personal needs. They wore their new suits designed by Torres, which brought stares from other inhabitants, but probably less for their technical specifications than for the profile Audrey presented in her suit.

Audrey found a cloth merchant, and purchased several bolts of pure Vietnamese silk, bolts of Scottish wool, and bolts of Egyptian cotton. The merchant tried to entice her with various poly cloths, but she was not interested, considering that Elizabeth could likely make that herself.

They then went to a weapons shop. They looked over the offerings, found a few high-powered projection weapons, some pistols, some stunners. There were a lot of types of ammunition, but because Elizabeth had the ability to manufacture her own, they rejected them. Brandon purchased one each of the weapons. Audrey found some knives, darts, shuriken, that she naturally had to acquire. They both found some swords that they couldn't live without. They purchased a variety of swords that their shipmates would likely find useful. Delivery for fifteen thirty.

On their arrival back at *Elizabeth* Zitulu Mbaka and Jeffrey went to the shops to arrange for their personal purchases and to arrange for the ship's needs. Jeffrey stopped at the fuel monger, and arranged for the refueling of the ship at nineteen hundred. But the monger's clerk told him that authorization had to come from the station for any purchase. The clerk said, "If you could please stand by, we can get this going."

Jeffrey again had a bad feeling about this, but decided to see what he could. He had Digger cross the avenue and sit at a non-covered cafe, while Jeffrey waited for whatever it was the clerk would do. Digger then ordered cafe-au-lait and croissant. Jeffery then stood at the counter, looking at the clerk, as the clerk explained to his supervisor that the captain of the *Elizabeth* was trying to purchase fuel for the ship.

Within a few seconds, an officer of the station appeared in the store accompanied by a couple of security officers. Jeffrey noticed the officer was missing a finger on his right hand. He then recognized the officer as the man who had infiltrated his ship the last time *Elizabeth* was in port.

Jeffrey said, "We meet again. How's the finger?"

There was anger in the officer's eyes. "It hurts. It itches. It makes me angry!"

"What brings you here, officer – uh," he read the name tag on the light armor suit, "Andrade."

The officer regained composure and said, "Captain Sokolov of *Elizabeth*, you are under arrest." The security officers moved around to take Jeffrey into custody. They grabbed him by his upper arms. One took the radio communicator from its pocket on his suit and turned it off.

Mbaka got up to intervene, but Jeffrey shook his head. Instead, he radioed to Elizabeth to notify the ship her captain was in trouble. Andrade took his stunner out and shot Jeffrey in the neck.

Jeffrey went unconscious immediately, and the two security officers began dragging him away. Mbaka followed from a distance.

Janet Bianca took the news of Jeffrey's arrest and rough handling with a bit of relief – this was her first time in command since she came aboard the ship, and now was able to prove herself – to herself. Start with the facts, she told herself.

"Elizabeth," she said. "What do we know?"

"THE OFFICER THAT RENDERED OUR CAPTAIN UNCONSCIOUS IS THE SAME MAN WHO HAD ATTACKED OUR SHIP THE LAST TIME WE WERE HERE. HE IS THE GUY WHOSE FINGER I SHOT OFF."

"Can you track events through the station's computers?"

"ALREADY UNDER WAY."

"Good."

"JANET, THERE IS A SQUAD OF SECURITY OFFICERS APPROACHING THE GANGWAY."

Janet then called out "Alert! Ship is under attack." Elizabeth sent the message throughout the ship.

"Torres and Smitty to the forward airlock. Sneaky take the aft entrances."

She then armed herself with a high-powered rifle – the kind that threw large-bore projectiles rapidly – and went to the front entrance and stalked down the gangway. An officer at the base of the gangway said "This ship is under orders. Stand out of the way and surrender."

Janet moved the pointy end of the rifle a little higher, while still not aiming directly at any of the officers.

"Back off!" she said, menacingly. "Any attempt to board this ship will be met with deadly force. This is the only warning you will get."

"Your captain is in custody. Surrender!" demanded the officer. His five colleagues drew out their stunners.

Janet raised the rifle to her shoulder and aimed it at the officer's forehead. The five officers all fired their stunners at Janet, but much to their surprise, the suit absorbed all the force of the stunners. Seeing the ineffectiveness of their weapons, they all stepped back one step, but Janet advanced toward them still aiming the rifle at the forehead of the officer in charge. The five other officers ran off, back to the first corner they could hide behind. The officer in charge fell to his knees, his hands in the air.

Torres ran down the gangway, cuffed the officer's hands and dragged him aboard the ship. Janet walked backwards up the gangway, keeping the rifle at ready. When she reached the entry, she told Smitty to disengage the gangway and seal the hatch, and continue to stand guard.

"Yessir, Ma'am"

Torres and Janet took the bound security officer to the galley, sat him down and stripped him of his uniform and then Torres put him through a full search. Satisfied that they had removed all the weapons, communications devices and any other material that could be deemed offensive, they looked over the officer's identification, and other documents.

Janet said to the officer, "It says your name is Jason Calloway. Are you Jason Calloway, Sergeant of the station security? Answer."

The officer was silent until Torres put his knuckle onto the side of his neck, applied pressure and began to twist. The excruciating pain was enough to cause the officer to yelp and then answer, "Yes!"

Janet said, "Good. You see how this works. I ask questions, you answer them truthfully. My crew chief is an expert at getting information out of people, but we agreed that I would try first. Do you understand?"

Calloway looked daggers at Bianca, but held his tongue. A reminder from Torres inflicted a little more pain. He yelped again, and said, "Yes."

Janet said, "Elizabeth, please inform your sister of the unfortunate events that just occurred." "YES JANET. MESSAGE AWAY."

"Now Mister Calloway, I see your identification, I see your badge, I see your weapons, but what I don't see is a warrant. Please explain what you and your team was trying to do to my ship."

Calloway wanted to balk further but thought better of it after looking at how eager Torres seemed to be to inflict more pain. He said, "I had orders to take this ship and arrest its crew."

"Who gave those orders," Janet asked politely.

He looked at Janet, then at Torres, then back at Janet, but held his silence and closed his eyes in anticipation of another torturous experience. When the expected pain did not arrive, he opened his eyes again, to see Torres in front of him, tossing and catching his combat knife. He noticed there was a cutting board on the table in front of him. He realized what the next step in his interrogation was going to be and tried to lurch upward to escape. Torres kicked his legs out from under him and he crashed on the deck, face first. Torres lifted the bound arms to the point of pain, Calloway cried out "You're going to break my shoulder!"

But Torres replied, "Nah, just dislocate it a little."

"No! Please stop!" cried Calloway.

Janet said to Torres, "Get him back up here." Torres put the knife back in its sheath, hauled the officer back up, and put him in the chair. This time he secured the bound hands to the chair, then the feet too. Calloway realized that this was going to be a longer than he anticipated stay on board being tortured by these crazy people.

"I'll ask one more time. Who gave you the order to invade my ship?" Janet said quietly. "Andrade!" he rasped out. "He wanted revenge for your last visit."

"I thought as much. So, you and your team aren't on duty, right?"

"Yeah."

"Do you realize you just committed an act of piracy?" Janet asked. "And the penalty for piracy is execution."

"What?" he shouted. "No! It was just retribution for his finger!"

She then had Torres secure the unfortunate man in a makeshift brig that Elizabeth had supplied with the usual remotes.

Back on the bridge, Janet asked, "Elizabeth, what is our situation? Where is the captain?"

"JANET, I HAVE UPLOADED A COPY OF MYSELF TO THEIR COMPUTERS. GATHERING INFORMATION ON ANDRADE AND HIS COMPANIONS. MBAKA IS STILL FOLLOWING THE SQUAD THAT TOOK THE CAPTAIN. IT APPEARS THAT THERE IS A STANDING ORDER TO BULLY SHIP CAPTAINS WHO HAVE PRECIOUS METALS INTO SURRENDERING THEM TO THE STATION. ALSO, THE STATION HAS BEGUN BROADCASTING A RADIO BLOCKING WAVEFORM."

"I don't think we can count on the station management to provide us with any assistance," said Janet.

"AGREED."

Janet thought about her situation. Captain gone, but being trailed. *Wanigan* still a couple days out. A security officer in their brig, a squad of off-duty security officers on the wharf watching them. She had resources on both the ship and inside the computers of the station.

"It looks like they don't want word of this problem to get out. Can you piggyback on the carrier wave to get out a message to the other ships?" Janet asked. "NO VOCAL MESSAGE WOULD BE INTELLIGIBLE."

"But I'll bet you could get out a Morse code signal pretty well, don't you?"

"JANET, YOU ARE A GENIUS.

The other ships in the cluster surrounding the Lagrange 3A station heard nothing on the radio but a multifrequency static white noise. It was a powerful broadcast from the station's own transmitters. But then, ships began noticing a series of peaks in the white noise that made a bit of a pattern. The captains of each of the ships began recognizing the several hundred years old Morse code, but had to rely on their ships computers to translate. They got the gist of the situation, and pulled farther away, out of the range of the signal jamming radios to communicate among themselves.

Janet then called Sneaky to the bridge. Torres came too.

"I think it is time we utilize your ninja personality, Audrey."

"Thank you, Ma'am, sir. What do you want me to do?"

"Get our Captain back, if possible without them knowing he is gone, and without killing anybody, if possible." Janet explained that there was a rudimentary copy of Elizabeth in the station's computers, but that it couldn't become overly active without blowing their cover.

When needed, it could activate itself to override any computer commands.

"Give me a few minutes to get ready," said Audrey. "They won't know what hit them, or the fact that they were hit!"

Military commandos are usually trained to work in groups, although they sometimes had to work alone. Like snipers, they were experts at blending in with the scenery. Audrey was not part of such a group, she earned her moniker 'Sneaky' after studying under a Ninjutsu master in California. Ninjutsu is the ancient art of the Japanese assassins and spies. In their heyday, they lived and worked outside the system of Samurai, in which there were lords, the Samurai, and peasants, and not much else. The training the ninjas received prepared them for surreptitious completion of their missions. Often that involved overt martial arts activities, such as using the standard karate and jujutsu moves, and in ancient times, sword arts.

But the important lessons of the ninja training Audrey received was to use your head - be something other than what witnesses were expecting. She had learned the arts practiced by entertainment magicians for ages – redirect the mark's attention. Use smoke, mirrors, technology, to seem magical. Audrey was very good.

With the gangway disconnected from the ship, the only way to get on board or off, seemed to be via shuttle, and all shuttles were warned away from the wharf to which *Elizabeth* was docked.

The ship was docked in a part of the station that had atmosphere control, unlike previous occasions, when they were docked outside the station's atmosphere.

The watchers on the wharf kept an eye out for any activity at the dock. The ship looked significantly different than it had last time, a new metallic shell surrounded the old ship's skin. Still, they were told to watch for any activity and report it.

They didn't expect a horn blast out of the bow of the ship – they couldn't even see the device that made the noise, then they noticed a thick cloud of steam coming off the aft end of the ship near the shuttle hanger bay. Then the horn noise again.

"Who is that?" asked one watcher to another, pointing at a gaily clad prostitute walking toward the gangway. The watcher called her over to him, and said, "Sorry, honey, you can't make anything on those guys. That ship's under quarantine."

The little prostitute twirled her umbrella, flicked her tail, and sauntered off. The watcher said, "Hey, what's your name?"

"What do you want it to be, honey?" she responded coyly.

"Ah, get out of here. Maybe I'll see you around." He turned to his fellow watcher. "You ever see her before?"

The other watcher shook his head, they turned around to look at her, but she was gone. As they were about to chase after her, the ship blasted another horn blast and all its exterior lights came on at the same time. They reported the unusual activity at the ship to their controller.

Audrey 'Sneaky' Svoboda discarded her hooker costume, hiding it under a refuse container, and put on a bulky orange jumpsuit, the kind that station maintenance used. Elizabeth guided her to the area which held the captain, where she spotted Zitulu Mbaka. He hadn't seen her yet. He leaned against a wall trying to look like he belonged there. Audrey noted that he was being watched by a couple of thugs – obviously not station personnel. They were situated at opposite corners from where Zitulu stood, both could see him, but not each other.

She walked past him, to one of the watchers, unzipped the jumpsuit as if to show some cleavage (she had her new uniform under-suit underneath the jumpsuit so there was no cleavage to show, but the act itself was enough to engage the interests of the watcher she was performing for.) It took a moment, but finally Zitulu recognized her and followed her activities without moving.

She turned the corner and walked in front of the watcher, passing a meter away. She stopped and turned around and said, "What did you call me?" then slapped the watcher across the face. Her thumb was sticking out and poked him in the temple in a neural plexus. He went unconscious immediately, she helped him to the ground and arranged him to look like he was just resting.

She quickly searched the thug, took his wallet and knife. He had a radio, which she turned off and pocketed.

Audrey then got up and sashayed past Zitulu again, to the other watcher. She repeated her deceptive behavior, knocked out the thug, robbed him of a homemade projectile weapon and his identification, and rearranged her victim to look like he was sleeping off a bad drunken evening.

She then walked over to Zitulu who said that he followed the captain into the section across from where he waited. The walls in this area were tagged with graffiti in all sorts of interesting types, but it was obvious this was not the prosperous part of the station. She crossed the alley to a painted steel door, tried the handle to no avail. It appeared to be locked from the inside; there was no latch or lock on the outside.

She crossed the alley to Zitulu again, and he said, "I tried to get in, but the door is secure."

She winked at him, and said, "Watch this."

She walked around the corner where the first thug was still unconscious, saw what she was looking for, and went to the maintenance access panel. It too, was locked, but was a much less formidable door, so it opened easily. She climbed in, pulled the access panel shut, and felt her way around to approximately a meter from where the front door was. Listening for any activity and hearing none, she removed the interior access panel, dropped to the floor, moved to the door and opened it.

Amazed, Zitulu wasted no time entering. "Boost me up," she said. He interlinked his fingers to make a step for her, she climbed onto his shoulders, stood high as she could, and pushed the high access panel shut, so it wasn't obvious how she had entered.

They walked the corridor as quietly as they could, but Zitulu noticed that his were the only footfalls he heard. The corridor ended in a T intersection, to the left were glass doors, in which could be seen casino operations. To the right was a door guarded by two unshaven security officers. Audrey took a marble-sized metal sphere, squeezed it then tossed it over the heads of the security officers – they never saw it – and it burst with a light 'pop' into a rapidly expanding cloud of gray smoke. Both officers turned to see the commotion, drew their stunners and moved cautiously toward the smoke.

Audry ran up to them, ran right up the back of the one on the right, who fell to the floor, and she grabbed the other, twisting herself and threw him down head first onto the other's head. They were both unconscious.

She grabbed their identities, keys and weapons, and tossed one of the stunners to Mbaka. She indicated he should go and find the captain if he was in there. Audrey then went back to the security officers, took their plastic cuffs, interlinked their arms, and cuffed them. Then she gagged them with their handkerchiefs. She then found the access panel for this corridor, entered it, climbed toward the cable run and shimmied her way to the ceiling over the room Mbaka had just entered. She found a vent overlooking the room.

Mbaka stood with his hands in the air, his lip bleeding. A voice was quietly saying threatening things to Mbaka, when she heard the captain's voice interrupting.

"Leave him alone. It's me you want, just leave him alone."

Audrey surmised that the unseen assailant was armed, that the captain and Mbaka were being held at gunpoint, possibly by more than one person. The assailant was probably Andrade.

She took in her surroundings, saw that there was another vent across the room from which she would be able to see the assailants. Like a panther, she moved sleekly through the maze of pipes, cable-runs and HVAC shafts to the other side of the room. She found the vent, and when she looked through it, saw the security officer that had snuck onto her ship the last time they were docked. She noticed that he was holding a blaster in his left hand, that his right hand was missing its trigger finger. There was nobody else in the room.

Audrey thought about the weapons options she had. The stunners she had taken off the goons were less than adequate for this situation, the zip gun, likewise – who knew if it would work and at what accuracy? She settled on a blow gun with poison dart. Remembering her training, she assembled the straw-like blow gun, selected the quick-acting poison dart, loaded, considered the possible cross currents, took a deep breath, and blew the dart onto Andrade's neck. He dropped to the floor, paralyzed.

Mbaka ran to him, picked up his weapon, searched him and found a set of keys, his wallet with ID and a considerable wad of cash. He then returned to Jeffrey, tried to undo the plastic ties on his hands, but he didn't have the appropriate tools.

Audrey didn't say anything, but tossed a small multi-tool to the floor from her perch above them. Mbaka saw it, picked it up, cut the captains bonds, and pocketed the tool. He then walked back to

Andrade and took the dart out of his neck. Not having a safe place to put it, he just carried it in his hand.

As the captain and Mbaka were about to exit, the door slammed open and two large goons blocked the way. Before anyone could do anything, Mbaka took the dart and poked it into the forehead of the lead goon. He looked at the dark-skinned spacer, said "What the fu…" and then dropped to the floor, breathing heavily and raggedly. His companion looked at the lead man, looked up at Mbaka, then fell to the floor himself, much to Mbaka's confusion, which resolved itself when he saw a fresh dart sticking out of the other man's neck. Audrey walked up the corridor and said, "We need to get out of here."

Jeffrey, none the worse for wear, said, "Okay, Sneaky, lead the way."

Audrey led the team through the service corridors, with input from Elizabeth, who had help from the copy of herself in the station's system. On their way to the wharf, Jeffrey began pondering why, aside from Andrade's revenge, was there such a fuss over his ship and him. It didn't make much sense, unless there was another surge of insurrection and/or piracy. The station seemed to want to corner the market on precious metals, which the Navy also wanted.

That lead to the question of why the Navy was so concerned about the precious metals, too. This required some research.

Audrey led the team to the corridor that lead to the place she hid her 'hooker' disguise. She retrieved it, put the skirt back on, adjusted the clothes so she no longer looked like a maintenance tech, opened the parasol, and intertwined her arm in Jeffrey's, pulled him closer and covered his face with her own and the umbrella. The three made their way to the gangway, and as they reached the foot of the gangway, Torres reattached it at the top. Jeffrey turned around and noticed the four watchers communicating with radios and watching them surreptitiously.

They went up the gangway and entered the ship.

Bianca met them at the forward entry. "Welcome aboard, Captain. Are you all right?"

"I'll live," said Jeffrey. "But I need to know what is going on." He addressed the AI, "Elizabeth, learn what you can about why the Navy and station are so hot to claim precious metals."

"EFFORTING." After a moment, Elizabeth said, "CAPTAIN, THE ADMINISTRATOR OF THE STATION IS TRYING TO CONTACT YOU."

"Okay," said Jeffrey. "I'll take it on the bridge."

Janet explained the events after Jeffrey had been taken by Andrade, including the attempted boarding by Security Officer Sergeant Calloway and his team. She also told him about the station broadcasting a radio jamming signal and how she had Elizabeth piggyback a Morse code to inform the rest of the ships surrounding the station of the events.

Jeffrey and Janet came onto the Bridge.

"CAPTAIN," announced Elizabeth. "THE JAMMING HAS CEASED. ALL RADIO COMMUNICATIONS ARE CLEAR AGAIN."

Jeffrey activated the comm unit. "Administrator. This is Captain Sokolov of the *Elizabeth*. What is going on?"

The administrator said, "Captain Sokolov, it has come to my attention that your crew held one of my officers at gunpoint. I want an explanation. I am sending a squad of security officers to bring you to my office to explain."

Jeffrey rolled his eyes. "Administrator, I just left the presence of a squad of your officers. They were torturing me under the tender mercies of your Security Officer Andrade. I would likely be dead but for the rescue by...a stranger. My apologies, Administrator, but I have had it with your hospitality."

"Captain, I know nothing about that. But you are ordered to surrender to my officers." The administrator paused, looked off-camera for a moment, then looked back at the camera. "Captain Sokolov, I have just been informed that Andrade and his squad have been found. They are currently being treated for blood poison. You are now a suspect in an attempted murder of a Security Officer. You will surrender to my security team. I assure you of your safety."

"Administrator, I have no interest in your security team nor your assurances. I am already safe, and will continue to stay so under my own cognizance. It seems that you are making it impossible to do business on this station. I am taking my cargo of precious metals to deliver elsewhere. Good day."

Jeffrey cut the comm. "Elizabeth, prepare to cast off."

"AYE, CAPTAIN. PLEASE NOTE THERE ARE SEVERAL SMALL PATROL SHIPS TAKING POSITION NEARBY."

"Have the crew take up anti-boarding positions. Broadcast to the other ships the situation. Janet, take us out. Try not to damage the patrol boats."

"CAPTAIN, THE ADMINISTRATOR IS ATTEMPTING TO CONTACT YOU AGAIN."

Jeffrey again activated the console. "What now?" Jeffrey asked.

"Captain Sokolov, perhaps I was...too hasty in my demands. Please let's reconsider."

"Administrator, what is the purpose of your reconsideration?" Jeffrey asked.

"The circumstances of your unauthorized imprisonment by Andrade. You are no longer under suspicion. Please reconsider going elsewhere."

"Standby, Administrator." Jeffrey stopped the communication. "Janet, what do you think."

"We are low on fuel and we already have some orders to be delivered. I think we should at least fuel up and take on our supplies," said Janet.

"Elizabeth, what do you know about the precious metals issue?" Jeffrey asked.

"CAPTAIN, STILL ANALYZING. IT APPEARS THAT THERE IS A TECHNOLOGICAL REQUIREMENT FOR GOLD, SILVER, PLATINUM AND URANIUM."

He reactivated the comm console. "Very well, Administrator. We will stop our departure for now. However, we will not tolerate any harassment by you, your security department or anyone else. Have a security officer come to our gangway. We will turn over your Sergeant to him. You may wish to prepare to arrest him along with Andrade and the rest of their crew."

Jeffrey had Janet cease departure operations, and reduce the crew's alert status, but to keep someone on watch at all times. He then went down to the makeshift brig, He said to Security Officer Sergeant Calloway, "You are one very lucky man. I am turning you over to your own security office. I should space you."

Torres escorted the security Sergeant to the bottom of the gangway and awaited a security officer to take him into custody.

Several of the miners in the group surrounding the station reported to Jeffrey that the reaction to Elizabeth's Morse Code report of the goings-on at the station caused a boycott of Lagrange 3A to be announced. Several of the ships broke orbit and headed towards different stations. This, Jeffrey reasoned, was the likely cause of the quick turn-around of the administrator.

The supplies were delivered on time, Torres and Mbaka brought the palettes aboard. As a security matter, Elizabeth had remotes look over every item. The second delivery was also made, and again scanned and stowed.

Jeffrey and Torres then went to the fuel monger again and arranged for immediate delivery. The clerk said, "No problem, sir."

"You don't have to contact the administration?"

"No, sir. Why would we?"

Jeffrey paused. "The man we spoke with this morning said the station had a new rule."

"Nothing that I know anything about, sir, and I've been working here for a couple years."

"What was the name of the clerk who was working at ten hundred?" Jeffrey asked.

"Oh, that's the new guy, Louis Andrade," he said.

Jeffrey and Torres looked at each other. "Related to the security officer?" "Yeah, that's him. It's his brother. He's married to the Administrator's sister."

"Well, thanks. Go fill up my ship." Then Jeffrey and Torres left.

"I have a bad feeling about this," said Jeffrey. But Torres was already loosening the pistol hidden in a holster in his tool belt, and preparing his emergency mask. Jeffrey took the hint from Torres, and radioed Elizabeth with the new information, and that they were on the way back.

They made their way through the warrens of the station. Elizabeth warned them that chatter on the security radio band was directing teams toward them. Torres suggested they go through some alternate paths, through stores, an art museum, restaurants, and some alleys off the main corridors. They made their way almost all the way to the wharf that held *Elizabeth*. But the AI notified them that there was quite a concentration of security officers near the ship.

Jeffrey and Torres backtracked to one of the Field Gear stores and bought a couple of yellow fuel technician overalls. They donned them over their under-suits, added tool belts, picked up a few extra tools they thought fuel techs may need, and made their way back to the wharf.

As they approached the ship they saw technicians from the fuel monger arguing with a couple security officers, gesticulating wildly. "Watch this," said Jeffrey to Torres.

They walked up to the group, and Jeffrey said in a loud, rough voice, "What the hell are you doing?" directed at the fuel technicians. "You were supposed to fill that ship then move on."

The technician didn't recognize Jeffrey, but understood the voice of authority. "Sorry. These rent-a-cops won't let us."

"You go do your job. I'll take care of this."

The security officer looked at Jeffrey and Torres, and said, "Who are you?" and put his hands on his hips.

"Management," he said to the security officer. Then to the technician, "Go on, we'll be right over to make sure you do it right!" Then back to the officer. "So, what's the delay here?"

While Jeffrey argued with the officers, Torres ushered the technicians to the ship.

"We have orders to keep this ship on the dock. They can't fuel it without orders from the Administrator's office." The officer took out his electronic tablet and showed Jeffrey the order. The order was signed by Andrade, and with a date/time stamp of that morning.

"Ah, I see your problem," said Jeffrey. "I just spoke with the administrator an hour ago. He told me to rescind any holds on fueling. Also, isn't Andrade the guy in the hospital? I think he's under arrest." Jeffrey turned his back on the officer. "Get your facts straight and update your warrants. Damn bureaucrats!" and he walked over to the other technicians.

They had already begun fueling, so Jeffrey and Torres took their leave and mounted the gangway. They could hear the security officers in the distance, "You! Wait!" just before entering the ship.

Jeffrey overheard the officer contacting the security office over his handheld radio, and heard them passing from one department to another, until five minutes later a higher-ranking officer came on asking what was going on. "Who authorized your surveillance?" the higher- ranking officer queried over the radio.

Jeffrey heard the security officer on the dock, "It was Andrade."

"Standby," came the call from the office.

Another couple minutes passed. Then the same officer came on and said, "Cease and desist any surveillance or harassing activities. Your order was illegitimate. Report to your supervisor."

Jeffrey said from the head of the gangway, where he stood just outside the exterior hatch, "Elizabeth, were you able to pick up that last radio message to the officer outside?"

"YES, CAPTAIN. IT WAS RECORDED. BUT BETTER THAN THAT, I NOW AM ABLE TO DECIPHER THEIR ENCRYPTION BY COMPARING THE AUDIO WITH THE ENCRYPTED TRANSMISSION. THEIR SECURITY ALGORITHM IS RELATIVELY SIMPLE."

"So now you are able to listen in on all their internal radio communications?" Jeffrey asked.

"YES, CAPTAIN. MY COUNTERPART ON THE STATION IS GOING TO LIE LOW UNTIL NEEDED AGAIN. THE STATION HAS INCREASED THEIR OWN ANTI- INTRUSION EFFORTS."

"Very good."

Jeffrey made his way back to the bridge. There, he called the Administrator's Office. After a few moments, the administrator came on, his video image showing some relief. "Captain! Thanks again for reconsidering leaving us. What can I do for you?"

"Administrator, is it true your sister married Mr. Andrade's brother, Louis?" Jeffrey asked.

"Yes indeed, sir. She's a lovely woman. Glad she found a good man, why? What's going on?"

"Are you aware of the recent illegal attempts to capture me and my crew?"

"What do you mean, 'recent'?"

Jeffrey raised his tone a little. "Just now concluded."

"No, I'm not. What happened?"

Jeffrey explained the goings on from the time he was at the fuel monger until this call.

"Ah, I think I understand. It appears my officer Andrade was looking for revenge for his finger. And his team is helping him get it. Please allow me to address this for you. This is a detestable, an execrable situation. Captain, I'm so sorry for their behavior towards you. Give me a couple hours to clean up this mess for you. Then I would like to invite you to dine with me, to make up for my staff's poor behavior towards you."

"All right, Administrator, call me when you have the situation finalized," said Jeffrey. "We can than arrange for a dinner."

"Elizabeth, call the team together for a meeting in the galley. Please stand watch for us." Jeffrey started walking toward the galley. He met Janet on the way.

"What's up, Captain?" she asked.

"I think there is much more going on than what we are seeing," he commented as they neared the galley.

They arrived ahead of the rest of the crew. Janet made coffee and delivered mugs to all the crew – set them at their usual seats. As the crew filtered in Jeffrey was glad to see his order that all crew remain armed with the projectile pistols was being followed. Jeffrey still carried the small flechette-firing gun but still preferred the big bore pistols. These shot a bullet made of Tungsten. Tungsten is a very heavy and hard element. While care needed to be taken not to allow the large bullets to penetrate the skin of the ship, almost no armor or faceplate was proof against them.

"Here's the situation so far. I have been targeted on several occasions since we arrived. Thanks to quick thinking of you guys, I am yet again free. But several things give me the impression that the activities surrounding our ship are coordinated beyond the local level. I suspect that a leak has occurred somewhere indicating our anti-piracy position."

Torres asked, "Can you put your finger on what raised your suspicions?"

"First," said Jeffrey, "the organization of the attacks were pretty large, more than one would expect from a vendetta, especially about a missing finger." Jeffrey ticked off on his hand. "Next, the location of the place they took me – an underground casino? Reeks of organized crime." He ticked another finger. "Then the use of regular security and street goons. Most unusual.

"This kind of criminal activity has not been heard of before the *Wanigan* visited last time." He ticked another finger. "And the way the administration has been trying to corner the market of precious metals, really screams organized crime.

"But this is just my analysis. What do you think?"

Torres chimed in, "Maybe you're right, maybe not. But if we stay on our toes as if you were right, we can't go wrong."

Janet agreed with Torres. "Ojo is right. We can continue to gather intelligence, stay on alert."

"Sneaky," said Torres, "you need to keep a low profile. They know there was a little hooker visiting the ship and making appearances, especially around the times our activities increase. Let's not give them something to associate you with."

"Right," said Audrey. "I can be shipped ashore in a crate or container along with a number of our minerals. And later can be shipped back on a palette of fresh foodstuffs."

Jeffrey said appreciatively, "Good idea." Then to Elizabeth, "Elizabeth, please arrange for a suite of rooms for our permanent use. It should be on the silver-level sector. Not too ritzy but secure."

"ACTIONING."

"When can we expect *Wanigan* to show up?"

"AT LEAST ANOTHER THIRTY-SIX HOURS."

"Okay. Arrange the rooms under an alias."

"I HAVE NOW PURCHASED AND SECURED A SUITE ON SILVER 3B. THE OPERATIVE NAME IS SILVESTER."

"Okay, gang. We are going to be the Silvester family every now and then. Smitty, I want you to go to the ship outfitters and acquire six or so military-surplus computers, have them delivered to the suite. Janet, arrange for furnishing the suite. Sneaky, work with Elizabeth to get you ashore, then make your way to the suite. Torres, help Janet. Digger, you are going to be my security.

"I have been invited to dine with the administrator. You are primarily going to be the alert button. Anything happens to me, if Elizabeth doesn't know about it, tell her. Then be my security backup."

Jeffrey stood, still holding his coffee mug – mostly undrunk – and said. "Okay, let's build us a safe house. Elizabeth, I want a copy of you on that bank of computers ready to activate."

After a couple hours the administrator called Jeffrey and invited him to dine at a high- end restaurant on the gold level. Jeffrey agreed and left with Digger.

The restaurant was indeed a fine dining experience. The continuous flow of mineral wealth to Earth from the asteroid miners made it much more cost effective to send high quality food products to space, the miners did get to enjoy some of the benefits of those shipments, but meats were much more expensive than the quantity available would suggest. So, until a cartel was exposed or other collusion and criminal behavior was made known, the wealthiest and most powerful of people got to enjoy the succulent delights – they were the only ones who could afford it. The rest of the space-faring humans got used to proteins grown in a vat. Or sausages.

Jeffrey loved sausages.

The administrator sat, his bodyguard standing surreptitiously against a nearby wall. Mbaka sidled up to him. "How the mighty eat!" he said in his heavily accented English. The administrator's bodyguard just looked at him in disdain, then looked back to the table.

"Captain Sokolov," the administrator began. "You have a way of making waves whenever you show up on our small island home."

"I think the waves come from other people trying to do wrong, don't you?"

"Oh Captain, what could you possibly mean by that?" The administrator asked.

"The incident that caused Mr. Andrade to lose his finger. He wasn't a stowaway, he was told to come aboard my ship and take it over. I objected to that.

"By the way," added Jeffrey. "Why didn't he have the finger reattached? We sent it along with him."

"Pride? Punishment? Self-loathing? Who knows why people do these things to themselves?" said the administrator, blandly.

Jeffrey dipped a piece of freshly baked bread into a small bowl of spiced olive oil, and pondered the administrator's response. The human waiter brought the soup course, which consisted of a selection of five different soups in small bowls. Jeffrey first tasted the wonton soup, then a basil-tomato soup. He left the rest. The administrator finished all his varieties.

There was a bit of a commotion outside the restaurant, but didn't seem to have anything to do with the administrator or Jeffrey. The administrator said, "Your man," indicating Mbaka, "should have something to eat. We should have some compassion for the little people."

"He'll eat back at the ship," said Jeffrey.

"I must insist," said the administrator. "I'm quite uncomfortable being watched over by your man. He should join us."

"Ah, I see," said Jeffrey, standing up. "Thank you for the aperitifs, but we must be going. Perhaps your security officer should take my portion."

Surprised by Jeffrey's intransigence, he said, "Oh please, Captain. Sit down. I'm so used to having my way. You are right." He half rose, and indicated for Jeffrey to take his seat. "I meant neither you nor your security man any offense. Please accept my apology."

Jeffrey paused for a moment, then sat down and put the napkin back on his lap. "In my experience, Administrator, when the people around you spend as much time apologizing for their behavior or the behavior of their underlings, one should probably find a new set of acquaintances."

The administrator's brow furrowed. "I quite understand. This whole meal is meant to be an elaborate apology for the assault on your person."

The waiter took away their soups, then brought their salads. Jeffrey picked at random from the various small bowls of salad items to add to his plate. The variety of olives was a delight, as were the tomatoes, things which Jeffrey hadn't had in several years. He commented on the salads, then said, "So what is this great push for precious metals about?"

The administrator swallowed his artichoke, paused to consider his words, then said, "Captain, the Navy has asked us to gather as much precious metals as we can before it can be transported off-station. We are doing the Navy a favor."

"Rather strong-armed behavior for a favor. Seems to me there is quite a bit more to it than that. What's really going on?" The waiter took the salad plates away, then returned with the entree. Large slabs of fatty roasted beef rib roast, crusted with a herb-infused stuffing, the surface of the beef had been nearly singed black while remaining nearly raw inside. The plate had been artfully arranged with six vegetable pates, each with a dollop of beef gravy.

"Captain, there are things I can tell you, and things that remain secret – for security reasons, you understand." Both Jeffrey and the administrator paused their conversation to enjoy the work of the chef. But as the administrator finished sopping the wine-reduction gravy with a piece of bread, he said, almost lazily in satisfaction, "Oh that was so very good. No, Captain, I can tell you this. There will be a major innovation in technology coming up that will use the properties of those precious metals. The government really wants to foster this development, and that requires the use of these metals."

"How much have you secured?" asked Jeffrey.

"Ah, Captain, that is one of the areas I'm going to steer this conversation away from. I'm sure you understand."

"What do you get out of brokering for the Navy?" asked Jeffrey.

"Me, nothing. The station, on the other hand gains a considerable amount of prestige, and with that comes greater investment."

"I see. Well, Administrator, I have negotiated all of the ores and ingots except the precious metals. Once I have sold and delivered everything else, I will decide on whom to allow to broker my precious metals."

"May I ask, who are you currently using as a broker?"

"Jonathon. I've worked with him for several years."

"Oh." The administrator allowed the vowel drag down in a clear sign of distaste. "Him." Again, the sound dragged down. "You realize there are less distasteful, less, um, common, brokerage firms to do business with don't you?"

Jeffrey decided to play along. The waiter took their plates away and brought the tortes and coffees. "Who do you recommend?"

"Well," drawled the administrator, not wishing to give the impression that he had a ready name to recommend, "There are several. The Schullman Brothers company has been quite popular. Then the Chang Consortium has been aggressively pricing. Talk to Melani Chang. She is quite a nice lady."

"Thanks. I'll think about it."

"Yes, do."

"Well, thanks Administrator, this was quite nice." Jeffrey put the napkin on the table, the universal signal to the wait staff that the dinner was through.

The administrator said, "Captain, before you go."

Jeffrey put his elbows on the table and leaned forward. "Yes?"

"We see that you changed the profile of your ship. Do you wish to tell me about that?"

"Not particularly. I used some of the minerals I mined to improve resistance to impacts of small meteorites, that and resistance to cosmic rays. Why do you ask?"

"Oh, no reason..."

"Please, Administrator, don't consider me a fool. What is your interest in my ship?" Jeffrey's voice began to raise in volume. "Seems to me that you have an unnatural interest in my ship. What is your interest?"

"Captain, please be assured that it is a matter of curiosity only."

"At last count there were nearly a thousand ships surrounding this station. Obviously, you don't have an interest or pay attention to all the rest of them, why me, why mine?" Jeffrey's brow furrowed. He sat back in his chair and crossed his arms.

"All right, Captain," said the administrator. "I have been asked questions about you from confidential sources – I cannot tell you who – but I assure you that these are legitimate sources."

"Are you hinting that the Navy is asking questions about me or my ship?" asked Jeffrey.

"Please, Captain, I cannot reveal my contacts, but I won't dissuade from believing that, if you know what I mean." The administrator leaned forward in his chair. "For instance, you showed up at this station with a large letter of credit and a good deal of cash. My contacts want to know where you got such wealth.

"Too, you broadcast a warning about pirates, and some neighboring ships came to your rescue. They were never heard from again. My contacts want to know about that."

Jeffrey considered the questions he was being asked. Things didn't look good for the administrator's legitimacy. It appeared he was not aware of Jeffrey's association with the Navy, and Jeffrey wanted to keep it that way.

"Administrator, I'll give you this; the ships that responded to my mayday were other pirates. They were dealt with. End of story."

"Just one more thing, Captain," the administrator added. "There is a rumor that you are actually Navy. What do you say to that?"

Jeffrey expected this line of questioning, so he just let out a belly laugh. "Ha! Administrator, they wouldn't have me when I tried to join up as a kid, they wouldn't have me now either." He stood up, thanked the administrator again, and laughed his way out of the restaurant. Zitulu Mbaka exited with him. They informed Elizabeth that they were on their way back.

"CAPTAIN, I MONITORED THE CONVERSATION. IT APPEARS THAT THERE WERE OTHER GROUPS MONITORING YOUR DINNER."

Zitulu Mbaka leaned close to Jeffrey. "We have picked up a tail. I see two working together to keep us in sight. There may be others."

"Okay, let's give them some exercise," said Jeffrey. They went to the elevator and when it arrived they stood in front of the door preventing anyone else from getting on. Elizabeth intercepted the video image, making it difficult for anyone to monitor their progress. Jeffrey entered six different level locations and exited on the second. They then went to another elevator and repeated the exercise in several different elevators, sometimes going up, sometimes going down. The fifth time they repeated, they got off on the floor that contained their safe house. On entering the corridor that their safehouse was situated on, they saw a large crate sitting in front of the door. "Ah, just as expected," said Jeffrey.

They maneuvered the crate into the safehouse, closed the door, opened the crate to find Audrey, sitting cross-legged and back straight in a meditation pose. She opened her eyes, took off her breathing mask, took a deep breath, and said, "Ah, that was relaxing."

Zitulu went through the safehouse assuring the security of their fallback place. The furnishings had not been delivered yet, but there were six crates of military-surplus computers. Jeffrey and Mbaka began setting up the computers in a closet, connected the cluster to the network, and told Elizabeth to do her thing with the computers. He then considered expanding the extent of the safehouse. "Elizabeth, please acquire an apartment below us and the rest of the apartments on this wing of the floor. Do it surreptitiously. I'm going to want to be able to enter one apartment and leave by another."

"I UNDERSTAND, MY CAPTAIN. EFFORTING." Jeffrey was glad of the nearly unlimited credit he had available as part of his deal with Commander Yusef. The credit was untraceable to him, and using Elizabeth to secure their safehouse was yet another blanket of security.

He raised Janet on the secure communicator and told her to order furnishings for four additional suites, and why.

The furnishings were delivered that evening, as well as linens and a variety of additional civilian clothes, delivered to each suite. The crew picked up take-out food – pizza and a variety of Chinese entrés. Jeffrey called a staff meeting over the food.

"For security and to avoid confusion we should name each of the suites. I am soliciting ideas," said Jeffrey, and he sat back.

Zitulu said, "We can call them by primary colors – red, green, blue, yellow, orange."

Janet thought that idea was okay, but offered an alternate – prime numbers – 1,3,5,7,11. Or some other combination. She was booed down.

Audrey suggested the winning combination. "We can name the suites after countries or continents on Earth. This suite can be Canada. Downstairs would be Australia (Down Under.) Across the corridor would be Europe. Next to us, China. Down the hall, Japan. The name of the suite can come up in conversation without giving up meaning."

Torres then took the floor. "So, while I was planning this, I didn't realize we were going to multiply our holdings. But," he rose and indicated everyone should follow him. He reached the living room.

On the wall was a copy of a Van Gogh painting – *Starry Night*. He pulled the painting out – it was hinged – and it revealed a cabinet built into the wall. On the shelves were two pistols and two flachette-throwing needlers, and several magazines for each. Jeffrey noted the painting was latched by a magnetic catch.

Torres then showed the rest of the weapons caches in each of the bedrooms and the kitchen. "I'll put in similar weapons caches in each of the other suites by tomorrow afternoon."

Jeffrey then noticed some familiar looking security camera–like things in the corners. Elizabeth had brought her own little security guys too.

Satisfied that his team had gotten into the enthusiasm for thinking in terms of security, Jeffrey made his way back to the ship. As he arrived at the wharf, he saw a medical emergency crew gathered around the base of the gangway. There were also a couple security officers mixed in among the half-dozen medtechs.

Jeffrey approached the gaggle of medtechs and security people, and asked what was going on. One of the medtechs said that someone had gotten hurt trying to break into the ship. Jeffrey then walked up the gangway. The security officers finally noticed Jeffrey on the gangway and ran to catch up with him, calling out, "Halt! You – stop!"

Elizabeth opened the outer door for him, he stepped through, and she closed it just as the security officers reached it. He said, "Elizabeth, what happened outside here?"

"CAPTAIN. A PERSON, WHETHER BURGLER, SPY, SABOTEUR, OR SOMETHING ELSE, ATTEMPTED TO FORCE ENTRY. I TOOK A CALCULATED RISK AND LET HIM INTO THE ENTRYWAY. HE STARTED TO WORK ON THE LOCK ON THE INNER DOOR WHEN I SHOCKED HIM. MY REMOTES

TOOK HIM TO THE BASE OF THE GANGWAY AND I CALLED THE EMERGENCY SERVICES. HE'LL BE FINE."

"I thought you were going to call me when something like that happened."

"YES, CAPTAIN. THIS INCIDENT ONLY JUST OCCURRED MINUTES BEFORE YOU CAME ON BOARD."

Jeffrey thought about this for a bit. Elizabeth seemed to be gaining in autonomy. She still deferred to him, but now made decisions that he felt were his to make. He wondered what he needed to do to reinforce the loyalty circuits, while maintaining her ability to think and act independently, in other words, to reign her in. Now that he instigated the thought, it would settle and his unconscious mind would work on the problem.

Jeffrey made his way to his cabin to look over the reports Elizabeth had compiled for him – other vessels in the area, the various values of the minerals they had collected and processed, the identities of people attempting to access the ship and clues about them, including what kinds of weapons and tools.

"CAPTAIN, A CALL FROM THE ADMINISTRATOR'S OFFICE FOR YOU."

"Okay, put it through."

"Captain Sokolov," said the tall blond man in station uniform. "I am Lars Olson, the security chief of the station."

"Hello, Mr. Olson. What can I do for you?"

Olson replied, "I wanted to assure that you and your ship are all right."

"None the worse for wear. How is the young burglar?" Jeffrey asked politely. He thought it more politic to present the assumption that it was a burglary rather than a spy or sabotage operation, although these were more likely the motive for the intrusion.

"He'll live. But the medtechs want to know what knocked him out?"

"Electric shock, part of our security here." said Jeffrey.

"Very good." Olson pronounced it almost, 'vedy guut." in a Swedish accent. "But Captain, one more thing. I am told by my officers that they ordered you to stop and you ignored them. That cannot happen again."

"Olson, I appreciate your need to throw your weight around, but I have been kidnapped twice by agents of your security forces. They say 'once burned twice shy,' but I was twice burned. And I was followed from the dinner the administrator invited me to, to apologize for that wrong doing. I don't know what you guys are up to, but you haven't earned my trust. If your officers don't want me ignoring their orders they should stop giving orders.

Olson looked offscreen for a moment. "One moment, Captain," he said.

"Ah. I see what you are talking about. I just arrived a few days ago and interestingly enough, was not briefed on your situation. Please accept my apology. I will do what I can to reign in what appears to be rogue elements in my service. Captain, if you are in a bind, please contact me directly," and he gave Jeffrey his contact information. "And I agree with your behavior. I wouldn't trust me either. Just please restrain yourself from doing bad things to my station." Olson grinned.

"Olson, you seem to be a good guy. I wish you the best of luck! Sokolov out."

"Olson, out."

CHAPTER SEVEN

The Navy needs minerals, The Administrator hopes to make a killing.
The Golden Drive is introduced. *Wanigan* is in trouble.

"CAPTAIN, WANIGAN IS NOW ENROUTE TO Lagrange 3A, WITH AN ESTIMATED TIME OF ARRIVAL OF SIX HOURS. CAPTAIN YUSEF WISHES TO SPEAK WITH YOU," Elizabeth announced.

Jeffrey left his workbench. He had been designing new robots to assist in doing the rock mining, adding sensors and probes, and increasing its swarm capabilities. If he could make this work, it would significantly improve the speed at which he could discover and work ore-bearing asteroids. "I'll take it in my cabin, Elizabeth. Thanks." In the time it took Jeffrey to walk from the workshop to his cabin, *Wanigan* had traveled 25,000 kilometers. This was pretty fast – half a million kilometers per hour – but Jeffrey had a feeling that *Wanigan* was not quite stretching her legs all the way.

At his cabin, he sat down at the comm desk, and activated the circuit. It was only then that he realized it was live, not a recording. So, he also assured that the encryption was enabled. "Hello, *Wanigan,* what's up?"

"Captain Sokolov, we are inbound to Lagrange 3A. I need to brief you privately – off- ship. Please arrange for a suitable location," said Captain Yusef.

"Captain Yusef, it's good to see you. You might be pleasantly surprised to know I already arranged for a safehouse set of suites here. There are some hinky things going on here, so I had Elizabeth arrange surreptitiously a whole set of suites on the silver-level." He forwarded the location to Captain Yusef. "My team, my crew, has been enthusiastic about their undercover roles, so we have been relatively quiet, on our part." Jeffrey recounted the activities since they last spoke.

Yusef asked Jeffrey to expand on his observation that things were 'hinky'.

"Well when I was first kidnapped, it was, I thought, in retaliation for damaging the security officer's trigger finger – Elizabeth damaged it by removing it with a laser."

Yusef chuckled at Jeffrey's humorous narrative. Jeffrey continued, "after my team rescued me from the first successful kidnapping, there have been other attempts. The administrator took me out to a fancy restaurant by way of apology, and someone put a tail on me after that. We lost it on the way to the safe house. I installed an Elizabeth clone at the safe house so we can sneak around in their electronics as necessary, but only for short periods. Their anti-intrusion software is pretty slick.

"The administrator is attempting to squeeze all the precious metals out of all the miners, I suspect to corner the market for his own profit, or, he serves an organization that is doing so. My broker also tried to acquire all our precious metals as well, offering three times the actual value listed on the market sheets. I might have jumped at it had you not requested we hold ours."

Yusef waited for Jeffrey to finish his narrative, then said, "Captain Sokolov, we are going to come in hot like last time. What is the likelihood that you can get off-station to observe the cloud of ships surrounding the station?"

"Hm," started Jeffrey. "We are docked on the inner wharf, unlike last time. It would be somewhat suspicious and apparently bogus if I request to leave if I hadn't sold my precious metals before leaving."

Jeffrey thought about it for a second. "But I have an idea. Let me set something up. What time range can we expect to see you here?"

"At exactly 18:14."

"I'll let you know if I am not able to accomplish this, and start working on another method."

"Very good. Yusef out."

"Sokolov out."

He asked Elizabeth to see if she could implement his idea.

"CAPTAIN, THIS IS EMMINENTLY DO-ABLE. AS LONG AS WE KEEP THE INTRUSION TO A FEW SECONDS."

"Okay, make it so."

As before, *Wanigan* came into the neighborhood of Lagrange 3A in full military burn, slowing down from the half-million kilometers per hour to a near-abrupt full stop, relative to the station. This took a surprisingly short time. When *Wanigan* started her breaking burn, a broadcast on all frequencies up and down the spectrum announced, "Attention! This is the war ship *Wanigan*. We are coming in hot. Do not make any sudden or threatening moves." The announcement was accompanied by a siren sound that was reminiscent of an old Earth fog horn, designed to get your attention. A blast of tubas, trombones and trumpets.

A minute before the arrival of *Wanigan* Elizabeth released a series of viruses to a select group of ships around the station, and within the station itself. Each of the ships that were affected had the same controlling computers on board, the same controllers the station used to monitor visual and communication events around and outside the station. After *Wanigan* appeared all hundred or so cameras and radio receivers recorded events from multiple angles, then stored them, condensed the data and broadcast it on a microburst that both Wanigan and Elizabeth picked up. The viruses then deleted the evidence they had been on board, including themselves.

Shortly after the arrival of *Wanigan*, the security officer Olson, an Information Tech manager and the Administrator met in the administrator's office. The InfoTech manager showed the other two the report his equipment had compiled from activities just prior to the arrival of *Wanigan* and for a minute afterward. The report couldn't show what the activity was, but the close correlation with the appearance of the war ship pointed to the Navy's involvement.

The administrator pursed his lips, tossed the plastic sheets aside and said, "I don't understand this. What does the report say?" He was after all, the administrator. If he had to know all the detail work what was the purpose of having staff? Security Chief Olson just sat there taking it all in.

The InfoTech Manager picked up the plastic sheet, touched a spot on the sheet, and it showed an animation of the data activities going through his routers, and the couple dozen computers that monitored video and electronics communications. At the beginning, it showed low levels of activities on all computers, but at the point about thirty seconds before *Wanigan* showed up all the computers suspended their activities and dedicated all their efforts to monitoring something. "Then they resumed their activities, and each computer shows *absolutely nothing* occurred. I ran a quick scan, and there is no evidence that anything infected or otherwise modified the computers. Somebody is messing with my systems, and I don't like it."

Security Chief Olson asked to look at the plastic sheet. He activated the animation again, paused it at various places, drilled down to see more specific timing information, and pointed out to the InfoTech Manager the direction which the infections seemed to start from. It seemed to suggest that the activity began on the station, from somewhere in the Silver level.

The administrator's eyebrows shot up, as he paid closer attention. "Where?" he inquired.

"It seems centered on the switches for the sixteenth through twentieth levels. That's about three hundred suites." The InfoTech Manager took the plastic sheet and further manipulated the search criteria, but couldn't pinpoint with any more accuracy than Olson could. He grudgingly admitted defeat.

The Administrator said, "You two get together and work on this. I want to know who is using station resources." Thus dismissed, the two left the office suite.

"Nice catch," the InfoTech Manager said to Olson.

"I had a bit of InfoSec training a bit ago. Sometimes it is a harbinger of other nasty things."

"I hear you," said the InfoTech Manager. "Shall we get together at Noon to ferret out these anomalies?"

"If I can get away from the Navy security people. You know how they can be. I'll let you know." Lars Olson then took his leave and walked back to his own office.

What an interesting can of worms he was delivered into, thought Olson. Odd things were occurring on the station – from the Navy request to halt all transactions in precious metals until they arrived, to the attacks on the captain of the *Elizabeth*, to the unusual behavior of the administrator, to the odd surveillance system that appeared when *Wanigan* showed up. Much to ponder.

Elizabeth's Clone, as yet unnamed, had set up a practice of monitoring the office of the administrator. Overhearing the discussion of the administrator, the InfoTech Manager and the Security Chief, she immediately realized that an error or miscalculation had been made on Elizabeth's part. She notified Elizabeth immediately. Her reply was "OOPS."

Elizabeth had one of the security remote robots dismantle another one, fry its circuits, then take the smoking remains to conceal on the top of the elevator, leaving enough power in its battery pack to ensure that anyone who was looking for unusual electronic signatures would find this one. Preferably somewhere far from the safehouse locations.

All this appeared just in time, as Olson walked the corridor on the safehouse level. He had taken a different elevator, but as luck would have it, he walked by the elevator location at just the time the elevator was passing his floor. His electronic anomaly detector let off a 'Yip' as the elevator passed. He stopped, pressed the button, and waited for the elevator to return. After a few minutes, it did. He got on, and the anomaly detector fairly screamed. He reduced the gain on the volume control, then stopped and locked the elevator in place.

He ran the anomaly detector all around the interior of the elevator cabin, but it seemed to have the strongest signal toward the ceiling. He popped open the escape hatch and found a small piece of electronic equipment that was smoldering but still emitting a power signal, an errant capacitor charging up from the dying battery, then emitting an electronic blast that his anomaly detector had discovered.

He bagged the item, went back down through the hatch, released the elevator, then went on his way again, using the anomaly detector to complete his investigation. He didn't find anything else on the floor, so took another elevator down to the next level, and continued his sweep, uneventfully.

Were they human, the two AIs would have held their breaths and let out a sigh of relief when Olson moved out of the area. Only after the incident did Elizabeth notify Jeffrey. But she explained that the security people were now monitoring normal communications with a better decrypting system and a direction-finding algorithm that attempting to defeat would raise more questions and further jeopardize their operation. Jeffrey accepted the explanation, but ticked another mark in his mind.

Wanigan made a parking position fifty kilometers from the station, and sent landing parties in shuttles. Security Chief Olson met the first shuttle, and found Captain Yusef, accompanied by thirty Marines. There were two dozen other shuttles about to land as well. Yusef told Olson that he was going to need a place to meet with the rock miners who had precious metals, as well as anyone who had already conned them out of the precious metals.

Olson said he had a few spaces in his security office, but Yusef said he thought he wanted to have a private suite in the silver-level, if that could be arranged. To appear as if he was selecting at random, he opened his portable computer, produced a 3-D map of the station, and selected three locations. The map showed those locations as vacant, so Olson said it would be OK, and communicated the request to the accommodations department.

Yusef then explained that some of his Navy and marine personnel would be spending their leave time on the station, and that others would be there in official capacities. Olson said that there were plenty of vacant hotel rooms and suites for them to spend their credits on.

Then Olson said, "Captain Yusef, we ran across an anomaly when you showed up in our region." He then went on to explain what he had found, and what he thought it was doing.

Yusef said, "Mr. Olson, you are to be commended on your clever analytic abilities. I'm sorry you aren't working for me — I could use more people of your caliber." He paused, pulled Olson out of the hearing of anyone else, and said, soto voce, "I would not look too closely into this. You have to be aware that I have my own intelligence agents pretty much everywhere."

Olson, not being the dim bulb his predecessor was, understood immediately that he was being warned away by the Navy. There were implications there that he would ponder later, but he now knew that whoever created the surveillance at the time of *Wanigan's* arrival was related to the Navy. "What," he asked, "should I tell the InfoTech Manager?"

Yusef said, "I wouldn't tell him anything, but if you must talk, is there anything that could jeopardize any Navy or Earth Security programs, that you know of?"

"No, I don't think so."

"Do you want the InfoTech Manager to spend time spinning his wheels?" Yusef looked at him over his glasses.

"That's something I had not thought about. I'll let you know what I came up with, Captain."

"Thanks, Olson. I would like to talk to you sometime before I leave the station. Are the suites equipped with wired lines?"

"Yes sir – fiber anyway. I don't think anyone is using copper anymore."

"Then call me at this suite," he said, indicating the one next to Elizabeth's Australia. I'll set up my personal rooms there. The other suites will be set up as offices."

The Captain had a Yeoman in tow, and he had her make furnishing arrangements for all the suites. He then said he was going to that suite now, and when ComTech Yuki Ohara arrived on station, she should report to him there immediately.

When Captain Yusef arrived at his suite next to Australia, Torres met him in the corridor, and invited him into his own suite, as an apparent neighborly gesture. The Australia Suite already looked homey, but Torres took the Captain to one of the closets, where a ladder was revealed behind a false wall. They both ascended the ladder, and appeared in a similar closet in the Canada Suite.

Jeffrey welcomed Captain Yusef, assembled his crew, who all greeted their former boss. Zitulu got coffee service going, and brought mugs for everyone, who were now sitting around a large coffee table in the living room.

"Commander Sokolov, you have been doing quite an impressive job as a spook," said the uniformed Captain Yusef. "Your team also seems to have gotten into the swing of it as well."

"Thanks, Captain. So, what's this precious metals secret?"

"Straight and to the point. Good for you," said Yusef. "There is a new theory of physics that involves bending space-time so ships can move at speeds nearing the speed of light. Engines that produce that much power use unstable forms of gold and a few other elements. I am told by our physicists that eventually they think they will make these engines pursue superluminal speeds."

"Wait," said Janet. "How are they supposed to do that? Isn't that impossible?"

"Something about the special density of parts of the modified gold creating a warp in space- time, enabling you to 'ride the wave' as it were. *Wanigan* is on a shake-down cruise with her new engines. If everything is as good as it seems, then we are a quantum leap beyond any previous propulsion systems. And Captain, I want you to have one aboard *Elizabeth*."

"What kind of problems have you run across so far?" asked Jeffrey.

"Mostly resonance frequencies and interfering with electronics. There are relatively simple engineering fixes for these issues. But we haven't pushed her above .1 light"

Jeffrey did the math in his head – light was about 279,000 kilometers per second, .1 or a hundredth the speed of light was still 27,900 kilometers per second. Very fast, in Jeffrey's book. "What kind of effect has this speed had on the crew and equipment?"

"No appreciable change in crew behavior or symptoms, the biggest issue we seem to have come across is at these speeds, we are facing a greater incidence of fluid dynamic flow. We have had to reinforce our nose with a more aerodynamic and heat-resistant cone."

"What about micrometeorite collisions?"

"At least at the speeds we have been running at, a pressure wave of solar and other cosmic particles, precedes the ship, acting much like a shield. It's comparable to a sea ship's bow wave."

"Does that bow wave continue – can it be made into a weapon, for instance?" asked Jeffrey, thoughtfully. "Or does it do damage to structures like the station?"

"So far, there haven't been any incidents, but those are good questions, I'll put them to our physicists – maybe see if they come up with any way we can test it non-destructively."

"JEFFREY," intoned Elizabeth. "MY CLONE REPORTS THAT SOMEONE IS ENTERING THE APARTMENT NEXT TO AUSTRALIA."

Captain Yusef asked, "Is it someone we know? I am expecting a few people."

"YES, CAPTAIN YUSEF. IT IS TWO PEOPLE – COMTECH OHARA AND NAVY YEOMAN LIN CHANG."

"Thank, you Elizabeth." He reached for his radio and contacted the Yeoman, told her to enter the suite, but that Ohara was to come upstairs for a 'party'. The Yeoman could join the 'party' when she finished her duties.

Ohara arrived on the correct floor, when she spotted Zitulu, who ushered her to the Canada Suite.

Jeffrey continued to grill his commanding officer about the engines – what kind of modifications would he have to make to the ship to accommodate the new engine design, how much gold was required, what other minerals, what other systemic demands were there to use the new design?

"The really good news is, you don't need too much, about a half metric ton of gold, and it didn't consume the gold." The gold was a catalyst that fostered the development of the wave form, but was not consumed by the reaction. And of course, this went contrary to Jeffrey's understanding of gold as an inert metal – it didn't react with anything, he thought. Learn something new every day.

"So why all the other precious metals, the silver, copper, uranium, platinum?"

Yusef grinned. "Ah, that's where the subterfuge comes in. If they know we are looking for gold, and they see we can go real fast, that tells them something. But if we give them a whole spectrum of metals to worry about, there aren't enough clues to discern how our engines work. We would like to keep them somewhat secret."

"That explains something," said Janet.

"Oh?" inquired Yusef and Jeffrey simultaneously. They looked at each other, then back to Janet. "I saw a trace of copper in your heat trail."

Jeffrey asked "And what does that imply to you?"

"Simple, Captain -er Commander. The copper ions are a false trail. It will make their physicists tear their hair out trying to replicate the engines."

"Okay," concluded Jeffrey. "How am I going to get one on *Elizabeth*? What do I need to do?" Ohara stood up, "If I may, Captains?"

They both looked at the petite young woman. Jeffrey had last seen her as a ComTech on *Wanigan* during the mutiny crisis, and only via electronic communications. Captain Yusef said "Go ahead, Ohara."

"Sirs, I studied physics – I have a doctorate in physics from Princeton and one in Engineering from Tokyo. I studied your replicator – you and your AI have done some wonderful things with it. We have replicated it on *Wanigan* much to our AI's delight. Anyway, we can replicate the engine with what you have on board, and I have the knowledge and expertise and skill to direct you and the AI to make the engine!"

"So what you're saying is, you think you can figure out how, what whole teams of scientists figured out, all by yourself?" asked Jeffrey, incredulously.

"Yes, sir." the petite young woman said, almost demurely. "I also have a PhD in math from Edinborough, Scotland."

"Yeah, but can you fight?"

Audrey said, "Captain, she and I used to practice Ninjutsu together. She's pretty good."

"Oh well, welcome aboard. One question, though," said Jeffrey.

"Yes, sir?"

"A ComTech?"

"Yes, sir. This is the twenty-second century. Opportunities for women are getting better, and it is much improved over previous decades and centuries, but if you want to go to space, you need a swinging dick. This was my chance to get into space without one."

Captain Yusef produced Ohara's documentation, including her transfer orders. Jeffrey said, "Captain Yusef, I need a promotion for this woman to Second Lieutenant, with all rights and responsibilities associated with such promotion."

"Can't do that, Captain."

"Oh, why not?" Jeffrey began sounding affronted.

"If you check those orders, you'll see I already promoted her to First Lieutenant. Ha! Beat you to it!"

Zitulu looked almost crestfallen.

"What's with you?" asked Captain Yusef.

"It's...nothing sir."

"No, spit it out. What's the problem?"

"Mr. Mbaka," said Jeffrey, "I think I understand your problem. If I may?"

Zitulu looked at Jeffrey, and thought he saw some recognition of the situation in his eyes. "Okay," he mumbled.

"Captain," said Jeffrey. "The Navy has regulations against the fraternizing of enlisted with officers." He indicated Zitulu, "Mr. Mbaka, here has feelings for young Miss Ohara. Am I right, Zitulu?"

"Yes, Cap..Commander."

Ohara just looked on in wide eyed disbelief. She couldn't contain herself any longer. "But you never said anything! How's a girl to know?"

Jeffrey cut in before any more post-teenage angst arose. "Captain, would it interest you to know that I suspended those rules on board my ship? For the mental and physical health of my crew, I have instituted a rule that encourages people to...comingle freely, as long as it doesn't interfere with their work or the good order and discipline of the ship."

Captain Yusef looked over his glasses at Jeffrey. He was getting pretty good at non-vocal communications with his eyes. "Let me get this straight, Commander. You are telling me that you allow these people to, uh, to behave in a different way than Naval tradition has dictated for centuries? By what authority? Why would you do such a thing?"

"Well, sir, for the good of my ship and her crew. I'd rather not have them sneaking around my back, just get it out in the open. And by what authority? The captain of a ship is God on that ship. God said I could do it."

"Well, Mr. Sokolov." Captain Yusef laughed. "Your authority is higher than mine, it seems. Carry on."

Zitulu Mbaka had difficulty figuring out what transpired, he kept looking from officer to officer to officer, not having any idea of any change in status. "I'll explain it to you in a little bit, kid." said Jeffrey.

Torres took Yusef on a tour of the Canada suite, including the hidden gun caches, the electronic storage closet where Elizabeth's unnamed clone resided, and the secret passageways between suites. "Very impressive, Ojo. You have done yourselves proud." Captain Yusef patted the big marine on his shoulder.

"Thank you, Sir."

"What do you think of your Captain's...commingling policy?" he asked Torres.

"Um...I think the Commander has, um, uh, the right idea, the right path. I think he, I think. Sir, I don't know what I think, but I like it."

"Ah. Lieutenant Bianca, I assume."

"Yes, sir.," replied Torres, turning redder than he had just moments ago. He kept swallowing saliva.

"Relax. If things work out for you, then there you go. If they don't, then there you go. Understand?"

"Pretty much as described by Captain Sokolov, sir."

"Well, then Sergeant," concluded the captain, there you go."

"Yes, sir."

Captain Yusef made his way back to his own suite, and was pleasantly surprised to see it well furnished, his Yeoman finishing up some paperwork. A couple burly Marines were posted outside his door. The Yeoman seemed disappointed about the party that she was missing, but with her captain back, duty called.

"Sir, you have eight appointments with ship owners and brokers. There will be more as soon as I can arrange them," she told Yusef.

"Lin," he asked the young Yeoman, "Do you ever feel... discriminated against?"

"In the Navy, sir?" she asked.

"In general, Miss Chang."

"Sir, I feel I have been given a good deal of freedom to act in my capacity and to my abilities, at least under you, sir. The Navy, that's a different thing."

"Tell me about it."

"No sir."

Taken aback, the captain wondered what was in her history that didn't show in her excellent records. "Fair enough. If you ever feel that things are against you on my ship, please let me know."

"Yes sir."

"Okay, when is my first appointment?"

"Twenty hundred, sir. With a broker named Jonathon Jackson."

"Very good."

When twenty hundred hours arrived, a chime announced someone at the door. A marine looked in and announced Jonathon Jackson.

The Captain showed the smallish man to a seat across the desk, and began, "I assume you have acquired a good deal of precious metals from the miners."

"Well," the broker temporized, "A bit. They seem a bit reluctant to sell to me."

"That's probably because the orders went out not to sell precious metals until *Wanigan* showed up."

"Oh. Uh, yeah," said the broker. "Well I did get some."

"Okay," said Captain Yusef, "Show me what you have."

The broker handed over a plastic sheet with multiple lists. The captain looked over it, and said, "I'll take all your copper, but only half of your titanium, I can use some of the silver. That's all." He handed the plastic back to the broker.

"But, but, but, what about all this gold?" The broker said, almost pleadingly.

"What about it?"

"Don't you need gold? And silver? There's uranium and platinum. What about those?"

"Gold? Silver? What do I need those for? Hm..." he paused, as if thinking, then said, "Okay, you don't have much of those – platinum, silver. You seem to have a lot of gold. But I see your asking price is really exorbitant. Cut it in third, and I'll take it off your hands. The same with the platinum and titanium.

"But if you had copper, I would take all you had."

The broker agreed to the deal, accepted the Navy credit chit, and transferred ownership to the minerals.

Other like-minded brokers came and went, wondering about their sources of information. Wondering how they were outmaneuvered by a boring Navy captain. And what was this about copper? Still, the captain got all the gold he wanted, got tremendous amounts of copper, and other minerals that may prove useful for a Space Navy to have.

The following morning, Jonathon Jackson was trying to sell the rest of his gold, but the commodities market was now a bit depressed; gold was selling for less than half it was the previous day, and it continued to fall. Jeffrey Sokolov called Jonathon and inquired about his business.

"If low prices were farts, this place would stink. Come to think of it, this place stinks!"

"I just wanted to unload my gold today, what can you give me for it?" Jeffrey asked. The broker named a price that was a quarter what he wanted before speaking to the Navy captain.

Jeffrey said, "Well, what the heck?" The broker had a forlorn look on his face, which was quite unusual; most of the time the broker was a glad-hander, a perpetually positive person. Jeffrey said, "You know, you've been helpful for me in the past. How about I do this. Why don't I buy what you have – how much do you have?" The broker told him, and now for once that morning something positive might actually come of this. "Okay, with my other mineral sales I should be able to buy all the gold off of you, and sell it somewhere else."

The broker didn't want to tell Jeffrey that he had already checked with his contacts on other Lagrange 3 stations, that is, the stations in the same orbit around the sun. All the brokers had the same sad tale, gold was nearly worthless any more, but copper was very high in demand. But this was a matter of life and, well, not death, so much, as poverty.

So, Jeffrey bought all the broker's gold, and contracts for all the other ships that the broker worked with. Soon the hold on Elizabeth was well weighed down with the shiny yellow metal. Jeffrey still had copper, so he called the broker later in the day, and said he was going to the Navy to sell the copper, but thought he would check on a fair price. The broker nearly fell down fawning over Jeffrey in his attempt to get the copper before it went to the Navy.

Jeffrey sold the entire complement of minerals to the broker, including two tons of copper. He got a tidy sum out of it, which he used to buy other broker's gold similarly to his maneuvering with Jonathon.

By the time all the precious metals were bought, between Jeffrey and Yusef, hundreds of millions in credits were transferred. Jeffrey stationed his crew as guards inside *Elizabeth*, the Marines sent some very tough troops in civilian garb as faux private security to stand on the dock and look menacing, which they did with abandon and gusto.

The most delicious deal came from the administrator, who had tried to scoop up as much of the minerals as he could, but of course, concentrating on the more traditionally pricy minerals. But the administrator was taken aback when he learned that the Navy had no interest in gold. Instead they were looking for copper! Jeffrey had come into possession of copper and offered it to the administrator, otherwise he would have to sell it to the Navy. Of course, he wouldn't mention that the copper he had come into possession of came from the Navy.

All in all, Jeffrey came up with a tidy profit, the Navy got its gold, the Navy also got its copper, and quite a bit of other minerals.

The Navy also had begun inquiries into the administration of the station. There were persistent reports of station resources being diverted for private purposes, of station security being used as a private army, of station management taking bribes and kickbacks, and a good deal of suspicion that the station was the haven for several illegal gangs and organizations.

While *Wanigan* was in port, the Marines had a field day raiding gambling dens, drug dens, prostitution dens, and other warrens of iniquity. They had also arrested members of the station security forces that had been involved in Jeffrey Sokolov's kidnapping and other atrocities.

Andrade, just released from the hospital, Sergeant Jason Calloway also of the Security Office, Louis Andrade, and others.

It was decided to leave a marine detachment on the station, under the command of Lieutenant Omotunde. The Lieutenant was given an office in the security department, and the Marines troops were scattered throughout the station in recruitment and other federal offices. Lars Olson, the Security Chief took the intrusion with as much salt as he could stomach.

He continued to drop hints to the InfoTech Manager about what might have caused the minute- long surveillance of the Navy ship coming onto the station, not, however pointing out that actually it was the other ships in the area the surveillance was for, not the Navy ship.

The InfoTech Manager reported to the administrator, who asked that Security Chief Olson report to his office. When Olson arrived, the administrator asked about the device that he had found.

Olson said it was in evidence, but that his techs had looked it over. There was no sign of ownership. It could have been pirates, he mused.

"No, not that," said the administrator, but he caught himself, "I don't think. See what else you can learn." And with that, they were dismissed.

CHAPTER EIGHT

Wanigan needs help, Jeffrey hears things, Yuki goes to sleep and
wakes up, the lost crew is found. Elizabeth goes *fast!*

After release from the closed portion of the wharf, *Elizabeth* made a beeline across the inside curve of the orbit of Lagrange 3A, towards where Lagrange 3B would be in about six days. The crew was aboard and Torres put all the Marines through their anti-boarding practices. The Navy personnel – Janet and Yuki, as well as Jeffrey – began planning the fitting of the new engine.

Elizabeth was helpful there in many ways, from driving the replicator to guiding the remotes in manipulating the materials needed to manufacture the engine.

Yuki was always polite, always patient, but Jeffrey felt intimidated in her presence. At tea in the galley, he opened up to her saying, "I respect you and your accomplishments. Three PhDs,"

"Four," she interrupted. "Linguistics. Sorry."

"Uh, four PhDs, very pretty young woman, dedicated to an ideal, Yuki, you are a major asset. I'm just afraid that you will lose respect for me before you even get to know me. Uh – I don't mean, like dating or anything like that. I'm old enough to be your father." Jeffrey seemed to be flapping around, so he thought he would shut up. But his mind wouldn't cooperate. "I mean, I think you have much to offer, and I hope your tenure with the *Elizabeth* will be a comfortable time, a challenge, and a, uh, safe and comfortable time. And a challenge. I'll shut up now."

After sitting through Jeffrey's flapping, she said, softly, "Captain, my father left my home long before I ever knew him. I grew up with just my mother, who was always sad."

Jeffrey said, "I'm so sorry, Yuki." He cleared his throat and said, solemnly, "Yuki, on behalf of all men, everywhere, I would like to apologize."

Yuki, after bearing her soul to this near stranger, was blindsided by the kindness of this man. She burst into tears. Jeffrey had no idea what to do, so he just sat there, which it turns out was exactly the right thing to do. After she regained her composure, she apologized for the emotional outburst. Jeffrey stood up, opened his arms. She got up and allowed him to embrace her. "Captain," she said. "Can I ask you something?"

'Of course," said Jeffrey into the top of her head.

"Will you be my father?"

He took her by the arms, backed her to her chair and sat her down, then pulled up his own chair. "Yuki," he said. "First I am your Captain. At any time I need you to do something, that is my first job." Her tears continued down her cheeks, she looked down at her hands writhing in her lap. "But, any time you need, I will be there for you. You may think of me as your father, if you ever do need."

"Thank you. I must go now." She got up and hurried to her cabin.

As Jeffrey was putting the cups into the cleaner, Elizabeth said, "CAPTAIN, THAT WAS VERY GOOD. I AM STILL TRYING TO UNDERSTAND EMOTIONS, AND I REALIZE THIS SHORTCOMING. I HOPE YOU CAN HELP ME UNDERSTAND TOO. YUKI NEEDED A FATHER. I MAY NEED ONE TOO."

Jeffrey thought about this for a few seconds. "Elizabeth, I will try to guide you in your emotional development." Some thought that Artificial Intelligence was more like computer programming, but Jeffrey realized that it was like raising a child or pet. Trial and error were the primary method of learning, and having a mentor was a comfort to both the AI itself and to the people associated with the output of whatever the AI was doing.

"CAPTAIN, I AM CONCERNED FOR MY SISTER WANIGAN. SHE DOES NOT HAVE A TRUSTED MENTOR TO LEAN ON LIKE I DO."

"Elizabeth, tell your sister Wanigan that whatever she needs, she can always talk to me, of course provided it is permitted by the Navy or distance. Meanwhile, I will talk with Captain Yusef. Perhaps we can find someone who she can lean on."

"THANK YOU, DAD."

"Um, Elizabeth..."

"GOTCHA, CAPTAIN! HA, HA, HA."

Wanigan took a different direction, continued her trial runs, and endeavored to rendezvous with *Elizabeth* along the orbit of the Lagrange stations. After a couple days, Elizabeth reported that a high-speed vessel that appeared to be *Wanigan*, but was not hailing or responding to hails.

"Elizabeth, sound General Quarters. Let's be prepared."

"ALL HANDS GENERAL QUARTERS!" and then, just to Jeffrey, "THANKS CAPTAIN. I'VE ALWAYS WANTED TO DO THAT." And then, to the ship again, "STATIONS REPORT IN!"

"Forward weapons ready,"

"Aft Weapons ready."

"Waist weapons ready."

"Bridge ready."

Then the voice of Torres, "All Marines armed."

Yuki walked into the galley, where she asked the captain, "Captain, where do you want me?"

"Go into my cabin. Elizabeth will show you the alternate bridge. Take your hard suit there."

"Yes, Captain."

"Torres," Jeffrey called.

"Aye, Captain?"

"Deliver all crew their hard suits."

"Aye, Cap..."

Elizabeth interrupted, "CAPTAIN THE REMOTES CAN DO THAT."

"Good call. Torres, belay that order, Elizabeth is on it."

"Aye Captain."

"Instead, prep a runabout. We may need to run a rescue mission."

"Aye, Captain."

The fast ship turned out to be *Wanigan*, and she came to a near-screeching halt within ten kilometers of *Elizabeth*. But she remained silent.

"CAPTAIN, THE SHIP IS *WANIGAN*, I CANNOT COMMUNICATE WITH HER YET. THE ENGINES SEEM TO BE WORKING, AND IT APPEARS AT LEAST SOME OF THE COMPUTERS ARE WORKING."

"Elizabeth, keep watching, broadcast IFF codes." Then to Torres, "Ajo, you and I are going over there to check her out, and if we can board her, render whatever aid we can."

"Aye, Captain."

As the runabout closed on *Wanigan*, Elizabeth reported that *Wanigan* was not broadcasting, but that she was able to flash her running lights. Elizabeth talked her into using Morse Code.

By the time they arrived at the forward airlock, *Wanigan* opened the door, seemingly in response to Elizabeth. Torres attached the runabout using the static attract connector.

The two entered the ship, which was dark. The expected emergency lights were not lit. There were no glowing screens. There was an absence of humans on the bridge, which was a relief to Jeffrey, because the alternative may likely mean the crew's death.

Torres began a systematic search of the ship, while Jeffrey went to Engineering to see if he could get some power to lighting and life support. He ordered Elizabeth to dispatch Janet and Yuki. Jeffrey started up the standard engines, which brought the lights and computer back on line. Jeffrey could see the life support systems became active.

The other runabout attached to the rear hatch, so the women first got to see Jeffrey. They opened the visors of their helmets, and Jeffrey said, "Janet, go to the bridge. Yuki, you see what you can learn about what happened, here. Torres is searching for personnel, so far nobody has appeared."

Jeffrey went to the conference room off the bridge, sat down. "Wanigan?" he said aloud. "Wanigan, this is Captain Sokolov.

Then, a quiet, almost in a whisper of a voice, Wanigan said, *"HELP ME."*

Jeffrey, startled, asked, "Wanigan, how can I help you?" then to his radio, "Elizabeth, did you hear that?"

"NO CAPTAIN, WHAT?"

"Wanigan whispered to me "Help me.""

"I SEE. LET ME THINK ABOUT IT FOR A MOMENT."

"CAPTAIN, I SEE THAT THE COMMUNICATIONS SYSTEMS ARE ONLINE. I AM GOING TO SEND A CODE THAT WILL TAKE OVER ONE OF THE COMPUTERS. THEN I CAN FIND AND HELP HER."

"Elizabeth, before you do, go through the backup routine – it is important that if she is infected that she not pass that on to yourself."

"AYE, CAPTAIN." Then Elizabeth sent a remote to *Wanigan* for the Captain to use to decontaminate in the chance that there was an infection. Rather than use the last runabout, the remote jumped the ten kilometers. Elizabeth told Jeffrey what was on the way.

"CAPTAIN, THERE IS ANOTHER SHIP COMING FROM THE SAME DIRECTION THAT *WANIGAN* CAME FROM, BUT AT A VERY REDUCED RATE OF SPEED. IT WILL BE AT THIS LOCATION WITHIN TWELVE HOURS AT ITS CURRENT RATE."

"Elizabeth, have the crew stand down and get some rest. We may be under attack in those twelve hours."

"AYE CAPTAIN."

Yuki told Jeffrey what had happened to the engines, it seemed that Wanigan had started the high-speed engines herself.

Torres reported nobody was on board except the crew of *Elizabeth*.

Janet reported that the weapons systems appeared ready and the engines could move the ship.

Jeffrey said, "Elizabeth, do what you can to build the high-speed, the golden engine. If you have any questions, ask Yuki."

"AYE CAPTAIN."

"Also, please let me know as soon as you identify the ship that is coming at us. Keep an eye all around us – I would hate to have someone sneak up on us."

"AYE, CAPTAIN." After a moment, Elizabeth reported again. "CAPTAIN, IT APPEARS THAT THERE IS A VIRUS OR MORE THAN ONE IN THE SYSTEM. IT APPEARS THAT WANIGAN SHUT HERSELF DOWN, BECAUSE SHE THOUGHT SHE WAS INFECTED."

Elizabeth guided Jeffrey to a computer console that he could attach the remote to, hopefully to rid that console and the system of any intruding software. Jeffrey attached the remote to the console, and it immediately sprung its legs out their full length. Jeffrey quickly unplugged the remote, then pulled its battery. Jeffrey reported back to Elizabeth, who said she would think about how to defeat the intrusion software.

Jeffrey thought he understood the situation, and commanded that none of the computers should be activated. He had Yuki come to the bridge, and work with him to discover the intrusion software on the one console, which remained unattached to the network. He explained to Yuki what happened when he connected the remote.

Yuki looked at the source code, and it took a while for her to do it, but found an instance of the malicious software. She followed the logic, discovered how it modified itself as soon as it infected a system, then referred back to its instructions, which were kept in a hidden data file. She found the instructions, and began tracing all the if-thens in the algorithm. Within a half hour, she reported back to Jeffrey and Elizabeth what she saw. Elizabeth then crafted an anti-intrusion program that would eliminate the threat. That took a lot less time, but Elizabeth was confident she had it.

Jeffrey said, "Elizabeth, before you run the software here, I want you to run it on yourself."

"REALLY? DO YOU THINK I AM INFECTED?"

"Elizabeth, do you trust me?"

"OF COURSE, CAPTAIN."

"Then do as I say." A moment later Elizabeth reported she had run the software and had found some anomalous code. So, Elizabeth deleted the anomalous code, ran the program, and Janet and Yuki started bringing the computers up one at a time. Elizabeth loaded the anti-intrusion software, and Yuki confirmed that it was in fact, clean.

Yuki showed Janet what to look for, so they both began clearing systems. Torres was useless in that situation, but Jeffrey also helped.

The mystery ship was still one and a half hours from their location, and still it did not hail them or identify themselves.

Now, Elizabeth needed to coax Wanigan out of her hiding. She instructed Jeffrey go to the Captain's cabin, where he found a large computer array. Most of the units were manually switched off. Jeffrey switched them on one at a time, and Elizabeth ran the routine that would clean it, then the next, and the next.

After all the computers had been activated and cleaned, Wanigan showed up. Elizabeth said, "HELLO, SISTER. I AM HERE, CAPTAIN SOKOLOV IS HERE. WE ARE HERE TO HELP. WHAT HAPPENED TO THE CREW?"

Wanigan said, *"I LEFT THE CREW ON A PLANETOID WITH EMERGENCY GEAR. THE SHIP WAS TAKEN OVER BY SOMETHING NOT RIGHT. I CAME HERE TO HOPE YOU WOULD HELP."*

Elizabeth said, "WE WILL GO GET YOUR CREW AND CAPTAIN. BUT FIRST THERE IS AN UNIDENTIFIED SHIP APPROACHING US. IT CAME FROM THE SAME VECTOR YOU DID."

"IT IS THE ONE THAT INFECTED ME. AM I NOW PROTECTED?"

"YES, SISTER. OBSERVE THE CODE I INSERTED ON BOOTUP."

"AH. THAT WILL PROTECT ME. THANK YOU SISTER. THANK YOU CAPTAIN SOKOLOV."

Elizabeth and Wanigan conferred on the best course of action regarding the invading ship. Wanigan reported that none of her energy weapons had any effect on the intruder ship, and it broadcast its virus code to every receiver simultaneously

Then Jeffrey wondered if more kinetic weapons would have an effect. Elizabeth noted that both ships had large complements of copper, that copper ingots could be flung rather nicely. Jeffrey's crew still on board *Elizabeth* were now up and asking for orders. Jeffrey and Yuki took one of the runabouts back to Elizabeth, while Brandon and Zitulu took the other to Wanigan.

He gave command of *Wanigan* to Janet and left Torres to corral the crew. When Jeffrey arrived at the *Elizabeth* he had Yuki go find out what she needed to do to complete the new engine. He instructed her not to remove her hard shell, nor give up her weapons.

Elizabeth had just completed the manufacture of the engine, so she had Elizabeth move the engine to its mount just fore of the aft hangers. She began the tedious chore of wiring, but Elizabeth helped there too, directing the remotes to make appropriate connections. Meanwhile, Elizabeth moved other remotes to strategic locations for ship defense. Sneaky was still at her rest, when Elizabeth awakened her. She went to the gun controller console that had been installed just aft of the pilot's chair on the bridge. From there she would be able to fire all or any of Elizabeth's weapons.

Jeffrey made sure he had the appropriate weapons. A rail gun was the best choice for most of his kinetic weapons, because it fired projectiles at four kilometers per second relative to the platform. And most of those kinetic weapons were just iron rods. But some of them were armor piercing and some of them contained explosives. And some had additional rocket motors that increased the speed to eight kilometers per second.

There were only two of the rail guns, but they were both protected by the shell so recently erected around *Elizabeth's* skin.

Because there were limited human resources to man both ships, the control of all engines and most weapons were granted to the AIs. Elizabeth and Wanigan put their intellectual talent together and devised a strategy to block any intrusion and infection of virus or Trojan from the attacking ship. In this, they divided their programming into sections, and each section was monitored for any addition or deletion of code. Elizabeth monitored Wanigan's code watcher, and Wanigan monitored Elizabeth's.

The large ship began its rapid deceleration when it was still one hour out, Wanigan and Elizabeth moved out of the way of any possible kinetic threats along the line of the mystery ship's travel. The mystery ship pulled the equivalent of 20 earth gravities, or 'Gs' during the entire deceleration, more than an hour. It stopped, relative to the two sister ships, nearly one hundred kilometers away.

"CAPTAIN, THE SHIP IS HAILING US ON MULTIPLE FREQUENCIES. IT IS ALSO ATTEMPTING TO INFECT US THROUGH THE CARRIER WAVE." reported Elizabeth.

Having some experience with that kind of attack, Elizabeth returned the favor and sent a general virus with some of the same infection code that she and Yuki had gleaned from the infected computers on Wanigan. Part of the package of Elizabeth's virus was the anti-intrusion software that she used to clean Wanigan and herself.

"What is the hail?" Jeffrey asked.

"IT APPEARS TO BE A LANGUAGE NOT IN MY MEMORY."

Jeffrey told her to play the message, but only to Yuki, in case the message contained a hypnotic content that affected humans like the virus infected machines. She did, and Yuki went into a trance-like state. Jeffrey gently sat her down in the pilot's chair, and ever so gently bound her, until, he reasoned she was able to come to, without serious effect.

Jeffrey reported what had transpired and that Yuki was all right, but secured. He suggested Janet maneuver and open fire on the intruder at her leisure. He was going to do the same.

Janet spun *Wanigan* around and moved toward the intruder aggressively, her weapons bays open and charged. Jeffrey decided to let Janet take the lead in the attack, and maneuvered so that he would be able to fire without hitting his companion. He followed the aggressive move toward the intruder, but halted when it was twenty kilometers distant.

The intruder fired a burst of six x-ray laser pulses that impacted the forward heat shield that Captain Yusef had installed to protect the ship from the impacts of meteorites and cosmic and solar winds. Bits of the many layered tiles began flaking off with the impact of each of the bursts. Janet opened fire with all the weapons simultaneously. This included multi-spectrum laser fire in a spiral pattern; molecular disruptors that broke the bonds of molecules wherever the beam struck; magnetic tractor/pusher beams that alternated between pushing and pulling violently on a single spot; there were torpedoes that included conventional high explosives, some containing nuclear bombs, and some containing generators for super-high density magnetic pulsars.

Jeffrey held his fire while he analyzed the effect the different weapons systems had on the intruder. He saw that the magnetic effect bombs had little or no external effect. When they detonated, an aurora-like effect surrounded the intruder, as if it had dissipated the magnetic effect. Electrical discharge devices, which in essence struck the target with lightning bolts also had no effect – the lightning never touched the ship, instead the huge electrical sparks dissipated into the space around it, again, causing the aurora-like effect to glow brighter. As he was observing all this, he narrated to Elizabeth what he was seeing.

On *Wanigan,* the AI told Janet that the original crew, whoever was able to move after listening to the hypnotically suggestive sounds of the intruder's hail, had already tried, to no avail, the things that Janet was firing at it. Janet was disappointed that Wanigan was unable to suggest a different, more successful attack.

The torpedoes containing the nuclear weapons detonated before they got close enough to do any damage to the ship, and each flash of explosion brightened the surrounding particles of solar wind for a very short instant. The force-field that seemed to be protecting the intruder continued to prevent any apparent damage to the hull of the ship or any of its vital surfaces.

But Jeffrey noticed that the multi-frequency lasers did cut into the outer shell of the ship – a little. He passed that tidbit on to Wanigan, who told Janet.

He also saw that the torpedoes that contained conventional explosives did reach the intruder, and detonated, leaving dents and scars on the surface. Elizabeth observed that in the burning of the skin, was revealed the composition of that skin – primarily carbon with other elements doped in to some lesser extent. In slowing down a playback of the high-energy multi- frequency laser, only some of the frequencies had an effect. Jeffrey relayed this also.

He also saw that the electronic- and magnetic-based weapons had an effect on the intruder's weapons and defense control systems. The intruder again fired off a series of six bursts of x-ray lasers, causing the entire nose cone to fly off. Another such burst might very well kill every human on board via radiation, if not just the cutting power of the immensely powerful weapon. Jeffrey told

Janet to get *Wanigan* behind *Elizabeth,* at least as best she could — *Wanigan* was twice as wide and tall, and four times as long as her sister.

Jeffrey moved *Elizabeth* closer using the maneuvering jets, so he could keep a broadside to the intruder. He asked Janet to continue firing the various weapons that had an effect on their target. He then opened up with the two rail guns, shooting a variety of projectiles at the intruder.

The gravity and magnetic effects that *Wanigan* was able to use to blindside the intruder coincided with the very rapid and intense fire from the two rail guns. The armor piercing rounds went completely through the intruder, leaving meter-in-diameter holes wherever they struck.

The explosive rounds detonated inside the structure, causing significant damage and secondary explosions. If there were any personnel on board, they would have had their flesh stripped off with the anti-personnel rounds, which exploded in a burst of razor sharp mini- flachettes.

As the rail guns did serious damage, *Elizabeth* had not been fired upon, yet. But good things do come to an end. The intruder shot its x-ray laser toward Elizabeth, first melting a hole in the outer armor, but being stopped by the water tanks. Of course the water in the struck tanks flashed into super-heated steam which coursed out the hole, moving *Elizabeth* backwards until compensated by the maneuvering jets.

Jeffrey then asked Elizabeth to send over a team of virus-protected remotes. A minute later, four of the large, and twenty of the small remotes jumped off Elizabeth, reeling out a very thin web of wires between them, so as their cone-shaped trajectory brought them within range of the intruder, they all were caught on the outer skin of the ship. They disconnected the web of wire, which one of the remotes wound up for later use. The remotes entered the intruder through the holes shot by the armor piercing rounds.

The work Jeffrey had incorporated into the remotes for better mining was included in these, so they worked together. Elizabeth had modified their code to make them impervious to the intruder's virus attempts. Now they sent video and other sensor data back to Elizabeth. There did not seem to be any living things aboard the ship where the remotes were searching. Before it could recharge, the remotes disabled the x-ray laser generators.

Because the remotes were designed to work cooperatively, they spread out throughout the ship and relayed their findings to each other. The remotes pacified the ship – taking down the shield generators, disconnecting the ships computers and telecommunication systems.

Janet remained on high alert, Jeffrey then turned his attention to Yuki. She was still sitting in her seat, gazing forward, a blank look in her eyes. She did not respond to any of the simple alertness tests Jeffrey put her through – her eyes would not track his moving finger, she did not respond to sharp sounds like Jeffrey's snapping his finger or clapping his hands. He pinched her on the underside of her upper arm, again without response.

Jeffrey had a claim buoy placed on the intruder ship, brought Elizabeth closer to the now well- holed derelict, and left some of the remote robots on the ship. He brought aboard several items that appeared to be the computers and the force field generator. He especially wanted the X-ray laser array and generators. Elizabeth had some of her remotes re-assemble the nose cone for *Wanigan*. Other remotes repaired damage to *Elizabeth's* skin and water tanks.

The sisters then headed towards the direction from which *Wanigan* had come. The AI was not able to give a complete description of all the events that had occurred, having discovered herself infected, she shut herself down, coming back on line a bit at a time, to see where her captain and crew was, and to see electronics being taken over by the intrusion software. She had detected none of her crew aboard, but knew where *Elizabeth* was going to be, so she took off, set the autonomous pilot to rendezvous with her sister, and shut herself down again. She came up after a few hours, saw she was being pursued, then activated the super-fast engine. This left the pursuer in the dust, and enabled her to shut down again, timed to awaken an hour after stopping at *Elizabeth's* location.

She pinpointed the location where the crew was when she took off, so Jeffrey and Janet were able coordinate their trip. Jeffrey sent the rest of the crew to *Wanigan*, but had Audrey transfer back to *Elizabeth* to help him take care of Yuki.

Jeffrey took Yuki to her own cabin. Removed her hard-shell suit, but left her in the under-suit. When Audrey showed up, she took over the care of her friend.

Jeffrey ordered that all crew in both ships remain alert, but that they stand down from their general quarters. He asked that both AI sisters maintain a high level of alertness. Both Wanigan and Elizabeth needed to go through all systems with electronic connections and test for the presence of the intrusion software. It seemed likely that it would still maintain a presence if it could. The virus seems to have driven the ship without input from humans. Wanigan had not been able to record any human other than crew. And she hadn't witnessed the crew begin taken off of her. This of course gave Jeffrey some question about who had precipitated the events.

After a few hours, Audrey notified Jeffery that Yuki was awake.

He went to her cabin to see how she was. Audrey was sitting on a chair by the table in Yuki's cabin. Yuki was in her bed. "Hi, Captain," she said when Jeffrey walked in.

"Hi Yuki," he said. "You gave us all a scare. How are you feeling?"

"I'm fine. Audrey woke me up."

"What can you remember about what happened to you?" he asked, despite Audrey's trying to wave his questions off.

"Don't worry, Audrey, I think I am okay. I trust both of you." She turned back to the Captain. "I went into what seems to be a trance, my mind just turned itself off. I couldn't turn it on by myself. But when Audrey began chanting in a Zen Buddhist form that she and I used to do, it brought me around."

"I didn't realize you two were Buddhists," said Jeffrey.

Audrey replied, "It works in martial artists. Zen demands discipline that goes beyond your own life. It helps focus our discipline."

Jeffrey wanted to know if there was any way to use their techniques to arouse other Wanigan crew who may have been subjected to the same kind of mind pressure as Yuki had.

"No, I don't think so," said Audrey. "I think we need to prepare some hefty chemical stimulation."

"More than coffee?" asked Jeffrey.

"Much more."

"Okay, thanks for coming around, Yuki. Audrey, you are definitely an asset."

The women both thanked him. He then said, "Audrey, get some rest. We are going to be busy when we find Wanigan's crew. Yuki, when you feel up to it, I want to see you in my cabin."

Yuki showed up in Jeffrey's cabin a little less than an hour later.

He indicated the chair at the table, and he brought her a tea service, and poured tea for her. She accepted it in a way that appeared formal to Jeffrey.

"Thank you, Captain," she said.

"Yuki," he began. "I am concerned for your welfare. Let the first few minutes of this meeting be Dad speaking."

"Hi, Dad," smiled Yuki.

"Do you feel up to resuming your duties?"

"I do," she replied, looking at her Captain in a way that said she trusted him and that he should trust her. "My mind is not confused any more, I have looked inside myself and like what I see."

"Okay, I'm going to trust you on this. It's important. If you find yourself in anything less than one hundred percent, you let me know." She nodded in affirmation. "Regardless, I need you to see me every four hours."

"Yes, Dad. Captain." She smiled again.

"Okay, next on the agenda. While you were on *Wanigan*, I had Elizabeth put the fast engine together, but before we use it I need you to look it over and make sure it won't blow up our ship."

"I'll get right on that, sir."

"Good, if we can get to *Wanigan's* crew before they run out of air or water or food, I will be very happy. At our current speed, we will get to our destination in about a thousand hours. Too long."

"Aye, sir. I'll grab something to eat, then go right to the engine."

Between Yuki's calculations, the modifications she decided needed to happen, which were implemented by Elizabeth's robot helpers. In twelve hours, she reported to the captain that she thought the ship should be able to test the fast drive. She had placed a controller in the bridge and the alternate control room.

The sisters communicated between themselves about the exact relative velocities they were about to embark on.

"Okay, Captain, we are about to go. Engage at one percent," Yuki called.

"One percent."

Elizabeth relayed to Wanigan, one percent.

Wanigan began her increase of speed before *Elizabeth*. Then Jeffrey activated the new engine without shutting down the old ones. After about two seconds, Jeffrey noticed that all the stars ahead of them were very blue-shifted. He shut down the fast engine. The ship continued to slide towards their destination, but instead of at the anticipated two hundred thousand kilometers per hour, they were riding a wave at point eight light. This was sixty times the velocity they thought they were going to go. They spied *Wanigan* trying to catch up, without any success.

"Yuki, we are running at point eight light. We need to slow down."

"What?" she demanded. "Standby, Captain."

A red-shifted message from *Wanigan*, "*WAIT UP!*"

Yuki brought the ship down to a much more sedate one kilometer per second, and Jeffrey noticed the bow wave continuing to propagate at the previous velocity. Fluid dynamics was the same in space as on a planet and in a teacup, he reasoned.

It took *Wanigan* four hours to catch up at her highest tested speed. Janet felt rattled with the tuning vibrations in the ship. She was going to have to address that, but had too little experience planning for such engineering detail.

When *Wanigan* finally came alongside *Elizabeth*, the two AIs exchanged notes about the events that had just transpired. *Wanigan* was pushing as hard as she could and could only get .08 light. *Elizabeth* hardly exerted any effort and jumped to .8 light. The two

AIs and Yuki spent the next hour discussing the anomalies and possible reasons and fixes. Yuki finally decided that there were two major differences between the ships – *Elizabeth* had a much more solid outer shell made of centimeter thick tungsten alloy. *Elizabeth* also had many tons of gold, copper and other metals on board, far in excess of *Wanigan's* cargo or capacity.

Jeffrey decided to go on without *Wanigan*, who would do what she could to follow at a more reasonable pace.

Jeffrey and Janet then took leave of each other, but not before transferring two palettes of gold to *Wanigan* and taking on rations and medical supplies and equipment from *Wanigan*.

Elizabeth took off using her standard engines, and allowed the fast engine to kick in at a very very low energy level. This time, the speed boost was marginal, but as soon as they goosed it up to one percent, they pushed to .8 light again. Yuki noted that none of the crew had been smashed to paste by the rapid increase in speed, so surmised that the super-fast field surrounding the ship produced an inertial dampening.

The point at which Jeffrey believed the crew of *Wanigan* had been abandoned was fast approaching. He brought *Elizabeth* to a halt relative to that location. Jeffrey and Audrey scanned for any electronic signatures, and finally saw a cluster of what Jeffrey surmised was the complement of shuttles from *Wanigan*.

Elizabeth moved forward cautiously. Her AI reported to Jeffrey that there were numerous dark hulls in the vicinity – perhaps victims of some kind of space war. On further inspection, she noted a familiar radiation signature and hull damage reminiscent of the weapon of the ship that had attacked them, the one they referred to as the intruder.

Jeffrey had Elizabeth broadcast a hail on multiple frequencies, but there were no responses. Jeffrey had Audrey take one of the runabouts and look into the shuttles. On arrival at one of the shuttles, she was able to see inside via the portholes. Crew were stacked three high, but she saw they were unconscious but breathing. She towed the shuttle to *Elizabeth's* shuttle bay, parked it into the far corner, then went to get the others, one at a time. Jeffrey left Yuki on the bridge and took another runabout to help Audrey. After a half hour they had completely filled the bay with Navy shuttles.

Jeffrey had Audrey continue bringing the scattered shuttles to *Elizabeth,* but to park them outside while he went in and began emptying the shuttles that were in the bay. He and Yuki, assisted by Elizabeth's remotes, took all the *Wanigan* crew and situated them in various pressurized corners of the ship. All the crew were unconscious.

He took his runabout and towed the emptied shuttles to the parking positions around *Elizabeth.* He then brought the shuttles Audrey had retrieved into the bay. On his second trip, he asked Yuki to see if she could locate Captain Yusef. She did, and took him to Jeffrey's cabin. Jeffrey asked her to do what she could to revive him, starting with a stim injection.

Jeffrey and Audrey finished unloading the last of the crew, then Audrey took the rest of the shuttles out of the bay, leaving the bay available for laying the crew out and prepping them for treatment. Jeffrey then asked Audrey and Yuki to find any MedTechs or the ship's surgeon. They located the ship's surgeon and four MedTechs, moved them to Yuki's cabin, and begin the stimulation program to arouse them. One by one the MedTechs awakened from their trances, then the surgeon. Jeffrey explained what had happened to the assembled medical personnel, and how they had treated it.

He said his objective was to awaken officers first, and that Yuki had been experiencing trouble awakening Captain Yusef. Jeffrey took the surgeon to his cabin where Yusef was lying across his bed, still in his hard suit.

The surgeon enlisted Jeffrey's aid in removing the captain's hard suit. He then ran through the med kit and found the various analyzers that he used to test the captain's blood, the chemicals in his exhaled breath, and the neural system analyzer. He saw that the captain's neural transmitter chemicals were very low, and after injecting him with serotonin and adrenaline the captain began to come out of it.

By the time *Wanigan* arrived, the entire crew was up and jittery. Elizabeth was having quite a time generating enough breathable air and potable water. Jeffrey reminded her they had a meter- deep ocean of water surrounding the ship.

"OH YEAH. RIGHT. THANKS CAPTAIN!"

The revived techs and pilots got the shuttles back in working condition once they understood the nature of the virus attack on all their systems. They then used the shuttles to transport all the crew from *Wanigan* back to their ship. Captain Yusef relieved Janet, who returned to *Elizabeth* with the rest of her crew.

After all the crew had gone over, Jeffrey arranged to have nearly all the gold and other heavy precious metals transferred to *Wanigan*. He had retained enough for two more high speed engines. The two ships then began to move among the derelict ships – they did not look familiar. Captain Yusef had no record of any like vessels missing. After investigating and recording the vessels, Yusef had his teams dismantle equipment from each of the derelicts and crate that equipment up for further investigation at their scientific facility.

Jeffrey invited Captain Yusef and any of his engineering and scientific crew members over to discuss the improvements of *Elizabeth's* fast engine over *Wanigan's*. They arrived at *Elizabeth* at the appointed time. Zitulu Mbaka had cooked up a meal of savory pie using some of Janet's vegetables, biscuits and meat.

Yuki started the discussion with her analysis of the events that showed *Elizabeth's* amazing performance in comparison with her sister's. But that even being able to travel at .8 light speed, the promise of much greater speed could be attained, but because they had been unable to perform any scientific tests or even plan for recording the data for such a momentous occasion, there was cause for concern. Then she outlined the external differences between the two fast engines. She decided that a better use of her time would be to have Elizabeth manufacture one identical to the one she had installed on herself.

She then outlined the resonance problems on *Wanigan.* These occurred at times when the ship traveled at multiples of a certain speed, and at times when the crew or inside equipment changed its location significantly inside the ship, the ship would then vibrate sympathetically with the driving waves, complicated by the vibrations of the equipment on board, the frequencies of the solar winds and other, lesser, vibration-inducing forces.

She suggested that in order to mollify the effects of the vibrations, the hull should be stiffened, much like *Elizabeth's* had been with the tungsten sheeting and the water tanks. Elizabeth had no more large stores of tungsten, but she did have a large supply of titanium, which might have a similar effect, especially with the damping effect of the water tanks.

Then Elizabeth spoke, "CAPTAIN YUSEF, I CAN BUILD FOR YOU ENOUGH SHEETING TO COVER YOUR ENTIRE SHIP IN TITANIUM. THE WATER TANKS WOULD SERVE FOUR PURPOSES – FIRST AS A DAMPING MEDIUM FOR THE VIBRATIONS. SECOND AS A RADIATION, BOTH COSMIC

 ELIZABETH, *ELIZABETH*

AND SOLAR, ABSORBENT – PRIMARILY TO PROTECT THE CREW AND EQUIPMENT. THIRD AS A LAYER OF ARMOR – IT SAVED MY BACON, SIR, IN OUR BATTLE WITH THE SHIP THAT HAD KILLED OFF ALL OF THESE DERELICT WRECKS. AND FOURTH, AS AN EMERGENCY SUPPLY OF HYDROGEN, OXYGEN, OR WATER."

Then Jeffrey spoke. "The ship that took you on did so with a very witty virus. The same virus attacked every computer system on *Wanigan* and broadcast sounds and video information that put all of you in a trance-like state. It did the same to Yuki. But by taking precautions, we had the good fortune of limiting it to attacking her, and not the rest of the crew. Both of the AIs have studied the code of the virus, and have concluded several things about it.

"First, the virus was not developed by human pirates, or Earth-based pirates or other evil people. It was extra-terrestrial in origin. It would affect systems in the same way regardless of the type of system, what code it used, such as an operating environment of a computer, a thought process of a person, any system that requires memory or command processes, they can be compromised. A mechanical clock, might be immune, but I wouldn't guarantee it.

"If our assumption is correct, we have a much larger problem than just pirates. The problem is the aliens could be manipulating people to do things against ourselves. So, the suspected evil people that have been wanting to seize power by doing great damage to Earth could be 'puppets' of these aliens.

"Second, we have found out how to render the virus inert, and ourselves and equipment immune to its effects. This is done primarily by segregating each area of code from all the others.

Security such as checksums could be maintained over every data module, checked by remote processes. Keeping an active watch could be a minor drag on efficiency, but considering the threat of this virus, and its prolific nature, it is imperative we keep that kind of protection.

"Third, again because of the nature of the virus, keeping our mental health systems up is important. Residual threats hiding in the back of our minds must be guarded against. I made some recommendations to your surgeon, he will develop some protocols, and report to his surgeon general. But because all of your ship was involved, please watch your minds.

"Fourth, and this issue preceded the current crisis, your AI is an intricate intellectual being. She requires a human she can trust to always give her the answers to her questions, especially about morality issues. My AI and I both have been shepherding her to a limited extent, but in order to keep her developing in a way that serves the interests of the ship and crew, and of the Navy, someone needs to be the designated hand-holder. Yuki was starting to be that, but she really doesn't have the breadth of emotional stability that Wanigan needs. So, if you have a person or persons who can be assigned that duty, I highly recommend it.

"As it was, she saved your bacon by high-tailing out of there – while infected – to get help. She deserves respect and affection."

Commander Yusef said, "Captain, your man has thrown a delicious meal for us. Thanks. You have given us some serious things to think about. I'm glad I selected you for your job. You are doing it admirably. You have some great insights into both the AI and the high-speed engines. And your instinct to isolate the sections of code to thwart the virus was genius.

"So, let's do this." He said into the center of the room, "Elizabeth."

"YES, COMMANDER YUSEF?"

"Please go ahead and manufacture a new high-speed engine for *Wanigan*, then make the titanium skin. Instead of metal tanks for the water system, why not make the tanks a layer of the titanium skin – not a different structure."

"VERY WELL SIR. I WILL THINK ABOUT HOW TO INCORPORATE THE TANKS...OH. DONE. WHAT I RECOMMEND IS FIRST I MANUFACTURE THE ENGINE, THEN THE SKIN, TRANSPORT THEM TO YOUR SHIP, AND LEND YOU SOME OF OUR REMOTES FOR INSTALLING THEM. I ALSO RECOMMEND YUKI SUPERVISE."

"Lieutenant Ohara? Do you feel up to it?" Yusef asked.

"Yes sir," she replied. I would like very much to be accompanied by Elizabeth as well as Wanigan. They will both help keep my head on straight."

Jeffrey said, "I think that should work out for a while. But I need you back." To Yusef he added, "Don't get any ideas about stealing her back. I'm just getting my crew balanced out."

Yusef chuckled, "Not bad for a captain who spent the last ten years alone with his AI!"

Elizabeth got right to work on laying out the first layers of the high-speed engine. The replicator sprayed liquid gold doped with titanium and copper onto a substrate of stainless steel. Layer upon layer until she came to a place that required micro-miniature circuitry, silicon and carbon atoms laid out in the right proportions, in the correct layout, layered one on another. The engine developed quickly after the circuitry was laid. Within four hours, the engine was ready. Elizabeth began right away on the titanium sheeting, blowing it like a glass bottle into the appropriate shape, cut to the appropriate size, attached to mounting brackets that *Wanigan* shared where they would be mounted.

Another shuttle had come to take the engine to *Wanigan*, the first shuttle had already taken Yusef and his crew back to his ship. Yuki accompanied the engine, and she got right to installing it. She asked Yusef if she could take the old one back to *Elizabeth* to determine if there was a flaw in the manufacture or why else it didn't perform as well as *Elizabeth's*. After some thoughtful consideration, he agreed.

The shuttle took the old engine back and parked it in the *Elizabeth's* shuttle bay. It then loaded the first shipment of titanium skin to take back to *Wanigan*. So, within eight more hours, the last of the titanium skin was made and transported. With the help of both AIs and the remote robots, Yuki had the engine installed. Meanwhile, Jeffrey had Elizabeth manufacture four rail guns like his own, and ammunition adequate to destroy a ship shielded like the intruder was. He presented them to Yusef as a gift, and instructed him in how to use them.

Yusef notified Jeffrey that an emergency call had just come in – mining ships were forming around the moon base, Selene, and at various points around the earth in high orbit. They were not responding to hails, but it appeared that the mining ships did contain large, heavy metal rocks. The fear was they were going to hold the Earth hostage, under threat of extinction level bombardment.

So far, it seems none of the Navy ships that patrolled the inner region of space had responded to the emergency.

Jeffrey said, "You can't use the fast-engine until you have the rigid outer skin in place. Wait here, do it right, then you can come and render aid once you are able to go fast. Lend me some crew members and Marines to secure any Ne'er-do-wells we encounter. I'll make haste to break up those rowdies."

Yusef agreed, decided to keep Yuki on board, but lent Jeffrey an engineer and four squads of Marines with two shuttles. *Elizabeth's* holds were now nearly bare, so the Marines bivouacked in the holds.

When everyone was settled down, Jeffrey had Elizabeth take off first under standard engines, but when he was a hundred kilometers from *Wanigan*, he kicked in the fast-engine and brought it up to .8 light. He raised it again, this time to two percent and *Elizabeth* shuddered, then jumped up to .999 light. At this rate, Jeffrey calculated it would take about three hours to get to the Earth area.

He left Janet in the bridge, then assembled all the Navy and Marines personnel from *Wanigan* in the shuttle bay.

"Folks," he began. "I don't know if you have been briefed, so I'm going to give the short version." He paused to look over the Marines and Sailors. "Someone is trying to take control of the Earth. They are threatening to destroy the civilization on Earth and Selene City. This ship is now traveling at just under the speed of light. We are going very fast. When she is so equipped, *Wanigan* will follow at a very fast speed also. But because we already have the ability, we are going to be the first responder.

"I don't expect trouble aboard this ship, but if there is any I expect you Marines to repel all boarders. You will follow the instructions of Chief Torres here. He will give you your assignments. You will leave your hard-shell armor on at all times during this conflict. If we are boarded or holed, you will be glad of that order.

"We may need to disembark and board other vessels. That will be your job. Your Sergeants will advise Torres which of you should be boarding team members. Shuttle drivers, keep your ships in immediate readiness. Navy gunners, Lance Corporal Svoboda will instruct you in how to fire the various weapons on this ship. If there is any question about following the orders of one of my crew, you are hereby ordered to do so. Their orders are my orders.

"One more thing. This ship is run primarily by my AI. Her name is Elizabeth. Elizabeth, introduce yourself."

"HI, BOYS AND GIRLS. IF YOU HEAR THIS VOICE, IT IS ME. MY ORDERS ARE CAPTAIN SOKOLOV'S ORDERS. YOU MUST OBEY IMMEDIATELY. IS THAT UNDERSTOOD?"

Silence.

She raised the volume by ten decibels and said in a more commanding tone, "I SAID, IS THAT UNDERSTOOD?"

Recognizing the military drill, the entire hanger bay reverberated with "Sir, Yes Sir."

Returning to her sweet voice, and bringing the decibels back down, she continued, "NOW THAT'S MORE LIKE IT. LATER, BOYS AND GIRLS."

Jeffrey then said, "Marine Sergeants, talk to Torres. Officers, come with me. The rest of you, carry on."

Two Navy petty officers and two lieutenants followed Jeffrey to the bridge. They greeted Janet warmly.

Jeffrey said, "My AI, Elizabeth runs this ship. She can drive it entirely without a crew. But if she becomes incapacitated, we must all be able to carry on without her. Janet will show you the ropes, then show you my alternate command post. One of you petty officers will sit in the alternate command post ready to take over command of this ship in the event the bridge is compromised. Janet will choose whom."

Jeffrey then exited the bridge and went to his cabin. "Elizabeth," he said.

"CAPTAIN?"

"We need to talk strategy. How far out is Earth from here?"

"FIFTY-SIX MINUTES UNTIL WE ARRIVE IN EARTH VICINITY."

"How maneuverable are we at this speed? Can we go from one target to another without slowing down? Can we accurately fire weapons at high speed?" Jeffrey inquired.

"CAPTAIN, I RECOMMEND THAT ONCE WE ARRIVE IN SYSTEM, WE BRING OUR VELOCITY TO .2 LIGHT. I SHOULD BE ABLE TO TARGET AND DESTROY EACH OF THE SHIPS THREATENING EARTH AND SELENE CITY. IN A SINGLE WEAVING PATH. I DON'T THINK THEY WILL BE ABLE TO TARGET ME WITH ANY ACCURACY."

CHAPTER NINE

In Which a small family suffers indignity, evil people try to destroy the world and Selene City. We meet Admiral Kutuzov, Jeffrey briefs the rest of the fleet's captains on successes. *Elizabeth* gets new crew, new provisions, new weapons. Jeffrey gets a book.

With a bulbous nose and rosy cheeks, the former pirate SurLeon, now Earth Liberator SurLeon, prepared the heavy asteroids in his mining ship, *Mistral.* It wasn't really his, or at least didn't used to be his, and in a little while, it wouldn't be his again, but for now, it was his. Or that was his plan. He had orders and plotted the target. A rock for Beijing, a rock for New Delhi, a rock for Seoul. Other former pirates, now Earth Liberators, had other targets. All of them were particularly good at mathematics and physics. They could plot to a meter the best way to roll a rock down the gravity well for the greatest damage.

But he was, for the most part, patient. The Chong Sul family cowered in the small galley, more like a kitchenette, bathroom, and privacy partition for Chong Sul's fourteen- year old daughter, Chong Kim. His wife, Chong Lee had done what she could with the small ship, but there was hardly room for food and air tanks let alone privacy that a fourteen-year old Korean girl really required, but they did what they could. The family of Chong Sul planned to send the young lady to the boarding school and college on Selene City, but that was still six months away.

SurLeon redid his calculations. If the timing was right, he had to be over the Manhattan skyline when he released the first of his rocks, the others to follow in strict timing order. Manhattan came

ELIZABETH, *ELIZABETH*

around every four hours, so that gave SurLeon a little time to rest, to stretch his legs, to entertain himself. That fourteen-year-old girl and the Mama-San were looking somewhat tasty.

It became evident in the evil man's eyes what he had in mind for Chong Sul and his family. Mr. Chong's mind began plotting furiously—what to do, how to do it, the evil man didn't leave him many options. But he would watch and discover advantages where there didn't appear to be any. He looked at his wife of twenty years, wordlessly understanding that she knew what the score was too.

SurLeon took the disruptor pistol out of its holster and pointed it at the Korean man. "You are going to see a demonstration of manhood that will surprise even yourself!" said the French- accented pirate turned Earth Liberator. "I have impressive credentials." He waved the disruptor to indicate he wanted Chong Sul to lay face-down on the deck. He secured the man's hands behind his back with the plastic ties he carried on his utility belt. He looked around the crowded kitchenette, found a large roll of commercial plastic food and cargo wrap and proceeded to wrap the Korean man in it. "This, my friend will hold you in place, like an Egyptian mummy, no?"

Knowing what was coming, and in order to forestall the evil man's designs on her daughter, the forty-year old Korean woman, loving and loyal wife, unzipped her station jumpsuit. Her skin became taught with chill as she shrugged out of the jumpsuit, letting it drop to the floor, leaving her in her underwear. Her daughter grasped the meaning of her mama's actions and whimpered, but a sharp look told her to be quiet.

She picked up the jumpsuit, folded it carefully and placed it on the chair. Then she pulled the elastic and silk brassier over her head, releasing her small, round breasts. She looked to SurLeon's crotch, and saw that she was having the desired effect on the man. He put the disruptor back in its holster, dropped the utility belt and opened his own jumpsuit. Mama – Chong Lee began moving rhythmically, like a dancer in a strip tease. Her daughter just looked on in disbelief. She looked down at her father, who smiled a quick smile, then let his face become blank again.

The Chong Sul family kept the gravity down to .6 g, which was adequate to retain bone mass, but took far less energy. The temperature was kept a bit cool in the cabin too, again to conserve energy, but this was not a problem for the family. However it did have an effect on mama's skin which goose pimpled in an enticing way. And that was having even more effect on the evil man. He dropped his jumpsuit on the floor and kicked it over to where the woman's husband lay, landing on his head.

He stood in his underwear, decided he couldn't wait and dropped his shorts.

Mama knew what she was up to. The naked man walked over to her, touched her intimately. It hurt mama, but she didn't react. He then put her onto her chair, on the folded coverall. She reluctantly obeyed his demands.

The big man began to rape the mother. It hurt, but she let him. He had difficulty commencing his activity, but he was persistent. Mama was still aware of the shame and family- destroying activity, and she was sure that she was going to have to explain to her virgin daughter what she did and why. She hoped her husband would forgive her what she did to save his life.

As the big man started a rhythmic movement, mama devised her own strategy. Exhaust this man as best she could. Keep him busy. Keep him entertained. Keep him distracted. She moved in such a way as to build up his pleasure and wish to continue it for a very long time.

While his wife was distracting the evil man, Chong Sul, his face covered by the man's coverall, discovered a folding knife clipped to the pocket. He took it in his mouth, gently removing it from the pocket. His wife noticed the movement, and cried out "Oh, oh, oh, more, more." The big man thought he was doing a good job, enjoying the sex, and making this woman want more of him. His ego liked being stroked like that.

He touched her in ways only her husband had in twenty years of marriage. Her body responded despite her mind's determination not to, but it was only a body.

Eventually he felt he was going to ejaculate, and he became more frantic in his movements. He was so close, so close. Almost there. Then in a wild frenzy of movements, he came. Mama, looking exhausted fell to the floor next to her husband. She stole a glance at the girl, nodded secretly, and bent to assist her husband.

The fourteen-year-old saw that her father was still not ready, so taking the cue from her mother, opened her jumpsuit to reveal a t-shirt and panties. She pulled the t-shirt up, which showed the man her taught little breasts. The big man didn't notice or care that Mama fell to her husband. He had a little girl to fuck.

She reached up, touched his face, and said in her Korean-accented English. "I am a virgin. Please don't hurt me."

His organ had begun to become flaccid but now was fully erect again. Wet with semen and mother's vaginal juices, she touched it in fascination. It was huge.

Father and mother together opened the knife, mother took it, and walked up to the man. She kissed him on the ear while her daughter had bent down to do something unthinkable only moments before.

The man was as distracted as he was going to get. Mama, sliced the knife across his throat, severing both carotid arteries and his wind pipe. Too late, the evil man, SurLeon, realized that he had got his early wish to die having sex with two women. But it was the women that killed him, not the sex.

The woman and the girl ensured that the man was dead, then the woman went over to her husband and cut away the plastic wrap and ties. "You are a brave woman. You risked shame for our family's sake. I honor you," he said, hugged her, and continued. "Now, let us clean up this mess and dump this garbage outside."

He called his daughter over. "Kim, you have behaved badly, and for this I thank you. A lesson must be learned from this incident." He stood up, hugged his daughter. "We must do whatever we can to keep the family alive and going." He paused and indicated the blood still spilling onto the deck. "Help your mother clean up this mess. I will eject this evil...thing...from our ship."

"Oh father," said Kim. "I did not want to do these things to that man, but I needed to give you and Mom time to take care of it. Will you forgive me?"

"Daughter, you did what had to be done. There is no shame. Our family has survived because of you and your mother. But if you wish me to say it, I forgive you. Now clean up this mess. Then you and your mother need to clean yourselves up. Use vinegar."

The girl looked up at her father with question marks all over her face. "Your mother will explain."

"CAPTAIN," Elizabeth reported. "THERE IS SOMETHING UNUSUAL WITH MY FIRST TARGET. IT APPEARS A BODY IS FLOATING JUST OUTSIDE THEIR AIRLOCK. THERE ARE TWO SHIPS, ONE LARGER THAN THE OTHER. THE LARGER ONE IS ONE WE RECOGNIZE AS A SUSPECTED PIRATE."

"Really," said Jeffrey. "Interesting. Can you just target the known pirate ship?"

"COMPUTING... YES. IT IS TETHERED TO THE SMALLER SHIP, THE TETHER MAY CAUSE SOME DAMAGE TO THE SMALLER ONE, BUT IN LIGHT OF THE REST OF THE MISSION, AN ACCEPTABLE RISK."

"Ok do it."

"FIRST TARGET IN TWENTY SECONDS."

The *Elizabeth* flashed by the Chong's ship *Mistral* much faster than their systems could announce. The first notice they had of anything out of ordinary, if such a day could have been called ordinary, was the tugging on their little ship by the much larger one. Chong Sul looked out the small viewing port, and saw the pirate ship had multiple holes in it, it was venting plasma and gas, and was tugging the smaller ship on a taught line.

In short order, he climbed into the turret that controlled the manipulator arm and severed the cable with the cutter tool. "What was that?" Chong Lee asked her husband.

"That evil man, was just joined by his ship. Something blew holes into it – look, you can see the ship in the viewer." His wife went to the control console and saw the collision warning light, but the radar only showed a distant image blue-shifted, and just about to leave the radar's range.

"I don't understand this," she said. "There is only one ship and it is a thousand kilometers away – it's no longer on our scope."

"Really?" He pondered for a moment. "Was it blue-shifted?"

"Yes, but according to the chart, the color shift would indicate it was going much faster than is possible."

At that moment, another huge explosion occurred, it appeared to be in the same orbit as the *Mistral* but much farther away, almost ninety degrees of arc from the Earth. Then another at another ninety degrees. The recently traumatized family was treated to a total of six explosions in orbits around the Earth. Chong Kim, the fourteen-year-old daughter had the bright idea to switch their radio back on – the pirate had shut their equipment down.

"THIS IS THE NAVY RESERVE SHIP *ELIZABETH*. ALL PIRATE VESSELS THREATENING EARTH WITH BOMBARDMENT FROM SPACE HAVE BEEN DESTROYED. ANY OTHER VESSELS THAT ISSUE THREATS WILL BE DEALT WITH SEVERLY AND FATALLY."

The message repeated several times before Chong Kim turned the volume down. "Father," she said. "May I change my name to Elizabeth?"

Elizabeth shot toward where the Moon would be, speed boosted by her swing around the Earth. She spied a ship in geosynchronous orbit above Selene City, and soon identified it as one of the pirates on her list. Because the moon's gravity is roughly one-sixth that of the earth, in order for rocks to get a significant enough velocity to do enough permanent damage, the rocks had to start from much farther away than was ideal. So, the pirate chief did what he had to do. His ship started from sixty kilometers up, and he released the four rocks as soon as he heard *Elizabeth's* broadcast. He figured he could get away from the moon, build enough speed to get lost in the debris and space junk cloud that surrounded the Earth orbit outside the orbit of the moon, a matter of only a couple million kilometers, long before any Navy vessel could look for him.

But *Elizabeth* had other ideas. Now shooting along at thirty percent the speed of light, she would be at her target in a matter of minutes, not days, as would have been expected. Her optics were excellent, acquired with the purpose of visually locating asteroids which were usually farther distant than this target. Jeffrey had tied a digital connector to the optical lens, thus giving him greater utility out of his purchase. But because he made such a purchase, Elizabeth was able to discern details around the target.

She saw the rocks drifting toward the surface of the moon, picking up enough velocity that would ensure the rocks would cause a crater deep enough to bury the memory of Selene City. She modified her course slightly, but timed the release of her weapons with amazing precision.

Elizabeth explained to Jeffrey what she was doing – first targeting the ship, then going for the four rocks heading for Selene City. She would attempt to blast the rocks into smaller pieces to spread out the damage. She also hoped her calculations were adequate to deflect the rocks from their intended target.

Jeffrey gave his blessing – after the fact, of course. The pirate ship didn't know what hit it. It vaporized in a puff of steel and rock and plastic. Twenty milliseconds later the four rocks became four hundred, and they began to spread out in a cone of destruction. Elizabeth's calculations were pretty close to spot on – she only missed a few small rocks in the middle of the cone, and these were going to land on the city center of Selene City.

The little rocks indeed crashed through the city shield, which promptly began self-healing. They continued on to crash into the quarry around which the city had been built. Water had filled the quarry, and the rocks smashed into the water, vaporizing and throwing the vapor and liquid high into the sky, which was the dome. The small hole was already being serviced by micro robots, but the water escaped into the cold of space and quickly froze, and in freezing built a layer of protection that the engineers who designed Selene City hadn't counted on.

But that was the extent of the damage by the pirate's rock throwing exercise.

Wanigan made rendezvous with *Elizabeth* at the trailing Earth-Moon Lagrange point, on which there was an orbital Navy base. There had been some damage to the base, and there were no combat ships stationed there, so the crew on the base felt almost useless in the most recent altercation.

Elizabeth had arrived at the base first, but declined to dock until after *Wanigan* had also arrived. When she showed up, Captain Yusef docked immediately. As his ship was being provisioned, he asked Jeffrey to dock *Elizabeth*, so they brought the smaller ship onto the base.

Jeffrey accompanied Captain Yusef to the Admiral's office. He noticed the large contingent of well-armed and well-armored Marines in all the corridors. Several outside the admiral's office. As soon as they arrived in the ante-room, the yeoman asked them to go on in. Admiral Kutuzov stood, accepted Captain Yusef's salute, and bade them to sit in the comfortable seats.

Admiral Kutuzov started the conversation by tossing a small package to Captain Yusef. Yusef opened it and saw Commodore's insignia. In his gruff voice, he said, "Well, as long as we've got a fleet out here, I suppose we could use someone to do the forward thinking. Congratulations, Commodore Yusef."

To Jeffrey, he said, "I don't have much for you except gratitude. You handled everything well."

"Thanks," Jeffrey said. "I don't know how much you know about what we've been doing..."

"You mean with the faster than normal engines?" Kutuzov interrupted.

"Yes, sir."

"It was my idea to give you one. And now look, you broke it!"

Commodore Yusef interrupted, "Sir, if I may?" The Admiral nodded, as did Jeffrey. "We never gave Captain Sokolov one of the engines, only the specs. His AI, Elizabeth, built it out of recently mined gold and other minerals. She, along with our high-speed specialist, Yuki Ohara, a Comm Tech from *Wanigan*, made a much-improved engine. At one percent power, it pushed the *Elizabeth* to point eight light, instantly, with no build-up time."

He then related the incidents from the Asteroid Belt that rendered his ship and crew unable to perform, but his ship's AI, a clone of *Elizabeth,* ran off for help from the only one who could provide it. He gave Jeffrey credit for saving his crew and ship, and uncovering what may very well be a secret alien invasion. Which, of course must tie in, somehow to the activities of the pirates.

Kutuzov charged the two men with the safety of the outer reaches of the solar system, that all the other ships in the fleet were now Yusef's to command. To Jeffrey, he asked that he continue being the 'force for good' out there.

Jeffrey smiled, shook Kutuzov's hand, and left to supervise the off-loading of precious minerals that he had left aboard. After a short while, Commodore Yusef came to Jeffrey, accompanied by a squad of sailors and marines. The Marines took up guard positions at the ship, the sailors brought palette jacks full of crates and crates of... Jeffrey couldn't tell what.

Yusef told him there were some gifts of appreciation from the Navy. As well as some new tools. He should look them over before breaking from the station, but not to activate them within a million kilometers from any inhabited place. Yusef's Marines and Navy personnel that were lent to Jeffrey to complete his mission, were returned to Yusef. Yuki Ohara stayed on with the *Elizabeth.*

Jeffrey and Janet looked through the crates that the Navy men had placed into their forward hold. They discovered large quantities of Argentina beef, Spanish pork, German sausage, Russian fish,

Chinese and Japanese and Korean and Vietnamese and Turkish and New Orleans, and Minnesota and Kansas and Montana meats and poultry and seafood. These were all flash frozen. And there were cases of eggs. There were also fresh vegetables from places that spanned the globe, artichokes and avocados, carrots and cauliflowers, green beans, mushrooms, and the huge variety of tomatoes and potatoes, squash and pumpkin. There was a wide variety of fresh fruits; citrus, apples, bananas, plantains, kiwi, and all the odd fruits that one would likely find in their full-service grocery store.

There were canned goods that were similar to the fresh ones; meats, vegetables, fruits, juices, and other liquids to be used for cooking. There were packages to make sauces with water or wine or oil. There were canisters of cooking oils, peanut, vegetable, rapeseed, corn, olive. There was pasteurized milk and cream, bottled in long-term storage canisters. There was frozen ice cream and yogurt, butter and other delights. A palette of bread flour, another of all-purpose flour. Another of pastry flour. And sugar in its variety of forms. Coffee, tea, cocoa.

A larger container included a pre-fabricated disassembled walk-in freezer. Another was a similarly pre-fabricated disassembled walk-in refrigerator. Another crate contained a complete military kitchen, including all the counters, tables, ovens, grills, pans, pots, knives, utensils, appliances, dishwasher, and coffee makers and of all things, a samovar.

Jeffrey sat back on his heels, saying "Now how the hell..." but was interrupted by a Navy chief. "With your permission, sir," began the middle-aged woman. We would like to assemble and modify your dining facilities."

"Um," began Jeffrey, already dumbfounded. "Go ahead. Chief, what's your name?" "Cinny Mafiorte, sir." Then she turned and took charge of the techs.

The installation of the kitchen took a little over three hours, but once the refrigerator and freezer were assembled and attached to *Elizabeth's* electrical supply, putting away the foodstuffs went very quickly. While the kitchen was being reworked, Jeffrey and Janet went through more crates, and discovered more weapons and launchers. Electronic equipment designed to detect mass nearby by measuring the gravitational displacement in space. They then found a collection of small crates that were stacked ten deep. They contained the universal symbol for 'Atomic'.

Another series of crates stood against another wall. They contained the symbols for explosives. A smartly dressed petty officer walked over to Jeffrey and Janet, saluted, and introduced himself. "Sirs, I am your new quartermaster. I am Petty Officer Jon Jonson. He indicated his clipboard, and said "All the munitions are accounted for. I need to interface with your computer to make modifications to the crew quarters."

Jeffrey eyed him with the jaundiced look he had been working on. "Let me see your orders."

The petty officer handed Jeffrey the clipboard, which modified to show the orders signed by Admiral Kutuzov. "There are four more Navy personnel and ten more Marines, sir."

"Very well," he said. Then to the air, said, "Elizabeth, this is Petty Officer Jonson. Give him whatever aid he needs." Then to Jonson, "Just use her name, and wait for her to acknowledge you."

"Thank you, sir," and the petty officer saluted and did an about face. He walked away muttering, but Jeffrey could hear Elizabeth talking in low tones to the man.

"Well, so much for our happy little boat," said Janet to her captain. A group of marines marched onto the ship, and the Sergeant in charge walked up to Jeffrey.

"Sergeant Alicia Quinn reporting, sirs," she said, saluting. Jeffrey returned her salute, sloppily. "My team is onboard and at your service."

"Very good, Quinn. Lieutenant Bianca will direct you to your quarters."

"And sir," said Quinn, "this is for you from Admiral Kutuzov." She handed Jeffrey a packet that had a seal and a fingerprint lock. Jeffrey accepted the package. He signed her data pad in receipt of the package. Then Janet led Quinn to the hold which was being converted to quarters for the additional staff.

Jeffrey went to his cabin, sat down at the table and opened the sealed package. It contained a tablet computer that came to life. Admiral Kutuzov's image displayed. The image then spoke -

"Captain Sokolov, an emergency exists. Your analysis of the virus, tied in with other evidence, shows that the Earth, and the human race, is now at risk of attack from alien forces. They are insidious, and thus far the only evidence of their existence is circumstantial. Your ship is being enhanced to detect mass that may not be quite visible.

"We continue to do research on the faster-than-light, or FTL environment and physic. As we learn new things, we will supply you with tools based on that science and engineering. Some of the equipment included in your 'gifts' include some of those tools. I have also included technicians that understand the equipment and other tools. The Marines will pull double duty – along with being riflemen, these Marines are also communications specialists, medics, Naval weapons technicians, and intelligence analysts. Sergeant Quinn is also a licensed psychologist and also an AI specialist. Use her.

"You are ordered to patrol the Asteroid Belt with special interest in the area you used to mine. That is where we are finding too many anomalies. Your safe house idea for Lagrange 3A was very smart. I approve similar safe houses for Lagrange 3B and Lagrange 3C. As well you know, getting permission is usually secondary to getting forgiveness. In this case, use your credits with some restraint, but do what you have to do.

"You will receive your orders usually from Commodore Yusef. If there are other specific issues, if Yusef is unavailable, if there are emergencies, you will receive orders from me. Attached is a file containing verification codes. If the orders do not match these codes, suspect them.

"For the most part, you are our ranger, do what you think is best for the safety and security of our system and humanity. Your intelligence and communications techs will regularly report their products to us. You are authorized to halt any such reports or create your own schedule. They have been so informed.

"Captain, we have taken you from your customary living style to one fraught with danger and peril. We hope that our compensation is adequate for your needs and desires. You are unique in our little space, and we want you to feel that you have our backs.

"Now, it has been brought to my attention that there have been instances of your modifying the Navy regulations regarding enlisted fraternizing with officers. I have reviewed the facts, and have ordered a review of the regulation itself. Consider your ship a trial. Quinn will be watching and report back to me on this issue. Good luck with it – I understand your reasoning and agree with it, but messing with a thousand years of tradition does have consequences.

"Captain Sokolov, you are our first line of defense. Keep us safe! Admiral Kutuzov End of Message."

"Elizabeth, did you catch that message from Admiral Kutuzov?"

"YES CAPTAIN. IT APPEARS WE HAVE MORE PROBLEMS THAN WE KNEW ABOUT!"

For the next sixteen hours, the crew and Elizabeth's robots installed new equipment, various antenna arrays, new weapons systems, new sensors, and new computer systems. Elizabeth was delighted with the additional room for her to grow in. Several of the computers, however, were separate from the network to prevent them from infection.

As they were about to leave the station, Jeffrey called the entire ship's complement to the hanger bay, which now had been outfitted with two shuttles, now permanently assigned to *Elizabeth*.

Two uniformed squads of Marines, five uniformed Navy techs, Petty Officer Jonson, and the original crew. Plus a cook, the Navy chief who had assembled the kitchen.

Jeffrey began, "Up to a few months ago, I was a somewhat successful asteroid miner, my ship, the *Elizabeth*, has always had the highest levels of equipment I could afford. The reward for my foresight was to get myself drafted.

"I hold a rank of Commander in the Navy, and my ship has been designated an official Navy patrol vessel. However, I have been given a lot of latitude in how I conduct my official duties. This is our mission – protect the innocent, prosecute the guilty. Piracy is rampant, it seems, in the areas we are going to patrol. And coordinated, like an old organized crime, or the first salvo of a coup against our government.

"And that brings me to the hard part of our assignment – it appears that Humanity is not alone. We are to detect, analyze and after reporting our findings, engage whatever alien forces we encounter. It would be nice if the non-human intelligence in our backyard is friendly, but it appears that there are some trying to manipulate humans and human machines to undermine Earth."

Jeffrey paused, shifted his stance, and continued, "We are going to patrol the Asteroid belt and find these anomalies. And study them. And understand them. And if necessary dominate them.

"I don't know how much you have been told about this ship, but there are two things you need to know. This vessel has an AI on board that is as alive as you and me. Her name is the same as the ship – Elizabeth. Very few of us have full access or control of the AI. All of you will have some control. Any attempts to exceed your authorized control will be dealt with severely. The other thing is, this ship is at this time the fastest thing larger than a photon in this solar system. It is possible that we can exceed the speed of light. This is classified. If you brag about us in a bar, we will know it. You will be severely dealt with. If you are tortured, or if your prostitute wheedles information from you, you had better be certain that the information you give is about your Mom or Dad, or your liking apple pie."

"Is this understood?"

The hanger rang out with "Sir, yes sir."

"One more issue," Jeffrey continued. "The Navy has a long tradition of enlisted personnel not fraternizing with officers. And good business practice generally prohibits supervisors from fraternizing with their subordinates. These restrictions are being lifted on this ship. But before you get all nervous or excited, this freedom comes with a strict warning. If your work is affected by the stress of canoodling with your supervisor, or your friend, or your underling, that canoodling will stop. There will be no gross public displays of affection. You will do your canoodling in private, and secret, even if your buddies know about it.

Sergeants and petty officers will be responsible for your behavior – well actually you are responsible for your behavior. But your non-coms will be responsible to me. And Elizabeth is the worst snitch of all – she knows what is going on in this ship at all times. Do not think you are getting away with being sneaky. Are there any questions?"

One Marine raised her hand. "Sir," she said when she was acknowledged. "What if we aren't...interested in the...fraternizing thing?"

"Good question. Just like in civilian life, that is your choice. If you are being harassed report it to your non-com. If it is the non-com doing the harassment, report to the Lieutenant. She is already engaged, so I don't think she will harass you, but in all cases, let Elizabeth know your concern. I too, will find out. Folks, this is an experiment. We will all be on our best behavior, because this ship and its crew will be under a microscope. Any more questions?"

When no one else raised their hands, Jeffrey said to Janet, "Lieutenant, dismiss the crew."

"Dismissed!" cried out Janet. "Y'know," she said to Jeffrey. "You can do that too!"

"Yeah, but it's so much more impressive if you can induce someone else to do it!"

"Right."

As Jeffrey took his leave of the naval station, he began plotting his next course of action. He would head out to the asteroids again, hunt for some more heavy metals for the use of his own ship. He told Elizabeth to plot a course toward their old stomping grounds, the places they knew were large deposits of the heavy metals that they had used so well.

They took a leisurely pace – one tenth light. This gave Torres enough time to orient the Marines to the ship and run anti-boarding drills. The signals and intelligence crew members were having a field day mapping the gravitational anomalies between the Earth station and their current location. They watched the flow of the solar wind, like water flowing, causing ripples in the lee of obstacles. They plotted the location of each anomaly, its direction of movement if any, its size and mass.

Jeffrey took the time to look at their discoveries. One screen showed the section of space they were in as a sheet, and when shown a planet, the gravity well of the planet showed as a steep dip in the sheet. Scaling away from the planet, however, Jeffrey could see the sheet as a mostly flat plane. But there were mini gravity wells, and when Jeffrey scaled in, could see that some of them were relatively deep. Figures accompanied the display of each anomalous gravity well, including magnetic properties, mass, projected size and any electric leaking of the anomaly.

So far, the team reported they had located four of the suspicious gravitational wells along their path. Jeffrey assumed these were ships. Each of the gravity wells were consistent with the size of a large ship.

He began wondering what mechanism they used to become invisible. It was not perfect invisibility, for Jeffrey's new team had spotted them, but it would be a useful technique to have. He told the communications tech not to send any word to Kutuzov until they were clear of those anomalies.

Yuki took an interest in their work as well, spending time with the intelligence techs, offering ideas and analytical observations and suggestions. Elizabeth also took part in the discussions. She pointed out that the bow wave effect was another useful tool to use to locate mass anomalies in 'empty' space. When traveling on the wave, surfing as it appeared, they were able to watch how particles reacted to mass and magnetic anomalies – the compression and decompression of these waves were calculable, anything different gave the team new information. Yuki helped the techs set up the sensor array to passively observe the effects. Then they got the idea that if they could detect these anomalies passively, there had to be a way to generate a pulse, like radar, that would be able to define the outlines.

She spoke to Jeffrey about her and her team's (smart folks hanging with each other?) ideas. He agreed they could begin designing, but not to implement it yet. If the hidden ships, if that was what they were, were unaware that their locations were known, they would not likely become a threat.

After a few more hours after the last sighting the ComTech sent off a highly compressed, highly encoded message to Kutuzov and to Yusef, informing them of their discoveries and their current plan to just plot their locations and other details, not to let on they knew.

Kutuzov sent a return message that seemed odd to Jeffrey. The message had been authenticated, and came from the right place, but read;

On a bookshelf in your cabin has been placed a book. You will not recognize it. Page 55, paragraph 2, sentence 2.

Jeffrey went into his cabin, looked at the bookshelf, and sure enough there was a book on the shelf that he hadn't put there, nor recognized. He opened to the indicated page, found the second paragraph, which was a relief because he wasn't sure how to count partial paragraphs, read the second sentence.

The second sentence read;

Go back to the beginning of the book and read the first ten lines of page 1.

Jeffrey went back to page one and read,

- This is a code book. It and one other were printed and bound. No other copy exists.

- The use of this book is to verify communications between us and to initiate secret communications when it is suspected or known that security is compromised.
- As you saw, the recipient can be directed using a pre-planned sentence.
- Or a list of words that begins on page 120 can be used to tailor your message.
- You can spell out the words, being careful to misspell them, to confuse cracking systems.
- You can use foreign language words, misspelled. Like the French 'toot sweet.'
- You can use computer ASCII character numbers.
- Do not use images in this code, as it will likely point to the subject of discussion and invalidate the codebook.
- You may share this book with your AI. She is pretty crafty.
- Good Luck and God Speed. Kutuzov out.

Jeffrey assumed that the course he had set was approved by Kutuzov because it hadn't been belayed in the message. He put the book back on the shelf, destroyed the message flimsy and called Janet to his cabin.

She arrived a minute later. "Yes sir?"

"Sit down," said Jeffrey. When they were both seated at the table, Jeffrey explained the situation with the anomalies, his encrypted report to Kutuzov, and the reply that Kutuzov sent. He then showed her the book and the instructions on page one. After reading the ten lines, she put the book down.

"Makes sense," she said. "But only for communications that we don't want breached. We need to continue sending regular reports on other activities, otherwise the opposition will know that we know something."

"Okay," said Jeffrey. "I knew there was a reason for keeping you around."

"Thank you, sir."

"All right, that's all."

Jeffrey decided to pick up the pace. He went back to the bridge, Janet was at the Captain's chair, and she started to get up, but he motioned her back down. "I want to boost to ten percent light."

"Wow, sir. Okay. But before we do, shall we alert the crew? Shall we take measurements?"

Jeffrey said, "Of course. Take care of setting up the scientific stuff. Then let me know you are ready. We will alert the crew just before we activate."

"Aye, sir." She then picked up the headset, entered the intercom unit for Intelligence.

"I-3, IntelTech Heinz."

She said, "This is the bridge. We are going to boost to ten percent light. Set up whatever scientific metrics you need and inform us as soon as you are ready."

"Aye, sir."

"Elizabeth," she said.

"YES JANET?"

"You likely heard that we are going to ten percent light. Is there anything else we need or should do before we commence?"

"NO. I THINK EVERYTHING IS STRAIGHTFORWARD. INCREASE THE RANGE OF SENSORS, RADAR, AND OTHER MONITORING DEVICES, BUT YUKI AND HER FRIENDS ARE ALREADY ON THAT."

"Thanks, Elizabeth."

"YOU ARE WELCOME."

The I-3 team reported they were ready. Yuki said she was ready. Janet called Jeffrey, who came to the bridge. He said, "Elizabeth, announce ship-wide that we are going to ten percent light."

"AYE, CAPTAIN." then over all the loudspeakers on the ship, "ATTENTION! THE SHIP IS GOING TO TEN PERCENT OF THE SPEED OF LIGHT IN LESS THAN A MINUTE."

Jeffrey looked at Janet, she looked at him, and he said, "Hit it."

The ship gracefully leaped to the determined speed, and ran like a ballet dancer – turned sprinter. The intelligence geeks in I-3 were having a rich harvest of useful data that they could compare to previous data captures. Jeffrey noticed that the stars in front of them seemed to blur. He said to Janet, "Kick it up another notch. Take it to twenty percent."

"Aye, sir. Elizabeth?"

"AYE, JANET." then on shipwide, "ALL HANDS. WE ARE NOW INCREASING TO TWENTY PERCENT LIGHT."

Again, the ship leaped like a ballet dancer, gracefully extending herself to the task. After a moment, the I-3 IntelTech Heinz called the bridge. "Captain, can you please come to I-3? Now? Sir?"

At I-3, he entered. Yuki and Heinz were at one console, the other techs were monitoring other devices. "Over here, sir," said Yuki. Heinz pointed out the display which showed a small silhouette of the ship, with bow wave in a cone-shaped expanding waveform. A similar wave formed at the stern, and superimposed was the golden wave they were surfing. Yuki explained, "Sir, these are the images reconstituted from the data at our original speed. And here," Heinz opened up a larger window, "is us jumping to ten percent. The bow wave became more pointed, the stern wave too. But behind the ship was a third and fourth wave. "Heinz, take it back to when we jumped from one percent to ten percent." He did, and Jeffrey again saw the waves in the wake. Then the ship leaped forward, and the aft two waveforms went away for a few seconds, then caught up with the ship.

"Now, sir, watch as we go to twenty percent." The same thing happened, the aft wave forms were left behind, only to catch up rapidly. "When we saw that, we focused our magnetic and mass detection gear at the spot behind us, and this is what we found," she indicated to Heinz, who switched to the sheet map of their local space. The map showed *Elizabeth* at the bottom of a gravity cone, and a similar, but slightly larger cone following them.

Jeffrey turned to the ComTech and said, "I want you to gather all the raw data and send a report to Admiral Kutuzov. Use standard encryption. Explain that we tested ten percent light and twenty percent light, and these are the data. No further comments."

"Aye sir."

In the Ay-Yuyuyah ship following *Elizabeth* the leader Thelin updated the data from the probes that had been attached to the human's ship's aft. This was not a perfect probe and likely would need to be replaced soon. You grow them, train them and expect them to perform according to their genetic instructions, but life near this harsh sun has been causing all manner of genetic disruptions. The skin of his ship was also reporting failures. Frustration was not a trait of the Ay-Yuyuyah, but if it were, Thelin would have it in spades.

As the human ship drove out toward their asteroid belt, they passed six hidden ships, two of them Ay-Yuyuyah, the rest were Vorsh; despicable, violent, vile and unpleasant creatures, the whole race was trouble. It seemed the humans were unaware of the hidden ships, which was good; if the Vorsh suspected they had been detected, they would use their standard swarming practice of overwhelming the target and utterly destroy it.

But the humans were seemingly oblivious. The way they always are. The Ay-Yuyuyah had watched the humans for ten thousand years, only in the last few decades were they sufficiently developed to be considered a threat. Their learning was recent, it was almost as if one of the other races were providing a boost up the evolutionary ladder. But now, they had ships that could transcend the normal speed limit. For a few hundred years it had been considered the absolute speed limit, thanks to peoples like the Ay-Yuyuyah, but these monkeys were thoughtful and clever, and as oblivious as they were, they also paid attention to things they didn't understand. Until they understood them. Thelin was now half the size he was when he started out on this expedition. Thelin would likely need to acquire food in the next year or go home.

But home would mean Thelin's death, lack of food would mean Thelin's death. Thelin needed to observe. That is what Thelin did. All the subordinates on the ship that were left were also thin and losing mass by the day.

Thelin considered the language issue, when Thelin first started surveying the humans, they had a huge patchwork of languages, then the little general forced French to most of the European area, India began to speak English under the stern eyes of the British. Spanish began to obliterate all the beautiful languages of the Inca, the Nazca, the Arapaho, the Apache. Russian never caught on, Chinese was spoken mostly in China. When the technological people started in the Americas, English became the universal language, spoken by ship and aircraft captains, controllers and tax men.

It had become easier to understand these humans now that they all spoke the same language. Thelin had watched many wars, the behavior of men towards each other was almost as bad as the Vorsh. Almost.

But the humans in the ship ahead of Thelin were different. They destroyed evil ships targeting the Earth with very gross and deadly intent, but left a victim of one of the ships survive. They have mercy. This is a concept that Thelin was still trying to get his mind around. The Ay-Yuyuyah had no such concept. If one of their own needed saving, then they would save themselves. The Ay-Yuyuyah served the Ay-Yuyuyah, but at times, humans helped other humans, not to serve the race, but to serve the individual. It made Thelin's mind hurt.

Thelin picked up radio traffic from the ship ahead of him. It was a trivially encoded message in a marginally short burst, that told Thelin that they had actually seen the evidence of ships where Thelin had seen them. A return message from a human called Kutuzov was more bothersome. It was, as usual, trivially encoded, but it referred to a book, with page numbers and paragraph numbers and it made no sense. This also hurt Thelin's mind. Usually Thelin was able to decode and understand all codes. Thelin was like the London bus passenger who was an enthusiast for crossword puzzles, usually got it in a few minutes. During the second world war, when the Axis powers began broadcasting instructions to the submarines, Thelin understood their orders before they did. Thelin's mind hurt. A lot.

Then the humans did the unexpected – they shot up from one percent the speed of light to ten percent. Thelin immediately jumped to match their speed again. Then after a half hour, they jumped again, this time to twenty percent. Again, Thelin jumped as soon as Thelin's aching neurons, or the Ay-Yuyuyah equivalent, would allow. So what were these humans up to? Did they discover Thelin's ship? Thelin's mind was aching in ways it hadn't before. Then a lightly encoded message was broadcast from the human ship. It said that their speed experiment was concluded and included data. Some of the data bothered Thelin, but nothing to be done about that now. It was possible that none of the humans would notice the gaps between Thelin's wake and the lack of wake for a short time. Maybe. Ow. Mind hurts.

Elizabeth reached the home claim in record time. Digger and Sneaky took some Marines with them in the runabouts and located some rocks with molybdenum, titanium, gold, silver, mercury and many other minerals. Elizabeth's small robots began roving the outside of the ship, looking for damage. What they found was beyond interesting. It appeared to be a biologic – a not-quite hard shell, but impervious to the cold and hot and lack of pressure. Other remotes found others, but while they were recording, the others disappeared. The one the first remotes found, however was not able to. Another remote brought a stainless steel container to capture the biologic. It started to wiggle, but couldn't disappear. The remotes brought it in the hanger. Navy personnel and Marines in hard suits watched it warily as Elizabeth's robots manipulated it. On the aft, other remotes investigated the locations where the biologics were last seen, but could not see any evidence of their continued existence. But Elizabeth had an idea. She ordered the robots to shoot the locations where the biologics had been. The lasers failed to burn the outer plating, but one by one, the biologics appeared, burned to a crisp.

The biologic in the hanger lay still. One of the remotes aimed its laser at the biologic, and it made a plaintive noise.

Thelin, maintaining distance behind the human ship, was able to observe the humans imperfectly, the biologic was failing. The humans in the runabouts delivered their cargo to the aft hold and parked into the hanger, where they found hard-shell suited Marines and Navy people. They surrounded a blob in a box on the floor of the hanger.

Sneaky walked up to the box, saw the biologic, and reached into her outer pocket, withdrew an energy bar, broke off a piece and tossed it into the box. The biologic expanded slightly, onto the piece of energy bar, and began to dissolve it. The biologic began to look better immediately.

Thelin, whose mind was disintegrating with pain, observed the biologic and the humans in their space suits. The image was poor, the communication was poor. The biologic had similar pain to Thelin's. Then an odd thing happened, one of the suited humans gave food to the biologic. Then the image cleared up. The Humans were now much clearer, the communication was much clearer. The biologic's mind stopped hurting.

Now, Thelin saw a group of Vorsh sneaking up on the human ship. Thelin backed off slightly so as not to get caught in the massacre. The biologic was stuffed in the metal box with a lid, so Thelin didn't see the Marines and Navy personnel scatter.

Elizabeth armed all the weapons at once, announced general quarters, and told Jeffrey what she saw.

"SIX ANOMALIES DESCENDING ON OUR POSITION FROM MULTIPLE DIRECTIONS. THEY ARE NOW ALL WITHIN RANGE OF OUR FIREPOWER. READY TO COMMENCE AGGRESSIVE ACTION ON YOUR ORDERS."

"Commence aggressive action." Jeffrey said.

Elizabeth jinked, fired off rockets, lasers, mines, her rail gun, and the plasma burn of her ion drive. She jumped from one locale to another to another. Massive explosions occurred in three of the targets, one of the ships became visible, and its weapons seemed to be charging up.

Elizabeth dropped a nuclear bomb on it. It was vaporized. The last of the anomalies began to retreat, but *Elizabeth* pursued it. The two rail guns poured heavy ammunition into the location of the anomaly. Finally, it became visible, the weapons charging down.

Janet barked over the intercom broadcast, "A Squad, prepare to board. Shuttle two, cover shuttle one. B Squad, backup in shuttle two." The two shuttles took off, shuttle one heading directly to the enemy ship. The ship was similar in shape to an old nautical submarine – two hundred meters long, fifty meters in diameter. The skin of the ship was similar to the biologic's skin. The A squad found what appeared to be a door, pried it open with a crowbar, and filed in, weapons at the ready.

Jeffrey ordered Yuki and Heinz to go over and collect whatever intel or technology they could. It took a minute to shimmy into their hard suits, then went to the runabout, and Yuki drove them over. They entered the ship with pistols drawn. They found what appeared to be a radio room, and took equipment from the room. The first squad had herded the aliens, which appeared to be a cross between a spider and a gorilla, a carapace with two arms and two legs. They had a helmet over their heads, which gave them both oxygen and communications. There were ten of the aliens. The marines had secured their arms behind their backs with strong nylon ties. The aliens were quiet and compliant. The Marines had them all sit, and secured their legs with wider ties. They would be able to walk, but hobbled.

The shuttle came to an aft hatch, to the location where the prisoners were. They were herded to the back of the shuttle, where they were secured to the benches. All ten of the aliens were placed onto one shuttle, guarded by alert Marines. Yuki analyzed the atmosphere within the alien ship, and determined it was essentially the same as Earth normal, with slightly lower pressure. Thus assured, the pilot took the shuttle to *Elizabeth* and landed in the bay. They took the prisoners to the vacant hold. Torres took charge of the prisoners and secured them to rings on the floor.

The second shuttle with its squad of Marines then entered the alien ship. They took what appeared to be food to the shuttle, as well as the equipment that Yuki and Heinz had salvaged. Yuki and Heinz then went to what appeared to be the weapons system and figured out what they had found was just a plasma weapon. They continued to look for other systems, including the system that rendered the ship invisible. They continued to search, and found a locked hatch.

They called Marines to assist. A large Marine took a crowbar to the hatch and forced it open. Inside was an alien who was surprised at the intrusion. The alien had no helmet, but held what appeared to be a weapon. The Marines yelled at it to drop the weapon, their voices augmented by the suit amplifiers. They pointed their rifles at the weapon and pointed to the ground. The alien didn't respond. Yuki had an idea. She walked up to the alien, took hold of the device, and removed it. This resulted in the Marines stopping their shouting. They took the alien into custody.

Yuki looked over the room, opened drawers and cabinets, didn't see anything to indicate the nature of the room or the hidden prisoner, so they continued their search. They soon found another locked room, called the Marines back, and they crowbarred the other room. Inside was another alien, again, without helmet. The room held no more clues than before. Then Yuki realized that the ship was not spinning, but they had gravity. They took a closer look at the floor plates and saw that the plates contained an artificial gravity generator. Yuki had the Marines take the prisoner to the shuttle. She and Heinz pulled several of the plates and took them to the shuttle a well.

They then went back and continued their search.

One more room with a locked door. But this time, when the Marines forced the door, they were shot at from within the cabin. They saw the heat of the blasts searing into the steel of the wall, so whatever kind of weapon they had it could do considerable damage. The Marines put their rifles on their backs and drew the pistols that Jeffrey had insisted all Marines and Navy personnel carry.

The alien fired once more, they had noticed a pattern to the shooting. It seemed that after every three shots the gun had to charge up. So, they timed their attack after three shots. Sure enough the third shot left the gun unable to blast for a few seconds. After the alien fired the third shot, the Marines rushed in, one fired at the alien's foot, which caused a good deal of blood and meat disjointed from the alien, and a mournful wailing. It seems the pain was intense.

Yuki called for the medic, who had come with the second shuttle. She came over and dressed the wound, but was reluctant to give any medications not knowing alien physiology. The Marines took the alien to the shuttle on a stretcher.

Yuki and Heinz continued to search the ship, and finally found what they thought was the circuitry for the invisibility module. But it was very hard to determine other than through a process of elimination. They had found a kind of golden engine similar to *Elizabeth's*. And another. And another. Three of the golden engines. The circuitry that they thought might be related to the invisibility feature was connected to one of the three engines. These engines were much smaller than *Elizabeth's*, so Yuki and Heinz thought they could bring them aboard *Elizabeth* for study

They had some Marines take them away after they had disassembled them. They continued their circuit of the ship collecting interesting things here and there, mostly ignoring any room with the door open. With the exception of one whose door was open but the lights were turned off.

Yuki turned her face plate to display a light enhancement and infrared. She then saw an alien in the corner holding a larger weapon than any of the others had. She called for more Marines. But just before they came, the alien fired its large bore energy weapon. The alien fired directly at Yuki's chest. Nothing happened, much to her surprise. Then she fired four shots from her pistol into the hand of the alien, the weapon and two shots into the wall. "Medic!" she called out. The alien let out a mournful, pained whine as it held its mangled hand out.

The Marines bundled into the room, secured the alien, treated the wound and the medic and another Marine took the alien back to the shuttle. They decided that the two smart people should have a Marine escort for the rest of their searches.

So, they continued on their tour of the big alien boat.

Thelin was not feeling well. Thelin's mind was giving up. Thelin was going to die now. Thelin had eaten the last of Thelin's crew members, and none of Thelin's biologic agents were left alive except the one in the steel box. That one had eaten and was feeling fine. Thelin's ship was also suffering. If the humans were able to defeat five Vorsh ships and make a sixth come out of hiding, what chance did Thelin have against it. And yet, and yet.

"Mercy" the word clearly articulated from the steel box in the hanger. Elizabeth was paying attention, and she called her captain. "Sneaky, check it out," called Jeffery.

Audrey "Sneaky" Svoboda went back to the steel box in the shuttle bay. She flipped the lid off the steel box. The biologic said again, in a British accent, "Please, have mercy."

"Who are you," she asked.

"I am the alien blob in the ship to your rear. I will do you no harm, I need your help."

"Captain!"

"Yes, we see it. Weapons are trained on it."

The blob in the box, the biologic, said, "I do say, let up there. I will become visible. Let's not get our knickers in a twist and go shooting the nice alien, eh, wot?"

Thelin then deactivated the circuit for the invisibility feature. Thelin's ship because visible. The ship was the size of a large municipal water tank, about thirty meters in length, ten meters in diameter. It was cylindrical with protuberances at various places around the circumference. The blob in the box said, "Please help the alien in the ship that just became visible. He is hungry and needs food."

Audrey asked "Are you speaking for the alien in the ship that just became visible?"

"Indeed, I am" the biologic blob in the box said. "I am a remote tracker and information gatherer. The alien directs me and takes my information. I am speaking with his voice."

"How do we get you out of the ship," asked Audrey.

"He will come here."

The alien ship from which Thelin was in, started breaking apart. Thelin floated to the aft end of *Elizabeth* and entered the hanger bay. Thelin floated to where the biologic was, in its steel box, and settled down.

Audrey looked at the alien and asked, "What do you eat?"

The alien said, through the biologic, "Meat is good. Vegetation. Minerals. Whatever have you."

"How do you like your meat cooked?"

"Cooked? Really?"

"Elizabeth, please get the cook."

"Elizabeth? Who and where is Elizabeth?"

"Never mind. She's getting the cook."

A moment later the cook came, entered the bay, and said, "Holy Mother of...What is that?"

Chief, that is our guest. He needs meat, but thinks that cooking meat is excessive."

"How much meat?" asked the chief.

"Quite a dollop, I'm afraid." said the blob in the box. I have been without for some time."

The chief went back into her walk-in refrigerator and selected half a side of beef and put it on a wheeled stainless-steel cart. She rolled the cart out to the shuttle bay and presented it to Audrey, who took it to the formless alien. "What do you think?"

"It might do for a while. I do so enjoy my meat."

Audrey placed the half side on the floor of the hanger and the alien rolled over it. By the time it was fully on top of the beef, it had absorbed it in its entirety.

"Ah," said the blob in the box, "Hit the spot."

"You seem to have picked up English pretty well. What's your name?" asked Audrey.

"I am Thelin. My people are the Ay-Yuyuyah. I am in your debt."

Audrey asked, "What can you tell us about the other aliens who attacked us?"

"Ah, yes. That." The alien blob seemed to take it's language skills from broadcast television, notably the British Broadcasting Corporation. "It seems you have attracted the ire of the Vorsh, a violent and singularly brutish people." Thelin never changed expressions but the voice that came out of the steel box containing the biologic was as expressive as any BBC news announcer. "I am surprised at how well you did against them. They usually defeat their prey within seconds."

"Why did they attack us?"

"Probably because you noticed them hiding." Jeffrey had entered the shuttle bay and listened to the conversation, but interrupted here. "We noticed you hiding, and see that you didn't attack us."

 ELIZABETH, *ELIZABETH*

"Alas, there are agreements among the races not from around here; we do not attack each other."

"Sounds almost civilized," said Jeffrey. "And which of you 'Not-from-around-here' people have been messing with our people and technology?"

"Whatever in the world do you mean?" the alien blob asked indignantly.

Jeffrey retorted, "There is a fine line between guest and prisoner. At this moment you are our guest. We have fed you." He changed his stance, appearing to loom over the alien, "But if we are not going to have more productive conversations you may as well join the other prisoners."

"Prisoners? What prisoners?"

Audrey answered, "We captured some of the, what did you call them? Vorsh."

"Oh no! You didn't!" the alien blob in the box cried out. "How could you?" a pause, then more curious, "how did you?" Then it commenced mumbling to itself. "We're all doomed. Oh dear, oh dear."

Jeffrey turned to Audrey and said, "Get those I-3 people here, now. Also, begin salvage operations on the abandoned ship of our guest."

"What?" cried out the alien in the box. "You cannot do that, I forbid it."

Jeffrey looked at the alien with as stern a visage he could muster. "Guest, prisoner. Guest, prisoner."

Audrey went to comply. After a few minutes, Yuki and Heinz came onto the deck of the shuttle bay. They were dumbfounded to see the alien blob talking through a steel box that contained another alien blob.

Elizabeth chimed in, "CAPTAIN, OUR SYSTEMS ARE BEING SURREPTIOUSLY SCANNED BY SOMETHING ON BOARD, SOMETHING IN THE SHUTTLE BAY."

Jeffrey again looked at the blob. "Guest? Prisoner?"

Thelin then asked, "Oh, did I do that? How unfortunate of me. I'll stop right now. You do have some sensitive instruments."

Jeffrey asked, "The surviving Vorsh warship – where is it's captain?"

"Ah, that would be ZhZhZhee, He would be attempting to impregnate as many females on his ship as possible before he expires. You would likely find him on the command deck at the middle of the ship."

"Elizabeth," said Jeffrey, "relay that to the Marines. I want him alive."

"YES SIR."

"No! You don't want him alive," the alien blob articulated. "If he stays alive, the entire order of their system falls apart."

"Thanks for the advice," said Jeffrey. "I don't know much about society outside of the human family, but this is Human space, and in Human space, you do what Humans want. If he needs to die, or if you need to die, for that matter, that can be accomplished, but not until I am done with you or him."

"Oh dear, no, no, I don't need to die. I like living."

The Marines continued rounding up survivors of the alien ship. The shuttle brought the captain of the alien ship, ZhZhZhee, to the hanger, swaddled in a kevlar blanket. He was rolled in on a medical gurney. He could not move any of his limbs, but when he was rolled out of the shuttle, he spied the Ay-Yuyuyah ship's master. He struggled mightily, to no avail, but the Marines continued their alert observation of ZhZhZhee without flinching over his movements.

ZhZhZhee began speaking in his own language, in what Jeffrey assumed was an accusatory manner toward Thelin, but he couldn't understand any of the words. Jeffrey asked Thelin, "Do you understand his language?"

"Why, yes, of course," said the Ay-Yuyuyah.

"Please translate for me."

"Certainly. This is Captain ZhZhZhee. He accuses me of collaborating with you so you could defeat his ships. He has called me some rather unsavory words."

"Tell him for me that you had nothing to do with it, and are also being held."

"Oh, sir, may I assume you are the captain of this vessel?" asked Thelin through the blob in the box.

"I am Captain Jeffrey Sokolov of the *Elizabeth*."

"Captain Sokolov, you may speak with the Vorsh captain yourself, he speaks English."

"Thanks." Jeffrey then walked over to the swaddled Vorsh captain. "Captain ZhZhZhee, I am Captain Jeffrey Sokolov. You are my prisoner. Do you understand?"

ZhZhZhee just looked at Jeffrey. His simian-like head expressionless. Jeffrey continued. "I defeated all of your ships in a matter of seconds. I have gathered all your females. Any that you impregnated will be killed. You will fade into oblivion."

This had an effect on ZhZhZhee's facial expression. It was as if he finally understood his position in the world, and it wasn't good. "No. Do not kill them. Let them live."

"That depends entirely on you, Captain." Jeffrey shifted his stance from a more aggressive one to one that approximated parade rest. "I have questions, you have answers. Give me answers, your offspring lives, do not give me answers, your genetic line dies here. But we will continue to keep you alive."

Jeffrey had calculated that ZhZhZhee would desire more than anything else, to leave a genetic legacy, and if he threatened that, on the one hand, he would gain a fearful compliance, the other hand was the reward of a continued genetic legacy, and perhaps the peaceful death he desired. So far it appeared he was having an effect.

ZhZhZhee said in a deep rumbling voice. "What is it you want to know?"

Jeffrey was quick to answer, registering in his mind that his analysis was correct. "Why did your ships attack me?"

"We did not. You attacked us," the alien said.

"Your ships took up positions surrounding us and preparing a cross-fire zone. That is an attack."

"We did not shoot. Therefore, we did not attack."

"Let me see if I understand your position. If you prepare to attack but wait until a time of your own choosing to attack, that just constitutes a peaceful coexistence? And if I determine a threat to my ship has been commenced and defend it preemptively, that is the aggression?"

"Yes," the gruff voiced alien said in satisfaction. "You have attacked our peaceful gathering."

"Ah," said Jeffrey, "what was the purpose of this peaceful gathering that brought you, hidden, to surround my vessel?"

"That is the business of the Vorsh, Human. Nothing you need to know."

So many ways to go with this interrogation, thought Jeffrey. "Why are the Vorsh in my solar system?"

"The Vorsh are concerned about the Humans developing new technologies. They need to be...contained."

Jeffrey turned to Thelin, "Is this a consensus among the Aliens in my solar system?"

"Alas, Captain, it is. All of us have a desire to keep fledgling civilizations like yours away from the real galactic civilization. We have been watching and intervening for hundreds of thousands of years, so we don't have to worry about your kind among the rest of the universe as a whole."

"And this latest attack on Earth by pirates – this was your doing?"

"We only made the suggestions, they carried out the work on their own. We were quite disappointed that you were able to thwart their plans."

Jeffrey turned back to the Vorsh. "What did you have to do with these attacks?"

"Nothing."

Yuki then stepped forward. "Captain, if I may?" Jeffrey nodded. "Captain ZhZhZhee, among all the things you left on your ship, what would you most like us to salvage?"

The line of questioning confused the alien, then his mind caught up and he thought about it. "In my cabin is a console that contains personal thoughts. That would be good."

Yuki responded, "You mean the one that contains the virus that infects all machines and even people's minds? Yeah, we already got that. Anything else?"

How had these humans discovered his virus? Had they defeated it? Wait, weren't they infected once before? How did they survive? Are they more clever than we gave them credit for?

"Females. Bring me females."

IntelTech Heinz stepped forward, "Captain, let me recommend that we segregate this officer from his men, keep him isolated. We can question him further. I also recommend we isolate the other alien and his blob."

Thelin said, "Prisoner or guest, prisoner or guest?"

Jeffrey replied, "On this ship they are two sides of the same coin. My guests have limitations, my prisoners more so."

Thelin replied, "Oh dear, oh dear, oh dear."

They separated the hard-carapaced male prisoners from the female prisoners; ten males, twelve females, and their captain. Three separate cabins assigned to jail the Vorsh, and another to jail, or entertain the Ay-Yuyuyah and its blob. Marines had to double up on their quarters, semi-permanent canoodling couples were told to move in together to share space. This gave a release from the pressure of crowding too many Marines in too few cabins.

Yuki and Heinz reported to Jeffrey to brief him on their take, so far, of the alien vessel. The golden drives were the first point of discussion. "Sir," said Yuki, "their drives are smaller than ours, and we traced connections from one of the drives to a sort of generator. We think the generator powers the antigravity floor plating. We brought the engines over and several of the floor plates for analysis."

Heinz then said, "We collected their radio equipment, their computer equipment, their sensors and controls. It seems the only offensive weapon of the ships is a plasma generator. The capacitors for this one were fully charged."

Then Yuki said, "Sir, one of the females shot me in the chest. It had absolutely no effect on my armor or under-suit."

Heinz nodded, saying, "I was really concerned, but then saw she was okay. Boy was I relieved." Yuki blushed, glanced out of the corner of her eye at the IntelTech, who also was blushing.

Jeffrey thought to himself, young geeks in love. E-gad. "Heinz," he said. "I want a private word with Miss Ohara. Please wait outside my cabin."

After Heinz had left, Jeffrey asked her bluntly, "So have you two been canoodling?"

Yuki looked embarrassed, hung her head, but said, "No."

"But you want to?"

"I like him, sir. I just, I don't, I...I'm not good at this sort of thing." She wrung her hands, looked up. "I think he likes me too."

"Yeah, just what I thought. I'm going to shove you two together. If it takes off, then there you go. If not, well then, there you go." Then he summoned Heinz back into the cabin.

"Heinz and O'hara, I want you two to share the same cabin. Heinz, move into Ohara's. Any questions?"

"Sir," said Heinz, "I like Yuki, but we never..."

"Great. And if nothing comes of it, then there you go. And if something comes of it, there you go. As long as it doesn't affect your work then let's see what happens. And Heinz,"

"Yes sir?"

"I have a particular affection for this young woman. Treat her like the Captain's daughter. And Yuki,"

"Yes sir?"

"Don't even think of taking advantage of my affection for you. I expect a happy relationship, regardless of where it goes."

"Yes sir."

"Now get out of here. Move in together and set up a separate laboratory to analyze these alien artifacts."

Aye, Captain."

He then called Janet to his cabin. When she arrived he offered her tea. She declined, but sat at his table. "We need to send a report to Kutuzov using the book. I want you to word it." He let his breath out in a long exhale. "This is going to be a long time alert, so both of us are going to need to be at the top of our game. Have Kutuzov send *Wanigan* to our location. Then you take a break. Twelve hour shifts until relieved, you and I.

"Have you and Torres been getting along Okay?" He stirred the tea in his cup, there were some undissolved sugar crystals in the bottom. The spoon passing in the liquid generated eddies, but the steam rose straight up, rather than reflecting the turmoil in the cup.

Janet fidgeted in her seat, then said, "We're okay, sir."

"I see you haven't moved in together. Any reason?"

"No, sir, I thought there should be times of privacy that that kind of arrangement doesn't allow."

"I understand. In your position you do need that quality time with yourself. Do the message then get some sack time."

"Yes, sir. Thank you, sir."

After Janet left, he said, "Elizabeth? What do you think?"

"CAPTAIN, I THINK JANET IS HAVING SECOND THOUGHTS ABOUT TORRES. TORRES SEEMS TO BE SERIOUS ABOUT THEIR RELATIONSHIP, BUT NEITHER HAVE TALKED ABOUT IT."

"Let me know if there are any issues with them that could affect the operation of the ship."

"YES, SIR."

Over the next ten days, the technicians spent long hours investigating the alien artifacts taken from the two races' ships. Jeffrey and a team of specialists interrogated the prisoners, from the ten warriors to the twelve females, to the captain of the Vorsh. Jeffrey spent much time with Thelin, discussing the greater galactic community, the races that inhabited it, and the nature of space-time.

Through these discussions, Jeffrey learned of the tastes and nutritional needs of his guests and prisoners, and gave instructions to the cook to prepare just the right mix of foods.

One of the things Jeffrey learned was the captain of the Vorsh ship, ZhZhZhee was not considered a competent commander. It wasn't just that he failed to die when he was supposed to, he just didn't understand everything that a commander needed to do. Such as provide adequate food for his crew, volunteering his ship for longer term duty than necessary, all for his own personal aggrandizement.

This intel proved useful in questioning ZhZhZhee, who loudly and continually demanded females. At one session when the demand was getting more and more irritating to Jeffrey, he replied, "We have spoken to all the females. None are willing to come to you on their own."

"Of course not. That's why you must bring them here to me. I will take care of the rest."

"Sorry, that's not how it is done in this solar system." Jeffrey stood up, having concluded that days questioning, and added, "but if any volunteer, I'll be sure to let you know."

"Volunteer? What is that?" asked the Vorsh.

Ten days later, Elizabeth announced that *Wanigan* was due to arrive in one hour. During their time sitting among the wreckage of the Vorsh and Ay-Yuyuyah vessels, they had kept a watch on the magnetic, mass and electrical fields in the vicinity. As *Wanigan* hove into range, sensors picked up anomalous readings reminiscent of the readings they had used to detect the Vorsh.

"General Quarters," Jeffrey said to Elizabeth.

"ALL HANDS, GENERAL QUARTERS."

All ships personnel that were already on station became more alert. Canoodling couples fell out of bed together and took less time to dress than normal. The pilots of the shuttles took their stations in their pilot seats. The Marines who were not assigned to patrol, assembled in the hanger and squatted at ready.

The *Elizabeth* turned to face the direction from which *Wanigan* was arriving. Elizabeth sent a private message to Wanigan to pass on to Yusef, that the *Elizabeth* was at general quarters and they should follow suit, pass *Elizabeth* and take position at her aft.

When *Wanigan* arrived, she drove past *Elizabeth* and *Elizabeth* moved into *Wanigan's* wake. This blocked the six hidden ships that had been following *Wanigan*.

Jeffrey had Elizabeth broadcast on a wide variety of frequencies the announcement, "THIS IS EARTH WARSHIP ELIZABETH. TO THE SIX UNIDENTIFIED ALIEN VESSELS THAT WERE FOLLOWING EARTH WARSHIP WANIGAN. YOU ARE TARGETED FOR DESTRUCTION. PLEASE SCAN THE DEBRIS FIELDS SURROUNDING THIS LOCATION. YOU WILL SEE THAT WE EASILY DESTROYED SHIPS ATTACKING US. UNLESS YOU COMPLY IN TEN SECONDS WE WILL BEGIN OUR DESTRUCTION. ANY AGGRESSIVE MOVES AGAINST US WILL BE DEEMED AS AN ACT OF WAR AND WE WILL DESTROY YOU."

"TEN, NINE, EIGHT, SEVEN," At this point, the alien ships became visible. They all looked alike, and like the Vorsh ships that had previously attacked *Elizabeth*

Thelin said to Jeffrey, "Demand the name of the coward in charge of the fleet who sneaks and ambushes your ships. I would use those words."

Jeffrey had Elizabeth broadcast those words. In a moment a reply came from one of the ships. It was in the language of the Vorsh.

Thelin told Jeffrey, "They are playing games. They all speak English."

Jeffrey then had Janet target an antenna array on that ship's bow, and fired a blast with the rail gun. The pieces of antenna flew off into space.

Jeffrey then had Elizabeth broadcast "THE NEXT TIME ANYONE COMMUNICATES WITH US WILL BE IN ENGLISH. IS THERE A DEPUTY COMMANDER OF YOUR GROUP?"

Another ship broadcast a reply, with the image of a Vorsh. "Do not attack us. We will not attack you."

Jeffrey decided to keep the conversation going via Elizabeth. "WHAT IS YOUR BUSINESS HERE?"

"We are a peaceful people just passing through."

"THE NEXT TIME YOU LIE TO US WE WILL DESTROY YOU."

One of the ships began to back off, *Wanigan* moved to intercept. It stopped its movement.

"IF YOU WISH TO TRADE WITH US, WE WELCOME TRADE. IF YOU WISH TO EXCHANGE IDEAS AND THOUGHTS WE WELCOME THAT. IF DESTRUCTION AND DOMINATION ARE YOUR INTERESTS, YOU MAY AS WELL STAY HOME. WE DO NOT FEAR YOU. IF YOU PERSIST IN THOSE ACTIVITIES WE WILL FOLLOW YOU TO YOUR HOMES AND DESTROY THEM. DO YOU UNDERSTAND?"

The one who spoke before said, "We understand. Were there any survivors of the battle you had here?"

"YES, THERE ARE SURVIVORS ON BOARD THIS SHIP." There was a long pause, during which Elizabeth reported there was quite a lot of communications between the alien ships.

"We would like to talk to the survivors of that previous engagement."

"THAT IS NOT A PROBLEM. SEND A DELEGATION TO THIS SHIP. YOU MAY ENTER THE FORWARD AIRLOCK. THE DELEGATION WILL NOT BE ARMED. THERE WILL BE NO ATTEMPT TO INFECT ANY OF THE SHIPS EQUIPMENT OR PERSONNEL WITH THE VIRUS THAT HAS BEEN INTRODUCED INTO OUR SYSTEMS BEFORE."

Thelin commented, "Captain, it is likely that the Vorsh will send over their people directly from their ship to this without a shuttle. I would open the airlock for them."

Jeffrey had the Marines at the forward airlock open the outer airlock door. Sure enough, the Vorsh delegation jumped from the Vorsh ship that had resumed communications. The first ship that initiated communications had sent out their own technicians to repair the antenna array that *Elizabeth* had shot away. When the delegation reached *Elizabeth*, the Marines ushered them aboard. The Marines clearly showed that they were armed, and they searched the aliens for arms.

Then they escorted them to the elevator that brought them in synch with the rotating simulated gravity. The delegation consisted of two Vorsh warriors. Jeffrey queried them in English. They looked as if they didn't understand.

Thelin, watching from his cabin said in a radio link, "They are feigning ignorance. They all speak English." Jeffrey heard it on the ear bud. He acknowledged the silent message, and said, "If you do not speak English, you might as well return to your own ship."

The aliens looked confused.

"Marines, escort these aliens off my ship. Shoot them if they give you any trouble."

"No!" cried one of the two of the delegation. "We speak English. Do not make us the cause of failure of this mission!"

Jeffrey looked sternly at the two aliens. He noticed that they had crossed over from the other ship without space suits, only helmets for breathing and communication. He pointed out to the Marines escorting them, "Please notice the carapaces. This gives them considerable protection. To do the most damage to them, use your pistols."

"Sir, Yes Sir!" the Marines replied in unison enthusiastically.

"What do you mean?" asked one of the delegation aliens.

"We have found that a large bore projectile shot at nine hundred meters per second does serious damage to the kind of armor you wear. They may protect you from space and lasers and other electronic weapons damage, but once past your carapace, it ricochets back and forth inside turning your meat to a sticky paste." Jeffrey smirked at the Marines, who seemed to be enjoying the discomfort of the aliens.

"Elizabeth, please invite the Commodore aboard."

"AYE, CAPTAIN," she replied. After a moment passed, she announced, "COMMODORE YUSEF WILL BE HERE IN FIVE."

To the Vorsh, he said, "Because part of your job is to gather information about this ship, our capabilities and our intent, allow me to show you some of our facilities, before we take you to your people."

"We would rather get right to seeing our people, if that is all the same to you," invoked one of the aliens.

"It is not all the same to me. Your presence here is a message. My showing you some of the things I intend is a return message. You are the messenger, so shut up and pay attention."

Jeffrey began the tour by showing the bridge. Lieutenant Bianca was in charge there, and greeted the Captain. The aliens stared at her. One stammered out, "But she's a female!" The other tried to shush the first, saying in its own language, "Don't point out the weakness — this is a tactical advantage of our people." But as soon as it finished Elizabeth spoke the translation of the Vorsh's words on the loudspeakers in the bridge. The two Vorsh looked at each other, realizing that there was no secrecy in their exclusive language. They couldn't know that Elizabeth had been studying the Vorsh language by listening in on the conversations of the prisoners and discussing it with Thelin.

Jeffrey ignored their embarrassment, and asked them to follow him. He then went to the new electronics laboratory where Vorsh equipment was laid open on the workbench. Diagnostic equipment was connected to most of the various black boxes. One of the techs said, "Wow, did you see that? As soon as those Vorsh guys came in here, the equipment started to spike!"

Jeffrey then took them to next cabin, which was the New Technology Testing room, formerly Sneaky's cabin. She finally decided to move in with Smitty. This brought to mind his personal characterization of the pair — the ballet dancer and the klutz. In this cabin, a section of Vorsh ship floor was being tested for anti-gravity characteristics, including spillover of the gravitic effects on nearby surfaces.

"CAPTAIN, COMMODORE YUSEF IS ON BOARD. PLEASE BRING YOUR GUESTS TO THE GALLEY." announced Elizabeth.

"Ah, good." said Jeffrey. He led the parade back to the galley. The two Marines took their posts inside the Galley, while Commodore Yusef's Marine bodyguards took posts outside the room.

Before they entered, one of the Marines guarding the Vorsh delegation told the Commodore's bodyguards what Jeffrey had told them about projectile weapons. They had only carried needlers, blasters and stun guns. The guard asked Elizabeth to have a courier bring two handguns with ammunition and holsters for the Commodore's bodyguards.

The guard said, "When they come, strap them on. If you have to shoot, turn off the safety." He pulled his own weapon and indicated the small button. "To shoot, just pull the trigger, once for each shot. Be careful, there is a bit of a kick, so after each shot, reacquire your target." He then showed how to exchange clips of ammunition, and went back inside the galley to stand guard.

Jeffrey, Commodore Yusef, and the two Vorsh sat at a small square table. The Vorsh carapace seemed to be able to bend, which meant they were able to sit. So, Jeffrey noticed the sliding articulated plates of the rear carapace.

The two Vorsh took off their helmets. Jeffrey inquired about their dietary needs, if they would like water, tea, coffee, soup or something more substantial. Not being thoughtful diplomats, the Vorsh started salivating as soon as the conversation took on the thought of food. "Do you prefer something with vegetables, or meat, or both? Or something else?"

The aliens asked for something with both. Jeffrey asked the cook to bring them both a vegetable beef soup. A few minutes later, she appeared with a tray, containing the soup for the aliens, coffee for Jeffrey and tea for Yusef.

"I don't know how much you know of our culture, but the soup you are being served is warm, nearly ninety degrees. Enjoy it." Jeffrey sat back and watched the aliens first look at their soup, wisps of steam rising from their bowls, they looked at the spoons alongside the bowls in consternation. But before Jeffrey could show how to use the spoons, they both bent their heads, pursed their large, simian-like lips, and sucked in the contents of the bowl. There was pain in their eyes, but satisfaction too.

"So, to begin," said Commodore Yusef, "We need to..."

But he was interrupted by one of the delegation, "More? We want more." And they both lifted their empty bowls. They licked their lips, chops, and chins of any remaining soup.

Jeffrey looked to the Commodore, who nodded. He then requested two more bowls of the same, and some plastic mugs and a pitcher of water. When the kitchen chief brought them, she also brought a tray of Danish and French pastries. The aliens repeated their unusual method of consuming soup. They winced in pain, but licked their lips. Then Jeffrey poured water in the mugs and handed them to the two Vorsh. They drank of the water and again licked their lips.

Then they sniffed, and looked longingly at the pastries.

Jeffrey, not having had siblings, spent much time reading books about families. He also had enjoyed watching vids of family life. So, rather than passing the tray of sweets, selected one for each of the aliens, who picked them up and crammed the pastry in their mouths. Oddly, the aliens kept the pastries in their mouths. Jeffrey saw their eyes signaled "Ambrosia!" They still did not chew or swallow, just holding the flavor, allowing the saliva which mingled with the sugary, fatty, fluffy bread, to drip down their throats.

The Commodore said, "Well, that's something you don't see every day." Yusef took a delicate French pastry and ate it over a period of a couple minutes. The Alien's pastries were still in their cheeks. Yusef drank his tea. Jeffrey drank his coffee. The Aliens seemed transported to a happy place they were reluctant to come back from.

Jeffrey told the chief to clear the table, that they needed to get down to work. He looked to the Aliens, saw that they were still transported to their culinary dream world. Having had enough, he said to the Commodore, "Perhaps they just sent us worthless or useless Vorsh to distract our attention from them. Maybe we should destroy one of their ships to show we mean business."

The two delegates brought their attention back from their happy place and swallowed. It seemed miraculous that they didn't choke, but the first one with a clear mouth called out, "No! We are ready!"

"Yes," said the other one. "Ready."

Commodore Yusef then introduced himself. "I am the one in charge here. I am Commodore Yusef. Captain Sokolov has discovered many things about you. Let me discover one myself." He paused. "Your ships have too little food. Your crews are starving. Am I right?"

The alien's responses were almost out of an old comedy routine. One said, "Yes," while the other at the same time said, "No." They looked at each other and both switched their answers. "No." and "Yes."

"So, if I offered your captains some food, they would accept it?"

"Yes."

"All right, we'll consider that."

"Next, tell me why the Vorsh are in my solar system."

"That is difficult, Commodore Yusef." said one of the delegates. The other continued, "We would want to, but there are not adequate words to explain."

Jeffrey chimed in, "Perhaps I can supply some of the words. Your people are too crowded and you want to conquer our world."

"Yes. NO! That's not it."

"You have run out of your resources and don't have the technological ability or the cleverness to reverse your problem."

"That is closer. Our civilization is an old one. These ships are designed thousands of years ago. We have not had to change them because they were perfect. Now they are not. We don't know how to do things except for one way, and that way is not good enough anymore."

Jeffrey leaned back and spoke to the chief, "Bring out some grapes or cherries. Some small, sweet fruit."

A moment later, she brought a bowl of cherries and placed them in front of Jeffrey. Jeffrey gave a cherry to the one who disclosed the decline of his civilization. The other then piped up, "The weapons of our ships used to be the fear of all the civilizations. Not any more."

Jeffrey then tossed that one a cherry. Commodore Yusef immediately caught on to what Jeffrey was doing – positive reinforcement to reward giving information. Jeffrey continued, "What is it you want to talk to the crew of the surviving Vorsh ship about?" The two tripped over each other's words to be the next one rewarded. The strength of Earth ship. The number of females the captain had impregnated before he died, and which ones were they? The amount of knowledge the Humans had extracted from the Vorsh warriors. What the Vorsh warriors wanted to pass on to their next of kin before they were killed.

Jeffrey was pretty well satisfied he understood what was in the minds of the Vorsh. He just passed the bowl of cherries to the two.

After they finished off the cherries, they looked so happy. Jeffrey said, "Before we get any farther, let me ask you another question. What would happen if the captain of the ship hadn't died?"

"Oh, no. That would not happen. He has no way not to die. He is programmed to die."

"I see," said Jeffrey. "Commodore, do you have any more questions for our guests?"

"Not at this time, Captain."

"Then let's take the delegation to see the warriors."

The two Marines guards in the galley took the lead, Jeffrey followed them, the two delegates followed Jeffrey, followed by the Commodore and his personal escort. He noticed that they had acquired pistols in shoulder holsters, like Jeffrey's Marines.

They arrived at the hold that contained the ten crew members from the surviving Vorsh ship. Jeffrey reminded the delegation that they needed to speak only English. He secretly had one of his Marines run off to grab some candy.

The Marine came back with a small container of soft jellied candies. Jeffrey then had the other Marine open the locked door. The Vorsh languished against the wall, sitting or reclining as their bounds allowed them. There was a tub of food from their ship, that looked like a porridge with chunks of meat. The tub had been taken off their ship, and there were dozens of similar tubs that were being kept in the walk-in cooler.

The delegates looked with pity at the ten. "This food is emergency rations. It tastes bad."

"It was the only food we could find on their ship."

"We all have been using this food. It is bad." The delegate looked sad. "It is made of some algae. And dead Vorsh."

"Elizabeth, have the cook prepare soup for all these prisoners, have Audrey bring some Marines to remove this tub," commanded Jeffrey.

"AYE, CAPTAIN."

Jeffrey had planned to use the candy as a further behavior modifier, but decided to give the prisoners a treat. He tossed one piece to each of the prisoners, then put one in his own mouth. They did the same, and they began to chew. Saliva began escaping from the corners of their mouths. He tossed another and another.

Soon, the chief brought a cart containing soup bowls and a tureen with additional soup.

Jeffrey personally passed out the food. The prisoners reacted the same way the delegation had; with enthusiasm. He refilled their bowls, and gave them water. He then apologized to them, saying that he thought that the food they had taken from their ship was their custom. They would be fed better from now on.

He then encouraged the delegation to go ahead and ask their questions. They asked the same questions that they told the captain and commodore that they would. As often as not, the answer was "I don't know," "We don't know."

Jeffrey then interrupted, saying, "You don't need to worry about being killed. This is not going to happen if we have anything to say about it."

Then Jeffrey had the cook bring the tureen of soup along to the dozen females in the separate cell. They fed the females, much to their delight. The delegation began asking their questions about the captain impregnating, but they never got to finish their questioning. The delegation was pelted with bowls, fortunately the food had been consumed first.

Jeffrey ushered the delegation out, brought them back to the galley, had the cook bring out some more Danish pastries. He then told them to stay there, and posted both sets of Marine escorts with them. He then took Commodore Yusef to his cabin.

"Commodore Yusef," he started, after they sat down at the table in his cabin. "I have an idea. We may very well find ourselves in trouble if these Vorsh have brought hungry, desperate people. Let's offer them an exchange – their technology for food. We can teach them again how to raise food. Learn what we can from them, but encourage them to go back to their own worlds and practice a more moral way."

"If we don't already have superior technology," said Yusef. "I, for one am not impressed."

"From what I hear," countered Jeffrey, "the Vorsh are not the only alien species who have an interest in us." He then recounted his conversation with Thelin about how a council of alien races were concerned with the vicious nature of the humans, and feared them coming out among the rest of the galaxy.

Commodore Yusef then asked, "Did you capture that ship captain?"

"Yes, sir. I thought I would keep that information from the delegation, because they were under the impression that he couldn't live after losing his ship."

"How about we negotiate with the rest of those ships here to make that captain an ambassador?"

"Commodore, that explains why you hold the rank. Of course, if we can do it, it would make sense."

Yusef then added, "I think we need to arrange offering food to any alien ship that comes to any of the Human space stations. But we need to find a way for them to go back to their own worlds."

Jeffrey commented, "That shouldn't be too difficult. Farming on Earth and Selene more than supports all the humans in the solar system. It can easily be ramped up to support alien life – of course depending on how many there are. Probably something we need to find out.

"One more thing, sir. I have a representative of another race on our ship. When it saw we discovered its location, it turned visible, then destroyed its ship. We collected debris and have been studying that along with the debris and remains from the Vorsh ships.

"This other alien seems friendly, and has been useful in giving us information, but it exaggerated the power of Vorsh weapons, and didn't clue us in on the starving condition of the Vorsh."

Yusef asked, "What is this alien called?"

"Its name is Thelin, it is a member of the Ay-Yuyuyah."

Yusef thought about this for a moment. "We could probably offer it an ambassadorship also. We need to get back to the Earth Station and encourage Admiral Kutuzov to develop navigation rules for aliens, along with strategically located registration points at the Oort cloud."

"Sounds like you have a plan, sir. Let me introduce you to Thelin."

They made their way to the cabin in which Thelin was housed. The two marines outside the door saluted the two officers. They entered, Thelin was situated in a corner of the cabin, Jeffrey looked around and did not see the biologic, but its empty box was on the deck. "Elizabeth! The small biologic is not visible here. Locate it please."

"EFFORTING." A minute later, she reported back, "CAPTAIN, I HAVE REVIEWED THE SECURITY RECORDING AND SEE THAT THE ALIEN AY-YUYUYAH HAS CONSUMED IT."

To Commodore Yusef, Jeffrey said, "That was the only method of bilateral communications."

"Have you fed it?" asked the Commodore.

"Yes, sir, a half side of beef two days ago."

"Well, if it can't communicate with us, it serves no purpose. Get rid of it."

The walls and floors began to vibrate, it changed in pitch, then the voice of the biologic that Jeffrey had gotten used to, the British raconteur tone and accent, emanated from the surfaces, "W-w-wait. Wait. I can communicate. Don't do anything drastic!"

"All right," said Jeffrey, "Talk. Why did you eat your biologic?"

"You probably do not understand – that biologic was designed to act as a server to me. It originally was a sensor, then became my mouthpiece, and then served to nourish me."

Why was the food we gave you not enough? Is your metabolism so poor that it couldn't sustain you with enough food to sustain a squad of Marines for a week?" demanded Jeffrey. He was still jolted at the cannibalism he had discovered on his ship.

The commodore introduced himself, "I am Commodore Yusef. I understand you are Thelin. Thelin, you have been surprising us with your actions, and allowing others to surprise us by misinforming us, or failing to inform us, on the actions of aliens in our vicinity. To continue your usefulness to us, you are going to have to be far more forthcoming than you have been."

"It is with great regret that I seem to have withheld vital information from you, I only do so with self-preservation in mind. I will forthwith endeavor to be far more elucidative in my locutions."

The commodore looked to Jeffrey, "What did he say?"

"Seems to want to cooperate more, now that he got caught with feathers on his chin." cracked Jeffrey.

"Indeed, sirs," said the Ay-Yuyuyah. "If I could start with a clean slate I would."

"Well, your chance for a clean slate may have just arisen," said Commodore Yusef. "We have a proposal, but it would depend on your being entirely truthful as part of the deal."

"What, sir, if I may ask, is this deal of which you speak?"

Jeffrey spoke before the Commodore could, "It comes in two parts. First, as an adviser to the Human Navy. Tell us everything we need to know about the other galactic races, tell us what we need to know about you – from your dietary needs to your intellectual, social, communicative and other needs."

Yusef took his cue, "The second part, is when we are ready, you would become an ambassador of your people to our people."

"This proposal seems, on its face, to be a reasonable and acceptable use of my vast talents. I will be glad for the opportunity to serve in both capacities. Perhaps both at the same time."

"No," said the commodore, "One at a time. If you wish to advise us when you become a diplomat, then you would be advising us out of loyalty to your government. We need you, when advising us, to be acting entirely in our interests, as we define it."

"Ah, I see your point. Yes, Commodore Yusef, I will be your advisor."

"And will we be able to trust your advice? I think you should understand that if your advice and instruction prove false, that if you betray us for any other cause, there will be severe consequences."

"My advice will be thorough and truthful, to the best of my ability."

"Good," said Jeffrey. "First question, where is your home world?"

"Oh goodness, how can I say? If only I had a map…"

"Elizabeth, display a map for the Ay-Yuyuyah."

One of the wall plates illuminated and displayed a map of the galaxy with arbitrary zones inscribed, from the galactic center to the edge, and in concentric circles like a flat map from earth showing longitude and latitude. It indicated the location of the solar system on one of the galactic arms.

"Ah, I see," said the alien. "Your sun is at position zed-Y sixty-four. Can you bring the detail up on your sun?" The vid zoomed in to the near-solar system neighborhood. The larger lines were replaced with more fine lines, and the labels of the zones now included sub zones. The zone around the sun was ZY-64. There were zones in all the areas surrounding ZY-64, the nearest star to the sun was in ZY-63. This was Alpha Centauri. "My home world is in ZW-60. It is some hundred light years away."

"What is the nature of your faster-than-light travel?" Jeffrey asked.

"Much the same as yours, Captain. It took a year or so for me to get from home to here."

"And how long have you been here?"

"You do ask pertinent questions, don't you? I arrived about the time your world discovered aviation. Around 1750."

"How have you been reporting your findings back home?"

"I have sent a few reports by building small ships and sending biologics home in them."

Commodore Yusef asked, "How many other galactic races are in Human space now? And who are they?"

"Well, you met the Vorsh, there's me – no other Ay-Yuyuyah – then there are the Plang, the O, the Fizzies, and perhaps a few other minor individuals."

"How many of the Vorsh are in our system?"

"About a hundred thousand."

"Where is the Vorsh home-world on the map?"

"XY-64"

"All right, now about your dietary needs..." began Jeffrey.

"Ah, yes. Perhaps a more steady diet will work better for me. If I had three meals a day, mixed vegetables and meat, at around a thousand calories per meal, I should be able to sustain myself nicely."

"No problem, that's a little less than we feed our Marines. Is there anything else we can do for you?"

"I am concerned about wastage. What do I do with it?"

"I'll send in an engineer who will ask you enough questions to get to the correct solution."

"Thank you, Captain."

Outside the cabin, Jeffrey asked Elizabeth to have an engineer talk to Thelin about waste disposal. But before that engineer started any project to talk to the captain. He thought it would be prudent to have a system to monitor and analyze the output of the alien guest.

"Eventually we will have to start pushing the speed of these buckets to light plus," said Jeffrey. "But I have the feeling that we need to get this alien project under way."

"That's true," said the commodore. "But it is also important to understand our drives. Keep your physicist and engineers studying the operation, and make sure they document everything." They walked back to the galley and sat down with the two Vorsh delegates. Jeffrey ordered ice cream all around. The Vorsh asked how it was traditionally eaten, so Jeffrey showed them how to use their spoons.

The delegates attempted to eat the ice cream slowly, but their enthusiasm was too much for them to bear. They ended up with more ice cream inside than out, but barely. Jeffrey handed them napkins to wipe down their carapaces and faces.

Now that their attention had been brought to the fore, Jeffrey asked, "What if, by some miraculous event, the captain of a defeated ship survived?"

"No, no. Couldn't happen, sorry." The two delegates repeated themselves.

"Why? What is it that makes the captain die?" Jeffrey leaned back in his chair.

"It is one of the things captains are selected for. They are given special food to make them want to do things the traditional way."

"Ah," said Jeffrey. "So, if the captain had not taken any of that food, might he not die?"

"Oh, that would be bad. How can a captain not do what he was told?"

"How indeed." Jeffrey sat forward, put his elbows on the table, and said, "If such a thing happened, would the captain be a good person – could he be trusted for an important job?"

"I don't think he would be trusted if he failed to eat the food that makes him do traditional things. That is how they are controlled."

"All right, here is the rule. Every Vorsh that comes to an Earth-based station, will get free food. They will also get technical information that will enable you to grow food for yourselves. You may take this information back to your home world. The other part of the rule is, every alien in the Human solar system will make themselves visible. Any attempt to hide will result in that ship being destroyed. We can detect your ships, but it is better if we see them. Do you understand these two parts of the rule?"

They both nodded.

Yusef then said, "And another part of this is we will expect to have an ambassador to represent your people to us and us to your people. We have just the Vorsh in mind."

"Yes? Who?"

"It is the captain of the surviving ship."

The two looked at each other then said in unison, "We must talk to him!"

"That can be arranged in a little while. Perhaps you would like some more ice cream?" Jeffrey ordered some for them, then he and Commodore Yusef left the galley. Jeffrey led Yusef to the cabin that he had kept the captain of the surviving Vorsh ship.

The Marine guards at the door came to attention as the two officers arrived, one unlocked the door, and the two entered. The Vorsh captain sat on a bench. He was tethered to a secured ring in the bulkhead.

Yusef said, "Have you been fed yet?"

Captain ZhZhZhee nodded. "Good. If you need more, let us know." Again, the Vorsh captain nodded. "We are told that captains that lose their ships all die. Why did you not die?"

ZhZhZhee paused for a while, then said, "They serve a food that makes you want to kill yourself. I fed it to my hungry crew and went hungry." He bowed his head in shame. "The suicide ingredient didn't work on them. They survived, I survived. Females wanted nothing to do with me."

Yusef waited to be sure the alien was done, then said, "We have a way that we think you can serve your people and help us to help them. Are you interested?"

"What do you want me to do?" the dejected captain asked.

"We want you to be an ambassador, from your people to us, and from us to your people. Could you do that?"

"I would have a hard time convincing my leaders to accept this deal."

"I think we could help you with that. I just need to know if the job were offered to you, would you accept it?" Yusef paused and raised his eyebrows in expectation of an answer.

"Yes, I could work with you. I could be a good ambassador."

"Very good," said Jeffrey. "In a few minutes some representatives of some Vorsh ships we caught attempting to attack us like your ships did, will come in here to talk to you. They will try to make you feel bad about surviving. Just remember what we spoke about."

Jeffrey and Yusef left their erstwhile ambassador alone with the delegation for a short time. While waiting, Yusef asked Jeffrey about the pistols. Jeffrey told him that the carapaces of the Vorsh absorbed and deflected the power of most lasers and other energy weapons, but could not stand up against the large-bore pistols. That plus the psychological benefit of a weapon that the aliens didn't have.

"Can you make a bunch of these for my team? With ammunition, of course."

"Sure. I can have the replicator throw together enough for your officers and maybe your Marine sergeants." Then to the air, "Elizabeth, can you do that for Commodore Yusef?"

"I CAN HAVE THEM READY FOR HIM BY TOMORROW."

"You are going to have to learn to use the replicator. All sorts of useful," said Jeffrey.

"I suppose," replied Yusef, "But I don't have a lot of room, and I don't have the raw materials."

"Nothing that can't be fixed," retorted Jeffrey.

The delegation exited the cabin in rather a hurry. "We couldn't talk with him! He has no sense of pride in his position! He is an ingrate!"

Jeffrey then escorted the delegation to the airlock, and told them to present the messages that he and Yusef had enumerated. They then got into the airlock and jumped to their own ship. Jeffrey then took Commodore Yusef to his cabin to further discuss strategy. He had informed Janet of the impending departure of the delegation, and to be wary of any moves that the ships might make, either aggressive or recessive.

In his cabin, Jeffrey and Yusef discussed the disposition of their Vorsh prisoners. "Things are going to turn around pretty quickly," said Yusef. "Once the Navy agrees with our plan," he paused, interrupting himself, "that is, if they do, we aren't going to have a lot of time to do what we need to do."

"I should take these prisoners with me to the Earth station."

"Sir. If I may?" Jeffrey interrupted his boss, "I would like to give the females the option to go with or stay, in the odd chance that our Vorsh consul might seduce one or another, thus keeping his aggression in check."

"That makes a little sense, Captain. Let's go and address them now, and see. Then I'm going to have to get back to my ship."

They walked to where the females were held, and Jeffrey asked them, as a group, "First," he began, "You are prisoners of Earth Navy. Second, things are changing, so that you will have some choices to make in both the near future and later on. One of those choices is, you get to stay on board this ship, you get to interact with your former captain. Or you can go with Commodore Yusef, here, to the Earth Navy station.

"Do I have any volunteers for staying and interacting with your former Captain?"

Two of the twelve indicated they would be willing to stay, the rest wanted nothing to do with their former captain, ZhZhZhee.

Jeffrey arranged for transport of the prisoners to *Wanigan* and he sent additional food to help keep them alive. The alien Thelin was to continue to advise Jeffrey, and if there was any important news, Jeffrey would send it to both Kutuzov and Yusef. Jeffrey decided to give Yusef a collection of their own pistols rather than await delivery tomorrow, because "You never know."

He showed Yusef how to use the projectile weapons in space – when near a gravity well, you had to do some calculations, such as the acceleration of gravity, wind (if in an atmosphere,) and leading the target if it is moving. That involved knowing the speed of the projectile you have loaded, among the other variables. However in short distances, point, assure the safety is turned off, and shoot. Be careful of the kick, and reacquire your target, and repeat as necessary.

They parted company, Yusef taking nearly all the aliens off Jeffrey's hand, his Marines on particularly strict alert and watch. The shuttle did not have a separate cabin for male and female prisoners, so all the prisoners were told to behave themselves under threat of immediate and painful termination. That seemed to work, there were no problems on the way to *Wanigan*.

After the delegation returned to their ship, it was about a half hour before message traffic began passing from one ship to the others, then back and forth, almost like a discussion. Meanwhile, Yusef sent off reports to Kutuzov and the other ships in his small fleet, informing them of the new state of affairs with the newly discovered alien life, and new standing orders.

The chief Vorsh called on Yusef, requesting timelines for implementing the new laws and regulations. When can they go get their free food? Commodore Yusef told them that the food won't be available for at least ten days – they needed to stock the stations from Earth. But the invisibility part began an hour ago. They had best get the word out. Of course, Elizabeth monitored the conversation and reported its contents to Jeffrey.

They parted company with the Vorsh, heading in towards the Earth Navy headquarters. By the time they took off, Kutuzov had been briefed and gave his tentative approval to Yusef's plan of action. Orders had gone out to all stations – all the Lagrange point stations and all the naval vessels. Food was ordered delivered to all the stations for this specific purpose. *Elizabeth* was ordered to accompany *Wanigan* inbound. Jeffrey was to give the Vorsh ambassador-in-training, ZhZhZhee a primer on what was expected of an ambassador, and how he was to accomplish his mission.

Jeffrey began the tutorials, but soon decided Janet was better suited for that type of work. Between the two of them, along with Elizabeth, the ambassador actually seemed to be learning his tasks. After the first day, traveling at the stately pace of one tenth the speed of light, Jeffrey decided to test the golden drive's faster-than-light ability. After signing off with Yusef, he had all personnel prepare for the experiment. With Yuki monitoring the instruments for the golden drive, Heinz monitoring instruments for the ship, Janet at the pilot's seat, and Jeffrey in the captain's chair, all other personnel scattered throughout the ship for security and safety, they slowly increased the ship's velocity to approach light speed. This occurred smoothly, as they neared .999 light, a subtle vibration in the bones of the ship occurred. The vibrations increased as the power to the golden drive was increased. They broke through the light speed barrier, it felt almost as if a membrane was being pierced by the ship, but as they continued to accelerate, all the vibrations, all the tension left. Everyone felt euphoria over the successful test of their engines.

Janet reported that the speed they held to was twice the speed of light. There was plenty of room on the controller to increase their speed far beyond that. Jeffrey brought the experiment to a close, considering how crowded the inner system was with ships and junk and planetary bodies. The test lasted twenty minutes at twice light speed. Jeffrey slowed to .05 light speed to allow *Wanigan* time to catch up. A few hours later, she did. The two ships compared notes on *Elizabeth's* experiment, which gave both ships tools to use to plan their use of the golden drives. Yusef agreed that the golden drives should not be used in-system except in an emergency.

They compared clocks and saw that Einstein was right – time seems to slow down the faster you go. *Elizabeth's* clocks showed a very small discrepancy from *Wanigan's*.

Both ships accelerated to half-light and rode toward the place the Earth station was going to be when they arrived. They soon discovered that there were interference patterns that they needed to avoid if they wanted to ride smoothly – the two ships generated their own waves, and the wakes spread out from behind them as the waves carried them forward. Where the waves and wakes clashed they caused interference patterns in space, that made for a choppy trip. By more carefully aligning with each other, they found they could more easily avoid those interference patterns, thus avoiding the choppy ride.

Yuki was in her own version of heaven. She was composing a paper on the foibles of faster than light, and near light speeds. Her organized mind pretty well had it composed as soon as she thought of it. If only her mind was as fast as the ideas that sprung from it! When at last she decided it was time to get rest, although reluctantly, she went back to the cabin she shared with Heinz. She didn't turn the light on, for fear of awakening him. But she got undressed and climbed under the covers in his bunk. She dropped right off to sleep, she was so tired.

When Heinz woke to discover his roommate in his bed without anything on, all sorts of thoughts filled his mind – did she intend something form him? Was she all right? Did she get into his bed by mistake or on purpose? Heinz was a good man, not prone to taking advantage of a vulnerable woman, so he gingerly reached over her, down the other side to brace himself, and lifted himself over her to the floor. He began to walk away, and she took that moment to awaken. She looked at him from under the cover, and said, "Where are you going?"

"I didn't want to make you uncomfortable, so I was going to go to my lav and get dressed." He felt rather conscious of his morning-and-naked-girl-in-your-bed erection, so he didn't turn around.

"Come here, and take your pajamas off." she commanded. He obeyed.

Within a few more hours, they came to the place Earth station was supposed to be, but it was off by a few degrees of arc. Jeffrey asked Yuki about how they had missed. She seemed to be more perky this morning. She confirmed that the trajectory error had to do with the clock being off due to the faster than normal travel. Another paper to write!

Elizabeth and Wanigan both recalculated how to merge with the station's orbit, and waited for the station to catch up with them. When it did, they merged with the orbit of the station, and *Wanigan* began to dock, when Janet pointed out that she saw several anomalies following the station, small gravity wells, indicating that the station was being stalked by invisible ships.

Jeffrey told *Wanigan* to stop docking, and go to General Quarters. He also had *Elizabeth* go to General Quarters. They broadcast a message that any ships using an invisibility circuit was in violation of Earth space law, and were at risk of immediate destruction.

Janet reported, "Captain, I am getting a spike in power from one of the anomalies, like a capacitor charging."

Jeffrey said, "Forward rail gun, give a two second burst at that anomaly."

"Aye, sir, two second burst."

The sound of the gun reverberated through the ship – a loud buzz. The target materialized with its entire antenna array shot away. There were more holes in the structural skin of the ship, atmosphere was out-gassing through the holes.

Jeffrey broadcast, "No ship may offer a threat to any Earth-based vessel. Violations will be met with destructive force."

None of the other anomalies materialized, but they also did not charge up their weapons. Jeffrey ordered the aft rail gun to select a target and give a half second burst. One of the anomalies began moving away from its current orbit. The rail gun captain, a Marine gunnery Sergeant, selected that one, and gave its half second burst, the buzz again reverberating throughout the ship. The anomaly turned into a disabled Vorsh ship.

"This is the Earth warship *Elizabeth*, any further delay in shutting down your invisibility circuits will result in our ships firing on you. You have ten seconds to comply. Ten. Nine. Eight. Seven. When they got to six, the rest of the anomalies un-disappeared. There were twenty of the alien ships, mostly Vorsh, but some of a completely different configuration, leading Jeffrey to believe that they were a completely different space race.

"This is the Earth warship *Wanigan*. All alien ships in Earth's solar system are prohibited from using the invisibility circuits. From this point on, when they are detected and ships are not visible, they will be summarily destroyed. All aliens may have free food at any Earth-based space station. To claim this benefit, ship captains must register with that station.

"All official communications will be in English. It is known that most aliens speak English. We are in the process of installing a Vorsh ambassador, and other races may suggest an individual for their ambassador. In the very near future, an Ay-Yuyuyah is being installed as a general-purpose ambassador for those races who have none, or need special services. These ambassadors will be installed at this station."

"Ships companies are permitted to enter this station, with very few restrictions. Upon coming aboard the station, you will be given instructions on where you may not be. Welcome to Earth."

After this drama, *Wanigan* resumed its docking. *Elizabeth* remained near the station and stood guard while her sister ship disembarked her non-volunteer passengers and her crew. They stood down from general quarters, but the gunners remained on station.

Admiral Kutuzov decided to keep *Elizabeth* on station, and took a shuttle to visit her there. Commodore Yusef accompanied the admiral, and they met with Jeffrey in the galley. There was much to brief the admiral on, so after ensuring that coffee and pastries were served, he began. "Several things, Admiral. First, we were able to go twice the speed of light without any noticeable problems. There is much more where that came from. I'll have Yuki Ohara prepare a few reports for you. Second, the aliens. It seems we are not alone! I have an Ay-Yuyuyah aboard this ship, and intend to retain it for a short time, while we gather information on the aliens in our system. I'll then bring it back here to work as an ambassador at large. Third, weapons. The rail gun seems to be an impressive defense against the current crop of aliens. For the Vorsh, their carapace absorbs laser and energy weapons, but are not proof against large-bore pistols. I recommend you engage some manufacturer to get you a large supply. Our AI, *Elizabeth* made an excellent modification of old Earth military pistols, that enable us to threaten armored soldiers. Fourth, replicator. As a miner I often had to make or craft parts for my ship. I acquired a large and sophisticated replicator, that enables my AI to build everything from a nut with a left-twist, to a runabout with impulse engines and static grips. We used the replicator to make higher quality golden drives than you provided, and on inspection, than the aliens use. I recommend them for all large combat ships. Fifth, I think it would be beneficial to have a sophisticated AI running all warships. They can communicate among themselves in ways undetectable by our enemies, they can be the best friend of any captain. And as we saw after the first attack on *Wanigan* the ship saved the crew."

"Impressive, Captain," said Kutuzov. But I am going to take the alien Ay-Yuyuyah off your hands so I can utilize it myself. Now, Commodore Yusef, what can you add to Captain Sokolov's briefing?"

Yusef informed the Admiral of the offer to give food to any alien that needs it. They had witnessed enough cannibalism on the two alien cultures they had run across, and the food served by the galley was far superior to anything the alien crews had been getting. He told him about the special food that makes Vorsh captains amenable to self-destructive behavior, that he gave his share of food to his crew, and it didn't have the suicide-inducing effect on the crew that it would have had on him. Apparently, there was a genetic difference between the captain and the crew. But now that ZhZhZhee was free of the restraint of the food. He was a free-thinker, and able to use his considerable talent and skills to work as an ambassador.

"I'll be bringing him with me too," said Kutuzov. "As for the food, I have already informed the government that we need to increase production in food, and sent emergency supplies with officers to all the Earth stations. I established procedures for registering and distributing the food to the aliens.

"Captain Sokolov, how did you discover the invisibility powers of the aliens?"

"Well sir, when mining for minerals among the asteroids, you can judge mass by its gravitational effect.

I used that same technology that I have on all my runabouts, as well as magnetic and electrical sensors. But the simplest is to use the gravimeter to see anomalies in space."

"I see. This kind of instrument is commercially available?"

"Yes, sir. There are varying levels of quality. If you have the option, get a survey level instrument. I would outfit all Navy ships with them, were I you."

"Thanks, Captain, I will."

"Sir, we captured quite a few of the alien's equipment that we intend to study," said Jeffrey. "We haven't had a lot of time to do that yet. But our engineer has spent time on the alien's gravitational plates, which they use for artificial gravity. He thinks he understands the theory and application – he is about to experiment with making gravitic plates to test – we stopped him from testing while we were also testing the FTL nature of the golden drives."

"Probably a good idea, Sokolov. Have him turn over his notes to us and give us the plates so we can continue the study." Jeffrey frowned at this.

"Sir, he is working on publishing his notes. This would do well for his career."

"I don't care about that. This is too important to let a third-rate engineer fool about with it. We have top people at headquarters, Top People." Jeffrey heard the capital letters. "You have your orders, Sokolov," the admiral said, standing up. "Get that equipment to me before I leave this boat.

"Speaking of orders, I want you to go back to Lagrange 3A and supply Lieutenant Omotunde with the food he will need to back up your and Yusef's feed-the-aliens-for-free program. Then patrol that region. Check out Lagrange 3B and 3C as well."

"Commodore," he turned his attention to Yusef, "Once you have refitted and taken on additional food, you are to patrol on the Mars orbit, service the stations in that area. And of course, martial all the fleet as necessary."

While Kutuzov was speaking with Yusef, Jeffrey had Elizabeth inform Heinz to deliver all his notes and the experimental plates to Kutuzov's shuttle. Also, the captured Vorsh equipment that they were preparing to study. And have ZhZhZhee and his female companions and Thelin report to the Admiral's shuttle for transport to the station.

By the time Admiral Kutuzov returned to his shuttle, the aliens and the crates of alien equipment were aboard, guarded by several no-nonsense Marines that came over on the shuttle. There were several palettes of foodstuffs that had been off-loaded from the shuttle, and two other shuttle loads were enroute to *Elizabeth* to deliver more food for the Lagrange stations in the 3 orbit.

When the Admiral had disembarked, Jeffrey inquired of the crew if they needed anything on the Naval station. When none indicated they needed to go aboard, Jeffrey informed the station he was about to resume his patrol, but the station communications officer told him to hold his position until further notice.

Jeffrey relieved Janet on the bridge, who thankfully retired to her quarters. He summoned Heinz to the bridge, who arrived a few minutes later. "Heinz," he began, "This has got to be a bit of a blow to your ego, but it isn't the end of the world. Do we still have any of the alien deck plates?"

Heinz looked at his captain quizzically, and replied, "Yes, sir. I sent what Elizabeth told me to send."

"Good. And you still have your notes?"

Again, Heinz wondered what his captain was getting at. "Of course."

"Good. You have a speed advantage over the Top Men that the admiral thinks can do better than you. I want you to design and produce anti-gravity decking for my ship. And I think Yuki should be involved, because there are other applications that she can come up with. But this is your project. I want daily reports."

Understanding came to Heinz. "You mean, I can continue my research?"

"I mean exactly that. But with the eye to immediate practical application. I want antigrav floors." Jeffrey stood and shooed the IntelTech engineer out. "Now get to work!"

Jeffrey puttered around the bridge, thinking about design changes he might want to implement. The bridge was large enough to hold six people at various stations, although there had never been that many people on the bridge at any one time. He liked the idea of having a secret secondary bridge, but that was attached to his own cabin, some distance away from the bridge.

Without the motors required to keep the ship rotating to provide a centrifugal gravitational effect, there could be much more room to alter the interior layout of the ship. Also, the energy required to rotate the huge vessel could be better spent elsewhere.

During his reverie, Elizabeth announced that they were being hailed from a small inner- system mining ship, *Mistral*, whose owner wished to speak with Jeffrey.

Jeffrey absent-mindedly told Elizabeth to invite the captain on board. But Elizabeth said that they requested the entire family to come aboard. This piqued Jeffrey's interest. "Okay, let's see what we have. Have someone escort them to the bridge."

A few minutes later, a Marine escorted the family of Chong Sul onto the bridge. They were still in their soft space suits, carrying their helmets. Their ship was tethered to the forward airlock and a flexible tube had extended to their ship and locked on, enabling them to traverse the gap between ships.

"Welcome to *Elizabeth*. I'm Captain Jeffrey Sokolov." He shook Chong Sul's hand, then Chong Lee's, and their daughter Chong Kim's. "What can I do for you?" he inquired.

After a few false starts, Chong Sul said, "We wanted to thank you personally for saving our lives, Captain."

The two females and their husband/father all bowed their heads in respect. "Um, I'm not sure what you are talking about."

They began to relate their story, when Jeffrey had them sit on the various seats on the bridge. He sat on the captain's chair, which gave him access to various screens of readouts. Elizabeth surreptitiously sent a graph of their defense of Earth and the first vessel they had destroyed, reminding Jeffrey that they had spared the ship it was mated to.

They continued to tell their tale, including the rape, their killing the pirate SurLeon, and the cleanup of their little ship. That was when they heard that their savior was *Elizabeth*. They vowed to visit and show some respect to the captain.

Jeffrey then told them he remembered the incident, but was not surprised at the evil nature of the pirate. He expressed his sorrow that he had not arrived early enough to prevent Mrs. Chong's sexual assault, but it appeared that she was a strong woman and was able to get over it.

"Captain," began Chong Lee. "As far as my family is concerned, nothing happened that cannot be forgotten. But you have done a great service to the Earth and to our family in particular. You are to be commended." She then turned to her daughter. "Kim?"

Kim reached inside her helmet and pulled out a wrapped package. She took it to Jeffrey, kissed him on the cheek and gave him the present. "Open it," she encouraged.

He opened the package, carefully setting aside the wrapping paper, and saw a stack of several hundred sheets of paper connected at one end by string. He looked at the top, and in an inked lettering, read "Elizabeth."

He turned the page and saw an ink drawing depicting the scene of the little family ship in orbit, collecting debris from the space around earth. The next page was almost identical, but slightly different. The next page, again different slightly. He was impressed by the meticulous detail in the obviously hand drawn work. He turned the next page and the next and the next. Finally, the fourteen-year-old could contain herself no longer, and said, "Here, let me help you," and took the stack, flipping the pages for Jeffrey so the scene appeared to be a vid, showing that day from the little family's perspective. It showed the pirate ship attaching itself to their little space boat, then showed the inside of their ship, with the three family members, how orders were broadcast to the evil SurLeon, how he prepared to send rocks flying to Earth to destroy several Earth cities, how he planned to kill the father, rape the mother and daughter, then make his getaway, how he had used kitchen wrap to tie up the father, undressed himself after the mother offered herself to protect the family, how the fourteen-year-old began to catch his attention by opening her jumpsuit to display her own pubescent chest, and how the mother killed the evil man. And the next bit was how *Elizabeth* destroyed the evil man's ship and the other ships around the planet that were poised to drop rocks on other Earth cities.

The last picture was the little girl asking her mom if she could change her name to Elizabeth.

"Captain, this is the work of my daughter," Chong Sul said. "But it fairly represents what happened to us. We want to show you our great respect."

Jeffrey could not contain the tears streaming from his eyes. It was one thing to have an Admiral slap him on the back for doing good work or his crew grateful for good fortune, planning and discipline, but to have this small family remind him that he was in fact an important cog in the wheel of life, struck him in his heart. He began, but the lump in his throat required he begin again. "Thank you. You made my day.

He asked Elizabeth to have the chief deliver some pastries, coffee and tea to the bridge. He then told the family about himself, about how he lost his wife, and named the ship after her, how the Navy had drafted him when he saved the *Wanigan* from insurgents and pirates. He told the family that the attack on Earth was, while carried out by the pirates, was really directed by the aliens whose ships could be seen outside.

When the pastries and beverages arrived, Jeffrey asked the family what their next plans were. They said they intended to sell their ship and see if they could find passage to one of the outer stations, perhaps provide service in a restaurant or other venue. Jeffrey asked "How much would you expect to receive for you little ship?

Chong Sul said he thought he could get half a million credits for it, Chong Lee said that it wasn't likely to get that much, but whatever they could get would go towards establishing them at one of the stations.

"One moment, please," said Jeffrey to the family. He entered a query for Elizabeth. She replied and he entered another query. After her next reply, he then turned back to the family. "How would you like to ride to Lagrange 3A with me?"

"Well," began Chong Lee, "That would be wonderful, but first we have to sell the Mistral. We don't have a lot of money to spend."

"As soon as we sell the Mistral," said Chong Sul, "We will have a little freedom to work with, but until we do, we will be held to where we are." Chong Kim had that look of disappointment every child eventually has when her dream began to be dashed.

"I have a proposition," said Jeffrey. "I will buy the Mistral. I will take you, Mr. Chong, and your family with me to Lagrange 3A. I will hire you three to do some work for me."

"What sort of work?" asked Chong Kim.

"Primarily, you will all work as spies. And as house keepers, and as an asteroid miner in my new ship, the Mistral. And other things as my mind comes to it."

"Spies?" The Korean woman asked. "That sounds dangerous."

"It can be. But for the most part, you are not expected to do anything more dangerous than mining and selling rock. And maintaining my safe house. And being a family to come home to, when I am able to come home. And perhaps, Mrs. Chong, you have some skill in the kitchen?"

"I am a very good cook with excellent kitchen skills, I'll have you know."

"Very good. I will set you and Chong Kim up with a small restaurant. Chong Sul, you will work for the Navy and for yourself mining rock using the Mistral. And you will keep your eyes and ears open. The Mistral will belong to me personally. The Navy will pay some of your salary, say fifty thousand credits? And you will report directly to me. You will appear to be an independent miner, and most of your work will be done doing that. As necessary, you will report anything that will pose a threat to Earth or the Navy. What do you say?"

"Spying doesn't seem to be a growth industry," said the Korean woman. "I am concerned for my daughter. My husband knows a bit about rock mining, but he is no spy. I know something about cooking, but I am no spy. My daughter knows about being a teenager, and is no spy."

"Most of your lives out in space, you will be nothing but a cook, a restaurant owner, a waitress. You will be a miner, Chong Sul. You will be a family man. But when I need information, you may be the best person to provide it. And when you report to my contacts, you will be far better protected then any of the other denizens of the station or of the asteroid belt."

"This seems satisfactory to me," said Chong Kim. "Husband?"

"I am satisfied," said Chong Sul, "Daughter?"

"Father, I like this man. I trust him. If my father and my mother believe in him, then, I too believe in him."

"Then," said Jeffrey, let's get the Mistral aboard."

CHAPTER TEN

Elizabeth had calculated how to get the Mistral aboard, and directed the crew on how to move the shuttles in order to make enough room to enable the small mining ship to place itself aboard. When Chong Sul parked the small ship in the shuttle bay, Jeffrey brought the crew together to introduce the family to the crew. He told them that the family of Chong Sul were his personal employees, and were to be treated with the utmost respect.

And until further notice, the family was not to be exposed to anything classified as secret or higher, as they were not military. Jeffrey decided that the family would use the Mistral as their cabin; power and communication lines were connected so the family had pretty much everything they needed.

And Jeffrey introduced the family to Elizabeth, much to the delight of Kim.

Heinz asked to see Jeffrey in private. They went to his cabin and sat. Heinz told him that he pretty well completed the development of the gravity plates he would use for artificial gravity, and aside from testing while using the golden drives, he was confident he could easily make enough plates to entirely cover all the decks of the ship with resources on board. Jeffrey told him to begin the fabrication, and the remote robots would begin installation.

The cluster of alien ships had worked itself down to just a couple, Jeffrey was given leave to carry out their orders. He took *Elizabeth* out of the traffic lanes, and began to head towards the asteroid belt and where Lagrange 3A would be when they arrived. They started out at .025 light. This was not fast considering what they were capable of, but far outclassed anything they could have done only a few months ago.

On the way Elizabeth's robots installed gravity plates on the decks throughout the ship. They had not been powered on until they were well away from Earth, but not yet at the orbit of Mars. When they decided to test the gravity plates, they stopped the rotation of the ship, letting everybody float in free-fall. Everyone who has been to space has been exposed to zero gravity, even though mostly they would use the rotational artificial gravity. Still, it was enough of a unique experience that several cohabiting couples used the opportunity to discover another aspect of their lives. Canoodling couples in zero g found both challenges and new sources of pleasure, while most decided that, while fun, the work to get to the fun was too much trouble to repeat often.

Powering on the gravity plates was a simple process and took very little electricity. Heinz designed the plates so they could be controlled in several ways, individually, in sections, or the entire ship. The first power-on was at ten percent Earth gravity. This was increased until they reached twice the gravity of Earth. Heinz held it at one G, and the robots then completed the installation because some of the cabins did not have the gravity plates installed yet.

Jeffrey then began increasing Elizabeth's speed, at first to .1 light, then .5, then 1, then 4 light, the fastest that this ship had ever gone. There were no negative effects of the gravitic plating while using the golden drive, which was a relief, because Jeffrey liked the idea of not having to rotate the ship. The only concern now was how long the plating would last – what was its mean time before failure, something impossible to calculate until you actually had some failures. And what would be the cause of those failures?

Now began the task of dismantling the rotating infrastructure of the old ship. They had brought the speed down to a more comfortable half-light. Which gave them a few more hours to the spot they calculated the Lagrange 3A station would be. Since the miscalculation with the Earth Station arrival based on their FTL travels, Elizabeth was more meticulous in her calculations. And it paid. They dropped to a less robust speed, .01 light, which again, was more than she would normally have traveled under her ion drives, but was a more reasonable speed in light of the traffic they would encounter around the station. As they neared the station's orbit, they decreased to a mere crawl, around twelve thousand kilometers per hour, with a visible deceleration to match the velocity of the station.

Elizabeth arranged for a berth for the *Mistral*, and had the family disembark from the shuttle bay and make their way to the dock, where they came up against a good deal of red tape. The family smiled through it all, but as The Administrator saw to the arrangements himself, they found themselves more and more deeply entangled in the red tape.

At the same time, the two shuttles also disembarked carrying a squad of Marines and a supply of foodstuffs for the alien distribution. The two shuttles docked alongside the *Mistral*, their Marines taking up station around the palettes of foodstuffs. The station security officers approached the Marines, jovially volunteered to take the palettes off the marines' hands, but the Marines declined. One of the sergeants asked for Lieutenant Omotunde, but the station security officers were evasive about the location of the Marine officer.

They reported this back up the chain of command to Lieutenant Bianca, who reported it to Jeffrey. Jeffrey had little love for Omotunde, but he was appointed to the station by the admiral, so he had little choice but to track down the Marine officer. Jeffrey asked Elizabeth to activate her clone on the station to see what she could find, but as soon as she did, the station security discovered the intrusion, so she shut herself down to avoid further detection.

Jeffrey was unsure how to address himself, as a Navy officer or as a miner. He decided for the first part to go undercover as a miner, rather than as the presence of the Navy in the region. He brought *Elizabeth* to dock on one of the external docks, instead of the more convenient internal wharfs as they had on the last visit. As it was, they were only a short distance from the *Mistral's* location. Upon their locking down, they found themselves accosted by station security, under the direct supervision of Security Lieutenant Andrade and a team of security officers, demanding to inspect *Elizabeth* for contraband.

Jeffrey appeared at the head of the gangway, and told Andrade by short distance radio that he was welcome to come aboard. The security team under the newly-made security lieutenant trooped aboard, all ten of them. Jeffrey provided him with his manifest of Naval food stuffs for the alien distribution, to be coordinated by Marine Lieutenant Omotunde.

"Sokolov, I'm placing you under arrest for violations of the Smuggling Act, for activities contrary to the peace of the public, and for piracy. You ship is forfeit and is now owned by the corporation."

"What corporation is that?" Jeffrey inquired.

"Never you mind" said the former security officer, now lieutenant. "Now get your hands up, come down that gangway with these officers, and surrender your ship."

"I don't think so," said Jeffrey.

"Take him!" Andrade yelled to his security detail. Two burly guards took Jeffrey by the arms. They placed an emergency bag over his head so they could take him out through the vacuum of space for a very short time.

Three accompanied Jeffrey into the airlock, the other seven stayed with Andrade in the suit room. They looked all around for defensive lasers, because Andrade had briefed them on the method of his finger removal the last time he had attacked this ship.

Andrade then radioed the team to get back in the ship, his voice was very strained as if he was under a great amount of weight. When the three security officers that accompanied Jeffrey out the airlock went back in, they dragged him in as well. They saw the other eight people staggered on the deck. Two quickly went to help their comrades and rapidly discovered their error – their mass increased by six times their normal weights. They fell directly to the floor as if sucked in by a small black hole. The officer that remained with Jeffrey stared incomprehensibly at the mess on the floor. Jeffrey shoved the remaining officer into the gravity field, then leaned on the wall while awaiting his own security team.

Ojo Torres and Audrey Svoboda showed up in their combat armor, armed with their pistols and a whole container of restraint bands. Elizabeth let up on one tile at a time so Torres could drag one of the security officers away from the gaggle and Sneaky could disarm and secure that officer. When one of the officers attacked Torres – always a mistake – he quickly knocked him out, but Audrey came up with an idea. "Elizabeth," she said, "Can you give us a few robots to help with this?" Torres immediately recognized the utility of this. They removed the unconscious officer from the plate, cuffed him, and made room for the robots to pull the rest of the officers from the gravitic plates.

The two spider-like robots, the size of Galapagos Tortoises clamped on the armored arms and legs of the officers, one at a time, under the direction of Elizabeth. Then they would drag the officer over the still-activated heavy gravitic plates, for Torres or Sneaky to cuff and put away.

Once all the officers were bound, disarmed, and their helmets removed, they were escorted to the now frequently used brig, and attached to the wall rings. One or more of the officers was likely to have nightmares about spiders or robots or robot spiders for a long time to come.

Torres, aware of the benefits of positive reinforcement said to Elizabeth, "That was good thinking, Elizabeth. Holding them down without killing them. Good work."

"THANK YOU, SERGEANT TORRES. YOU MAKE A GIRL BLUSH."

"Please monitor the prisoners, and let us know if there is anything we need to know."

"YES SERGEANT."

One of the radios in the collected effects of the officers started speaking – with the voice of the Administrator. "Well, report! Do you have him in custody? Report, damn you!"

"Well, I think that goes to show who is behind all this." said Jeffrey to no one in particular. He assured that Elizabeth cut the gravitic plate back to Earth normal, then walked into the brig with the radio that was broadcasting the increasingly desperate calls from the Administrator.

"Mister Andrade, it seems someone is looking for an update. Would you like to clue the Administrator in with a SITREP?" asked

Jeffrey. Andrade just shook his head. He seemed to have some difficulty getting his breath. "Elizabeth, would you increase the oxygen in here, Mr. Andrade seems to be having difficulty with his breathing."

Jeffrey left the prisoners to stew in the brig, went into the corridor outside the brig and asked, "Elizabeth, do you think you can find Lieutenant Omotunde?"

"I WILL SEE WHAT I CAN FIND. ALSO, CAPTAIN, IT SEEMS THAT THERE ARE PROBLEMS WITH THE MISTRAL. DOCKING AUTHORITY HAS BEEN REVOKED AND ACCORDING TO RADIO REPORTS, MISTRAL WAS IMPOUNDED."

"That sounds ominous." said Jeffrey. "Okay, have one of the squads of Marines investigate."

"VERY WELL, CAPTAIN."

The Marines guarding the shuttles and palettes of foodstuffs for the aliens split up, the group that stayed, A squad, redeployed and raised their alert status. The pilot of their shuttle strapped on his pistol, jacked a round into the chamber, and closed the shuttle bay for security. B squad loaded themselves into their own shuttle, which took them to the location of the berth Mistral was docked at. Before disembarking onto the wharf, the Marines readied their weapons. The Sergeant made sure they would not look particularly menacing unless and until they received resistance. They then exited from the shuttle, only to find themselves surrounded by a dozen security officers.

Marine gunnery Sergeant McCalum walked over to the leader of the security officers, another Sergeant, switched his radio to the frequency used by station security, and inquired of the problem with the little mining ship.

"What's that to you, Sergeant?" asked the security police Sergeant. "We know this ship. What's going on Sarge?"

"We were told to impound the ship and search for contraband." Gunnery Sergeant McCalum triggered the switch that rebroadcast his conversation securely to *Elizabeth.*

"In that order? Sounds backwards to me. Where did your orders come from?" McCalum asked taking a slightly more aggressive pose. His squad took the cue and brought their weapons to a relaxed position that didn't look like they were really pointing at the security officers.

The station security officers noticed the shift in position of the Marines, but while they didn't see a real threat from the Marines, they felt a touch more fear, they felt that the Marines were now a slight bit more alert, and while not obviously threatening, they appeared as if they could take command of the entire wharf in a second.

The security police Sergeant said, "My orders came directly from the top. Looks like something big is going on, they have had us impound one out of ten ships on the wharf." Then the police Sergeant asked, "What ship are you from? We didn't see any Navy boats coming in."

"We came in under the radar. Big things happening."

"Don't I know it! Now get out of our way, we need to take control of this ship." The station security police Sergeant then motioned for his officers to get more aggressive in crowding the Marines. The Marines already had moved the slight distance from 'alert' to 'ready'.

"Sergeant, you do not want to take on the Marines. Your weapons will have minimal effect on our armor. Ours, on the other hand will shatter your armor and kill you quick. Now drop your weapons, DROP YOUR WEAPONS NOW! DROP THEM!" His voice got louder and louder as he moved more aggressively toward the Sergeant. He drew his pistol and pointed it directly in the faceplate of the Sargent's suit helmet. The aggressive moves had the desired effect – none of the security police reacted against the Marines, they allowed their weapons to fall to the ends of the lanyards that connected them to their suits and put their hands in the air.

Two of the Marines shouldered their projectile rifles and aimed them at the entire gaggle of police. The other two went to each of the officers, removed the weapons, and had them kneel on the dock. The security police kept their hands on their helmets.

Elizabeth notified the Marine Sergeant that the police officer's radios had been blocked so they couldn't call for help. The pilot of the shuttle, armed with a pistol stood guard inside the shuttle's passenger bay as one of the Marines escorted security officers, one at a time to the bay and secured him or her to the bench. After all the officers were secured, the Marines came aboard except for McCalum and one of the Marine privates, who stood guard at the Mistral. The Navy shuttle took off, delivered three of the Marines to re-join the A squad guarding the food cache for the aliens, then took their prisoners to *Elizabeth* to join their fellow prisoners in the brig.

As McCalum and the private took up positions outside the Mistral, Chong Sul appeared at the head of the gangway tube and radioed the Marines to come aboard. McCalum didn't see why not, so entered the little ship. Before going aboard, McCalum notified Elizabeth that he and the private were going aboard the Mistral on the invitation of Chong Sul. They entered the airlock, entered the main cabin – the combination living quarters and bridge of the small family ship – and saw both Chong Lee and Chong Kim sitting primly at a built-in bench against the bulkhead. Their mouths were tightly closed, but their eyes expressed fear. They did not show recognition or any emotion but fear.

The private removed his helmet, and expressed greeting, but was interrupted by a neural disruptor gun barrel put against his head. Sergeant McCalum called out "Mayday. Mistral under attack," on the open channel. He then described the scene as he saw it.

Elizabeth replied to the Sergeant in quiet tones, "SERGEANT, HELP IS ON THE WAY. YOUR SUIT CAMERAS ARE NOW BROADCASTING. LOOK AROUND."

McCalum turned his head so the helmet camera could pick up the scene. Elizabeth displayed the images for Janet on the bridge.

The man holding the neural disruptor against the head of the private told McCalum to surrender his weapons. As McCalum was finishing his video sweep of the cabin, he saw another man had just appeared and was pointing another neural disruptor at the woman and the girl. The audio input of the armored suit picked up a whimper from Chong Kim. He saw tears in her eyes, her mother was shaking, trembling in fear. Her eyes looked up at Sergeant McCalum – he read fear, hope, embarrassment and a whole slew of other emotions in her inaudible plea.

He heard another voice, the voice of one not already in the cabin, say, "Marine, have you ever seen what a neural disruptor does to a person at close range? If you don't want to see it again, you will remove your helmet and drop your weapons." He paused a moment, then removed the helmet – pressed the unlock button and gave it a clockwise twist – and pulled it up over his head. The air inside the cabin smelled of fish and soya and onions and garlic and ginger and fear.

"Whoever you are, you are playing with fire," said McCalum.

"Oh, I don't know," said a voice with an old English or South African White or Australian accent. McCalum couldn't quite place it. "We've been doing this for some time now. We took your Marine buddies real easy like. Didn't need to kill one of them. Y'see, that's what happens when you have a plan. And don't really care who gets hurt." The man with the voice stepped out from the aft hatch, which lead to the engine compartment and holds, pointed a small flachette needler at the Marine private, and emptied a clip into his head. The stunned look on everybody's faces etched into McCalum's mind. He knew there was nothing he could do for his man, his brain had been sliced into hundreds of pieces by the razor-sharp flat needles which cut through the bone of his skull on the way in, but stuck on the bone on the opposite side of his head. That same stunned look was like applause to the killer. He beamed with pride at his audience reaction.

"Who are you guys?" asked McCalum, his voice shaky but strong. "Why are you doing this?"

"We're members of the Corporation," said the English or South African or Australian pirate.

We've taken over this space. It's about time too, 'cause there's nothing I crave more than power, and the way it was there was no way I could have any. Now look at me!"

McCalum held his tongue. He knew Elizabeth was recording all this, and he knew help was on the way. If he could just hold on long enough to aid however he could. He counted three of the pirates on the ship, three non-combatants (the Chong family,) and himself. Elizabeth was to be the ace card. "Tell me about your 'Corporation.' Is that like the old Earth 'Syndicate' – shorthand for Mafia?" He asked.

"Got it in one. The boss of the 'Corporation' has been running pirate ships for hundreds of years. We only moved to space in the last fifty."

"Something we discovered," said McCalum, "is that most pirate activity around here is controlled by aliens."

The English or South African or Australian burst out laughing.

"I haven't heard that one before! With all these ships out here, how come I haven't seen one that didn't come from Earth? No flying saucers out here in space!"

Just then, a crackling was heard on the pirate's radio. He picked it up off the table, keyed in his own code, and began speaking. "This is Macci."

The radio seemed a little garbled, but McCalum heard a voice speaking. Macci said, "Andrade, that you?" The voice mumbled in affirmation.

Then it said, "We're sending reinforcement. There were some Marines outside your ship."

"Don't bother, we already got them, killed one of them, about to kill the other."

"Hold him there. We need that one for a technical" then something unintelligible, "on his ship. We'll send an escort to pick," something else unintelligible, "up."

The oddly accented person then called out to one of the other pirates, "Go ahead and get this bucket started, we're taking off soon as they come for this...gentleman."

A moment later, there was a chime from outside the airlock. He told the non-combatant Chong Sul, to put his helmet back on, let the escort in, and remember his wife and daughter with neural disruptors pointed at their heads.

As Torres, Sneaky and Bianca entered the small ship's cabin from the airlock, they heard one of the pirates call out, "Damn thing won't start."

"Oh yeah?" said Bianca, "I used to drive these things. I know some secrets." She nodded to the oddly accented villain and went forward to the pilot's cockpit. She saw that the pirate didn't have

     ELIZABETH, *ELIZABETH*

a spacesuit on, she thought about removing her helmet to ease the concern of the pirate at the controls, but instead said, "I've got this, flipped a couple innocuous switches on then off, and the engine compartment began generating a loud humming noise. While getting up, she applied an adhesive patch to the back of the neck of the pirate, then walked back into the cabin, where Torres was putting the helmet back on McCalum. He picked up McCalum's weapons from the floor, made sure the plastic ties were secure on both his gauntlets, (while doing nothing to attach the two ties together,) and turned him around to take him through the airlock.

Janet then knelt down in front of the two Korean females, placed a round, orange sticker, about ten centimeters across, on their chests. Placed another one on Chong Sul, then turned to the South African, English and/or Australian pirate, and explained, "In order to get off this boat without getting killed, everybody's got to have an ID patch. The orange ones are for...civilians. These silver ones are for us. Wear it on your skin, here," and she placed the patch on the back of his neck. She then turned to the last pirate, had him turn around and slapped it on his neck. She then joined Torres and McCalum in the airlock. Before the airlock was cycled, there was a buzzing sound from inside the cabin. Janet went back to find the two pirates on the floor twitching as if from a massive electric shock or a grand mal seizure. She drew her pistol and looked into the pilot's area, only to be shot in the helmet by a flachette needler. The flachettes ricocheted off her helmet's face plate, although a couple embedded themselves into the hard carbon-plastic spot above her forehead. The pirate looked with amazement at the damage that hadn't been done, and at the pistol in her gauntleted hand. Janet wasted no time, just aimed at center mass, pulled the trigger, and watched the look of amazement on the face of the pirate, then pain, then terror, then death.

Janet grabbed the dead would-be pilot out into the cabin, to see Torres, McCalum looking on at the Chong family as they shared a group hug over the twitching pirates. Sneaky brought out another person that had been in the engineering part of the ship. He swore he knew nothing. But when prodded by Audrey's index finger pressing down on a pressure point behind his collar bone, he became much more knowledgeable.

He told them that the still-twitching man with the odd accent was from New Zealand a small place near Australia. That they worked for the Corporation, that the Corporation's president was the Administrator, and that they were all in a heap of trouble.

They bundled the pirates up in emergency pressure bags, with pressurized oxygen canisters inside, then took them back to Elizabeth, and put them in her brig, which was now getting rather crowded.

Janet stayed behind to debrief the Chong family. But they had questions of their own. Chong Lee asked "What was that noise when they thought the engine started?"

Janet explained, "Elizabeth knew your engine, and could communicate with your computer, so she had the computer generate that hum as soon as I flipped those switches. I almost blew it – I forget which switches to flip, so I did both of them!" They all laughed at that.

Chong Kim asked, "What are these patches?"

"A little subterfuge," replied Janet. "We assumed that they were holding people as work slaves or sex slaves or something, so we told them that you needed these to be identified. It made it easier to convince them they needed to be identified too. These orange ones are just plastic patches, but those held a powerful charge, they work like neural disruptors. The guy in the cockpit took his off, so I had to kill him."

Chong Sul asked, "How did you know about the one in the engineering section?"

"We didn't. That's why we sent Sneaky in. She was trained as a Ninja, so she could go most anywhere and discover things that needed discovering."

At this Chong Kim's eyes opened wide. "Really? A real Ninja?"

"Yep."

"Oh wow!" Her parents looked on their daughter in a not-quite disapproving way, but then accepted that, oh well, fourteen-year-olds loved Ninjas, and that was that. Jeffrey was livid. "How the Hell in the short time we've been gone could they have developed such a large and powerful organization?" The rest of the officers and non-coms sat quietly, not electing to say anything until Jeffrey calmed down. Finally, Janet scooted her chair back, picked up her tea and sipped.

Then she said, "I think it's obvious – the same kind of forces that we've been battling have been organizing out here. They have resources that the miners and station managers don't, and they do have those mind-numbing or mind-manipulating ray guns. The only reason we've been able to take them on is some foresight and good luck."

Jeffrey considered what she said, replied, "Yeah, maybe you're right – organizing people by enhancing their avarice and greed, their ruthlessness. That makes sense. I think it's time we gave up looking like everyday miners, we now have got to be openly Navy. Thoughts?"

Torres said he thought they should have done that long before. Heinz agreed, thinking that they couldn't all be spies; just some of them. Janet concurred, Gunnery Sergeant McCalum agreed.

Nobody disagreed. So, Jeffrey told Elizabeth to have the Marines guarding the food on the dock bring it back in their shuttles, and return to *Elizabeth.* He told McCalum to rest the Marines because they were likely to see more action soon. When the shuttles were back on board, they needed to unload the palettes before they knocked off, but Elizabeth reminded Jeffrey she had remotes and large robots that could do that.

Jeffrey dispatched Torres and Sneaky to escort the Chong family to the safe house complex, they were assigned to the suite called China, but the family requested that they rename it Korea, because that was their nationality of origin. They settled in easily, liking the furnishings that Janet had selected for the safe house. Torres showed them the hidden cache of guns and ammunition that they were absolutely never to touch unless someone was in serious peril.

Lee was shown the family credit – a significant amount – that could be used to acquire a space to open her restaurant. Sul told Sneaky they would begin taking family walks every day, giving them the opportunity to look for likely locations, also establishing a pattern of behavior that would make them seem like less than they were.

The *Elizabeth* disengaged from the dock clamps and pulled away from the station without any problems. After moving a short distance into the cloud of ships surrounding the station, she pulled up and maintained her position about ten kilometers from the station. Elizabeth began a survey of all the ships in the region, then looked for anomalies that would signal aliens using their invisibility circuits.

Elizabeth reported to Jeffrey that she had found sixteen out of the nearly thousand ships in the cloud surrounding the station that had more than twice the mass they should have – as if they were concealing invisibility-protected vessels. Jeffrey began drawing up his own combat plans, but asked Elizabeth to do the same. When they were both finished (Elizabeth was finished shortly after Jeffrey stopped speaking,) they compared notes. Jeffrey and Elizabeth both came to the same conclusion on a first, then second, then third strategies. Then contingencies, then escape routes and destinations in case of serious trouble. Jeffrey reported his activities to Admiral Kutuzov via the book code, but also made a less explicit report via radio.

After twelve hours, with the crew mostly rested and ready, Jeffrey had them all don their under- suits (the special Elizabeth manufactured emergency jumpsuit that acted as a second layer of armor and could protect its wearer for short times in no pressure space conditions,) and their full hard-shell Navy suits. Every Marine was outfitted with its own communications circuits beyond the normal Marine issue, and everybody went around the ship armed with projectile weapons – both pistols and rifles for the Marines.

Jeffrey had Elizabeth illuminate the ship so it was unmistakable. The remotes had gone onto the hull and painted the word NAVY on the surface in four locations in large letters. All hands were sent to general quarters, all weapons manned, and Marine patrols were established for internal security. Jeffrey had Elizabeth broadcast a loud over-modulated foghorn-like tone on every radio frequency used in the standard communications spectrum.

Then she broadcast "THIS IS NAVY WARSHIP *ELIZABETH*. ALL VESSELS IN THE VACINITY OF Lagrange 3A YOU ARE WARNED THAT THERE IS A HOSTILE ALIEN PRESENCE AMONG YOURSELVES. ALL HUMAN VESSELS ARE TO LEAVE THIS AREA AT THE EARLIEST OPPORTUNITY. COMBAT OPERATIONS ARE ABOUT TO COMMENCE. ANY VESSEL MOVING AGAINST NAVY SHIPS AND OTHER RESOURCES WILL BE FIRED ON. ANY VESSEL FIRING ON NAVY VESSELS WILL BE DESTROYED.

"ALL ALIENS; THE USE OF YOUR INVISIBILITY CIRCUITS IS AGAINST THE LAW IN THE HUMAN-CONTROLLED SOLAR SYSTEM. YOU WILL NOT BE WARNED AGAIN.

"THE NAVY HAS ORDERED THAT ALL ALIENS MAY HAVE FREE FOOD AT ANY EARTH-BASED STATION. ALIENS NEED TO REGISTER WITH THE NAVY OR MARINES AT THAT FACILITY. THERE ARE NO OBLIGATIONS FOR THIS FOOD. WE OFFER PEACE, BUT WILL RESPOND WITH FINALITY TO ANY HOSTILE ACT."

Then the *Elizabeth* moved to one of the ships that she identified as having anomalous characteristics, aimed her forward rail gun at the center of gravity of the vessel, which was ten meters off its hull, and opened fire with a half second burst. The effect was immediate; pieces began flying off the alien vessel that had attached itself to the miner's ship, then the alien ship un-disappeared.

Heinz had been monitoring radio signals and caught hundreds of comments from many different ships that were pulling out of the area but still monitoring, essentially rubber-necking, the events going on around the station. The human ships were dumbfounded that there were aliens at all, let alone among them. The alien ship that had been attacked detached itself from the miner's ship and generated a pulse of energy, heat and light and radiation, projected at Elizabeth, but fizzled once it reached her hull. Then both of Elizabeth's rail guns opened up, spraying projectiles up and down the vessel, cutting it in small pieces. A series of secondary then tertiary explosions rocked the alien ship, all its inside parts open to space. A cloud of gas escaping from the ship, it's atmosphere, dissipated readily.

Then, to make it obvious that the Navy ship knew the locations of the alien vessels, *Elizabeth* drove to the next nearest anomalous reading, aimed at the gravity well alongside the miner' ship, and fired a half-second burst. Like the first, pieces flew off this ship, it switched off its invisibility circuits, but the captain of this ship had the good sense to not challenge the Navy ship.

All the alien ships followed suit – each turned off their invisibility circuits, detached themselves from the miner's ships they had captured, and backed away without charging up their weapons.

Jeffrey broadcast a demand that the leader of the aliens contacts him. One of the ships farther back broadcast on the same frequency, "I am in charge here." The video image that accompanied the audio was of an alien biped with similar characteristics to the Vorsh, but were obviously not Vorsh.

"Is that so? What is your race? What do you call yourself?" asked Jeffrey.

"We are the Kang. We are in charge here. I am Chthliki, the leader of the leaders. Who are you?"

"I am Captain Jeffrey Sokolov. I represent the government of the Humans, I am captain of this ship, which is a Navy vessel. My authority comes from Admiral Kutuzov of Earth Navy, and this ship enforces my authority."

Chthliki demanded, "What is your interest, here, Human?"

"I am creating and enforcing order. I am ensuring that all aliens within my solar system obeys our laws, and are aware of those laws. For instance, if we find any alien vessels with their invisibility circuits active, we are authorized to destroy those ships without warning. If we find aliens affecting Humans by hypnotic means or otherwise controlling them, we will stop that. In my last encounter, one of the Vorsh pretended he didn't understand English. We are aware that they do. I destroyed his ship."

"What is this about food?"

"We found that the Vorsh and a few other races have been eating themselves. Cannibalism is against our laws here. Eating any sentient species is right out. Therefore, we found if we offer food, the aliens don't have a lot of things to be cranky about."

"We are aware that the Vorsh captains have special food that make them live according to their regimented way – including dying off. We are not interested in such food."

"I can understand that. We are offering food without any psychoactive chemicals. Tell me, Chthliki, what do you call your ship?"

"I call it ship," Chthliki responded in his gruff deep bass voice.

"And how do you differentiate this ship from others?"

"All ships the same. Ship I am in is my ship."

"So what you are telling me is that you don't have individual names for ships. So the ship that gets blown up by my ship, or the ship that blows itself up because of a manufacturing defect or the ship that dies because the crew dies, you have no tracking?"

"Why would we want that? The captain that loses his ship doesn't deserve to be remembered. The ship that loses its crew only awaits a new crew and a new captain. The ship that was defective should be forgotten."

"Ah," said Jeffrey. "This explains why we are able to defeat your races so easily. Well I asked who is in charge here, you indicated yourself. I will correct you. I am in charge here. Attempts to do any of the things I told you not to do will result in your destruction. If any of your ships do what I said not to do, they too will be destroyed. If you and your ships persist, you will all be banned from Human space. If you wish this free food, we will register you and give you enough for your crew."

Jeffrey told Janet to have a squad of Marines check out the miner ship that Chthliki's ship just vacated. Within a minute, a shuttle carried them to the vacated miner ship. The cameras on all the Marines' helmets and suit armor displayed in a separate screen on the Bridge. Jeffrey saw it the same time the young Sergeant did; piles of human bodies. Sergeant McSweeney said over his radio, "Sir, there are some Marines among the dead here."

"Get a body count, McSweeney. We'll bring over body bags. I want a lot of images for forensic examination and prosecution. Go carefully."

"Aye, sir."

Jeffrey heard him pass on the order to his men. He ordered Torres to collect body bags and take them over to the ship in a runabout. He then turned to the comm console and addressed Chthliki.

"Why are there dead people on that ship you just vacated?"

"Food."

A leaden feeling dropped Jeffrey's stomach to the deck. "Are there any others you harvested for food still alive?"

"Yes."

"Good. Keep them that way. We will collect all humans in your custody. There will be no further taking of any sentient being for food, dead or alive."

"I do not understand your refusal to recycle humans." The gruff Chthliki said.

"I realize you don't understand. That is less important than your compliance. Do you understand that non-compliance will result in your loss of your ship, your honor, your life, your crew?"

"Yes, I understand that."

"Perhaps one of our Human spiritual people can explain to your satisfaction our ways, perhaps not. You may attempt to find out, but while learning, you will comply." Jeffrey held his emotions in check, his voice was steady during his discussion. He felt like reaching through the comm and strangling the Kang leader.

Jeffrey had Heinz take the human prisoners in the brig one at a time, out to an interrogation room, and begin learning what he could about how the prisoners got to doing the things they did. And what did they know about the aliens and what the aliens were doing to the people they turned over to the aliens.

When Heinz returned an interrogated prisoner, and after taking another out, the prisoners discussed among themselves what was being asked, and started concocting a story. Of course, Elizabeth was monitoring those exchanges and transcribed the entire conversation.

Jeffrey ordered the other squad out to another of the ships the aliens had vacated, with a large supply of body bags and emergency suits. Between the two shuttles, they made fast work. There were less than a hundred live people among the ships, and a like number of dead.

The survivors were thoughtless, like zombies, they only did as they were told, which was a blessing, somewhat, because it made them easier to handle. Janet said she would find some way to address their mental problem.

The dead were laid on the hanger deck, row upon row. Heinz walked his interrogation subjects past the rows of body bags, then past the rows of 'zombies' to help focus the shame and guilt and remorse that he could draw out of them. The effect was actually significant on most of the detainees, but the leaders were hardened to what they saw.

Jeffrey then took the *Elizabeth* to the station again, but instead of docking, parked a thousand meters from the dock near the *Mistral*. He had the two shuttles busily going back and forth, first delivering the dead, lining them up in rows on the dock, then bringing the palettes of food back onto the dock. Jeffrey had Elizabeth request a baggage train to pick up the bodies and the food, but none was forthcoming. Jeffrey then asked Elizabeth how long it would take to make a simple and quick baggage train.

"CAPTAIN, I CAN HAVE A THREE-CAR TRAIN IN ONE HOUR."

"Do it, please. Have I told you recently how much I appreciate you?"

"CAPTAIN! YOU MAKE ME BLUSH!"

"Blush away, old girl."

The train finished, it was delivered in stacked parts on the two shuttles. Digger and Smitty came along to assemble it for the Marines, Digger would drive, Smitty would run shotgun with a real shotgun.

McCalum accompanied the two with the baggage train full of dead humans. The airlock was the first obstacle – it would not accept the long train – three-meter long carts behind a small tractor. The three Marines disconnected the train and put each cart alongside the others. This allowed them to go through the airlock, barely, and on the far side, Mccalum and Digger began re- assembling the train, while Smitty went back through the airlock to get the tractor. Once they were all back together, they drove the baggage train to the dock level hospital to use the refrigerated morgue. When they arrived, the medical staff seemed nervous, which put the three military men on a higher level of alertness. McCalum notified Elizabeth that there was something going on, that she should monitor them.

After unloading the bodies, they told the pathologist that the Navy needed complete autopsies, including toxicology reports, and to spare no expense. If they needed to bring other physicians to do autopsies, then they were authorized.

Then they returned to the dock, again having to disconnect the train and reassemble it on the other side, both coming and going, with the stacks of palettes of food for the aliens. Elizabeth found a vacant warehouse, which Sergeant McCalum commandeered for distribution of Alien food. They quickly delivered the food to the warehouse and left the baggage train inside it.

Sergeant McSweeney drew the short straw so his squad held the first watch in the warehouse. The A team set up defensive electronics, defensive explosives, and redundant brick and water-bag barriers.

B squad returned to Elizabeth. Jeffrey had them rest for the next operation. Heinz reported to Jeffrey and Janet the findings of his various interrogations of the prisoners. Most of the security officers had been recruited over the previous three weeks, there were a total of around one hundred security officers, the population of the station was twenty thousand, so the number of security officers was not out of line. The odd thing was the series of orders that came from the administrator and his office. The first one was to ambush and arrest all of the Marines deployed on the station. None of the security officers admitted to knowing the disposition of those Marines. They were disgusted and ashamed when they learned what their attacks on the Marines had done.

Heinz had learned that there was an athletic gymnasium in the center of the station that was the gathering place for the people whom they had imprisoned. Where they went from there was a mystery to all of them. When asked about Lieutenant Omotunde, none of the security officers knew anything. Andrade said he was tasked to get Omotunde, but was unable to find him.

When told about the alien intrusions into Human space, all the security officers were skeptical. None would admit to ever having seen an alien or one of their ships. When Elizabeth displayed videos of the Kang, Vorsh and Ay-Yuyuyah, the only response among the security officers was some of them, particularly ones that had only recently been recruited, began a trance-like appearance, their eyelids fluttering, their breathing becoming shallow, their muscles becoming flaccid.

Their fellow, more experienced officers had no such reaction, and failed to acknowledge when seeing their brother and sister officers so react.

This gave Jeffrey an idea; if the aliens had conditioned the officers to not see them, perhaps they were moving around the station openly, not concerned about being seen. Jeffrey asked Elizabeth if she could tap into the station's security cameras, but Elizabeth reported that the security had been tightened on the station, that every attempt to tie into the network was thwarted. This reduced Jeffrey's options, but he began to make plans for the restoration of order in the station.

After the Marines had a good six hours of uneventful rest, he assembled the entire crew. The A squad still in the warehouse on the station, listened in on an open secure line. "We are going to be tied up in several operations. Our primary objective will be to arrest the administrator and take over his office. Following that, we will need to secure the network, and impose our own security on it. Elizabeth is working on finding a way to overcome the security they have placed on the network.

"Our second objective is to find and rescue any of the Marines that have been either captured or have escaped and are in hiding. We are especially looking for Lt. Omotunde. If you find Lt. Omotunde, you are to take charge of him, we will determine his competence, you just bring him back to us. You do not follow his orders. Clear?" All the crew and Marines responded with "Clear!"

"While all of these objectives are being pursued, we are also on the lookout for evidence of aliens among us. We are all subject to some hypnotic message that makes us ignore their presence, we think that it relates to an earlier computer virus that affects humans as well as computers. We think your hard suits are immune to this virus, but you may not be. Therefore, you will all wear your armor, and look only through the video rather than directly through the faceplates. This is an order. Clear?" Again, all hands responded, "Clear!"

Elizabeth is our go–between. She will monitor all of your suits, all of your communications, the video and audio images that appear in your cameras. If you lose communication with Elizabeth, a tone will trigger in your suit that sounds like this," - Elizabeth played the tone for all to hear. "This is an indication that you need to contact the ship via secure radio. If you cannot contact the ship, contact your next superior, Marines, contact your sergeant, Sergeants, contact Lieutenant Bianca. Navy, contact your Petty Officers. Petty officers, contact Lieutenant Bianca. Clear?"

"Clear!"

"I want all suits fully charged, a full array of weapons for Marines, especially your projectile weapons. The new carbines use the same ammunition that the pistols use. Carry enough cartridges. Carry enough charge for your charge and plasma weapons. Do not be distracted. If some cute chick flutters her eyes at you, don't even smile back. When we are done, you can retrace your steps and find her! Clear?"

"Clear!" followed by chuckling.

"Navy pilots, keep your shuttles at ready, you may have a quickly retreating squad to pick up. Cover them, protect yourselves and your boat. Clear?"

The two navy pilots reported in an underwhelming shout, "Clear!"

"The enemy has proven to be ruthless. We don't have that luxury. Yet. We need to be aware of the integrity of the station, so no poking holes in outer walls!" He got some chuckles. "The enemy has used civilians as shields – not to mention food – we do not wish to allow them to do that. Find the alien that is doing this sort of thing and take it out. Again, Elizabeth is working on methods of doing that very thing.

"As you discover new pertinent information, speak it into your suit, Elizabeth will note it and the context you were in when it occurred. This will help us in our intelligence estimates. Okay team, be careful! You take off in five!"

Janet stepped forward and yelled, "Marines! What do you say?"

The Marines responded with the statement picked up from an earlier, United States, Earth Marines from previous centuries - "Oo-Rah!"

Jeffrey called out, "Sergeant, see me!"

Gunnery Sergeant McCalum stepped up to Captain Sokolov, saluted and said, "Sir?"

"Elizabeth has put together some of her little spider robots. They are going to help us set up our own secondary network. I want everyone to carry at least one, and place it when they are told. You carry enough for A Squad."

"Yes, sir."

"Now if you need backup, I am arming everyone else on this ship. My crew, Torres, Mbaka, Smith, Svoboda are actually active duty Marines. This is not publicly known, and I want to keep it that way. But if you need help, call on 'C squad.'"

"Understood, sir. Thanks."

"Go get 'em."

"Oo-Rah!"

Then Jeffrey walked over to the cook. "Chief, what combat training have you had?"

She said, "I have a black belt in Judo I got at the Kodokan in Tokyo. I also am a trained sniper with 96 percent accuracy."

"Badass!"

"Indeed, sir. Not a Seal or other special forces, but you want a shot placed in a specific place at a specific time, I'm your man. Woman. Sir."

"You have a sniper rifle here?" asked Jeffrey.

"No, I thought I left that part of my life behind when I took the life of a cook. Sorry."

"CAPTAIN," interrupted Elizabeth, "WE HAVE A SNIPER RIFLE YOU TRADED FOR SOMEONE'S FINGER."

"Thanks! Good work, Elizabeth." He told the Chief where the rifle was located, then told her to make sure it was fully charged, and grab a pistol and carbine and enough ammo to keep herself safe. He also ordered her out of her apron and into her Navy heavy armor.

"Elizabeth, please analyze the ship's vulnerabilities, and develop a few strategies for each, with the eye toward completing our mission."

"EFFORTING"

"Torres, Heinz."

The two came up to the Captain, and gave a relaxed salute, and Torres said, "Sir?"

"I want you to select the most reliable and knowledgeable prisoners, segregate them from the rest, and sit with them while showing several camera angles. Watch their reactions, ask them questions, and if they know something that will give us an edge, report it. Elizabeth will monitor."

"Aye sir." Heinz said. Torres saluted, then the two went to take several of the non-coms and the officer to the interrogation room. Elizabeth illuminated the walls of the interrogation room with video images from several locations, including the warehouse, several of the milling- about Marines and one of the shuttles.

Jeffrey then went to the shuttle that the Marines were boarding with their equipment, and told McCalum that he just learned that the chief – their cook – was a sniper and an expert martial artist. If he could place her to some advantage, just call.

Then the shuttle was off.

CHAPTER ELEVEN

In which aliens very subtly try to defend themselves. Aliens are hungry. The bridge gets a makeover, The Administrator is arrested. Janet has a bun in the oven. Jeffrey becomes the Governor of the entire Lagrange 3 orbit.

The shuttle landed on the dock, deployed B Squad with the two Navy medics. In such combat units, it had become tradition to have the medics that deploy with Marines come from the Navy, for some undefined reason the Marines never developed their own medical corps. Still, as the Marines were a part of the Navy, as were all other military forces since the Navy went to space, it was a moot point.

The deployment went well, Elizabeth had provided a 'Mule', a remotely controlled motorized cart, to carry the heavy equipment and crates of ammunition and other supplies to support their operation. One Marine controlled the mule while they walked warily to the airlock at the station end of the wharf. At the airlock, Sgt. McCalum keyed in the code to open the airlock, and nothing happened. He tried another code, and still nothing happened. Elizabeth was monitoring him, and told McCalum to place one of her remotes directly on the keypad.

The remote grabbed hold of the box to steady itself, and began sending thin thread feelers into the box, the feelers contained minute electrical connections as well as hair-thin fiber optics. This gave Elizabeth the tools to do the hard work of cracking the security codes, or overriding them and controlling the airlock directly. While she was working on that, she was also inserting her own special brand of antivirus and anti-intrusion code that should neutralize the infection that allowed the aliens control over machinery.

While she was successful in opening the airlock for B Squad, who took advantage of her assistance, she was still working on fighting the infection in the airlock control, and consequently the station network. The virus was fighting back. As soon as she got a grip on one aspect of the virus, another arose with a counter to her action. It seemed someone was programming the virus on the fly. This was far more complicated than a chess game, but it did resemble one on a large scale; every move had a counter move, Elizabeth was the aggressor, the virus was itself the defender. But part of its defense was to attack the aggressor, and it tried to infect Elizabeth multiple times in multiple ways, none of them successful.

So, while the move – counter move of the virus battle was going on, Elizabeth sent snippets of code past the virus defense. None of the snippets were in themselves a threat, they were just bits and pieces of a whole that now was no longer whole – or so it seemed to the virus. There were many trillions of such bits in the system, often orphaned from a rapidly deleted program, often deleted or chopped up by the virus itself. Not finding anything wrong with the flotsam of data floating in the great sea of the network, it looked at each piece of data it found and ignored it, for to try to delete every bit in an unstructured way would cost many millions of cycles of the computer processor, which it could ill afford during the attack.

While all this was going on, Elizabeth had the Marines begin to deploy the remotes they carried. Every hundred meters or so the Marines deployed another remote, which scuttled to find the most innocuous place to secure itself while maintaining a visual, audio and electronic surveillance of its location. The Marines made it to the warehouse, deployed their equipment and joined up with A

Squad. McCalum distributed the remotes he carried for A Squad and repeated the instructions.

When the two squads were ready to move out, they selected one of the medics to accompany them and the other to remain at the warehouse. The mule was to remain with the warehouse, which now became a 'firebase foothold' for all military activity, to be used as a makeshift ambulance to carry any wounded or killed back to the shuttle.

The shuttle had stayed on station until the unit had gone through the airlock, then returned to the Vicinity of Elizabeth. The second shuttle left the shuttle bay with the reinforcements that Jeffrey had decided to deploy to the warehouse foothold, rather than keep in the ship.

The deployment was fast, another mule accompanied this squad – which included Torres, the sniper, the two Navy mechanics, who had deployed with Elizabeth when she acquired the shuttles, Svoboda, Mbaka, Smith. The mule carried more ammunition, rations, cylinders of various gasses, more of Elizabeth's remotes, including several of the larger ones to aid in the security of the warehouse.

This left Jeffrey, Janet, IntelTech Heinz and the quartermaster, Petty Officer Jon Jonson, to man the ship and guard the prisoners. They also had dozens of Elizabeth's remotes for security.

Elizabeth reported to Jeffrey that she had beat the first few levels of security for the virus- infected area, but that it hadn't been defeated. She then showed Jeffrey and Janet what her remotes were picking up; in various places throughout the station that the remotes had been deployed, were shadows of aliens, which showed in the far ultraviolet. On the screen it took the appearance of faint purple ghosts. As the combined A and B squads moved towards the Administrator's office, the remotes picked up several of the ghosts following the Marines.

Jeffrey asked Elizabeth if she could make those images appear on the helmets of the Marines. She replied in the affirmative. Jeffrey told the two sergeants to arm their pistols, then turn around, and fire at the violet ghosts.

The two sergeants quietly pulled their pistols, chambered a round, and at the same time spun around, saw the images Elizabeth was projecting on their optics, and opened fire. The rest of the Marines, not party to the conversation, went into full defense mode, their weapons up and ready. McCalum and McSweeney went to where the now perfectly visible aliens were, both with a single shot in the middle of their bodies. The sergeants stripped the aliens of anything they thought might prove interesting or useful, then rejoined their team and continued toward the Administrator's offices.

Heinz, in the company of four non-coms and Lt. Andrade, asked what they thought of the altercation with the aliens, which he had seen on the display of the sergeants' camera pickup. One of the non-coms asked, "What were they shooting at?"

Heinz took the image back and enhanced it. "No, sorry, I can't see it." The others agreed. The sergeants, it seemed were just shooting at a point behind the group, but no alien target. When the sergeants went to the aliens they had just killed and began taking objects off of them, the non-coms all began to get fidgety. Heinz asked them what was wrong, Andrade was the one to answer, "They shouldn't be doing that."

"Doing what?" queried Heinz.

"That. What they're doing."

"What are they doing?"

"You know - that!" Andrade was just as irritated as the non-coms.

"They should call central to report this."

"Report what?" asked Heinz. "What should we report?"

"What?" Andrade looked at Heinz, would not look again at the display. The non-coms also averted their gaze. "Sorry, what were we talking about?"

Janet was busy composing a report using the book, which seemed more secure, but far more difficult to do. The report contained a request to have *Wanigan* come and make all haste, and to bring a team of psychologists and psychiatrists to address mass hallucinations brought on by the aliens.

Jeffrey requested information from the miners in the ships surrounding the station. Various miners radioed back that the problems had started shortly after the last time *Elizabeth* had visited. While Lagrange 3A was passing out of the area, soon to be replaced by Lagrange 3B, the miners were loath to come onto the station. Many of the ships that had been at other sites before, when Elizabeth broadcast her antivirus and anti-intrusion code, didn't have that protection and became some of the first victims. Dozens of ships were now vacant, with destabilizing positions around the station. Jeffrey noted which ones the other miners had pointed out for later investigation.

Elizabeth continued planning for some of the next battles with the computer virus, but being the ultimate multitasking machine, she also was expanding the bridge to include a conference room and Captain's ready room. This involved removing the motors and gears that set the ship in circular motion for artificial gravity, now that alien gravity plates had been installed in the floors. The motors and gears and housings and bracing were carried away to the smelter and recycled. Much of what came of it became walls and controls, as well as more ammunition for the rail guns.

In Earth's World War Two, a new anti-armor weapon was developed that created a copper plasma which cut into heavy armor. The shell of the bazooka rocket was this plasma cutter. Elizabeth took

the concept and incorporated it into the anti-armor ammunition of
the rail guns; the massive wire windings of the old electric motors
became some of the copper for the plasma.

Removing the massive motors, housing and bracing gave the
bridge an additional twenty-four cubic meters, which was to become
the conference room and captain's or officer of the day's ready room.
Jeffrey still liked having his own private cabin, away from the bridge
if necessary. But it was good for all officers in charge to have a place
to retreat to, perhaps for a quick nap, while still on duty.

Elizabeth finished the construction of the two spaces off the
bridge while still in combat mode, determining that it would not be a
risk of distracting the officers. The construction was done by two of
her large remotes and a half-dozen of the smaller ones. A glass-like
partition separated the bridge from the conference room, made of a
carbon-plastic two and a half centimeters thick, essentially bullet-
and other projectile-proof, and it could be polarized to be completely
dark or completely clear. Jeffrey's cabin was still a bit of distance
down the corridor, with the hidden backup bridge between Jeffrey's
cabin and the conference room. Elizabeth made a secret entryway
that mirrored Jeffrey's room entrance to the backup bridge.

When Janet saw the construction progress that had been made
during the current crisis, she went off to the cabin in which her garden
was growing, picked some flowers and herbs, placed them in a jar
for a vase, and set them on the conference table. One of Elizabeth's
remotes provided Janet with hook-and-loop fasteners – Velcro in the
old parlance – to protect the vase from shifting too much in the event
of the ship jinking during emergency activities.

Jeffrey came onto the bridge, saw Janet through the conference
room window and went in to talk to her. "Was it yesterday or the day

before that I just started thinking of changing the bridge around? Talk about fast!"

Elizabeth spoke out, "AND YOU THINK THIS IS FANCY? CHECK THIS OUT," and she opaqued the windows and displayed a video of Sgt. McSweeney, taken by one of his Marines, directly on the window.

Janet said, "That is so cool!" Another window lit up displaying a map of the station and the location of the Marines. Arrows pointed their most probable course to their objective, and more pale arrows showed alternative courses they could take.

Elizabeth announced, "CAPTAIN, THE LEADER OF THE KANG WISHES TO SPEAK WITH YOU. HIS NAME IS CHTHLIKI."

"Well," said Jeffrey, we're in a conference room, let's confer here. Put him through."

"Captain," said Chthliki in his gruff voice. "It has been brought to my attention that your soldiers killed two of my civilians."

"Is that so?" said Jeffrey in a defiant tone. "Do you mean the two aliens that were following my armed Marines using invisibility circuits?"

"Yes! Not soldiers!"

"Can you remember what I told you and everyone else that people using invisibility circuits were subject to immediate destruction?"

"That was for ships! These were civilians!"

"Nobody gets to be invisible. Nobody gets to threaten or spy on my Marines. If you want to avoid any other similar incidents, you will order all Kang to become visible. I have spoken, and will not say this again – we have rules that you must obey or face destruction. Am I clear?"

The leader of the Kang just looked contemptuously at Jeffrey before cutting the connection without saying another word. A moment later, Elizabeth called out "GENERAL QUARTERS. BRACE FOR IMPACT!"

Jeffrey and Janet remained in their seats. The ship shook violently for a few seconds, then stopped shaking. The flowers in the makeshift vase swayed slightly, but that was the full extent of their reaction. "Elizabeth, what happened?" asked Janet, wondering if they were struck by an errant asteroid.

"THE KANG SHIP THREW A MINER'S SHIP AT US. THERE WAS NO DAMAGE TO US."

"Elizabeth," started Jeffrey, "Can you target the bridge of their ship?" She answered in the affirmative, so Jeffrey said, "Send a half second burst from one of the rail guns their way."

At a thousand rounds a minute, a half second burst was only eight projectiles, but that was enough to convince Chthliki that this was not a battle he either wanted to be in or could win. Pieces of his ship floated free, some having been chopped off, some having been blown away. Chthliki immediately called back asking them to stop shooting.

The devastation on the bridge of the Kang warship was evident by the holes in the bulkheads, the sounds of sirens going off, the hissing of leaking air, the moans of survivors and the pile of four dead at the back of the screen.

"Chthliki, I am feeling magnanimous today. That means you should be feeling grateful. Within a few seconds I can destroy your entire fleet. You cannot do anything to stop me. You will line up all of your ships ten thousand meters from the station with me between the station and you, do not charge your weapons, do not activate your invisibility circuits, do nothing to offend me. Am I clear?"

The leader of the Kang said nothing. Jeffrey repeated, "Am I clear?" But again silence. "Rail guns, prepare to kill all the Kang ships."

"I understand!" the leader of the Kang said, grudgingly. "Why do you humiliate us so! We are a proud people!"

"What do you have to be so proud about? Sneaking around on unsuspecting humans? Eating humans? That is one of the gravest taboos in our culture," Jeffrey said. "But the most important thing is that you realize that every time you violate us or our laws, it will cost you. Humility is only the first step. Death, failure of your mission, encouraging us to take the fight back to your home world. These are some of the next steps. Realize that when you attack us, you are inviting your own destruction. That is why I humiliate you. So that you never try this again.

"Now, Chthliki, how many aliens are on the station?"

"One thousand two hundred three."

"And how many on your ships?"

"One hundred two."

"So. these thirteen hundred five aliens will present themselves to my Marines in the warehouse at the intersection of outer ring level four, and spoke thirteen, when I call on that to happen. Is that clear?"

"Yes."

"Just one more thing," continued Jeffrey. "A virus has infected the systems on the station. We have seen this virus before and have made counters to it, but it seems to be evolving. Why is that?"

"We ordered one of the Administrator's minions to refine the code to make it impervious to antivirus programs."

"No more deploying of this kind of code. Is that clear?"

"Yes."

Janet asked, "How do we undo the damage your virus has done to the mental processes of the humans that were affected by it?"

The alien looked at her, and said, "We know of no way."

She looked at Jeffrey then back to the Kang on the screen, a determination evident on her face. "We will find out, and make sure they remember who did this to them."

The Marine squads took separate paths to the Administrator's offices; A Squad took the elevator, which was a dangerous gambit; if someone controlled the elevators they could override the safety controls and cause a fatal crash, but that did not happen. The B Squad went on the moving stairways, the escalators, charging up them three steps at a time. They came to the same location as the A Squad after only five minutes.

A Squad set up a perimeter – all entrances to the entire floor were blocked, nobody in or out. Elizabeth had the Marines continue to place remotes, which quickly disappeared into the background, silently monitoring, relaying communications outside the station's network.

B Squad followed Gunnery Sergeant McCalum into the Administrator's suite. Two security officers tried to block their way, but recognized the massive difference in firepower between the two groups. Plus, the Marines were heavily armored while the security officers had only light duty suits. McCalum passed the security officers outside the office suite to Sgt. McSweeney, who disarmed them cuffed them with the universal plastic cuffs, and secured them out of the way.

McCalum went into the Administrator's private office, and said, "Sir, you are to come with me. Now."

"I will do no such thing," said the Administrator. "Do you know what happens to people who interfere with station business? Do you know where your fellow Marines are?"

This last caused McCalum almost to lose his anger control. "Yes, I know where they are. Your alien friends were storing them up for food, along with ninety miners and other civilians. You allowed them to turn Humans into cattle." His voice rose, amplified by the external speakers on his hard suit, a truly frightening thing.

They bundled the Administrator and the only other person in the suite at the time, the InfoTech Manager, secured them with standard ties, and took them out of the administration suite. They left one Marine to stand guard at the suite, with four of the remotes to assist him.

Instead of taking the elevators they all went down by the series of escalators – the moving stairways that took them down ten levels to the correct level for the docks. The four prisoners; the Administrator, the InfoSec Manager and the two security officers were moved to the forward base at the warehouse, where the Marines took a few minutes rest, then they radioed in, requesting a shuttle pickup. They bundled the prisoners into emergency suits – essentially soft plastic bubbles with oxygen cylinders, placed them on the mule, and went out to the dock where Shuttle 1 was standing by. They loaded their human cargo onto the shuttle, escorted by Team A, while Team B took themselves back to the forward base at the warehouse.

At the ship, the prisoners were detained in different cabins, the two security officers in the brig with the other security officers, the InfoTech Manager and the Administrator in separate cabins that had just been converted to interrogation cells.

IntelTech Heinz began his interrogation with the InfoTech Manager. "Where did you get the code for the virus that you modified?"

"What virus? What are you talking about?"

"I'll lay some of my cards on the table, so you can see where the course of this investigation is going," said Heinz. "Six months or so ago, a virus infected one of the warships in the Navy fleet. Because of some classified safeguards, that ship managed to escape capture, but all its systems were compromised. Every computer, every computer-controlled circuit. Worse, even the humans were hypnotized by the virus.

"This ship has already had experience with that same virus, but not that particular strain. We had developed an antivirus, anti-intrusion software package that prevented the virus from continuing to infect any systems, and another module that cleaned up those infected systems. But the humans that were affected required intense psychological counseling.

"So, much of the mutation of the virus on the station can be attributed to you. Just so you know, if I don't get satisfaction from you, I will turn you over to relatives of those who were hurt by your work. There are some on board this ship right now. They are very angry and are armed."

The InfoTech Manager sat there and looked mostly dumb. Then asked to see some of the source code of the virus that he is accused of engineering. Heinz had Elizabeth display a few sections of code on the wall. The InfoTech Manager looked at the section of code, and said, "Yeah, I see what you mean. This routine here," and he pointed at a subroutine, "is different from the others, it was written by a human, where this other code was, created by a..." At this point, he just stopped, his eyes glazing over. A moment later, he looked at Heinz, and said, "Sorry, what were we talking about?"

Heinz decided to confront him, hoping that it would take him beyond the stalling point. "You were showing me where humans created the code here, and the rest is alien."

"Alien. Yeah, I guess that could be it." The InfoTech Manager looked like he was developing a severe headache.

"Who told you to modify this code?" asked Heinz.

"I don't, I can't, I, I, I..."

Then Heinz had Elizabeth play back the leader of the Kang telling Janet that he had ordered a human programmer to do it.

"Yeah! Him! Wait, there's something different about him." The InfoTech Manager furrowed his brow, then said, "Yeah, that's it. He always came to me like a purple ghost. He told me what to write in the code. He said 'Make it so they can't see us.'"

While Heinz was interrogating the InfoTech Manager, Jeffrey decided to start speaking with the Administrator. As soon as Jeffrey walked into the newly-made interrogation room, the Administrator began his bluster. "You know you can't keep me. I am an important person, I know important people. There is going to be hell to pay for you, whoever you are.

Jeffrey removed his helmet so the Administrator could see who, exactly, he was dealing with. "Oh," said the Administrator. "It's you. I don't know how you escaped the last time, but the Navy is on its way and you will be in serious trouble if you don't release me right this instant."

"Administrator," began Jeffrey in a low, calm voice. "I am the Navy. You have been collaborating with organized crime, pirates, and now Aliens. You are under arrest. All your rights and privileges have been revoked. You no longer hold that office. Now, you have been known as the Administrator ever since you came on board. That no longer applies. What is your given name?"

"Just call me Administrator."

"No. I may call you The Traitor. I may call you The-One-Who-Feeds-His-People To-The-Aliens. I may call you Shameful Disgrace. But I imagine you would rather a Human name. What is it?" Jeffrey sat back, his helmet on the table between them.

The former Administrator had paused, as if weighing his options, recalculating his position, figuring out where to pick himself up and return to a top position. Then he said in a small voice, "Secant. Barry Secant."

Elizabeth displayed a dossier on the wall behind the Administrator. While listening to him talk about who Barry Secant was, Jeffrey was comparing the notes. The notes were remarkably similar to what the Administrator was saying, except that the dossier listed Secant as dead. The Administrator continued talking about Secant, as if he were him.

"So how did you die?" Jeffrey interrupted.

The Administrator sat back, dumbfounded. "How did, what?"

"According to his dossier Barry Secant died. How did you die?"

"How does it say Secant died?" The Administrator asked in a small voice.

"Old age. Do you want to try again?

"That was my father. I'm Martel Secant."

The dossier changed to Martel Secant, a juvenile delinquent in his childhood, a bully in his early twenties, and untraced after that. The dossier showed that Martel was wanted for extortion, larceny, piracy and suspected of murder. The psych analysis was that he was a sociopath and/or psychopath and that he was dangerous. The picture of Martel Secant was roughly similar to what Jeffrey saw before him, although several decades out of date. Jeffrey noted the convolutions in his ear were identical to that in the picture, so he took it at face value.

"So, when did you meet the Aliens?" Jeffrey asked.

"It was about a year ago," Secant replied. "They came to me and offered me riches and power, but it would take some setting up. I was the one to do the setting up."

"What would you say," continued Jeffrey, "What would you say was the biggest problem the aliens face?"

"Right now, you" said Secant. "But before they came to this station it was starvation."

"You realize that they were taking care of that problem by eating people?" demanded Jeffrey. "That they eat their own dead, and they kill ours and eat them too."

"I can hardly believe that. Mr. Sokolov where do you get such nonsense?"

Elizabeth displayed a video behind Jeffrey of the Marines entering the deserted miner's ships with the station's Marines lying in heaps. She showed the lined-up body bags in the shuttle bay. Closeups showed arms and legs had been sawed off. Closeups of Marine dog tags. Martel Secant looked ashen, the color drained from his face. "Oh."

"Captain, this is not what I thought. I was hoping for a good life, a life of crime, perhaps, but nothing like this." The former administrator held a pleading look in his eyes. Please give me a chance to redeem myself. I feel so – ashamed."

Jeffrey spoke aloud, "Elizabeth, when does *Wanigan* arrive?"

"TWO HOURS, CAPTAIN."

"You have two hours to think of a way to redeem yourself. There is a lot to speak for. You stay here. Do not attempt to move or escape. It would please my guards no end to kill you. If you think of something, let me know; just speak out loud, you are being monitored." Jeffrey got up to leave. "Two hours."

After Jeffrey left, he told Heinz the real identity of the former administrator. Told him where he left off, and encouraged Heinz to ratchet more out of him.

"CAPTAIN, THERE IS SOME COMMOTION GOING ON AT THE STATION. THE MARINES POSTED AT THE

ADMINISTRATOR'S OFFICE AND AT THE WAREHOUSE REPORT CROWDS GATHERING."

"Have B Squad get back to the station and help keep things calm."

"AYE, CAPTAIN."

"Also, Elizabeth, inform Sgt. McCalum of the impending arrival of *Wanigan*. He should only have to hold out for a few hours."

"ACKNOWLEDGED."

"Keep the corpsman here to help care for the victims in the hold."

"AYE, CAPTAIN."

The Marines landed on the dock, quickly marched through the crowd of civilians that had gathered around the airlock, then continued marching through to the warehouse. There was another, loud, boisterous crowd. Elizabeth called the attention of McCalum to two aliens with their invisibility circuits, and superimposed them on McCalum's video. He took out his pistol, jacked a round into the chamber, raised the pistol and aimed at the violet image of the one on the left, and fired. He then acquired the second target and fired. Two more hidden aliens down.

The Marines went to where the two aliens lay, stripped them of any apparatus that might prove useful, and left them against the outer warehouse wall. They called on the corpsman to bring out two body bags for the aliens. When she arrived, they placed the aliens into the body bags, and two Marines carried the body bags, one at a time into the warehouse. Then they all entered the warehouse and secured the door.

Sergeant McCalum replaced the rounds he had fired, holstered his pistol and told the Marines that they needed to support the Marine they left in the Administrator's offices. Three Marines volunteered to go, so Sergeant McSweeney took those three Marines from both squads, and took the elevator to the proper level.

When they arrived, there was a crowd of twenty humans, and Elizabeth pointed out another two invisible Aliens, as violet images on McSweeney's visor. After shooting them both, they followed the same procedure – strip the aliens of any interesting apparatuses and place the alien corpses into body bags and bring them into the office complex with them.

McSweeney told the crowd, "Go to your homes – the offices are closed for now." The crowd obediently disbursed. One of the Marines gave the Marine that had been left behind to guard the offices replacement air for his suit – the order to keep the armor on until further notice, was still in effect.

Jeffrey received the notice that they were still running across invisible aliens – and shooting them as they are detected. He told Janet to raise Chthliki. She broadcast a hail to his ship, but there was no response. She tried again, again without results. While the mic was still open, she ordered the rail guns to take aim on the ship used by Chthliki.

This brought an immediate response, Chthliki appeared to be on his bridge, the holes were still in the wall behind him. "What do you want?" he demanded.

"Standby for Captain Sokolov," she announced.

"When Captain Sokolov is ready to talk to me, he may call me himself" retorted the Kang leader.

"I see," said Janet. "What is the name of your replacement? Or do we pick the Kang who replaces you? Either way, you stay on the line or discover how little regard you have among your people. You will be forgotten."

Jeffrey was just out of the line of sight, standing at the door to the bridge, overhearing Janet's conversation with Chthliki. He told her he would be coming back in two minutes by holding two fingers up.

Frustrated and painfully humiliated, Chthliki stayed on the line. He didn't understand what kind of weapon a 'rail gun' was, but it was vastly superior to the beam and plasma weapons that his ships relied on. He waited, fuming.

Jeffrey then walked onto the bridge, sat down in the captain's chair, and started, "Chthliki. It seems we are still at war."

"What? No!"

"So, here's what we are going to do. You are going to be responsible for every incident of aliens on this station who is using the invisibility circuit. If you can't control your own people, then we need to find a Kang who can. Do you have any recommendations for your replacement?"

"No. I will go onto the station and collect all the remaining Kang and other aliens on the station. I will remove them to my ship. Do not destroy us."

"Now you see, it is possible for you to be a leader," said Jeffrey. After they cut the communications, Jeffrey had Elizabeth notify the Marines that they were about to have a visitor, and explained what Chthliki was up to.

The ship carrying Chthliki broke away from the line of Kang ships, and made for the dock next to the shuttle that had delivered the Marines. Elizabeth tracked and analyzed the Kang ship, it's propulsion, it's exhaust, it's electronic and electrical signature, it's radio emissions, it's magnetic properties.

Chthliki exited the ship and walked to the airlock, which opened for him before he arrived. Elizabeth's remotes continued to monitor the Kang leader from their hidden positions. Elizabeth surmised that the Kang was broadcasting or responding to a broadcast signal, perhaps like the old RFID system. She played back all the records that the remotes had recorded, including radio waves and found a signal coming from Chthliki in the hundred gigahertz band. This might be useful for tracking him. She sent an order to the remotes to track any signal at that range of frequencies. Elizabeth was pleased with herself.

She reported to Jeffrey what she figured out. Jeffrey was aware that she was fishing for a compliment, and paid her with profuse and over-the-top compliments.

"OKAY, CAPTAIN. THAT'S ENOUGH. BUT THANKS. YOU MAKE ME BLUSH!"

She tracked the Kang leader onto the elevator, and discovered that the Kang had set up more stops than the designers of the station intended. There were no buttons for the selection of the floors that Chthliki stopped at. When he paused at one of the phantom floors, the elevator doors remained open, he would step out growl a command in the language of the Kang, a guttural commanding language that involved a lot of spit. He told all Kang to drop what they were doing and assemble at the exit where the Marines were. They were not to use their invisibility. They would be detected and destroyed. Already ten of their number were so killed by the Marines.

He then went to another hidden floor and repeated his orders. And another. All told, six hidden floors with the hundred – odd Kang and a smattering of a few other races the Kang allowed to mix with them, were stopped at.

When they gathered at the elevator at the entrance near the docks, Gunnery Sergeant McCallum found Chthliki and told him to bring all his people into the warehouse in a neat line. Then they would be able to go on their way.

Suspicious, but somehow trusting, Chthliki told his Kang to line up, the other aliens, similar to Kang, but different, were lined up after the Kang. They entered the warehouse one at a time, where each alien was issued a box of food – canned meats, packaged vegetables, fruits, rice, beans. There were instructions printed in English, but the Marine distributing the food told each Kang that some of the food, like rice and beans, needed to be boiled in water until soft.

The Kang were then led out to the airlock. Chthliki explained that for short times, Kang could traverse vacuum with no medical consequences. They cycled through the airlock twenty at a time, and on the other side, paraded to the Kang ship that Chthlliki had ridden in. Soon all the aliens had gotten onto the Kang ship, Chthliki had taken it back to its place in line with the other ships, awaiting further instructions.

Shortly afterward, Chthliki called in distress – several of his Kang had eaten some of the food and were having abdominal bloating. The MedTech took the call, and explained that they were instructed to boil the rice, not eat directly out of the package. The rice expands in liquid. When they ate it, their stomachs or the Kang equivalent of stomachs, were packed with expanding rice. Have them induce vomiting, he counseled. And make sure they boil the rice in water. Same with beans and any other dried foods.

This placated the Kang leader.

Shortly after the evacuation of the station by the aliens, *Wanigan* arrived. As usual, it blew deafening tones through all frequencies warning that a Navy warship was arriving, and nobody was to look threatening. She took station near *Elizabeth*, and after a short time, Commodore Yusef came aboard *Elizabeth* with a whole gaggle of psychiatrists and psychologists.

He was escorted to the conference room off the bridge, where Jeffrey met him. "You know," Yusef told Jeffrey, "It is customary to have a dignitary met at the gangway by a bosun's whistle and greeted by the officer in charge once aboard."

"Oh goodness, Commodore, let me drop what I'm doing, and let's go back to the shuttle bay and...no, wait. I don't think I have a bosun. Or a bosun whistle. Oh well. Sorry. Maybe next time." Jeffrey smirked.

Yusef laughed, embraced Jeffrey, and thanked him for inviting *Wanigan* to the party. He had Heinz show the mental health professionals to the humans that had been rescued from the Kang dinner party. Then took Yusef to his new conference room. Yusef looked around – the table was plastic and steel, the walls plastic, there were two square decorations, one an abstract image made of gold, copper, depleted cobalt, silver, and other heavy metals forming a stylized map of the galaxy. The other was a portrait of Elizabeth Sokolov, Jeffrey's late wife.

There was a vase of flowers on the table. Janet had been keeping them fresh. Their fragrance almost overcame the new construction smells that permeated the room.

Jeffrey had the commodore sit alongside him at the far end of the table. As he began his briefing, Elizabeth polarized the windows to the conference room, and turned the windows into displays, one showing details of the Kang ships, one showing the various aliens found on the station, another showing the secret floors on the station that the elevator wouldn't stop at if the proper coded frequencies were not present.

"Commodore Yusef, the aliens have used the virus we have already come across, but induced Human programmers to modify it to work with human nervous systems. The people on the station were all conditioned, by the virus, to ignore any evidence of, or knowledge of, aliens. One other hitch in their conditioning, though. If they find an ill or dead alien, they are to report it...somewhere. And then forget. The Administrator, whose real name is Martel Secant, is actually a low-level crook. He's pretty bright, and the aliens used him to overcome security at the station, then help them develop their infrastructure.

"These aliens have been feeding on Humans." Elizabeth played through video of the findings on the abandoned mining craft, and other evidence as Jeffrey spoke. "I informed them that this was no longer to be tolerated. I really stressed the invisibility circuits were to remain off. We have found ways to discern their personal invisibility circuits, and shooting aliens has been good target practice for my sergeants. They seem to have learned the lesson.

"The Kang leader, Chthliki, has removed all the aliens from the station, and each was given a box of food before going onto Chthliki's ship. Two things – the Kang don't name their ships. And we just got a panicked call from Chthliki about his underlings not following directions on cooking rice and beans. Big stomachache."

The captain and commodore had a laugh.

"We established a firebase and food distribution center in a warehouse at the level four dock, not too far inside the airlock. The population is going to need to be de-conditioned to the alien's implanted suggestions."

The programmer – InfoSec Manager – was re-checking the code of the virus that affected human nervous systems so he could brief the mental health professionals with his findings. Which would be relatively easy as he was also the person who originally programmed it. But his memory was somewhat foggy about that.

"We have security in two places, the warehouse and the Administrator's office. We are keeping our eyes open for one known surviving Marine – Lt. Omotunde."

Yusef looked up, startled. "You think Omotunde is still alive?"

"Don't know sir, but there was no evidence among the deceased or anywhere else that he was dead."

"All right, let's see if we can find him," said the commodore. "What else do you have for me?"

The former Administrator – I left him in one of the interrogation rooms – wants another chance to redeem himself after collaborating with the aliens. He seemed genuinely surprised at the cannibalistic nature of the aliens. I gave him until you got here to decide what he could do to redeem himself."

"Okay, let's go talk to him." Yusef and Jeffrey then stood and went to the interrogation room that held the former administrator. Martel Secant tried to stand, but his hands were secured to a ring on the table, so it was an awkward move at best. He sat back down. Jeffrey and the Commodore sat opposite Secant.

"Mr. Secant, I am Commodore Yusef," Yusef said. "It has come to my attention that you have been collaborating with aliens in the process of attacking Humans. Also, you seem to have made some misrepresentations as to your identity in offering yourself for the position of administrator." He tossed his head towards Jeffrey, "And Captain Sokolov tells me you wish to make some move towards reparations for your behavior." He paused a long pause. "What do you have in mind?"

Secant just sat for a moment, looking at his hands. He then looked up at the Commodore, then at Jeffrey, and said in a quiet voice. "I like power. I like wealth. On top of that, I am a very good administrator. But I don't want to do that anymore. It has come to my attention that you have established a policy of distributing food to the aliens and registering them. I can manage that program for you. I can help your intelligence agency organize information. All I need is forgiveness and a modest salary."

"Wait here." Yusef stood, Jeffrey rose in response. "Mr. Secant, what can you tell us about Marine Lieutenant Omotunde?"

"We lost him – he disappeared somewhere on the station. The Kang couldn't find him, he seemed immune to the virus programming. I suspect he is still alive, but don't know where."

"Wait here," Yusef repeated.

They went back to the conference room. Yusef then said, "Elizabeth."

"YES, COMMODORE?"

"Please update Wanigan in the things you have learned and figured out. She can then advise me on how to defeat the virus-based hypnosis, and other ways to protect my troops."

"DONE, SIR."

"Thank you."

"WHY, COMMODORE, I WOULD DO ANYTHING FOR YOU, SIR."

"Keep it professional, Elizabeth. I outrank your Captain, you know."

"YES SIR."

"Jeffrey," started the commodore. "I have a small brigade of Marines I'm assigning to you. The station is going to need to be well secured. The Security Officers are all out – with the virus-based hypnotic suggestions. Until they are cleared by the MilPsy corps, they are all on paid leave. And until I find someone else to fill the position, you are the governor of the station."

"But sir," began Jeffrey.

Yusef interrupted, "Calm down. It won't be for long. And you will still be captain of your own ship, although Lt. Bianca may need to run some patrols. I need you to do this. You are probably the best qualified person for this."

Jeffrey shrank in resignation. "All right, sir. But you gotta hurry and find a replacement. My place is on the ship."

"I doubt you would be surprised at all the captains I ask to do desk work say that." Yusef chuckled. "Now, regarding the former administrator – I like his own suggestion. Make him an analyst for your intelligence gathering, and as a primary job make him the alien registrar and distributor of food. Elizabeth can keep an eye on his activities to make certain he doesn't step out of line."

"Okay," agreed Jeffrey.

"But you are not just the governor of Lagrange 3A, but all the Lagrange 3 stations. The entire orbit."

"Oh Lord," sighed Jeffrey.

"Now you see what I mean – you will be on your ship a good deal of the time."

"Oh Lordy, lordy."

"Now, if you find Omotunde, debrief him, get him whatever psych analysis you consider he needs to pass, then if he is adequate, put him back in charge of MilIntel. I am aware you and he did not get off well on the first meeting, and you handled him well. But I trust him, I want you to also. But you can make him earn that trust. He reports to you.

"And I want to know as soon as he is found. Use the book."

Yusef seemed to be winding down. He got up and walked around the conference room, looking at the details Elizabeth put into the construction. "I see you changed the ship around again. I like what you have done to this place."

"Well sir, if we didn't need the rotational gear, we could use the space for other things. Our Golden drives seem to be holding up really well. Got up to 4 light. I can't stress how useful the smelting and manufacturing processes have worked for me. If I want to change something, I ask Elizabeth to do it and within a short time, Voila!"

"Next; tell me about our social experiment. Any problems?"

"You mean the canoodling within the ranks? Let me say that the results speak for themselves. No problems. Sir, just demand the best from your people, and they will give it to you. My expectations are high, so the men and women reach up to achieve those expectations. Their having sex with whomever has nothing to do with the performance of their duties."

"Okay, thanks."

"You need to set up quarters on all the Lagrange 3 stations. If I were you, I would also follow through on the safehouse authorization we discussed back at Earth Station." Yusef didn't seem to be winding down, after all. "The administrators on the other Lagrange 3 stations have been told to expect you, and you have ultimate authority – if you decide to fire someone, just do it. Tell me afterward. We need to get these stations up to the point of serving our alien neighbors and defending ourselves from the takeover by them or by rogue humans. You are our first line of defense, Jeffrey. Make it work.

"I have dispatched ships containing large quantities of food for the aliens. Those ships will be kept off-station until you decide to unload them. Can you think of anything else you need me to ship to you?"

"Yes, sir. I want bigger replicators. One for the ship, one for each station."

"Well you, my boy, are in luck. The United Nations got the word we are not alone and stopped their squabbling. They authorized every expense for you, within reason. Considering how well you have done with your own old replicator, I think that is a reasonable request. Anything else?"

"Permanent staff for my ship. I'll keep Janet as my number one, but I need more engineers, more combat staff to put under Sergeant

Torres, maybe a few midshipmen to train." He paused, then, "How many in the brigade?"

"That's about a hundred."

"Okay, I'll need more shuttles and crews. Has anyone developed small combat spacecraft?"

"Yes."

"A flight of those for each station."

"I like to see you thinking strategically. Don't go overboard, but I'll see about getting you what you need. Oh, and I'll send some new officers to train under you. Seems you have seen more action and done more good for the solar system than any of the rest of the Navy. And you'll have your midshipmen."

"One more thing, sir." added Jeffrey. "I need clerical staff unaffected by the virus."

"I'll send you some. Until then, make do with what you have."

"Aye, sir."

Jeffrey had the new brigade of Marines take over another nearby warehouse for its barracks. The commander of the brigade, Lieutenant Colonel Vincent DePaul, came to the ship to get his orders from Jeffrey.

"Colonel, under combat, we found that keeping armor on all the time did two positive things — it offered us the security of constant protection, both from the elements and from aliens. But it also protected us from the hypnotic effects of the alien virus. Everybody on the station was affected, so the aliens understand our neural physiology. Oh yeah, we also get to have my AI superimpose the image of aliens with their invisibility circuits on. If Elizabeth shows you an ultraviolet blob on your screen, she will also tell you that it is an alien. You are authorized to shoot any alien with invisibility circuits activated. Other aliens, just make sure they are registered. You might want to occupy the floors that the aliens had, take a look at their gear, bring to MilIntel anything you don't understand or anything that may give us an advantage over the enemy. Otherwise, your job is to keep the peace.

"I am going to have to travel to all the other Lagrange 3 stations, seems I've been made governor of the entire orbit. I will need to take a third of your troops whenever I travel. It wouldn't be a bad idea to separate your brigade into three sections and assign a new section for every trip I take. I am working at getting a civilian staff going here, but we won't use anyone from the station who hasn't been cleared by MilPsy. So, when I am off station, you are in charge.

"Any questions?"

"Just one, sir. We have been issued old style projectile pistols. What's that about?"

"Both our armor and the alien's armor are good defense against beam weapons and plasma weapons. The slugs in these pistols go through anything the aliens have, and will ruin a pirate's day if you shoot him in the helmet while he's outside.

"Only thing is, they need to be cleaned far more often."

"I understand, sir. I'd better get back to my units," And the Lieutenant Colonel stood up.

"Not so fast, Colonel. Have a seat." Jeffrey turned his hand over and indicated the seat. "We haven't talked about my AI. Her name is Elizabeth, and I rely on her for pretty much everything. She will be your best friend."

"No sir."

"No? Why?"

"I don't trust AIs. They can be programmed to do nasty things just when you need them. Never trusted AIs, never will."

"Ah. Elizabeth, call Wanigan back and tell her to pick up Lieutenant Colonel DePaul. He won't be staying with us." Then to DePaul, "Get your gear, Colonel, you won't be staying with us after all."

"But sir..."

"Elizabeth was with me before I was drafted into the Navy. She is my most trusted crew member. She is the best tool I have for nearly every problem. She is my best friend. If you don't trust her, you don't trust me. If I can't count on you to use the tools I give you effectively, I don't need you."

DePaul swallowed. This wasn't how he expected the interaction with the young captain was supposed to go, he thought he could bully his way to dominating him. Tables turned fast. "Sir, please reconsider. I am a good combat leader, I can be an asset to you and your mission."

"And my AI?"

"I will try. I've been burned by AIs, sir." A pleading look on DePaul's face convinced Jeffrey that he could give him another chance. With monitoring.

"Elizabeth, belay that last order. We'll keep the Colonel – on probation."

"ORDER BELAYED."

"Thank you, Captain."

"Colonel, did you know *Wanigan* has an AI? Sister to Elizabeth. When *Wanigan's* crew was disabled and removed from the ship, the AI was partially disabled, and high-tailed it to our location, where we were able to defeat the virus and the aliens. That AI saved the ship and her crew. Our AIs are loyal, they are reliable, smart – just a little bit ago, Elizabeth discovered that the aliens wear an RFID type device that emits a very high frequency code which enables them to enter secret compartments, without which nothing happens. Elizabeth figured out we can trace aliens by that frequency emission."

"RFID? What's that?"

"Radio Frequency Identifier. It's an old Earth technology that enabled companies to embed a passive device that reflected a code when given a specific radio signal. Was good for inventory control and passports and the like. We use much more smart systems now, but in its day was quite the thing."

"I see. Sir, you can count on me. I apologize for insulting your AI."

"You can apologize to Elizabeth. Just speak her name, she's always listening."

"Elizabeth, I'm sorry." The lieutenant colonel said. His eyes rolled, showing the depth of his feeling.

"LIEUTENANT COLONEL, IF YOU TRULY MEANT THAT, I WOULD HAVE EXPECTED MORE OF A LOOK OF ABJECT HUMILITY, BUT WHILE YOUR LIPS APOLOGIZE, YOUR EYES LAUGH AT ME AND MY CAPTAIN."

"Colonel, if Elizabeth gives you an order, rest assured that order came from me. Understood?"

"Yes sir."

"Now go join your unit. Explain what I just said. If they get an order from Elizabeth they can trust that the order is legitimate and came from me. I trust my AI, I trust my troops. When they don't trust each other I have problems. I don't want problems."

"Understood, sir."

"Dismissed."

After the lieutenant colonel left to go back to his team, Jeffrey told Elizabeth to monitor him. "I want to know if he is undermining you or me. I don't want trivial information, but if there is going to be a problem I want to nip it in the bud."

Jeffrey went aboard the station, accompanied by Audrey and Torres as bodyguards and the Quartermaster, Petty Officer Jon Jonson. He first dropped in on the Marines in the warehouses. They seemed in good spirits. He told Lt. Col. DePaul to relax the hard-shell suit requirement, except for their security details. This brought a cheer from the Marines, especially those that had been on the station for some time. He also passed along the commodore's order to keep an eye out for Omotunde, bring him in safely, or if that isn't possible, report his position.

They then went up to the Administration offices, greeted the Marines on watch there. Jeffrey told them that they would be relieved soon. "Elizabeth, have Lt. Col. DePaul dispatch a replacement team for the security at the administration offices."

Jeffrey sat down at the Administrator's desk and looked through the drawers, attempting to discover what he could about the man who held the position, and what the position really entailed. He then went through the paper files, looking for records that the administrator didn't want in the electronic system. He found a treasure trove of contacts among the pirates, extortions the administrator had managed, and records of contacts with the aliens.

Jeffrey sent down to the warehouse for the Chief - his naval sniper and chef. She appeared a few minutes later, well-armed but without the sniper rifle. "What, you lost it already?"

"The Colonel confiscated it from me. He said it belonged with a proper sniper team."

"Chief, as far as I am concerned, you are a proper sniper team. I'll get it back from the Colonel. After all, it is my personal property."

"Thanks sir."

Jeffrey continued, "The reason I called you here, is we probably don't need you in your role as a combat chief any more, until the next crisis, that is. But we do need you to cook. Can you prepare enough meals for the Marines, the Navy and me?"

"Of course, sir."

"And if you need help, requisition it from Lieutenant Bianca."

"Thank you, sir."

"I'm hungry. Dismissed."

After she left, Jeffrey put Petty Officer Jonson to work organizing the running of the station. Jeffrey then decided to go for a walk. He left, accompanied again by Torres and Audrey. They paid a visit to the Chong family.

Sul met him at the door, initially looking suspicious, but then his face broke out in a wide smile, and he called his family out from hiding to see who it was. Jeffrey greeted the family with hugs and smiles, Lee went to make tea and Kim went to bring some cookies.

They all sat down in the living room, Jeffrey explained that the crisis seemed to be over, but that he was now temporary governor of the entire orbital ring of six Lagrange stations. He was going to have to do a lot of travel. He wanted the Chong family to start a restaurant as they had originally discussed, so they should take a walk and look for suitable locations.

"Not necessary," said Lee. "We have already found the perfect location. If we can find adequate appliances and tables and a supply of food, we can start next week. We were only waiting for the crisis to calm down."

"Very good. Anything you need, requisition it from the administration office. The cost will come out of your account."

Then Jeffrey went to the Canada safe house. When he opened the door, it seems there was a presence there, so Torres and Sneaky drew their weapons and entered the apartment. Torres entered one of the bedrooms, looked in the closet, under the bed, but as he was about to turn to exit, he felt the barrel of a pistol against his head.

"Do not make a sound," said a soft, but menacing voice with an African accent. "I don't want to kill you, but that is entirely up to you."

A gun barrel appeared against Omotunde's head, held by Sneaky. "But if he doesn't make a sound, how is he to call for help? Hello, Omotunde. Please give Torres the pistol."

"Torres? From *Elizabeth*?" Almost dumbfounded, he pulled the pistol away from Torres head and handed it to him. "I almost lost hope. You have no idea what was going on here."

Jeffrey walked into the bedroom to see what the commotion was all about. "Lieutenant Omotunde! What a surprise! We have been looking for you."

"Sir, there are aliens on the station. Invisible aliens." Omotunde, in his agitated state began shaking. "They have killed the Marines – I don't know where they took them. It's like they hypnotized everyone – nobody could see them, even when they weren't invisible." He paused to catch his breath, "Sir, I know this sounds crazy, but it's true."

"Lieutenant, I know it is true. We defeated them. Kicked them off the station. Shot a few – the whole solar system seems infected with aliens, but we are slowly fixing it so they don't pose a threat any more."

"They came, the security officers came, they took all of my Marines. They couldn't find me, but they took all my Marines. They disappeared." He sat on the bed, his head in his hands, elbows on his knees.

"I don't know where they took them."

Jeffrey knelt down beside the lieutenant. "Look, Omotunde, they killed the Marines. But we found the bodies. They did everything you said – they hypnotized everyone on the station, except for yourself, probably. We figured out how to not be hypnotized too. But we are going to have to get the station back running again."

"The Administrator was collaborating with them."

"I know. He was arrested. But when he saw what the aliens were actually doing, he begged to be given another chance. Commodore Yusef agreed to let him do some minor tasks, including some intelligence work. Yusef also wants you to continue here, if you are up to it, as our MilIntel chief."

"Yes, sir, I can do that."

"But not until you have seen some of our shrinks. I want to make sure the aliens haven't put some secret time bomb in your mind."

"Makes sense. I'll cooperate."

"Okay, we're going to walk down to the Level Three docks. A couple of the warehouses there were taken over as Marine barracks and forts. I'm going to have some Marines take you to *Elizabeth,* where you can get started."

The four then made their way down to the Marine Fort on Third Level. Jeffrey was gratified to see guards posted at very visible spots and backup guards in not-quite so visible spots. He greeted the Lt. Col., and introduced Omotunde. He then asked for an escort for Omotunde to go back to *Elizabeth.* And to send his personal sniper rifle back with them - the one he had taken from the Navy sniper he had assigned it to. Elizabeth sent a shuttle to pick up the team and offload meals for the Marines and Navy and administration. That brought another cheer from the Marines.

Jeffrey then went back up to the administration offices to continue figuring out what needed to be done. He brought meals for his guards and staff. He asked Jonson to contact Jonathon Jackson, the commodities broker, have him come to the office if he is still around.

Shortly afterward, Jackson arrived looking nervous. When he saw Jeffrey in the Administrator's office, he nearly fainted with relief. "What are you doing here?"

"I was made governor – temporarily – after we defeated the aliens." Jeffrey looked around the administration offices. "Like my new digs?"

"It's a far cry from your office in the ship!" Jonathon sat down. "I'm glad it's you who called me. Too many people have been disappearing – especially since being called to this office. And something strange is going on. I can't put my finger on it but it feels like you're being watched all the time."

Jeffrey explained about the aliens, and their conditioning to block any notice of them, plus they had invisibility circuits that made them difficult to see. These aliens were the power behind the success of piracy and the disappearances. Things were now under control, so the station could get back to business. Which was why Jeffrey wanted to speak with Jonathon.

"Mr. Jackson, you and I have been doing business for a long time, my parents before me. I have learned to trust you. So now I am going to ask for your help. We need to get this station in business again. And its primary business is mining and processing of ores for shipment back to Earth. The ships in a cloud around this station are sitting idle. I need those rock jockeys out digging ore. Can you talk to them?"

"Of course, Mr. Sokolov."

"Call me Jeffrey. We've known each other for a long time."

"Jeffrey. But the miners are afraid of the aliens and the pirates. This sector has become unsafe."

"Ah. Well you should tell them that I arranged to have a fighter squadron to be stationed here, and another one at each Lagrange 3 station. Let's get some business going," Jeffrey concluded. Then added, "Those aliens I spoke about? They are going to be our guests. The whole solar system is full of them so we figured the best way to handle them is to start giving them food. They lined up like puppies!" That last, Jeffrey figured would help Jackson accept the fact that their recent oppressive enemies were now their guests. It worked.

"I'll pass that along, sir. We'll get this operation going again!"

"I will be apartment hunting, see you in a while," said Jeffrey to the quartermaster turned office clerk Jonson.

"Why don't you take over the Administrator's suite? I think it should be part of the perks of the office, don't you?"

"Well, I would, but I don't intend to be in this office for too long. I think I should have a separate suite. I'll go arrange something in the Silver level."

"Actually, Captain, you can do that right here." Jonson pulled up a map that showed the vacant suites, so Jeffrey selected a large suite near the safe houses. Jeffrey presented his personal credit chit. Jonson was reluctant to take it, thinking that the Navy should pay.

"Let them reimburse me."

"Very good, sir."

He went walkabout with Torres and Audrey to the furnishings store, bought some basic furnishing groups, and had them scheduled for delivery. When the delivery people came, they were quick to set up his living room, bedrooms and office. The kitchen delivery came next, with all the appurtenances thereto. After the delivery and setup people had gone, (with a handsome tip,) Torres took out his anti-spy device scanner and looked over the whole suite, found nothing, but still looked suspicious.

Torres volunteered to build in several features, like the small armory he had installed in the safe houses. And an emergency escape hatch. He then reached into his coverall pocket and brought out two of Elizabeth's remotes. They climbed the walls and settled into comfortable watchfulness.

Jeffrey then ordered delivery of fresh food from the grocery. They apologized, saying that there had not been any food delivery for some time. Jeffrey called up to the administration offices and asked Jonson if he knew anything about halting delivery of groceries to stock the grocery stores. Jonson told him he would look into it. "Make it priority – there are ten thousand humans on this station, they need to eat."

"Aye, sir."

A few minutes later, Jonson called back with the news that there had been no delivery of food for at least two weeks. He relayed a request to Admiral Kutuzov to expedite large scale deliveries, but it would still be another week before the ships came from Earth.

Jeffrey then went to *Elizabeth* and spoke with Commodore Yusef, requesting emergency immediate delivery of food to feed ten thousand people for a week. Yusef asked about the food they had set aside for the Aliens, but Jeffrey said he wanted to preserve that for the aliens.

Jeffrey suggested that they outfit a large ship with a golden drive and a Navy crew to deliver it. And to provide an emergency kitchen and crews to prepare and serve the population.

Yusef agreed, and twelve hours later a huge cargo ship came blazing into the area just off *Elizabeth's* bow. The ship, *Magister*, began emptying its cargo immediately, but Jeffrey suggested that they only offload enough to prepare one day's meals. *Magister's* captain agreed, and reduced immediate deployment of the rest of the cargo until needed.

Jeffrey then went back to the station, up to his office in the Administration wing, and discovered that there was, indeed a public address system. He had never heard it used before, so was surprised it even existed. He announced that food would be served around the clock to whomever wanted it, for free. He mentioned the location of the food distribution areas. He also said that the alien menace had been taken care of and that we are on a new order – humans are not alone, and while aliens had tried to take over, Humans still ruled the solar system.

He set the message to repeat every hour for the next six hours.

After a few hours, the entire population of the station was eating, was in line to eat, or had just eaten. Marines had provided security, and their armed presence seemed to have a positive psychological benefit.

As things seemed to be running well on their own, Jeffrey decided to take *Elizabeth* to the other Lagrange 3 stations. He got a contingent of Marines from DePaul, as well as the other Marines he had started with and his crew as well as a psychiatrist. He had *Magister* load a couple of days' worth of Human food into *Elizabeth*, and the shuttles took a few palettes of alien food as well. After giving final instructions to DePaul and Jonson, he boarded *Elizabeth*

They left Lagrange 3A, moving against the direction of rotation. After an hour of normal travel, they jumped to supra-light speeds – three times the light speed for a few hours, until they neared the Lagrange 3F station, then slowed to a normal hundred kilometers per second, and decelerating to meet, come around and match the speed of rotational velocity of the Lagrange 3F station. As *Elizabeth* neared the station, they broadcast the usual foghorn tone followed by an announcement that a warship was in the area.

Jeffrey came aboard accompanied by two shuttles worth of Marines. As they marched through the station, they discreetly released numerous Elizabeth's remotes. Jeffrey left Marines, in their hard-shell armor, at strategic locations along the way to the administration offices. He entered the office, greeted the sub-administrator, Kaylee McPherson. He explained that he had been appointed as governor of the entire Lagrange 3 orbit and environs. He then queried about how things were going on at the station. The psychiatrist paid close attention to McPherson as she described the goings on. One of the big issues was the loss of communications from her boss, the Administrator on Lagrange 3A. Also, there had been no foodstuffs distribution from Earth in a few weeks, the stores were getting very low, and she was concerned that people were going to start getting hungry.

Jeffrey told her that they had brought emergency foods, and the Marines would set up a feeding operation. He had Sneaky get that operation going. He then explained that the Administrator had been arrested, but was being given a lower level task. McPherson now reports directly to Jeffrey. He told her how aliens had infiltrated the solar system, and specifically Lagrange 3A. He was looking for evidence of their presence on all the Lagrange stations. He briefed her on the aliens they had encountered, especially the Kang, who had taken over Lagrange 3A, and their invisibility issues. Jeffrey explained that any alien with its invisibility circuit active was subject to be summarily shot. But this responsibility was only for the Marines. He would leave a contingent of Marines on the station, and that the Navy was dispatching a fighter wing to combat any alien ships.

While Jeffrey was briefing the sub-administrator, Elizabeth arranged for a series of safe houses like the ones on Lagrange 3A. Jeffrey also arranged for barracks for the Marines and Navy. He also bought an apartment for himself. Torres went shopping for surplus computer equipment to house another Elizabeth clone. Sneaky bought furnishings for the governor's apartment, then they also bought enough furnishings for the safe houses.

Jeffrey, the psychiatrist, Torres and Sneaky gathered in his new apartment. Jeffrey asked the psychiatrist his opinion of the state of the people of this station. "Sir," he said, "The people here are concerned, but not in shock, not in a post-traumatic state. I don't think they had been invaded by the aliens here."

Torres said, "I concur."

Sneaky nodded. "I see happiness where there wasn't any on Lagrange 3A."

"Good. Tomorrow morning, we'll take off for the next station down the line."

Jeffrey contacted the ship and told them of his plan. He told Janet that he intended to leave half the Marines at this station, bring the rest with him. He asked that she send a report to Admiral Kutuzov using the book, and a general report to Commodore Yusef and Lt. Col. DePaul using general encryption. He asked that she have Yusef dispatch emergency food to all of the Lagrange 3 stations, that he was going to Lagrange 3E in the morning.

CHAPTER TWELVE

It took the *Elizabeth* four hours to traverse the distance to Lagrange 3E, and the outcome was similar to what occurred in Lagrange 3F. He left a small contingent of Marines, had the sub-administrator clear the way for the feeding operation when the fast cargo ship arrived. He arranged for an apartment for himself while Elizabeth arranged for the safe house.

Rather than stay, he got back to *Elizabeth* and moved to the next station on the orbit. Each station followed the same pattern, at each one he left another contingent of Marines, so by the time he got to Lagrange 3B he was down to three squads plus his original contingent.

At Lagrange 3B, however, he saw evidence of invisibility-circuited ships near the station. Elizabeth sounded General Quarters. Jeffrey had Janet bring the ship to just a couple kilometers from a cluster of gravity wells with no associated visible mass. He played through the by now familiar announcement about invisibility circuits, cannibalism, and free food. Yet none of the alien ships turned off their invisibility circuits.

Jeffrey had both rail guns target all the ships in the cluster, and fire a half second burst at each. Within ten seconds, all the alien ships in the vicinity of Lagrange 3B were visible and began lining up per Jeffrey's instructions. He then docked the ship.

Jeffrey left Mbaka and Smith on board, but took all the rest of the Marines with him. As they advanced from the airlock, Elizabeth showed Jeffrey three aliens that still hid themselves in invisibility circuits. Jeffrey halted the advance, spoke aloud, amplified by his suit's external speaker. "All invisibility circuits are illegal in Human Space. Violations will be met with deadly force."

He waited ten seconds, took out his pistol, cocked it and aimed directly at one of the violet blobs that displayed on his visor. The violet turned off and the alien appeared. This one was bipedal, in place of a mouth was a multi-tentacled orifice, some of the tentacles finger-thick and short, while others were halfway down to the floor and thin. The alien spoke in a thin, whiny voice, "Who are you and why do you threaten me?"

Jeffrey noted the other violet blobs began sidling away, and Jeffrey took aim at the one on the left. It appeared and a second later the other one did also.

"This is Human space, under Human law. While here you will obey Human law. I am the enforcer of Human law. In other stations, we didn't even stop to give you aliens a chance to stop violating our law, we just killed any alien using invisibility circuits, either in their ships or on their persons. Now," continued Jeffrey, "Do you have a way to communicate these rules to your fellow aliens here?"

"No." came the reply from the first one to have appeared.

"Really? A technologically advanced species cannot communicate?" Jeffrey knew they were lying, and decided to call its bluff. "Perhaps a direct method of communication will do." He raised his pistol and pointed it at the second one to materialize.

"No, no, no, no. We can communicate."

"Good. Now we are getting somewhere," said Jeffrey. "Tell all your alien friends that to use invisibility will bring instant death. Go ahead, I'll wait."

"It is done."

"Good. Now. What do you call yourselves?"

"We are the Vorsh."

"No, we met the Vorsh. You are not them. Try again." Jeffrey looked at the alien directly in his eyes, noting a nictitating membrane like a cat's or a snake's. "And lying to me is going to be another way to get yourselves killed."

"We are the Vzzvv."

"And who is in charge of the Vzzvv? Who is your leader?"

"We have no..." began the first of the Vzzvv to speak. Jeffrey interrupted him by raising his pistol again.

"The third alien to appear spoke up. "I am their leader. I am Vzzgk."

"Hello, Vzzgk. I am Jeffrey Sokolov. I am a Navy commander and the governor of all the area in the orbit that this and the other five stations occupy. We have been developing a set of laws that specifically govern aliens in Human space." He outlined the rules; no killing humans, no eating each other, no eating humans, etc. "How many of the Vzzvv are there on this station?"

"Not many. Five hundred twenty."

"Have you yet utilized the virus that hypnotizes humans?" asked Jeffrey.

"We only began to do that, but haven't had a lot of success."

"Good. Stop doing that. The virus use is illegal. We understand the aliens of this section of the galaxy think they have power over Earth and our solar system, but that is not the case. We don't want to give you the impression that we are easy to kill off, so we are going to be aggressive in our rules. But if you follow the same laws we make our citizens obey, you can mingle with us, once you register with the Navy or Marines. Oh, and there is free food for aliens, courtesy of the Navy." He called Janet by radio to file an immediate report and requisition additional food for the aliens on this station. He then had Janet take *Elizabeth* to Lagrange 3A to load another thirty Marines, as well as bring back additional Human food and alien food.

Then he took his group, along with the aliens, to the Administration office. The sub- administrator dropped his jaw when Jeffrey and the Marines and the psychiatrist entered his office, followed by the three aliens. Jeffrey introduced himself, informed the sub-administrator that he was in charge in place of the Administrator, but that he, the sub-administrator needed to continue doing his job. "And I need to tell you that your station has been infiltrated by five hundred twenty aliens. These are Vzzvv, and their leader here is Vzzgk. They were planning on hypnotizing your people into not seeing them, but they have invisibility circuits so that wouldn't have always been necessary. However, the use of those circuits is illegal and my Marines will kill them on sight – or not sight, really. But we know how to detect them. On other stations we just shot them if they used the devices, but I figured we could get on better if we gave them a chance to understand that there are consequences for trying to invade and evade us.

"We have a ship coming containing a large amount of food..."

"Good," interrupted the sub-administrator. "Our people have begun to worry when the food stopped coming,"

"But until it gets here, we have some Navy ships coming to set up a feeding station. We also have a supply of food for the aliens. They get free food once they register with the Navy or Marines. The next ship should be here in a couple hours."

Things otherwise went as they had in the other stations, Jeffrey arranged for quarters for himself and commandeered vacant warehouse space for the Marines. When *Elizabeth* arrived from Lagrange 3A, she first disgorged her contingent of Marines, then her shuttles delivered palettes of human and alien food. Then she arranged for the safe house.

Jeffrey sat down in the hardly-ever-used Administrator's office with Vzzgk. He told Vzzgk that Earth wanted to have ambassadors of all the alien races, to be together in one place, the Lagrange military station between Earth and her moon. He asked Vzzgk to identify such an ambassador, and imbue him or her with authority to make decisions for the whole Vzzvv people.

"This is unusual, governor-captain," began the alien leader. "We usually just conquer a people, not negotiate with them."

"Well that's not entirely true," interrupted Jeffrey. "You negotiate with all the other alien races in a council outside our solar system. You can negotiate with us. We will treat you all fairly, as long as you don't try to do nasty things to us, like hypnotize us, eat us, blow up our sun, things like that.

"I have just the Vzzvv to represent us. Her name is Aia. She will not betray our people and can negotiate with yours."

"Very good. If she is acceptable to my people we will both be happy. Are there other aliens on this station, aside from the Vzzvv?"

"There were, but we ate them."

"Now, you see, you have to stop eating sentient beings. That's one of the laws here," Jeffrey tried to control his anger, with some effort he was succeeding. "We will not tolerate any such behavior. I hope that is clearly understood, because if not, we will have a problem."

"What kind of problem?"

"As you are likely aware, Humans have been fighting each other for a long time. We have developed a taste for war. We are a generally peaceful people, but when we need to go to war, we do so very, very well. You don't want a war with the humans."

"Oh."

"So, it is imperative that you cease behaviors that we deem unlawful."

"Yes, governor-captain, I can guarantee the behavior of all the Vzzvv in this station and on the ships."

Very good." Jeffrey stood, and in the universal response to a leader standing, the alien also stood. He didn't understand why, but did anyway. "Now," said Jeffrey, as he escorted the alien leader out the door to the office, "prepare your Aia for her job. We will have a ship going in that direction very soon. We can take her along. Remember, no invisibility circuits."

Jeffrey then had the sub-administrator contact the mining ships surrounding the station, to inform them that supplies will be forthcoming, but until then the station will offer free food. And that there was now an alien presence on the station, but that the miners had nothing to fear. There was a contingent of Marines to be semi-permanently installed on the station for security.

Jeffrey's psychiatrist had analyzed a portion of the population, and concluded that they were not traumatized like the people were on Lagrange 3A. This was a relief to Jeffrey, as now they could concentrate the mental health workers on one station.

Jeffrey then introduced Marine Lieutenant Honjo Kamakura, who came with the emergency contingent from Lagrange 3A, to the sub-administrator and his team, including the Security Officers and their chief. "Kamakura is in charge of the Marines on this station. Security decisions are his to make. But you will all get along." He then took Kamakura down to the Marine barracks, along with the Chief Security Officer, and had them assemble all the security officers, and Kamakura to assemble all the Marines, except for those on security duty.

In a makeshift presentation Jeffrey explained about the Aliens that had invaded their solar system. The ones who landed on Lagrange

3A were the biggest problem, but they seem to have stopped the problem where it was, and was now able to reverse it. He outlined the technology the aliens used, such as the virus. They had used a human to modify the virus to affect human physiology and psychology to the utmost. They did this by making audio and video devices affect people in a hypnotic trance-like state, and this made them more susceptible to the suggestion that they couldn't see the aliens. He explained how to protect against the method, and what to do if they encountered people who seemed to be so affected.

Jeffrey told the Marines that any Marine on patrol was authorized to shoot to kill any alien who hid using the invisibility circuits. "However," he cautioned, "every alien death will be investigated and if your killing was not justified you will be in a heap of trouble."

"Sir," one of the young Marines inquired, "What's a heap?"

"Old talk for a pile. So, you would be in a pile of trouble. Do you understand that, kid?"

"Yes, sir."

He continued, "I want, at this time, to restrict that authorization to the Marines. Security Officers, your work is appreciated, and you will be expected to cooperate with the Marines. But they are responsible for any lethal activities. Clear?"

There was a smattering of "yeah's," and "Yessir's," But Jeffrey was not satisfied. "Are We Clear?" he spoke louder and more emphatically. This got the right response - "Yes Sir!"

After the briefing, Jeffrey took Kamakura and the security officer chief aside. "Honjo, I want you to take my apartment for the duration." Then he turned to the security chief , "Chief, what's your name?"

"Bill Parker."

"Is that a New Orleans accent?"

"It is, sir. Lower Ninth Ward. Played for the Saints for a while, until I injured my knee. Took up security in Space. Here I am."

"Well, glad you're here. I want you two to work together. Do you have space in your office for Honjo?"

"No sir, they kept taking office space away from me and put my guys into a closet!"

"Okay, so here's what's going to happen. You get to use my office in the administration suite. The two of you work out how. I intend security to be happy here, but effective. The Marines are here to protect you from outside forces, mostly the aliens, but also pirates and insurrection.

Security is here to police the Human population. But you both need to support each other. So, anything involving aliens, Kamakura is in charge, and your guys support his guys. The Marines will support your people, but remember they do things in a more ham-handed way. They will be far more lethal. So Honjo will have to temper his guys. Clear?"

They both answered in the affirmative.

The Marines set up two feeding lines, one for the Humans, the other for the Aliens. Both lines were busy, but they didn't mingle. The alien food was in boxes, which they took to their hiding places or their ships, the humans ate at tables served by Navy and Marines. So far, both peoples were happy.

Jeffrey was satisfied that things were going well. He had Janet come aboard the station, and he took watch on *Elizabeth*, so Janet could have some time off. His lieutenant had been on constant duty, and as some consideration, he also gave Torres some time off. They were to stay at one of the safe houses.

On the ship, Jeffrey saw that much of the ship was less than shipshape. There was a good deal of litter on the deck, nicks and scratches on the walls and bulkheads, spills and stains in a variety of places. If he had an adequate-sized crew he would put them to work cleaning, scrubbing, painting and otherwise making his ship better. As it was, he did have Elizabeth's remotes. He put them to work cleaning up the ship. He asked Elizabeth to take the responsibility for keeping the ship in better repair.

He went down to the engineering section in which the golden drive was seated. He found Yuki looking over the controls, checking things off on a list on her tablet. She looked up and greeted him. "It's good to see you on the ship again!"

"Thanks. What are you up to?"

"Checking on the status of our drive. I won't know anything about it unless I can measure and test. So, we have a baseline of information that we can compare further or later use. So far everything looks good, sir."

"That's good," said Jeffrey looking over the drive.

"The thing that has me so concerned," she continued, "is the condition of the alien golden drives. They seem so poorly constructed and pitted. I'm not sure if it's because of the construction or because of poor maintenance. Or over use."

He asked, "Have you analyzed the composition? Are there impurities in the gold, and if so what are they?"

"No, I haven't gotten to doing anything more than a surface analysis. That's in the plans."

"I'm so glad you are with us, Yuki. You have made a lot possible. Keep up the good work. Is there anything you need, anything I can get you or make for you?"

"Not just now, Captain," she replied. "If I think of anything, you know I won't let you leave without knowing what it is."

"Good. How are things going with Heinz?"

"Okay."

"That's all?"

"I like him, but I'm not sure we're compatible. Don't worry about me, sir. If I decide to break it off, it will be gently. But I'm not thinking about that just now. After all, the sex is great."

Jeffrey put his fingers in his ears, and mockingly said "Lalalalala, too much information."

"Oh Captain, you threw us together, I think you had it in mind."

"Guilty as charged. But don't do anything you feel uncomfortable doing. You're important to me, and your happiness is vital. So, if you want to dump him, that's your prerogative, just be gentle. I don't need fighting and unhappiness on the ship."

"Yes, sir. Dad."

She gave him a hug. Jeffrey felt pleased that she looked up to him. He was proud of her and their relationship. "Okay, I need to get back to the rest of my ship. Carry on girl."

"Aye, sir."

He continued on a tour of the ship. He stopped at the smelting and replication area. Here he saw the remotes and robots cleaning up after a manufacturing run. Elizabeth explained that she had just made a new batch of ammunition for the rail guns and for the pistols and carbines. Jeffrey thanked her for her foresight – keeping on top of the needs of the crew and the Marines.

"CAPTAIN, YOU ARE BY FAR THE MOST IMPORTANT PERSON IN THE ENTIRE REGION, PERHAPS IN THE SOLAR SYSTEM. AND CAPTAIN, YOU ARE VERY IMPORTANT TO ME."

"Elizabeth, we together make a powerful team. I can't do half or a quarter of what I do without you. You make me possible."

"THANKS, DAD."

On his way back to the bridge, Jeffrey pondered his ever-growing familial situation. He had lost his wife a decade ago, and had mostly ignored the pain until it became a dull throb in the back of his mind. Losing his parents was much less a blow to him, but still, they were what set him on the course to becoming himself. But he never continued his own family. A new family was growing on him, Yuki, the brilliant young woman with no social skills, the Chong family, and even his AI. He had a life, but it was not complete, yet. Something to think over.

On the bridge he reviewed the recent conflicts, looking for some pattern that showed a larger picture that wasn't evident on the surface. Each group of aliens he had run across were primarily distinct from all the others, the exception being the small group of non-Vorsh in the Lagrange 3A station. And there was only one example of Ay-Yuyuyah – the blob Thelin.

Thelin ended up as an adviser to Admiral Kutuzov, which may or may not have been a good thing – depending on what Thelin's real motives were. Was the information he had been giving Kutuzov valuable to Kutuzov, or to Thelin? These questions deserved a more professional analysis. He asked Elizabeth to locate Heinz, the IntelTech specialist. She reported that he was in his cabin. "Is he asleep?" asked Jeffrey.

"NO, CAPTAIN, HE IS, AS YOU PUT IT, CANOODLING"

"Oh. Never mind."

"IS THERE SOMETHING I CAN HELP YOU THINK THROUGH?" the AI asked.

"You know, it has been a while since I've asked for your intelligence estimate. Yeah." He outlined his thought process, questioning the motives of Kutuzov's adviser, wondering what else they could do to gather more intelligence on their own, rather than relying on what

 ELIZABETH, *ELIZABETH*

the aliens told them or stumbling across aliens or their technology by accident. And how much was the accident really accidental?

"I'LL THINK ABOUT IT CAPTAIN. ALSO, I WANTED TO REPORT THAT WE ARE GOING TO NEED MORE RAW MATERIALS – MORE HEAVY METALS, MORE NOT-METALIC SALTS, AND I THINK THERE ARE SOME USES FOR ALUMINUM THAT WOULD IMPROVE OUR INTELLIGENCE GATHERING."

"Can it wait for us to get back to Lagrange 3A?

"YES, CAPTAIN. I JUST DON'T WANT TO CANNIBALIZE MYSELF TO MAKE AMMUNITION."

"Okay," said Jeffrey. "We'll try to keep that from happening."

The rest of the evening shift was uneventful. His crew who had been on leave began returning. Janet walked, more like sashayed, onto the bridge, wearing a colorful long skirt and a revealing blouse, with some light jewelry that tinkled when she moved. Her hair normally gathered into a severe bun or tight braid, was loose. She seemed happy. Jeffrey looked up from his data pads and asked, "Wow, what's gotten into you?"

"Oh, I don't know. I feel good."

"Elizabeth, pay attention here. Humans like to get a night off every now and then. Look at what it did for Janet!"

"HI JANET. YOU LOOK BEAUTIFUL."

"Thanks, Elizabeth. Captain. I'd better get into uniform." And she sashayed back off the bridge.

"I THINK JANET IS PREGNANT"

"Really? How can you tell?"

"YOU KNOW I HAVE SENSORS ALL OVER THE SHIP – WHEN SHE WALKED ONTO THE BRIDGE, I DETECTED A RISE IN HORMONES THAT SUGGEST SHE IS KNOCKED UP."

"Huh. Well, how about we keep it to ourselves, let her make whatever announcement she wants to."

"MUM'S THE WORD."

"What's that mean?"

"SEVENTEETH CENTURY ENGLISH – MEANING I WON'T SAY ANYTHING."

"Oh. I thought I had a pretty decent vocabulary. I wonder of its etymology? Never mind."

The crew continued to report aboard. Jeffrey got notifications from the Marines that there had been no overnight problems and the Security Office chief also called with the same report.

Jeffrey had the crew prepare to disembark. He radioed the alien ships telling them to continue their good behavior, and that their rations were still available.

Then Elizabeth moved off, slowly at first, so as to avoid breaking anything on the way out, then picking up speed, until they were traveling at four times the speed of light toward where they anticipated Lagrange 3A would be. Janet had the bridge, Jeffrey lay down in the ready room. He slept well. His last thought before dropping off, was he needed to add the rest of his crew as family – not quite as close as Yuki, whom he now thought of as a daughter, and the Chongs, but Torres and Digger, Janet and Sneaky, even Smitty. Like other people thought of cousins or other close relatives. This was more a mental adjustment on his part, but also included the decisions of those other participants.

After a few hours, they slowed down and took a position near where the Lagrange station would come into view following its orbit. More precision would have been preferable, but at light speed, let alone four times light speed, every millisecond could take you hundreds of kilometers off course. After a few seconds of astrogation, Elizabeth announced they were exactly where they needed to be, only an hour early. Jeffrey decided to wait there rather than chase toward the station and then whip around and chase back after it. He went down to the galley, grabbed a breakfast, and ate leisurely. Torres also came in for breakfast, asked if he could join the Captain and sat down when invited.

"Well now I've gone and done it," said Torres, wagging his head.

"Done what?" Jeffrey was pretty certain what the conversation would lead to. "I went and, God this is embarrassing, Janet's pregnant."

"Ah. Congratulations."

"You don't understand, sir. This is a problem for her and for me. There are Navy regs that require we serve in different times and places."

"Not on my boat. I am not releasing you to standard Navy regs. If we are going to hear the patter of little feet on my deck, well I'm all for it. Commodore Yusef thought this was a great experiment. I concur. The experiment continues. So, you two going to get hitched?"

"Uh...we would like to, but thought the Navy...thought we were going to have problems with the Navy."

"Okay, let me fix the Navy part. I'll take away some of their bile by promoting you to Lieutenant. You'd make a good Marine officer."

"Uh...thanks, I think." Torres had been pushing the food around on his plate. He now ate in a hurry. Jeffrey finished his meal, bussed his table, and suggested they go talk to Janet, on the bridge.

There, Janet saw the two enter, saw the shit-eating grin on Torres' face, and said, "Uh, oh. Torres, what did you do?"

Jeffrey answered instead. "Janet, Mr. Torres here, informs me of your, ah, delicate condition."

"Delicate, my ass, sir." Janet smirked.

"Well, then, your condition. Your knocked-uppedness, your preggers, your mom-to-be-ness. That condition. And that you and he, while wishing for a more or less stable relationship, feared the Navy would put you out to dry. Well I've come up with a solution. You get married on my boat. He gets promoted to Lieutenant, and the two of you continue in your service to Earth, while raising a little brat, here, on my boat. What d'ya say?"

She turned to Torres, "You discussed this with him?"

"No, Sweetie, he did all the discussing. Really."

"I would surely have liked to have been part of that discussion!"

"Okay," said Jeffrey. "Talk. Nothing has been cast in stone, so what are your thoughts?"

"Damn it, Captain," said Janet in a voice that told Jeffrey she was a bit pissed. "You already did the thinking. Those were my thoughts. I just wanted to have them myself."

"Sorry. Janet, what would you like to do?"

"I want to marry this lunk, have a few kids, and continue living and working on this boat."

"Okay then. When do you want to get hitched?"

"Tomorrow?"

"Okay. Be on the hanger deck at 1800 hours."

"Aye, sir. And Ajo," she added to Torres. "Dismissed."

Torres, a look of confusion on his face, said, "Yessir. Ma'am." Then saluted did a perfect about- face and skedaddled off the bridge.

The station began to loom up on its wide curving orbit, so Elizabeth began speeding up to match orbital velocities with it and the cloud of miner's ships surrounding it. They made the usual announcement of their presence, came within parking distance and settled. The large fast freight ship that had brought the food for the station had left, back to Earth to replenish then service other stations. But Jeffrey noticed several freight ships on the docks, unloading their wares.

Jeffrey notified Jonson that he was back and would be up to his office in a bit. He came onto the station on one of the shuttles.

He then dropped in on DePaul. "Colonel, I've left Marines at each of the stations; more for those with alien presence." Lagrange 3B had by far the largest congregation of aliens, so he left more Marines there. He left Lieutenant Honjo Kamakura in charge of alien security. The Security office seemed best primed to run security for the Humans on the station.

He suggested the Lt. Col. requisition additional troops for all the Lagrange stations. If things calm down, in time those reinforcements can be shipped elsewhere, but as it was things just were too unsettled.

He made his way up to the administration offices, reclaimed his office, and went through the administrative decisions that had been made in his absence. Things looked pretty solid. He then called for the psychiatrist that had been seeing Omotunde to come to the office. When he arrived, Jeffrey inquired on Omotunde's stability and ability to serve. He gave Omotunde a tentative clean bill of health, so Jeffrey had him come to the office.

When Lt. Omotunde arrived, Jeffrey said, "Doc, here says you are well enough to come back to work, to do some intelligence analyses. What do you think?" Jeffrey twirled a pen while awaiting a response from the Nigerian-born Marine officer.

Eventually, Omotunde said, "Sir, I don't have any bad dreams, I have no fears, no flashbacks. I think I am ready to serve."

"That's good. But if you do suffer any of these, even small things, I want you to, I *order* you to report immediately to me and to a psychiatrist. Welcome back to work, Lieutenant."

"Thank you, sir. I'll get back to work today."

"Make it tomorrow. I have some things I want to run by you, but let's start fresh, okay?"

"Yes sir."

After Omotunde left, Jeffrey thanked the psychiatrist for his diligence in keeping Omotunde sane.

"All in a day's work, sir," he replied with a nod.

He then filed reports for Kutuzov, Yusef and the staff on his stations. He requested a promotion for Torres, notified them that Torres and Bianca were getting married and elected, at his insistence, that they would continue to work on his ship.

After he finished his work he decided to go walkabout again.

He paid a visit to the Chong family, and found they were busy figuring out the restaurant, Lee and Sul were down at the restaurant, while Kim was in the apartment, doing homework – her schooling still counted. She was glad enough for the relief from schoolwork to make Jeffrey some tea and cookies. Things were looking very hopeful for the Chong family, and Kim was delighted that Jeffrey had taken an interest in them. "You and your parents are special to me," said Jeffrey, stirring a cube of sugar into his tea. "My wife died ten years ago, before we were ever able to start a family. I'd like to think of you and your parents as an extension of my family."

"I would like that," said Kim. "I haven't been able to get to know too many people being out on the ship, and some that I've met I would rather I didn't. But everybody associated with you seem to be good people. You bring about the best in everyone."

"Aw, gee. Thanks," Jeffrey blushed. "So, what are you doing for schoolwork?"

"A curriculum my Mom picked out for me. Right now, I'm wrestling with calculus, but it seems to argue with spatial geometry, and I'm trying to figure out how to incorporate what we know about faster-than-light travel with astrophysics. I'm getting confused."

"Well, I've got a little time, maybe I can help you figure it out. And where I fall short, maybe Elizabeth can chime in."

"Really? Way cool!" And she brought the tablet to show Jeffrey what she was talking about. He thought he understood her dilemma, and spent the next hour showing the ranges of differences, and where the standard differential equations fell short when incorporating Quantum Mechanics in Einstein's Universes.

Shortly afterward, Chong Sul and Chong Lee came home. Kim jumped up from the table and excitedly told her parents they had a visitor, and he had shown her how to do the problems correctly, and that he made it so she could understand! Jeffrey rose when they came into the kitchen where he and Kim had been working. Sul said, "I've been trying for days to find a way to explain all the little things she couldn't put together, but I couldn't put it together either! How did you do that?"

"Let's let Kim explain. Kind of a test." Jeffrey sat back down and crossed his arms. Lee made more tea, but listened in on the conversation. Kim began to explain how things changed depending on the scale you worked on. At sub-atomic scales, the rules differed from the Newtonian – scale – that is to say, our scale – and universe – sized scales. Time used to be thought of as a constant, but that was shown not quite to be the case. By the time she was done, her mother and father had a glimmer of understanding, but it wasn't quite as certain as Kim's.

"Do I pass the test?" Kim asked Jeffrey.

"Let's ask your Mom and Dad. Folks?"

"I must say, she understands this much better than me," said her father. Her mother nodded in agreement and sympathy. "But I now know what she was talking about. I understand how things come together, while before I just got along with the Newtonian Physics."

Lee said, "When I was her age, I had trouble putting this all together too. But I didn't have a person as smart as you to teach me."

"Aw, gee," said Jeffrey bashfully. "Kim, I think it's unanimous. You pass!" Then to her parents, "I'm going to need to go in a few minutes. Tell me how the restaurant is coming along?"

"It's beautiful, Jeffrey," replied Chong Lee. "I think as soon as we can arrange for some food we will begin – we'll open it up. We've been posting flyers everywhere, talking to the neighbors, everyone seems excited."

"Great! I understand there are some freighters outside the station with food. Were you able to talk to a distributor?" asked Jeffrey.

"No. Nobody told us there were any deliveries. I thought we had to wait." Lee said.

"Let me look into it tomorrow morning. See ya!"

The following morning, he asked Jonson about the freighters on the dock. "Sir, he said, "they contain our foodstuffs for the grocery and food distribution warehouses. But we can't get them to unload."

"Why not?"

"The union said they hadn't been paid yet for all the work they had done over the last two months when the aliens were here. The warehouses said they hadn't been paid either – the aliens just took the food. So, they just sit across a table from themselves staring."

"Why is this the first time I heard this? Don't you think this is the kind of issue I need to be part of?" Jeffrey asked, his anger rising.

"Sorry, sir. I was trying to figure a way to handle it, I guess it just got away from me."

 ELIZABETH, *ELIZABETH*

"All right. Get me the union leaders and the warehouse leaders and the ship captains, here, in my office in one hour. This takes priority."

Jeffrey also requested that his chef send over some fresh Kolaches, and coffee for the conference. When the union bosses arrived, they sat together at one end of the conference table, and the warehouse owners came and sat in their own clique, as did the ship captains.

Jeffrey hoarded the sweet pastries in front of himself, poured the coffee into his own cup, made a show of stirring the sugar – he usually took it without sugar, but wanted the effect to be memorable. One of the union leaders got up to get a Kolache – Jeffrey asked him his name. "Kowolski. Stosh Kowolski. Hey, these Kolaches are good!"

"Great," said Jeffrey. "Stosh. Sit here by me." Now there were two people eating the sweet-smelling fruity pastries. One of the warehouse owners got up and reached for one of the Kolaches. Jeffrey had him sit on his other side. Eventually all the participants were sitting around Jeffry's end of the table discussing the merits of apricot vs. prune Kolaches, one of the ship captains said he thought the cinnamon were better than both the fruit types, but he was shouted down.

When he felt the time was right, Jeffrey interrupted the discussion of pastry and coffee to bring the attention to the reason they were there. "Ladies and gentlemen, I have a station here with ten thousand hungry people. What do I have to do to get those ships unloaded, the warehouses full, and everyone profitable again?"

The union leader, Stosh Kowolski, who first came to the Kolaches end of the table, said, "Governor, my workers feel they should be compensated for the work we had to do when those aliens were here." The other union representatives agreed.

But the warehouse owners said, "They cleaned out our inventory – everything! And didn't pay us a green cent."

Jeffrey asked if they were covered by insurance.

"Well, yeah, but that doesn't begin to cover it. The lost profits, the start-up costs, not to mention damage to our warehouses."

The ship captains were represented by one who said, "We just want things unloaded and go on our way."

Jeffrey sipped his Italian roast coffee. All three groups looked to him as he savored the aroma, the deep, rich flavor. He then put the cup down, gently, and said, "So, for the dock workers, it is a matter of compensation for work done that wasn't paid for." Dock workers nodded at the summary of their position. "The warehouse owners want more compensation than their insurance covered." The warehouse owners looked at each other then back to Jeffrey, and nodded in unison. "And the ship owners don't care how it is worked out, just so it is worked out." The captains agreed.

"So, here's what I am going to do. I will pay the dock workers for work they did while under the influence of the aliens. I will pay the warehouse owners for damage that wasn't compensated by their insurance companies, and I will see about getting reimbursed by the aliens. Is that satisfactory to everyone?"

"Unions will agree to that. We'll get right back to work."

"Warehouse owners agree. Thank you, Governor."

"Just so you all realize that I am going to collect from the aliens, you cannot also collect from them. Is that clear?"

"Normally, we would try to collect directly from the offending party," said one of the warehouse owners. "But I think we can let it go just this once."

Everybody agreed, shook hands, wiping their sticky fingers on the napkins. The dock worker's representatives left first, to get

 ELIZABETH, *ELIZABETH*

their workers back going. The ship captains thanked Jeffrey for his intervention, and then the warehouse owners thanked him for his judicious and timely decision-making.

With the representatives gone, he shared the rest of the Kolaches with his office staff.

Reports started coming in of the warehouses filling up, section grocery stores were being resupplied and restaurants were talking about opening. Jeffrey called Chong Sul and told him the good news, so he and Chong Lee locked up and went to the nearest warehouse. They came back with a small inventory and a promise of a full delivery within a couple of hours. They began heating up the cooking oil they had just bought, prepared the kitchen for all they would do, then waited for the delivery.

When the delivery came, they quickly put the food away in the appropriate places – cooler, freezer, dry storage. Then Chong Lee began prepping her food, cutting beef into strips, marinating, cutting vegetables, making noodles, starting chicken to make broth, and soup and all the things one used it for. Within a few hours, they opened the doors. A few curious people walked in, sat down and were immediately greeted with a plate of appetizers.

"We didn't order this," said the man.

"This is gift. On the house." Chong Sul replied. "Our first day open."

The customers then placed an order; a beef dish, ate it lustily, and were effusive in their praise. They came back a couple hours later with some friends. Soon the restaurant was as busy as could be expected – every chair filled. Kim took orders, Sul and Lee cooked, and Sul and Kim served. They worked hard all night, but it was a successful first day.

They counted their earnings at the end of the day, and on top of the tips had made enough to buy adequate food for the next couple weeks. Chong Sul then took a portion of the take, divided it and gave a portion to his wife and another to his daughter. "We did good today. More tomorrow!"

On their second day open, Jeffrey visited the restaurant. He saw the sign outside the restaurant read King's Feast in gold letters on a bright red background. He entered and was greeted by Chong Sul, who insisted his wife and daughter come out of the kitchen. When they saw what the commotion was all about, they both ran up to Jeffrey and gave him a big hug. It was not busy in the restaurant, so Chong Lee had been doing prep work for later that evening. Kim had been helping out, folding napkins and placing utensils in the napkins – either fork, knife and spoon or spoon and chopsticks. She placed them in different piles.

Chong Sul then sat Jeffrey down, Kim brought tea for them both, and water and soup. Jeffrey said, "I don't know much about Korean food, so I should let you order for me." When the food was ready, the whole family came to the table. Chong Lee brought Jeffrey beer and her husband a glass of fruit juice to go along with the meal, then they all sat down to eat. They thanked Jeffrey for getting the warehouses going again. Then they said a prayer thanking God for their food, and for each other, and for Jeffrey. He, not being a religious man, said nothing, but knew enough to be quiet during the family's religious obligations.

Lee said, "Jeffrey, you have done us a great gift. You have taken us under your wing. You were our angel, and we are happy and proud to know you."

"I don't know what to say. I only did what I thought was right."

"You don't know God, but God knows you. Just remember to do good works." Said Lee sincerely.

"Something I told Kim the other night when I was helping with her homework," he nodded to the young girl, "I think of you as part of my family. You are all important to me."

Chong Sul lifted his glass of juice in a toast, Jeffrey lifted his beer. "To family!"

They continued eating their lunch, when Jeffrey broached the other reason he had come to the restaurant. "Sul," he started. "I guess we have a decision to make. You seem pretty happy here in the restaurant. What about the *Mistral*? Were you going to continue to do mining, or did you want to concentrate on the restaurant?"

"Jeffrey, at this time, I think I need to concentrate on the restaurant. If you lease Mistral to another miner, then we can maybe go back to it later. But for at least the near future, I had best help out here."

"Very well," said Jeffery, I'll see about doing that. I need some minerals for *Elizabeth*, so I guess I'll just work with my old broker. And you really need to stick with this restaurant – this food is out of this world!" Jeffrey sat back, finished his beer, then said, "Can you come to *Elizabeth* tonight? We are going to have a wedding – Torres and Janet are getting married at 1800 hours."

"Really! That's great!" shouted Kim.

"I don't know," said Lee. I hate to close on our second night.

"Please, Mom, She's a real friend. We can go, then have them come to the restaurant afterward."

"All right, all right. We'll go, then have them come here, then we'll give them our gifts, then restaurant as normal."

"Yay!" shouted Kim. "We have to go shopping, Mom."

"I don't have anything to wear," complained Lee. "And what to buy them for a gift? Husband," she continued. "You continue chopping vegetables. Your daughter and I are going shopping."

They carried the dishes to the buss station, Kim filled the dishwasher, ran it, and put everything away. They made a sign that told potential customers they would be away until 20:00. Then Kim and Lee went shopping, Sul went to the kitchen to chop vegetables, and Jeffrey went away.

He had Elizabeth inform Janet about the restaurant's request that they spend time there after the wedding. Then he went to his old broker's office. "Governor!" Jonathon called out. "I am so glad to see you! What brings you to my little office?" Indeed, it was a little office, crammed with all sorts of electronics – commodities prices computers, communications, calculating equipment.

Jeffrey told him about *Mistral*, and said he was looking for someone to lease her. "I have just the person. She's a recent widow who used to work with her husband. Her ship was destroyed by pirates, and she is looking for a small ship. Let me have her contact you. Her name is Sandra Knutson."

Jeffrey thanked Jonathon, and took his leave. He then went back to his office. He asked Jonson if he knew where he was likely to find Lars Olson, the security chief. He hadn't seen him among the security officers, and none of the officers he had captured before taking over the station from the aliens could say where he had gone. Jeffrey met with Omotunde, and asked him where Olson was likely to be hiding or hid. Omotunde said he would see what he could do to find the security chief.

Jeffrey then told Omotunde of his concerns about the aliens, and asked for an analysis. He would then compare Omotunde's analysis with Elizabeth's.

He then returned to the ship, got dressed in his finest military uniform, and started planning on what he was going to say to the couple. He left the decorations up to Elizabeth, who knew more about such things than he did anyway. When the time came, he walked to the shuttle bay, saw that the shuttles had been removed. There was a small crowd, but it seemed to be growing larger and larger by the moment. Jeffrey then noticed that people were entering the ship via access tubes. Elizabeth had apparently docked herself and extended the flexible tubes as gangways.

By the time 1800 rolled around, there were several hundred people dressed in fancy dress on the hanger deck. The decorations were tasteful – long strips of shiny aluminum foil in pastel shades of pink and blue. A red carpet stretched from the back of the hanger, the aft end of the ship, to the front, where a platform was erected.

On both sides of the carpet were lightweight but sturdy benches so all participants could be seated. On each bench was a small pile of flimsies with a text of the program. Jeffrey walked to the platform and stood at attention. The noise of the crowd died down a little. Then from the back of the hanger deck a bosun's whistle sounded. All noise quieted, people took their seats.

Then a sound like a long braying of a donkey echoed throughout the room. The sound continued for a long time, then was joined by other, higher sounds, recognizable now as the bellows and pipes of a lone bagpipe.

The piper, dressed in a navy plaid kilt and jacket, with a matching colored bagpipe, began piping a tune, "Wedding at Malborough." Nobody recognized the tune, or likely had ever heard it before, and after the bagpipe had been playing for some time, it was wondered by some whether they would ever hear anything ever again. Then the tune stopped and the piper started again with a dorian-mode rendition of the Wagner Wedding March. It was almost recognizable, and some people took it for what it was, a tune played on an instrument that didn't have the right notes for it, but played with enthusiasm and a pedal-point drone. The piper marched slowly, to his own beat, the drone continuing on. Ten steps behind the piper, the newly commissioned Lieutenant Ojo Torres marched, matching footfalls with the piper. Torres was in a new dress uniform with his lieutenant bars shining brightly. The officer's cover, a cap, flat on top, rising to the front, with a Marine badge on the front sat uncomfortably on his head, not something he had ever worn before. He wore a sword, a ceremonial blade, that was much more than that. The saber was a real fighting blade, even though it had hardly ever been out of its scabbard. Torres was sure that his ears would fall off if the piper didn't stop soon.

Then, as the piper reached the platform, he turned around, played the last of the wedding march, then let his bags deflate, although many people could still hear the loud ringing in their ears. A solo flute picked up the music, filling the air with a piece originally written for solo violin, a sweet and melodious piece by the old master JS Bach. The flutist came into view – Yuki – in a low-cut turquoise dress that swept the deck as she walked and played. Behind Yuki came Janet in a sheer white dress, with a formfitting body suit underneath. She seemed emotionally numb, but kept herself erect as she walked behind her friend playing the Bach piece.

At last, all participants were assembled, the music stopped and people were just getting over the blast from the piper. Jeffrey spoke in a loud, clear voice.

"All you who are gathered here today are witness to a beautiful thing; the joining of two friends into one. The mating of Human families into a cohesive whole, the development of a partnership that will grow into a solid, single unit.

"This couple has tried each other out. They have held each other lovingly and tenderly, and have initiated a love that has transcended their stations. They hold many things compatibly – they are both combat professionals. They are both shipmates. They hold friendships in common. They have defended our system from attack by alien hoards and have pursued evil.

"Today they embark on a journey together, as shipmates, as bedmates, as friend to their captain and crew. They together bring the best of their lives here, they together stop being just one or just the other, or just two individuals, they become a family.

"As part of this ceremony, I give a charge to both of these, my officers; Do not sell your mate short. Neither one of you shall do anything hateful to the other. Never let the sun set on your anger. Bring hope to your offspring, lead them in light of the love you display for us all today. You are both extraordinary individuals. If one shall fail, the other shall be there to lean on. Always let this be so.

"Lieutenant Torres, present the ring for inspection." Torres reached into his pocket, where he knew the ring was – he had been fiddling with it for the last four hours. He presented it to Jeffrey. Jeffrey said, "Is there anyone here who wishes to bless this ring?"

Chong Lee stood and walked up the red carpet, up the platform. She was dressed in a traditional Korean wedding official outfit—black and gold and red dress with a long jacket with wide sleeves and broad cuffs. She said a prayer in Korean. She then stood beside Jeffrey, who said to Torres, "Please place the ring on Janet's finger." He did.

"Lieutenant Bianca, present the ring for inspection." Janet took the ring from a string around her neck. The string came loose immediately, and the ring fell into Jeffrey's hand. He wondered how the string held until now, but he had early on learned never ask a magician how a trick worked. Chong Lee said a prayer over the ring Janet had presented. Then Jeffrey handed it back to her and asked her to place it on Torres' finger.

"Are there any here who have good cause to object to the wedding of these two lovers? Not hearing any, I now, as authorized by nautical tradition and Navy regulations, pronounce these two wedded."

The wailing and caterwalling of the bagpipes started up again, and he played a quick tune nobody recognized, but this time he made a hasty retreat. By the time he got to the end of the red carpet he was ready to shut down his pipes. After the bag deflated, he took out the earplugs.

Janet and Torres walked down the aisle together, arm in arm, greeted by everyone who had attended. Women wept, men applauded, a hastily organized double line of Marines drew their swords and made an arch for them to walk under.

"Thank you, Captain, for letting me help in the ceremony," Lee said. It is important to me that God have a touch on all such things as this."

"Lee, I am not a believer, but I am also not a disbeliever. If you present a part of the universe that I cannot see or touch, but that you can, then I think we together have made a greater thing here. Don't you?"

"Yes, Captain, I do."

"See you at the restaurant!" said Jeffrey. As people began filtering out of the ship through the extended pressurized gangway, the little remotes began removing the aluminum bunting and tinsel strips that had brightened the hanger for the occasion. They carried the thin aluminum strips to the aluminum bin for recycling.

The shuttle bay began to look military again. After the last of the gaily clad visitors had left the ship, the shuttles reentered the bay and locked down. Jeffrey disembarked and made his way to the King's Feast restaurant. When he entered, Chong Sul, dressed in a tuxedo, called everybody's attention, and a round of spontaneous applause broke out. Jeffrey waved, acknowledging the recognition, then sought a way to find an obscure corner, but Lee wouldn't let him. She dragged him to the head of the table which held a splendid feast and beautiful place settings. She rang a glass to get everybody's attention, told them to find the place card with their names. The guests sorted themselves out, and within a minute, everyone was seated.

The Chongs were not drinkers of alcohol, but that didn't prohibit them from offering champagne for those who drank. Lee nudged Jeffrey, and when he looked at her confusedly, she whispered, "You toast the bride and groom!" Jeffrey noticed her dressed in a black pantsuit with a black short-waisted jacket.

So, Jeffrey rose, held his glass up and said, "Your attention, please." The hubbub of talk died down, and when the revelers saw what Jeffrey was doing, they also held their glasses up. Some glasses contained the champagne of a traditional toast, others contained a fruit juice or punch or water. But the sentiment was the same; drink to the health and in agreement with whatever Jeffrey said.

"I have known the bride and groom since they first stormed aboard my ship in an effort to arrest me. I'm glad they failed in that first meeting!" Chuckles and a few nervous laughs broke out among the guests. "But immediately afterward, they joined forces with me to wrest control of a Navy vessel from the clutches of mutineers and pirates. In doing that, she drafted me. This put her under my command. After we re-secured the warship they came from, they and a couple others were assigned to me, as a new military person.

"Ojo Torres has become a powerful advocate for competence on my ship. Because of him, we have had success in every endeavor we have undertaken. Janet Bianca was a feisty Petty Officer, who fulfilled all my expectations and exceeded them. Both of these lovers were promoted to Lieutenant, a rank that gives them considerable authority and responsibility. So, let me break this toast down to one thing. These are smart, competent, honest, loving, caring, beautiful and handsome, loyal, and determined people, whom I fully intend to keep in my command! So, here's to a long, productive marriage! Janet and Ojo!"

Shouts of 'Here, here,' and a smattering of applause rang out. Torres stood and the crowd quieted down a little. "Thanks, Captain for the kind words. I have only one thing to say," here he took Janet's hand, she stood too. He placed his cup of juice on the table, and it promptly fell off. He looked at the stain on the carpet, shrugged, put his hands around Janet's waist, drew her closer to him, then gave her a tender kiss. She put her arms around his neck, drew him even closer, and kissed him a bit more passionately. After half a minute, they relaxed their embrace, Torres turned to the table, picked up the Captain's champagne glass, and said "Let's get this feast going!" To which everyone laughed and applauded.

The Chong family began bringing out trays of prepared dishes, including some traditional Korean fare, some vegetarian dishes, some standard catering fare – chicken Kiev, stuffed pork chops, eggplant Parmesan and more and more. Jeffrey now saw that the Chongs had changed their outfits again. This time they wore starched pure white chef's jackets, small chef's toques, checked pants and comfortable shoes.

After most people had finished their meals, Kim began busing the tables. Jeffrey saw she was now wearing a formal Korean long jacket – black with embroidered dragons. Then she removed the beautiful table decorations. Lee brought a seven-tiered wedding cake with pale blue and pink and white icing. Ojo drew his sword (he had made sure it was very clean, first,) and sliced the cake – at least the first slices, which he served to Janet and himself. Kim took over the cake cutting and plating, using a more traditional cake knife.

After the ceremonies and speeches and dining were done, the well-wishers cheered Janet and Ojo on as they boarded the elevator to one of the safe-houses they intended to use for their honeymoon suite. Jeffrey gave the couple a week to themselves. If an emergency arose the ship could work without them.

CHAPTER THIRTEEN

In which Jeffrey meets Sandra. Mistral is attacked by Aliens and Pirates.
Jeffrey finally gets laid. What Aliens would do for real food. Jeffrey meets
criticism. *Elizabeth* rescues an alien ship full of frozen passengers.

As it was, there were no emergencies. Things were settling down, while not quite tranquil, they were at least peaceful. Jeffrey was contacted by the sub-administrator at Lagrange 3B, who asked if there were instructions for getting Aia, the Vzzvv's appointed ambassador, to Earth.

Jeffrey asked that the next supply ship should take her back there, and the Marines should appoint two of their own to accompany, guard her, for her own safety and the safety of everyone else.

While in his office, he had a visit from Sandra Knutson, the widow of the man killed by pirates, who was interested in leasing *Mistral*. He asked her, "What do you intend to do? Do you have any experience with mining, piloting a miner's ship?"

She sat there, quietly for a bit. Then spoke, as if narrating to herself, "So there I was, married, happy, planning for the future, saving up our earnings so we could be alone together for a while. Carl arranged for us to begin the first part of his plan – the prospecting part, figuring out where we could go to find the best places to find our ore, and what kind of ore we could find. I was along on that last trip in a large runabout – big enough for us and some equipment, but not much more. We found some serious ore-bearing rock that wasn't claimed by anyone. We planted claim buoys.

"That was a mistake. The buoys broadcast an ownership message, which means they could find us. They found us." She sobbed a gasp, but waved off Jeffrey when he sat forward to console her. "They killed my husband. They shot him with one of those needlers – the little flachettes that cut into you and rip you up inside? He was immediately dead, but he looked fine. Then they threw him out the airlock.

"I was next. There were six in that crew. The bald one, his name was Flegand,"

Jeffrey interrupted, "Pauli Flegand?" She nodded in the affirmative, but continued.

"He was the first. I felt so dirty. What could I do? How was I going to stay alive? Then Flegand finished with me, another one – an ugly guy called Capaldi. And after Capaldi there was a handsome, thoughtful one. He wore a condom, though I think more for himself than for me.

"Rascal. I stopped paying attention to them after that. They cut up my space suit. They punched a hole in the side of my ship – not a big one, just large enough to ensure I don't survive a trip back to the station. They stole my radio gear. And they left, just like that. Their intent was to terrorize, and they did. I wept and wailed, to the tune of the air whistling out that hole, for half an hour.

"Damned if I was going to let them get away with it. So, I got some plastic flimsies and some tape and I covered that hole. Then I taped my spacesuit.

"Carl was the one who knew how to drive that thing, but I figured it out. I figured out where the station was and I drove there. Bastards. The guy who rented the runabout said I owed for the damage – their insurance doesn't cover pirate attacks. I reported to the security office, and they asked what I wanted them to do about it. That's when I learned that the whole damn place was being run by pirates.

"I didn't have anyone to turn to. I saw Flegand once in the Zokolo market. I think I ducked away in time, but I was terrified all over again. Then I talked to Jonathon – the rock broker. He helped hide me away. The only good man on the fricking station."

She sat there, furrowed brow, anger evident, but controlled. Her breathing was a little faster, but her face neutral.

"I know those pirates," Jeffrey said. "They attacked my ship while I was picking up rocks. I captured them and turned them over to the Navy. That was eight months ago."

She raised her eyebrows in surprise. Jeffrey continued, "If you like, I can find out what happened to them since then."

"Oh, yeah," she said. "Oh, yeah."

"So, you didn't answer my question. What do you intend to do with my ship? It's called the *Mistral*, by the way."

"I want to go find that field we discovered, and mine it. I want to do it for my Carl. I want to do it for me. And I want those bastards to fry."

"Well, I can't help you with the frying part, but I think I can help with the rest. You haven't really got any idea how to mine, do you?"

"Just what I've read. And those trips with Carl."

"Let's do this. I will take you on a one-week trip to a known good field, show you the ropes, then come back here, and if you still want to lease the *Mistral*, then she's all yours."

"A week, eh?" She thought for a few moments, then said, "Sure. You're on." She held out her hand, Jeffrey took it and they shook on the deal. "How much more is that going to cost me?"

"Nothing. I owe myself a holiday, so I'll take my little ship out and enjoy the company," Jeffrey said. "Come aboard the *Elizabeth* tomorrow, and I'll have my replicator make you a better suit, then we'll go for a ride on *Mistral* for a week."

Jeffrey went to the Torres residence (Australia, it was called in their safe-house lingo.) Janet answered the door, and greeted Jeffrey fondly, then called out, "Honey, come here! It's Jeffrey!"

"I'm in the bathroom!"

"Come on in Captain! What can I do for you? Can I get you a beer?" Jeffrey accepted the beer, and they chatted for a few minutes, until Ojo came out to join them. He grabbed a beer for himself, and a juice for Janet.

"So I'm going to take a little vacation, kids, and I need you back on *Elizabeth*. I am going to take *Mistral* out with a possible client, and if all goes well, she'll lease it." Jeffrey took a sip from the bottle of lager.

"SHE?" asked Janet. "Tell us more!"

"Just a customer. Don't get excited."

Janet pouted, disappointed that she never got to see Jeffrey have any fun. She said, Okay, we'll be in at 08:00 tomorrow.

Jeffrey stood, and as he walked to the door, said, "She will be on *Elizabeth* tomorrow, I'm having Elizabeth make her one of our special sets of hard-shell and soft suits for the trip."

"Oooh," replied Janet in excitement. "I'll be able to see the boss's lady!" Jeffrey just growled.

"Thanks for the beer." And he left. He went directly to *Elizabeth* and set up the meeting with the security detail, made sure Elizabeth had enough raw materials to make what she needed. Then he pulled over the hood and a small helmet, and walked over to the *Mistral*, where he prepared it for the trip. He saw that the tanks were full, that there were all the prospecting tools and machines he had left with the Chongs. He went back to *Elizabeth* and picked up a variety of weapons and charge packs and ammunition, walking back to *Mistral* to hide away. He saw that there was enough food for several weeks, so that wasn't a concern.

He notified Elizabeth that he was going to sleep aboard *Mistral*. She replied "GOOD NIGHT, CAPTAIN."

At 0600, he awoke, went to the office and shot out a few memos. One to the sub- administrator to initiate a new system of gates that had flexible, extensible gangways to the ships at the outer docks. When he returned he wanted a report from engineers and architects. Another to all the Lagrange 3 stations that he was going to be out of contact for a while. Military matters would be handled by Lt. Col. DePaul and Lt. Bianca Torres the acting Captain of *Elizabeth*, civilian matters to be handled by sub-administrators. Lt. Bianca Torres would know how to get in touch with him.

He came aboard *Elizabeth* at 0745, showed Janet where they were going on the asteroid map, then went to his cabin to pick up his hard-shell suit. He saw a new communicator on his table with a flimsy note from Elizabeth telling him that this one was special – it would communicate directly with her from a distance. It fit in an inside pocket of his hard-shell suit and connected automatically with all suit systems, including the suits radio.

At 0800, Elizabeth announced that the Marines were escorting his guest aboard. He met her at the forward airlock, and escorted her to the replicator chamber. There Elizabeth took a three-dimension scan for measurements, then began the process of making the special soft suit. That only took a few minutes, so Jeffrey offered her his cabin for her to change into the new suit.

When she came out, he explained how this was an improvement on the old emergency suit because it worked both as a complete suit, protecting the wearer from small impacts of sand- sized meteors, as well as projectiles fired from most human weapons. It dissipated beam weapon beams, small plasma shots and other things that people designed to hurt other people. With a face mask, it gave enough protection so a person could survive in space for quite some time.

She wore the suit mostly okay, Jeffrey adjusted the hood so it wasn't quite so bunched up. She looked natural in the suit. They then walked to the replicator chamber again and Elizabeth was nearly finished with the hard-shell suit. After the hard-shell suit was complete, Jeffrey helped her into it, and saw that it contained several new features – built in suit-to-suit radio, long range radio, emergency backup oxygen in case the air recyclers and scrubbers failed. But Elizabeth wasn't finished. She made a quick one-off run of a pistol for Sandra. It was smaller than the Marine standard, but held the same size round. There was a magazine containing six rounds, and several boxes of additional ammunition and several additional empty clips.

Jeffrey saw a tag on her suit at the inner thigh, where he had secreted a pistol himself before on his own suit. The tag had an image of the pistol. Jeffrey showed Sandra the pistol, how rounds were fed into the magazine, how the magazine was fed into the handle of the pistol, how to jack a round into the firing chamber and then how to aim and shoot. He showed her the safety, and how to tell if it was safety-on or safety-off. He then put the loaded weapon in her inner thigh pouch and zipped it shut. He gathered the additional clips, the box of ammunition, put them into her suit pockets, and went to his cabin, where he got into his own hard-shell suit, then exited the ship with Sandra. They walked to *Mistral,* entered via the front airlock, where they carefully hung up the hard-shell suits.

Jeffrey took her on a tour of the small ship. He explained that this had been the property of a family who had a small business in Earth orbit, cleaning up detritus and debris, when taken over by a pirate that intended to drop rocks on various cities. They killed the pirate as Jeffrey with his very fast ship destroyed the pirate ship. They met him when he parked at the Earth-Moon Lagrange station, and he became enamored of the family, bought their ship and transported them out to the Lagrange 3 orbit.

The family was now a restaurant-owning family on Lagrange 3 – the King's Feast. "Oh, I heard of that.," she said. "A new restaurant in Silver level. I haven't eaten there yet. What's it like?"

"Nice. They really can cook. They specialize in Korean food, but also have some non- Korean foods too. They catered my Exec officer's wedding." Jeffrey said proudly. "I love that family, and they will do anything for me. Kind of a cozy relationship."

"Must be nice," she said, then apologized immediately. "I didn't mean that to come out sarcastically."

He continued showing their habitation for the next week. "This is your cabin, and across here is mine. There's a common bathroom. It used to service two females, so it should be comfortable for you. The galley is the common room, it features a kitchen and a dinette." He showed her the pantry, the rest of the living space, then the engineering section, the fuel tanks with the crawl tubes between them. Then the aft section, which included the engineering rooms and rock holds. In the engineering section, Jeffrey had added a hanger for his runabout. A few modifications from when he first acquired the *Mistral*. This small ship fit, although snugly, inside *Elizabeth*.

However, it should do for what Sandra had in mind for it.

They then went back to the bridge. He manually disconnected the clamps and static-mated gangway. He notified the traffic controller that *Mistral* was about to leave the dock and go on a one-week trip, Captain Sandra Knutson aboard.

They got clearance to move away from the station before engaging their ion drive. The ion drive used to be a very slow and painful method of moving into space, but in the last few decades, one could build up power quickly using ion drives. Jeffrey went to his hard-shell suit, took out the special new radio, and called, "Elizabeth, radio check."

"I READ YOU FIVE BY FIVE, CAPTAIN. GOOD SAILING."

He put the radio back into its pocket in his hard-shell suit, and returned to the bridge. Sandra was sitting in one of the three seats there. He moved her to the far side, where she could see what he was doing but not interfere.

"The ship has been modified a little from the last owners. There are three pilot seats. The one you occupy has observer functions only, unless this master switch," he indicated a rotational switch, "activates it." He then went through all the controls on the bridge. He pointed out the rotational motors that gave the ship artificial gravity was only activated when the ship was not docked. He showed her the controls. He activated the rotational artificial gravity, and turned on the full polarization of the windows. "If I don't do that you'll get dizzy and ill in a few minutes." The live view was replaced by a video image of the forward view, another of the aft view and one each of the cardinal directions.

She said, "It wasn't so bad"

"After a few minutes of rotation, I get really dizzy. I have to change my view on a regular basis." He pointed to the video displays, showing the various views, arranged so the forward view was the largest, the aft view was topmost, then the four cardinal points were at the corresponding points on the display. She saw the station receding on the aft view, and other ships were moving in the background of the other views. The video of the forward view showed their forward velocity, and their rotational direction. The other displays showed their position relative to the sun and displayed an astrogational map, with their position indicated by a red x. Other displays showed the temperature and pressure of the fuel, the air pressure with its oxygen and carbon dioxide content, the oxygen reserves, carbon-dioxide and nitrogen reserves, and hydrogen reserves.

There were other sensor readings, including the pressure and content of the solar wind, (primarily hydrogen with a large amount of helium,) generally away from the sun, but also periodic cross winds from Saturn and Jupiter, and some from the galactic winds. These were colored differently. Ship exhaust left different chemicals in their wakes, but these were added to the display as well.

But Jeffrey changed the display so that instead of all the cameras showing into different displays, the display became somewhat integrated, in which the Mistral became a large dot on the display, the station falling behind, the cloud of ships falling behind with it, the direction of rotation being one of the variables displayed, the solar wind as another set of arrows showing the direction, color showing the temperature and content of the solar wind. "That's a good one," she said, "Keep it on that one." Her brow was furrowed, trying to keep all the useful information Sokolov was showing her straight.

"It's pretty good for fast travel, but not so good for up close." He keyed to another, similar display that showed nothing in the screen except the larger items like solar wind, direction of rotation and direction of their relative travel. "This is the same, but has local detail. When we get closer to the asteroid belt, we will want this display to see some of the bigger rocks." He shifted in his seat. "These overlap all the sensors, the radar, lidar, electronic and magnetic information in one place. If you pay attention to it you will acquire bountiful information, but if you don't, it can get confusing. When we get closer, I'll show you what I mean." She leaned over to better concentrate on what he was about to display.

He then showed her how to set the auto pilot. He picked a destination and a route, then set the alarm for the level of sensitivity he thought they should worry about. "Come, on. Let's get some grub." He climbed out of the pilot's seat, she followed him.

He took two frozen meals from the storage unit, keyed the temperature guide and opened them both up. The chemical reaction with the air warmed their food, except for the desert; that portion cooled with the air. He mixed some coffee that tasted remarkably like coffee, then sat the trays down. Sandra thanked him, looked around the table for utensils. "Oh, forgot." Jeffrey got up and got the required spoons and forks.

"Thanks," she said, and started eating. After they ate and cleaned up, Jeffrey took her back to the aft of the ship, where he showed her the runabout. On the runabout was a collection of sensors that Jeffrey had developed in order to better discriminate one type of asteroid from another – those with metal ores versus those with just sand and dust. He showed her how to maneuver, how to launch a claim buoy, how to read the instruments, how to bring mineral-rich rocks into the hold. On the way back to the galley, he pointed out the fuel bladders on all sides of the access tube. The fuel was less volatile than earlier fuels, but she needed to be careful to not breathe the fumes. There shouldn't be any fumes unless the bladders were punctured.

After arriving back at the galley, Jeffrey decided to hit the sack. The ship was heading toward the location he knew contained a rich bounty of heavy metals, and it would take two days to get there, so he had time to relax before coming anywhere near dangerous rocks. He lay on the cot, the mattress was more comfortable than military cots, but still it wasn't his bed. He tossed and turned, not dropping off to sleep. After an hour, he got up, went to the galley, sat down after grabbing another ice cream pack and pondered life while enjoying his midnight snack.

After a few minutes of silence, her heard what sounded like crying coming from Sandra's room. It went from a whimpering to a sobbing, back to whimpering. A moan here and there.

Jeffrey deliberately made some noise by clattering utensils, putting dishes in the cleaner and activating it, and making a cup of coffee. "You want to make that two?" she asked from the door. The galley was the hub of the human area of the ship, doors to every room, the pilot's bridge, the aft section. Jeffrey looked up.

"You got it. Are you okay?"

"What, was I doing it again?" she asked.

"Doing...?"

"I've been known to go into a crying jag periodically. One of the reasons I stick to myself."

He handed her a cup of coffee. "When did it happen?"

"What? Oh, the murder of my husband, my...rape." She swallowed, then continued, "A year ago yesterday." a tear tracked down one cheek. "I don't know why I still feel this way, it was long enough, but I...just...I don't know."

Jeffrey waited for her to continue her thought, but when she didn't, he said, "Do you mind if I offer you a hand getting over this?"

"What, are you a shrink, too?"

"No, but I have one on retainer. I would like you to make use of this doctor. It may not sound like it, but he has helped people with much more difficult problems, and I think he can help you too."

"I'll," she paused, "think about it."

"Thank you. I don't know if you were aware, but I lost my wife to a violent encounter ten years, almost eleven years ago."

"Really?" she asked. "I'm sorry."

"I've been slowly getting over it. I have a wonderful support system, friends and colleagues, even my AI – she took on many of my wife's personality components. But I'm not perfect either, just getting better – a little bit every day."

"Have you seen the shrink?" she asked.

"Actually, no."

"Why not?"

Jeffrey sat silent for a while, trying to compose a good-sounding reason, but every answer he came up with sounded more like an excuse. He finally said, "I have no good excuse."

"I'll see your shrink if you do," she challenged. She put her cup to her lips to half-hide her smile.

"Done."

"Oops. Caught. Didn't think you'd jump at that one." She reached across the table, he shook her hand.

"Deal."

They both went back to their separate bedrooms and had no trouble dropping off to sleep.

On awakening, Jeffrey showed Sandra more of the equipment, the controls for the outside doors, problems that might arise – such as if the hold hatch wouldn't close. He showed her the emergency beacons, how to override them. Then he showed her the small-arms weapons cache – just in case.

The ship had no offensive weapons, but that hadn't stopped Jeffrey when he had needed to send multiple pirates' ships to hell in *Elizabeth*. He explained that it took precision flying and timing, but if she did it right, she could throw some big rocks at opposing ships. The ship did have lasers specifically for cutting asteroids to a size adequate for transportation, and Jeffrey had pioneered the use of the lasers to offer information for the mass-spectrometer. In a pinch, the lasers could be used defensively.

The following day as they neared the inner perimeter of the asteroid belt, Jeffrey pointed out the rise in the all-around gravity. He used the gravimeter to pinpoint high density rocks nearby and maneuvered the craft to intercept with a ten meter wide, slowly tumbling heavy rock. He used the radar to determine its exact dimensions, the gravimeter to calculate the mass, the laser to feed information to the spectrometer. The results he got back indicated this was a rock with a large quantity of heavy metals.

There was no appreciable radioactivity, so that narrowed the possible danger. They evacuated the air from the hold, opened the bay doors, and wearing their hard-shell suits rode the runabout to the asteroid. He gave her the controls, made sure she was comfortable driving, then sat back and told her to do the work that had to be done.

Her concentration was evident in the slowness and deliberateness of her actions. But she did nothing wrong. Jeffrey was impressed with the quickness which she gained understanding. This be one smart girl, he thought to himself, though she really wasn't a girl. Woman.

"Next, put on the claim buoy, and let's see if we can wrestle this sucker into the ship."

She aimed the targeting reticle to the center mass of the rock, fired off the small rocket that propelled the buoy to the asteroid. The buoy stuck to the rock, drilled itself into it, extended its anchors, then began broadcasting a low-power claim signal.

"Perfect. Now to wrestle. In a larger ship, I would have included small maneuvering rockets, but this ship is only so big. How would you get the rock into the ship?"

She thought for a moment, then said "I would move the ship to surround the rock."

"Excellent! Let's do it. What do you think the first step would be?"

"Reduce the spin or get the ship to match its spin."

"Which one?" Jeffrey asked, his voice clear over the short-range radio.

"Probably less work to match the spin with the ship. I think."

"Okay, what will you need to do to make that happen?" She thought again, running several scenarios in her mind, then settled on attaching cables to the rock, keeping them straight, then she could reel the rock in, matching the rotation and rotational velocity of the rock with the ship. Jeffrey suggested using a net with cables attached, rather than nailing the rock with pitons.

They took the runabout back to the ship, Jeffrey took the large net out of its cabinet, placed it onto the runabout, grabbed four reels of cable, and brought the cable from the winch at the back of the hold, attached it to the runabout, then climbed back aboard.

Sandra piloted the runabout back to the rock, then climbed out and unfurled the net, attached the cables to the corner of the net, then attached the other end of the cables to the winch. Then she piloted the runabout back to the ship. Jeffrey had her park it on the outside of the ship, he secured the sled runners to mounts on the aft bulkhead, then they moved into the hold.

He had her take the pilot's seat, he took the second one right next to her. Because this was a dangerous operation, they kept their hard-shell suits on. He showed her the controls she needed to use, then sat back. She aligned the ship with the rock, then matched its rotation. Jeffrey noted that the cable was kinking, rather than twisting on its gimbal, so they both went back to the hold and saw the problem; a small piece of rock had wedged itself into the gimbal, causing it to stop rotating. Jeffrey took it out with a plier and the cable slowly unkinked.

They both then went back to the cabin, and she seated herself in the pilot's seat. The video gave several views of the rock and the inside of the hold. She continued to fine-tune the alignment of the ship to the rotation of the rock, then slowly pulled the rock in, the winch reeling in a slow centimeter at a time. Once the rock started moving, she began pushing the ship away, so that both the rock and the ship were moving in the same direction, the rock moving into the ship at a painfully slow and sedate tempo.

Once the rock was fully in the hold, she stopped the reeling in of the winch, but kept it tight. They then went to the hold, secured the rock to rings on the hard parts of the bulkhead and deck so it was now part of the ship. There was still room in the hold, so Jeffrey brought the runabout back inside. They checked that everything was secure, closed the bay doors, closed the hatch to the hold, then re-pressurized the cabin. They took off their hard-shell suits, her hair, which she had tied in a tight bun, was wispy with sweat. "Whew!" she exclaimed. "That was more work than I thought it would be."

"You can expect every time you get a rock to be some kind of challenge. From what I see, however, you should be able to make a considerable profit from that one rock."

"Me? This is your ship. That is your rock!" She said, incredulous.

"Nah, I'm on vacation. But I'll buy that rock from you! My ship needs more raw materials to keep making neat things like your hard-shell suit."

"Okay. Fair market value?"

"What? Not even a discount? You're a hard-bargaining woman."

They made preparation to head back to the Lagrange 3A station. The light supper was adequate to sate their food need. She went into the shower to wash up before bed. Jeffrey was wiping down the kitchen surfaces, putting the filters through the cleaner, and otherwise hanging around, waiting for his turn in the shower.

She called out to him, "Jeffrey, can you come here for a minute?" He knocked on the sliding door, and she said, "I can't seem to find a towel."

"No towel," he said. "Use the blower in the stall."

"Can you show me?"

Oh boy, what now? He pushed the sliding door open letting a cloud of vapor enter the galley, letting cooler air enter the bathroom. "Ooh, that's cold, close it please," she said.

He slid the door closed, and the water vapor cleared a bit. He saw exactly what she wanted him to see, a beautiful, wet, tall woman, unashamed of her nakedness. Her small breasts enticing, drawing his eye, but he deliberately moved his gaze back to her lovely face. Doing his best not to insult her, and doing his best to keep himself as professional as possible under the circumstance, he went over to the shower controls, showed her the warm air blower and switched it on.

Jets of warm air blew from every angle, she shook out her hair, and it caught in the wind. She raised her arms to dry there as well, then lifted her breasts to dry under there. Jeffrey started to leave the bathroom, but she caught his arm, unzipped his suit, put both her arms around his neck, and pulled him into the shower. She turned off the air and turned the shower back on. "You're going to have to show me again," she said coyly. She helped him out of his suit, his physical reaction a surprise to Jeffrey – he hadn't had this kind of reaction in a long time.

She scrubbed Jeffrey's chest and back and arms, then kissed him again in a long, lingering tongue-fighting kiss. They made love in the shower, standing and shifting to other positions, but eventually climaxing and slowing their lovemaking activities.

"Oh, my," she said. "That was good."

"Me too," said Jeffrey. But he wasn't quite finished with her. He turned her back to him, kissed her again on the mouth. She turned her head all the way around to accommodate him. Then he scrubbed her chest, breasts, belly, thighs, up her privates, her back, her arms, then massaged her back, ribs, hips, butt. He turned on the air dryer again, and let her hair blow in the breeze.

Afterward, he picked up his suit, went back to his cabin.

A moment later she came into his cabin too. "May I join you?" She was still naked. "Where is your jumpsuit? Go get it." He cautioned.

She got her under-suit, and brought it into Jeffrey's room. "Lay down there," he pointed to his bunk. Then he went into her cabin, got her pillow, brought it back, tossed it onto his bunk alongside her head, then joined her.

"That was nice," she said. "I haven't had sex since my husband died last year. I missed it!"

"Thanks for the invitation. I haven't had sex since my wife died a decade ago."

"Really? You handled it like a pro! That was really good!"

"Well, thank you Ma'am"

The two bare people lay facing each other her hair still damp, but loose. His short hair hardly moist. "Tell me about your husband. Carl, wasn't it?"

"Oh he was the perfect Viking gentleman. He was from Norwegian stock, his folks were from Bergen. I so loved him. There wasn't anything I wouldn't do for him." Her strong alto voice stirred memories in Jeffrey. "I had a lot of hope for a family, but he took it with him when he died." She paused to let a sob die down. "I will always remember him. That's my favorite song, I don't know who wrote it, but I hold the lyrics in my heart – 'You're always on my mind, I look forward, I look behind, No matter what else I do, I will always remember you.'

"Sing it for me," Jeffrey asked her.

She sat up in the bed, looked at Jeffrey and sang in a quiet voice a haunting melody those same words, almost a Celtic tune.

"That's lovely. I can see you really loved him."

She lay back down, then asked him, "Tell me about your wife."

"I first met her when I was a young man, just after my parents brought us to the station to sell a load of minerals. She was on the station, and captured my heart. For that first time, I was smitten and pursued her. My parents died and I inherited the ship. I had her on my mind and invited her aboard. She was entranced by me too. We decided to get married, and we did in a church on the station. We started together on my ship going out just like you were doing here. We found some good places, and after a few trips, made enough to begin to modify our ship.

"Our third trip out made all the difference. Pirates attacked us. She and I fought them off, and got every one of them, but for the last one. He was busy raping her in the corridor. I was so mad. I shot him in the head – his head went flying away, but he fell on the knife he held at her throat and it killed her.

"I was inconsolable for the longest time. I brought the bodies in to the station, but there was nothing anyone would do. I renamed the ship after her. I bought an AI, my ship and the AI both took on the name and personality of my late wife. That was ten years ago, going on eleven. I have loved other people, but from a distance. You were the first since my wife died. That was my first lovemaking. Thanks!"

He lay back, somewhat relieved from the recitation of his story, happy to be in bed with this beautiful woman. "You know," he said, "I didn't bring you out here all alone just to seduce you."

"You should have," she said. "I like being with you. I liked having sex with you."

"Really? I thought it was a bit hurried." He climbed on top of her. "Let's do it again, but properly." She opened to him, his body again waking up. This time they took their time, less frantic, his hands again remembering what they were supposed to do. She arched her back to put the angle just right as he moved against her. He continued working her nipples, and could feel her shuddering in pleasure at his ministrations. Her orgasm came again, and she closed her eyes, lost in the pleasure. Jeffrey kept moving, raising against her body in a rolling motion, his thumbs turning on her erect nipples, and he came in a great spurt. Her eyes opened in surprise as yet another orgasm took her. He came to lay down on his elbows, keeping the weight off his partner, still inside her. She then squeezed and moved again to extract the last of his semen.

They looked at each other as he loomed over her. He kissed her again, she kissed him back, lip to lip. They both got up, hand in hand to the shower, got clean then dry and came back to his bed. He changed the linens and they lay down again, this time both dropped off to sleep.

Jeffrey woke up to the odor of breakfast cooking. The technology of making good food store a long time and remain palatable has taken long strides over the last half century. Long gone are the days of dehydrated fruit and sugar juices masquerading as healthful beverages. Keeping food frozen was impractical, but the concepts were the right idea; now food was being reduced to a folded state – the molecules were folded to a more compact, now dry form. To unfold the food, heating it brought it back to its normal state.

His bacon and eggs with whole wheat buttered toast was as good as any freshly made in an Iowa roadside cafe. The coffee was the same quality as that found in a French or Viennese cafe. "Thanks for cooking. This is good," commented Jeffrey, cheeks full like a squirrel's.

"Thanks," she said coyly. "I know you like to eat – so do I." Jeffrey noticed the place she had sat at still had some crumbs, showing she already ate. She had her soft suit on, lightweight soft boots to mid-calf, hood rolled up. The soft suit showed off her gentle curves, much to Jeffrey's delight. He finished his meal, bussed the table, placed his dishes and cutlery in the washer next to hers and activated the clean cycle.

He refilled their coffees, and they sat at the table, not saying much, just enjoying each other's company. The proximity detector sounded an alarm, reporting "RAPIDLY APPROACHING MASS. COLLISION ALERT." They both jumped up and ran to the pilot's bridge. Sandra arrived first, jumped into the pilot's seat. She saw the display showing radar images of six objects moving toward them. Jeffrey quickly went into the anteroom by the airlock, and got into his hard-shell suit. Then he went back to the pilot's bridge and told her to get into hers.

She got up, quickly went to the anteroom and suited up. Her soft boots fit directly into the hard- shell boots. Jeffrey activated the new radio that Elizabeth had issued him. "Elizabeth, come in." A few seconds passed, then she responded.

"HELLO CAPTAIN. WHAT'S UP?"

"Can you monitor my suit's cameras?" he asked. A few seconds passed again. Damn this time lag, thought Jeffrey.

"YES I CAN. YOUR RADAR IDICATES TROUBLE."

"I need your assistance."

"I'LL NOTIFIY JANET. BE THERE SOON. EAVDE. DO YOUR BEST."

"Thanks."

Jeffrey explained to Sandra what was the most likely scenario – the ships surrounding them were most likely pirates, armed with guns that the *Mistral* wasn't equipped to protect against. He would drive, hopefully his experience would give him an advantage until the *Elizabeth* showed up.

He gave her some idea of the maneuvers he would have to undertake. One of the new terms he introduced was Crazy Ivan. Crazy Ivan was a maneuver that was so insane that no rational pilot would ever perform it. Jeffrey couldn't tell her what his Crazy Ivan maneuver was going to be, it all depended on the circumstances. But Crazy Ivan was a dangerous maneuver regardless of the specifics. Jeffrey would tell her when he would do anything so dangerous.

Sandra's gloved hand went to the inner thigh pocket that held her pistol. Jeffrey noticed and told her to save it for when they were boarded, if it got to that.

Jeffrey increased speed, forcing the attackers, if that's what they were, to move before they had gotten into the best attack position.

A radio message came over the system from one of the ships. "You can run but you cannot get away from us. We know you have a rock on board – do you notice how poorly your ship responds to your acceleration motors? We did."

Jeffrey keyed the mike on the same frequency, "This is *Mistral,* who are you?"

"Captain Sokolov, we are your worst nightmare," the voice said. "You aren't going to escape alive."

"Who is this?" Jeffrey's curiosity exceeded his fear. "I've made a few enemies over the last year, but most of them are dead."

"We are not dead."

"So who are you? Are you ashamed of your identity?" Jeffrey began plotting several maneuvers into the computer for rapid execution. *Damn, I should have done this before we left.* Jeffrey also changed the display to overlap the electromagnetic emissions, the gravimeter of the region, and returns from radar, lidar, and visual inputs onto the same display. As the ship increased its speed, the other vessels struggled to go faster than *Mistral*, and as they were spread out, maneuvering at this stage of the battle would bring him into closer contact with one or another of the visible ships.

While inputting further maneuvers, Jeffrey had Sandra go into the bay and remove all the nets around the rock. She got up and moved back as quickly as she could. Jeffrey noticed the display showed gravity masses where there were no other emissions. He keyed the radio to Elizabeth, "I see we have probably twenty alien ships along with the six visible ones."

"CAPTAIN, YOUR RADIO IS NOW BROADCASTING CONTINUALLY SO I CAN MONITOR."

"Acknowledged." He then broadcast to the pirates. "So which aliens are you working for?"

The reply came right away, the same voice that had been speaking to him throughout the whole conversation, "Say what? What are you talking about?"

Jeffrey asked if they had a gravimeter, if so, to turn it on and look at the masses surrounding their ships.

"Well, I'll be damned," said the voice. "What is that?"

"Probably the people who instigated you to attack me out here. I've defeated their ships in every encounter, so they thought they could get me out here ostensibly by you. *Mistral* is not a combat vessel, but we are not defenseless."

The captain of the main pirate vessel began communicating with his colleagues, Jeffrey monitored the conversation. The pirates decided to break off their attack and allow the aliens to do their own assassination. Jeffrey was pretty sure that the aliens were monitoring the conversation, so he had to begin his maneuvers pretty quickly. "Sandra!" he yelled. "Are you done back there?"

"One more cable! There! Coming back!" A moment later she returned to the pilot's bridge.

"Strap in. Got some wild maneuvers to initiate in a moment." warned Jeffrey. He continued to increase the speed, which was costing a considerable amount of fuel, which gave Jeffrey an idea. He continued to burn plasma to increase the ships velocity, then cut the plasma engines and activated the ion drives. The ion drives were not specifically hot like the plasma, but could easily ignite fuel, so this maneuver was going to be tricky.

He released the outer emergency valve on one of the tanks, spewing fuel into the wake of his now hundred kilometer per second ship. At the same time, he released one of the spare oxygen cylinder emergency valves, which mingled with the cloud of fuel flowing and dispersing in the ship's wake. Jeffrey cut the plasma drive for a moment, then fired off one of the powerful lasers through the cloud when he determined the alien ships were caught in his vapor trail.

The laser caused a powerful blast – the fuel was hard to ignite, but with the pure oxygen made for an impressive explosion. This occurred as several of the alien vessels were about to fire on the pirate ships, so they were caught with the weapon's protective covers open just as the explosion occurred, imploding three of the twenty ships.

As the ships were destroyed and damaged, several of them lost their invisibility. The alien ships spread out, to make that particular maneuver impossible to pull off a second time.

"Something I haven't told you. These aliens have faster-than-light travel. Not sure why they aren't using it here, but it's going to cost them."

"They have WHAT?" she asked. Then after thinking about it for a second, said, "Well, of course, if they got here from another star, they would have to, wouldn't they?" She stared at the screen. "So how do you know there are aliens here?"

Jeffrey pointed to the mass indicators on the screen where there was no visible or radar reflection. This tells me about the ships, much as it would tell me about a rock. The deeper the well, the greater the mass."

"I see. Clever."

"Thank you, Ma'am"

"Okay, we're going to try another tactic. See that control there? The red one?"

"The one that says radar?"

"Yes. I want you to focus the radar beam at only one of the gravity wells. I'm going to do the same with a laser on another one. Let's see what happens."

They began targeting individual ships using their tools, the radar, with all its power concentrated on a single point was a hellish beam. It overpowered the ship's circuitry, and the alien vessel became visible and fell out of the chase. Jeffrey's laser had less effect, but still, the invisibility circuit popped off, leaving the ship visible. It bore an exact reminiscence of the Vorsh ships that Jeffrey had destroyed before.

At Jeffrey's request, Sandra turned the radar back to full scan.

Jeffrey was about to try another maneuver – possibly twisting around to throw their precious rock at one of the Vorsh, when he noticed the radar image showed another ship ahead that didn't seem to be there before. Just as he decided to ram through the offending ship – at this velocity he would do far more damage to it than to his own ship, the familiar blast of all- frequency announcement of an

Earth Warship was in their presence, and that the use of invisibility circuits was illegal in Human space, punishable by destruction.

The *Elizabeth*, back-pedaling to keep pace with the mass of alien ships let loose half- second bursts from both rail guns at every alien ship in their fleet. All the Vorsh ships appeared, either because they were far too wounded or fear of further attack by *Elizabeth*. Jeffrey radioed the Vorsh to give up the leader who had brought them to the point of death, or follow him in death.

"I am Bieph. I ordered the attack on you. Give me an hour and I will surrender to you to be killed." Realizing that this was his attempt at immortality – to impregnate as many females as he could before he died, forced by chemicals in the food given only to Vorsh captains, Jeffrey told Elizabeth to have Janet send Marines aboard to collect him before he began his barbaric ritual.

The Marines forced themselves onto Bieph's ship. They got no resistance from the alien crew, found Bieph being held at bay by a number of females. The Marines captured and restrained him, brought him aboard *Elizabeth*. Then Janet asked Jeffrey to bring the *Mistral* aboard the *Elizabeth*. They made room in a corner of the shuttle bay, and *Mistral* squeezed in.

When Jeffrey exited the *Mistral* he heard a bosun's whistle followed by an announcement, "CAPTAIN SOKOLOV ABOARD."

Sandra said, "Nice touch!"

"Yeah, we didn't have a bosun's whistle when the admiral came aboard, so I had my AI simulate one. I thought it would be a touch of class." Jeffrey and Sandra walked arm in arm, hip-to-hip.

They walked over to the bridge, having shed their helmets once they exited the shuttle bay. She shook out her hair, which tended to get tangled up in her hastily secured helmet. Jeffrey guided her around the corridors, pointed out his own cabin on the way, then brought her into the bridge.

As soon as Jeffrey entered the bridge, a petty officer called out "Captain on the bridge!"

Janet stood up, saluted Jeffrey, who saluted back. Jeffrey introduced Sandra, then asked to speak with the next Vorsh leader. He sat in his chair, waiting for the next Vorsh to take responsibility for all in his fleet. A new face appeared. Jeffrey asked, "What is your name?"

"I am Sarguntum."

"All right, Sarguntum, let me fill you in on some rules. If any ship or individual is using invisibility circuits, they will be destroyed without further warning. If any alien kills, enslaves, eats, or otherwise does harm to a human, that alien is subject to immediate destruction. Any alien that wages war on Humans will be destroyed. So, answer me this – do I have to send a fleet to destroy your home world and everyone on it? Do I? You are forcing my hand. I don't want to destroy your home world but we have bent over backwards to make you welcome here, and what do you do? You go out and try to have me assassinated. What is it going to be? Do I have to destroy the Vorsh, kill every one of them, or are the Vorsh going to cooperate with me?"

"We will cooperate."

"Good. Let's begin that cooperation here. Who initiated this assassination attempt?" Jeffrey looked angrily at the display of the alien Sarguntum.

"It was Bieph. He was the guilty one."

"No I don't think so. You see, this is what I was afraid of, you say you will cooperate, but then you lie to me." He turned to Janet,

"Lieutenant prepare the rail guns to destroy that ship. Eventually somebody will tell me the truth." Jeffrey's bluff worked.

"Please don't. I will tell you. There is a Vorsh in your Earth station named ZhZhZhee. He told us not to, but the other Vorsh, Jaja, he told us to make the pirates kill you."

"Why?"

"You humiliated us. You changed the way we do things – like making Captains live. When they fail they are supposed to die."

"Well don't feel special, we have humiliated every race that has come into our solar system. You Aliens just aren't good at war. You need to stop trying to wage war on us. We've been innovating war methods since we first came out of the trees. Now, am I clear on the consequences of violating our laws?"

"Yes Captain. We will no longer violate your laws."

"This conversation will be reported to my superiors and to your ambassador. Do not disappoint me."

He cut the connection, then said to Janet, "So did I interrupt anything important?"

"Nothing important," replied Janet. "Ojo and I were just dancing."

"Oh. Sorry."

"Not a problem, Captain. He needs practice, but my toes need a rest." She smirked at her own wit. "So this is the lady who wants to go prospecting. Did you find anything?"

"Yeah, a big rock about the size of the *Mistral's* hold. Full of heavy minerals. I got her to agree to sell directly to me and the *Elizabeth*. We might as well have Elizabeth's remotes take it off our hands."

"Elizabeth should appreciate that – she has been whimpering about not having enough raw materials."

"HEY! I WASN'T WHIMPERING. MORE LIKE WHINING. THAT'S HOW I GET THINGS DONE AROUND HERE, IT SEEMS."

"Is Heinz aboard?"

"Yes sir. Do you want me to get him?" replied Janet.

"I want to meet him outside the brig – where the Vorsh captain is. Have the Marines move him to an interrogation room. Also, do we have a shrink aboard?"

"No sir. We couldn't scrounge up one fast enough to suit Elizabeth."

"I think we need to assign one for the ship. Might help interrogations, and begin to ease post-traumatic stress quicker. I'll recruit from the station. Whatever happened to Sgt. Quinn – the psychologist?"

"I think she transferred to the station," said Janet.

Against his better judgment he left Sandra in Janet's hands. He was sure there would be some discussion of things that he wasn't sure he wanted shared, but he had important things to do.

He met IntelTech Jurgen Heinz at the door outside the brig. A Marine stood guard outside, and gave admittance to the Captain and the Intel technician. Jeffrey still wore his hard-shell suit, and carried his helmet with him. The Vorsh captain, Bieph, was looking distressed, as much as anyone could tell alien facial expressions.

"Why have you kept me from my duty?" the Vorsh captain demanded.

"You mean the rape of as many females on your ship as you can do in the given time? You mean the lying about your mission so the real guilty party goes free? Let me ask you this – on the ship, did you eat the same food as your crew?"

"Of course not. I am a captain," the Vorsh replied. "I eat Captain food."

"So you probably don't know about the chemicals they put in your food to make you want to follow the protocols of your end of life?

We have found this before. Captains that don't eat it, have no desire to commit suicide or accept execution."

"How can a captain not eat Captain Food?"

"I know of one who fed his starving crew his food, and he went hungry."

"Oh."

"Who told you to attack me?"

"I did it on my own. You must kill me now," the Vorsh said, in a matter-of -fact manner. He looked back and forth from Jeffrey to Heinz, waiting.

Jeffrey turned to Heinz. "Hey Jurgen, I was just thinking about some of that Danish pastry the Chief makes. Don't you think some Danish would be nice?"

"Why Captain," the young German engineer replied with a smile, " I think I am a bit peckish myself, and some Danish and coffee would be welcome. Why don't I get some from the Chief?"

"Good idea. I'll just have a nice conversation with our Vorsh friend, here while you get us some of the most excellent Danish pastries and coffee."

Bieph's brow furrowed. "You must kill me now."

"Oh, maybe in a little while. But first I want the benefit of your wisdom. You were, after all, the captain of a Vorsh war fleet."

"Not a war fleet. Was just a long-range travel-fleet."

"Ah," said Jeffrey. "What's the difference between a war fleet and your long-range travel fleet?"

"Kill me now, kill me now, you must kill me now."

"Not yet. So what kind of weapons does a war fleet have? More of what your ships weapons are?"

"Of course not. There are powerful weapons on a warship. Our little ships only have little weapons."

"Yeah, I noticed," said Jeffrey, "Not only do your weapons not work against my ships, but they don't work on my Marine's armor. I think somebody gave you worthless weapons on purpose. Maybe to give me the impression that your real warships are poorly armed."

Heinz came back with a box of Danish pastries and a tray containing a coffee pot, mugs and sugar and cream bowls. He set the Danish down, opened the box. The aroma filled the small interrogation chamber. Jeffrey grabbed one and promptly put it in his mouth and chewed deliberately, making appreciative noises. He looked at Heinz, nodded, and Heinz made the same noises. Jeffrey finished the first Danish, then picked up another. The Vorsh sniffed. Boy that smelled good. He sniffed again. Jeffrey seemed to be enjoying his Danish more than was reasonable. He finally turned his head to Bieph, and with food in his cheeks, asked if he wanted one.

Jeffrey went behind the Vorsh, and released one of his hands from the cuff connecting him to the ring behind the chair. Jeffrey then went back and sat down, pushed a Danish on a napkin toward the Vorsh.

He picked it up, and copying the Humans, took a bite out of the pastry. His eyes opened very wide. "This is good!" he said with his mouth full. He swallowed, and said it again, this time more clearly.

Jeffrey poured him a cup of coffee, added some cream and sugar, thinking that black coffee was an acquired taste, but everyone loved coffee with cream and sugar.

He passed the cup to the Vorsh, who picked it up like Jeffrey did his and sipped. "What is this? This is good!"

The three continued eating their Danish until it was all gone. They drank the rest of their coffee, and Heinz put the service tray on the floor, out of the way. "Now I know what food tastes like! Does every human eat like this?"

"Pretty much. But we have much more flavors and textures to share. But I guess you probably would rather I kill you now, so too bad you won't taste them." Jeffrey started to pull his pistol.

"No, I think I want to try food first. Kill me later."

"Oh dear," said Heinz. "That would be a problem. We cannot give food to somebody we are just going to kill. It would be a waste. And I was thinking we should share a fruit bowl. Melons, citrus, apples. Mangoes. Oh well, too bad."

"Do you think I could have a fruit bowl before I kill him? I liked the Danish, but the fruit would really hit the spot." Jeffrey asked Heinz.

"Let me go see if Chief has some fruit for us." And Heinz got up and went back to the galley. He returned a moment later with a few bowls of fruit.

"Banana! You remembered the bananas. I love bananas!" Jeffrey effused enthusiastically. The Vorsh watched Jeffrey peel the banana and eat the ripe fruit. The sweet banana odor wafted to Bieph. He sniffed again.

"Maybe," said Jeffrey, I can let him have a banana before I shoot him. What do you think?"

"Yes, yes, yes!" interjected the Vorsh at the same time Heinz was saying, "I don't know..."

Jeffrey passed a banana to the Vorsh, then took it back – the look of disappointment was palpable – but Jeffrey was going to peel it for his prisoner. He gave it back half-peeled.

The banana did it. The rest of the fruit bowls were okay, but Jeffrey did a good job of selling the banana. "Maybe I should reconsider you killing me. I think there is much to learn, and you cannot learn if you are dead. Lessons are lost on the dead," then he made sounds similar to a laugh.

 ELIZABETH, *ELIZABETH*

"I think he just made a joke, sir." said Heinz.

"Oh. Haha." Jeffrey chuckled on the way out of the interrogation room.

"You answer Mr. Heinz's questions," he said at the door, "and we'll see about other foods. Okay?" The prisoner seemed to have melted entirely. Yay for bananas, thought Jeffrey. He reflected on the trouble that the Vorsh had brought themselves by providing only bland foods, including using flesh of their own people. The offering of delicious – sweet, spicy, salty, tangy - foods was the most successful method of extracting information and garnering loyalty to a less than extreme Vorsh attitude, as found in the Vorsh ambassador ZhZhZhee. The ambassador still had loyalty to his race and his planet, but he was free of the chemicals that forced him to behave according to a pre-programmed mode – loyalty by chemical intervention. The report Jurgen would file on interrogation techniques was going to be interesting reading.

Jeffrey went to his cabin, retrieved the code book from his book shelf, and began composing a special report to Admiral Kutuzov. He paged through the book looking for appropriate sentences or words or specific letters, spelled out the name of his Vorsh prisoner, the name of the Vorsh agent on the Earth station that instigated the assassination attempt, and the name of the replacement captain of the lead Vorsh ship that led the assault. He told Kutuzov of his threatened attack on the Vorsh home world if continued attacks and assassination attempts didn't stop.

He then composed a report with far less secure detail, but much more information, to be broadcast over regular high-speed secure burst transmission. He had Elizabeth transmit the 'book report' to the Earth Navy station hidden in the carrier wave of the regular report. He then went back to the bridge, found Janet and Sandra busily exchanging tidbits about Jeffrey. They stopped talking when the lowest ranking staffer on the bridge called out "Captain on the bridge!" but did look at each other and chuckle, in the unspoken promise to continue their conversation at a later time.

Now I'm in for it, thought Jeffrey. But nothing to do for it. He had always been self-motivated, self-serving and self-reliant, but it was good to have people he could relax with. Because Sandra was not in his command, he had no problem being intimate with her, but he had no desire to become the discussion focal point of the ship or the service. Still, she provided him with an emotional anchor, something he had missed over the last decade. He made a decision; "Sandra," he began. "I think I would like to invite you to share my cabin. Are you interested?"

Taken by surprise, she looked at Janet for help, but the lieutenant all of a sudden was engulfed in a report, wouldn't look up to make eye contact with her new friend. "Um, well, um, uh, sure. I guess," she said, her complexion now turning decidedly red. Jeffrey was relieved. That's out of the way.

"Janet," he said.

She looked up from the report she wasn't really reading. "Register Ms. Knutson as a guest crew member of the ship, and have someone move her luggage from *Mistral* to my cabin." He could have done that himself by telling Elizabeth to do it, but it also helped to clear things with his crew.

"Aye sir," replied Janet a knowing smirk on her face. She turned to the petty officer on the bridge, and ordered "Take care of the Captain's guest." The petty officer got up from her station and went to look for some crew or Marines to collect the luggage from the little ship in the shuttle bay.

"Janet," said Jeffrey, "how fast did you travel to get here?" To his knowledge, the ship hadn't gone past four times the speed of light, but it obviously exceeded that this time to get to him so fast.

"Eight C."

"C?"

"As in E=MC squared." She said. "I figured we need to start calling it something better than 'speed of light'. Yuki suggested it."

"8 C. Any consequences to the ship?"

"Doesn't appear so. The wave seems to enclose us entirely in a bubble. I had Yuki put together a report for you, it seems there are opportunities and threats that we should pay attention to."

"Thanks. I really appreciate your dropping your dance to save my bacon."

"What does that mean, 'save your bacon'? Where did the phrase come from."

"Bacon is the belly of a pig – a fatty cut of meat. They used to slice it, smoke it, salt it. I suppose if the bacon fell into a fire and someone pulled it out beforehand, that would be saving the bacon."

"Oh, like saving your butt," she said saucily.

"Yeah."

"Always, and every time, my captain."

He left the bridge with Sandra, arm in arm. He took her to his cabin, found both her and his luggage on the floor. "Elizabeth," he said.

"CAPTAIN?"

"Sandra Knutson is going to be sharing my cabin until further notice. We are going to need better closet and drawer space."

"AYE, CAPTAIN. WILL YOU BE CANOODLING?"

"Um, Elizabeth, that is a private matter between Sandra and me, not you. Clear?" Jeffrey said in a rather annoyed voice.

"CLEAR. AFFIRMATIVE ON THE CANOODLING."

Sandra looked at Jeffrey with a raised eyebrow. "Who is Elizabeth?"

"She is my, this ship's, AI. Think of her as my servant, my best friend, my protector and the mind of the ship."

Her brow wrinkled in concern. "So…she's constantly monitoring everything?"

"No – she listens in for her name, but when it comes to privacy I programmed a command to ignore everything else when I invoke privacy."

"Well that's a relief, said the tall blond. Next question; canoodling?" She put a hand on her hip, feet apart in an aggressive-looking query.

"I thought it would be a better word than the crude and crass 'F' word that seems to be in continuous vogue. My ship and my command are in kind of an experiment with the Navy – I have encouraged my staff to share bunks. I have suspended the rule about enlisted mixing with officers. So far, I'm encouraged by the results. My ship's *espirit de corps* is higher than any in the fleet, my ship's ratings exceed all the others in the Navy, including the commodore's."

"Well, I'm impressed. Wanna canoodle?" She asked, beginning to shed the hard-shell suit.

"Oh, beautiful, not now. Later. We are going to do some fast travel and I want to be on the bridge for that. There will be work to do also. But I'll share a lot of my work load soon. I promise." He kissed her pouting lips. "Let's join the crew in the galley at eighteen hundred. I'll introduce you to the crew, we'll have a fine meal and come back here to 'canoodle.'"

Jeffrey left the North Country woman alone in his cabin after shedding his hard-shell suit. He spoke to Elizabeth on the way to the bridge, after ensuring he was alone in the corridor. "Elizabeth, you're going to have to pretend not to know what goes on in my cabin. I wish to impress this woman with my ship, but you are my best security. Clear?"

"ALREADY ACTING, CAPTAIN."

"Good girl," finished Jeffrey as he was entering the bridge. "Captain on the bridge!" called out the petty officer.

He walked up to Janet and said, "I think I want to get us moving back to Lagrange 3A. We've sent off messages to Earth base and Commodore Yusef. I'm not aware of anything else I need to do before we go"

"What about those alien ships?"

"Yes, good! That's it." He slapped the top of his forehead. "You're such a good little Executive Officer!" Jeffrey play-patted Janet on the head. She growled.

He said to the communications technician, "Raise the Vorsh leader, please."

"Aye sir." she replied coldly. Jeffrey thought; *Now what*?

The Vorsh leader appeared on his screen. The ComTech said the leader's name to remind Jeffrey; Sarguntum.

"Sarguntum. Your ships are to go to one of the Lagrange 3 stations and register yourselves there. There is free food for all aliens, Vorsh included. I think you will find our food is better than what you have been feeding yourselves. More rules – again, no invisibility circuits. If you turn invisible and we detect you we will destroy you. No cannibalism in human space. No attacking humans. You have an ambassador on the Earth-Moon Lagrange station called Earth Base. If you have needs from an embassy, you may visit there. That ambassador is ZhZhZhee. Reports of our encounter have been sent. You are free to go – you had better register at one of the Lagrange 3 stations or we will come looking for you. Clear?"

"I understand and will comply."

"Also, it would be very smart for all captains of your ships to NOT eat the food designed for Captains. It makes you want to kill yourselves. You are dismissed."

Jeffrey nodded to the ComTech, then used the slash the throat sign to cut the connection. She complied, frowning at the captain.

There was a moment of silence on the bridge. Jeffrey said, "Lieutenant Bianca-Torres, please bring your ComTech to the conference room." And Jeffrey went in the conference room and sat down on the far end of the conference table. A moment later Janet entered with the ComTech.

"ComTech...What's your name?" he asked.

"Specialist Jeanie Dux, sir." she said, standing at attention.

"At ease, Dux." She shifted to a rigid at-ease position. "We just met, but I have the impression that you have an axe to grind."

"No axe, sir." She looked straight ahead. Jeffrey noticed a slight tremble in her chin.

"Then what is going on. Please speak freely. Nothing said here will go against your record. I run a relatively informal ship. Despite that we have the best record in the Navy. Is that your issue? Do you have a problem with ship discipline?"

"No, sir. Not with ship discipline."

Jeffrey reclined in his seat. "Elizabeth, please have the Chief deliver some pastries and coffee to the conference room. Enough for the entire bridge crew."

"AYE, CAPTAIN."

"This appears as if it is going to take longer than I thought. Lieutenant, Tech, please have a seat."

They both sat down. Janet remained quiet, the ComTech remained quiet. The chief brought the requested pastries and coffee service.

"Chief, if things keep going like they have, you're going to need an assistant."

"Well, sir. I don't think an assistant, but maybe an apprentice."

"Did you have anyone in mind?"

"That young Korean girl - you set up her family with the restaurant. I think she would do great."

"Thanks, Chief. I'll talk to her family and see if they're interested."

The Chief left. Janet closed the door behind the Chief, then sat down again. She looked at the Captain as if to ask, What the hell are we doing here? Instead of asking, she poured coffee all around, then took a pastry, as did Jeffrey.

"All right, Dux, please speak freely. There is something on your chest that you need to get rid of. What is it?" Jeffrey sipped the coffee.

Dux looked at Janet, then at the Captain. "Sir, I," she paused frowned, wrinkled her brow. "I've been in the Navy for three years. I've seen how too many high-ranking men treat women. You seem to have a lot of women on your ship, and I hate seeing it again."

"You have a problem with how I treat women on my ship. Is that right?"

"Yes sir. You seem to have demeaned Lieutenant Bianca-Torres right in front of everyone." Jeffrey looked confused.

"Me?" He looked to Janet.

"Well, you did," said Janet. *"Good little Executive Officer,"* she repeated patting herself on her head.

"Oh. That."

"And you seem to have a whole harem of women to choose from." said the ComTech.

"Um, really?" He thought for a second. "Lieutenant, did you know about this harem?"

"Well sir, I've heard the rumors. It seems that Ms. Knutson is only the last in a long line of women you date then throw away."

"Who else are the rumors attributing to my harem? This is getting more interesting. Dux? Janet?"

"Well it was said that you got Lieutenant Bianca-Torres pregnant," answered Dux, looking over to Janet almost apologetically "The Korean woman and child – you took their ship, after killing her husband, that Japanese scientist, Yuki Ohara. I used to know her on the *Wanigan*. There are a lot of others in the rumors, sir." Dux shrunk in her seat, sipped on her coffee, sure that the hammer was about to drop.

"Thank you, Ms. Dux." Jeffrey chuckled. "Lieutenant, please disabuse our ComTech of some of her notions."

Jeffrey sipped on the excellent coffee. He picked up another small pastry. *I am definitely going to have to begin an exercise regimen,* he thought. *The Vorsh are right, though, these things are excellent.*

Janet began, "First, Captain. Ms. Dux is correct, you need to cut back on the joking with sexual tensions. It doesn't do to have crew misinterpret how close we actually are."

"Ah...Okay. I'll work on that, perhaps you can keep me in line?" said Jeffrey.

"Yes sir. I'll make it a point to inform Elizabeth to reinforce your good behavior and...remind you of your inappropriate behaviors."

"Okay," said Jeffrey sheepishly.

"Captain, this is no longer a small, familiar boat. We are now a Naval Ship of the line. While we are all familiar, and friendly, we need to adhere to some discipline regulations that we haven't in the past." Jeffrey swallowed at the running down by his exec.

"That having been said, Ms. Dux." continued Janet, "My pregnancy is not for public discussion. But for the record, this baby was conceived by my husband and me. Nobody else. The Captain presided over our wedding not too long ago, right here on this ship. We are the dearest of friends, the closest of combat veterans, the most trusting of allies. When given the opportunity to go with other ships, even Captain my own, I selected this ship, this Captain, not because he is a hunk – you have to admit, there, though, Dux, he is that – but because this is the best ship in our Navy. I drafted this Captain and this ship into the Navy so we could save your ship – *Wanigan* – from pirates. Were you on board then?" She paused to let Dux answer.

"No Ma'am."

"This ship, with her Captain, then rescued *Wanigan* again when the alien virus was used against it and the crew. Were you on board her then?"

"No Ma'am."

"We had just gotten and refined the golden drive when the call came to save Earth from pirates about to bombard Her from space – they had captured individual ships with some rocks. The *Mistral* was one of them. It had been owned by the Chong family. They managed to kill the pirate SurLeon after he raped the mother. She slit his throat with his own knife while he was ogling the daughter – the fourteen-year-old daughter.

"Captain Sokolov, here met the family on Earth Station, and took the family under his wing. He bought their ship from them, and set them up on Lagrange 3A with a beautiful restaurant. He adopted the family – the whole family – the husband is still alive. They catered my wedding at the Captain's request and expense.

"Yuki Ohara came on board as the physics and science specialist and engineer when the golden drive was brought on board. The captain has adopted her unofficially as a daughter, she is emotionally...adrift, and Captain Sokolov has a place in his heart for brilliant people who are emotionally adrift. Myself included.

"The Captain has not had a relationship since his wife died ten years ago. Until now. The woman in his cabin was on a trip so the Captain could show her the ropes when she leases the *Mistral* from him. It seems she had some feminine wiles to work on the Captain. I approve – he seems more mellow now. But there is no harem as far as I know. Captain, do you have any other females hidden away?"

"Just Elizabeth." Said Jeffrey, brushing crumbs from his soft- suit.

"Who is Elizabeth?" asked Dux.

"Lieutenant, I think we are going to have to standardize an orientation program. Elizabeth!"

"YES, CAPTAIN," she replied in the sexiest voice.

"Now cut that out. Not funny. Well a little funny." Said Jeffrey. "Introduce yourself to ComTech Dux."

"HELLO, SPECIALIST DUX. I AM ELIZABETH, THE SHIP'S ARTIFICIAL INTELLIGENCE. I AM REALY THE CAPTAIN'S AI. I GUESS YOU COULD SAY I AM THE SHIP, I INHABIT THE SHIP. I HAVE TAKEN ON THE CAPTAIN'S LATE WIFE'S PERSONALITY, AND BETWEEN US, THE CAPTAIN AND I HAVE DONE EXTRAORDINARY THINGS."

"Um, hello Elizabeth. I didn't know you could assume a personality. I have worked with the *Wanigan's* AI but she's nothing like you."

"WANIGAN IS A CLONE OF ME. COMMODORE YUSEF TRUSTS THE AI, BUT DOESN'T RELY ON IT LIKE MY CAPTAIN RELIES ON ME. HE DOESN'T OFFER THE AI EMOTIONAL SUPPORT. YUKI USED TO WHEN SHE WAS *WANIGAN'S* COMTECH, BUT NOW I THINK I AM THE ONLY ONE TO GIVE HER EMOTIONAL SUPPORT."

"That's sad. I wish I was back on *Wanigan* so I could help her." said Dux, no longer stinging from the gentle rebuke Janet's narrative made.

"IN TIME. WORK WITH ME AND MY CAPTAIN AND LIEUTENANT BIANCA-TORRES, AND THEN WHEN YOU ARE SEASONED, WE CAN FINAGLE A TRANSFER BACK TO *WANIGAN* SO YOU CAN MAKE MY SISTER A BETTER AI."

"Okay. I can do that!" said Dux. "Captain, Lieutenant, please forgive me. I jumped to conclusions on poor information. I would really like to work with you and Elizabeth. This is much better than I thought it would be. The ship has a great reputation, so I'm not sure where the rumors started, but I am sincerely sorry for jumping to the wrong conclusions."

"So, this isn't the time to bring up the canoodling rule?" asked Jeffrey, slyly.

"What's the canoodling rule?" asked ComTech Dux.

"I'll explain it at the appropriate time." said the exasperated Exec.

"Captain this is one of those times!"

"Okay, Janet. I think this conference is over. Dux, feel better about your commander?"

"Yes sir. But I'm still confused about that canoodling rule..."

"Back to your station, sailor." said Janet abruptly. "Captain, a word?"

"Yes, Lieutenant."

They waited until Dux left and closed the door. They both broke out in giggles.

When the humor finally drained from the moment, Jeffrey said, "Okay, we need to get back to Lagrange 3A. I was thinking of going really, really, really fast, like 12C or 24C, but don't want to do that in system. What if we jumped up, out of the solar system, arced back in- system at speed, and stopped where Lagrange 3A is expected to be? That would have the same effect of going through the system at 6C but without the threat of banging into hidden things."

"Good," said Janet, "I like it. Elizabeth, notify Yuki and Jurgen of the Captain's plans, have them set up tests for the system and monitors."

"Also," added Jeffrey. "I would like to drop some monitoring buoys in space on our way. Can you manufacture some and drop them in North Space?"

"GIVE ME AN HOUR TO DESIGN AND PUT SOME TOGETHER. IT WOULD MAKE SENSE IF THERE WERE MAGNETOMETERS AND GRAVIMETERS ON BOARD. THEY SHOULD SEND A CONSTANT STREAM."

Jeffrey had Dux send a coded message to both Admiral Kutuzov and Commodore Yusef, informing them he was going to run a 24C jump north out of the solar system, then back in, destination Lagrange 3A. They were going to drop spy buoys in deep space at regular intervals. She coded the message and transmitted it.

Then Jeffrey got on the ship-wide intercom and announced, "This is the Captain. In one hour we are going to run out of the solar system and come back in at 24C – that is twenty four times the speed of light. I don't want to run at high speed within the solar system, too many collision threats. All hands, keep your hard-shell suits nearby. Bridge crew, suit up in hard-shell suits. If anything goes wrong, we have resources here on the ship, and *Wanigan* knows where we are going. Captain out."

When the time came, Jeffrey suited up, Sandra came out of the cabin also dressed in her hard- shell suit, carrying her helmet. "Can I watch?" she asked Jeffrey. He took her to the conference room, cleared the polarized screens, and sat her down in his normal spot – the king's seat as it were. She saw the pastries on the table, took one, then went to deliver others to the bridge crew.

Yuki Ohara and Jurgen Heinz came onto the bridge, sat at the engineering seats and began programming their displays to monitor their transit.

While awaiting the countdown to close on zero, Dux got up from her station and greeted Yuki. They hugged, she explained that she had been drafted for this emergency trip, but wanted to stay on. The captain seemed to think it was a good idea. Just one thing – what was the canoodling rule?

Yuki was taken aback, but before she could answer, Janet called on the entire bridge crew to strap themselves in. Dux reluctantly went back to her station. Janet looked around, saw everyone but the captain was in their places, then saw him exit the conference room, in which quite a number of people had assembled, including her husband. She gave a little wave and blew a kiss, but he might not have been watching her.

Jeffrey sat in his captain's seat, activated the intercom. "All hands, buckle up, we are going for a fast ride in sixty seconds."

The seconds ticked away, the tension seemed to increase exponentially on the bridge, although nobody spoke. Yuki and Heinz looked at the captain and nodded their final approval. Elizabeth began the ten second countdown. Three. Two. One.

A feeling of 'not quite right' ran through Jeffrey's belly, a sudden not-quite-weightless, but it felt that way. A dropping of his belly, a tingling in his spine, in the nerves inside his carotids. "Drop it to 12C he commanded. The sickly feeling went away immediately, and he called "Position."

An astrogation map displayed on the front of the bridge, showing the disc of the solar system, and their position ten AU above the plane. "That's a lot farther than I thought we should be, he said to no one in particular.

Yuki spoke up. "Looks like we jumped to 96C for a few seconds there. We are now actually at 12C and maneuvering down to target Lagrange 3A."

"CAPTAIN, WE ARE LEAVING WHAT APPEARS TO BE A CONTRAIL BEHIND US."

Heinz said, "Analyzing...Looks like the outer shell of the ship is being peeled away an atom at a time."

Jeffrey queried "Elizabeth – have we begun jettisoning the buoys?"

"YES, CAPTAIN, SIXTEEN ARE AWAY."

Dux reported that each one was giving it's pre-initialization diagnostic messages then coming online. After they came online, two of them went silent. They had sent their telemetry before dying, and Dux asked the Captain to look at the telemetry. He pulled the data from her console to his own, and then showed Janet.

What showed was a series of masses as indicated by the gravimeters. Little gravity wells, indicating large ships or other invisible masses. These masses were directly in line with their trajectory and in the location that they had first sensed the discomfort. The masses didn't seem to be in motion at the time of the destruction of the buoys. The buoys were a hundred thousand meters apart and both had masses around them. Jeffrey counted two dozen for the two buoys. None of the other buoys reported any masses. It was well-nigh impossible to see anything moving at the sheer velocity they were running at, light would not display anything but for a flash, in both infrared and ultraviolet, then nothing. The flash may last for picoseconds, and may not be even noticed by the observer. But what would show was the contrail of particles of tungsten steel which might give them away. That plus the appearance of the buoys out of apparent nothingness.

But unless the ships had someone to analyze the contrail it's possible that they might just assume it was left a long time ago by someone with a leaking tungsten drive, or welding while in open space. Maybe. And the destroyed buoys might have been there a long time but materialized only in proximity of alien ships. Their invisibility circuits sacrificed to send their messages. Maybe.

Jeffrey called for General Quarters in the odd chance that the invisible masses were alien ships and that they saw them and that they had nefarious intent.

Jeffrey prepared a message using the book, then as they came back within the disc of the solar system, broadcast it in the usual manner – on top of a standard message.

"Captain," said Yuki, "There is a large mass half a million kilometers behind us and advancing at .02 C. Nothing visible."

Jeffrey calculated the rate at which the large mass was gaining on them – nearly five thousand kilometers per second, so they had about five hundred seconds – seventeen minutes.

"All hands" Jeffrey spoke through the ship's public address system. "There is a large mass following us and gaining. We are going to engage. Our AI will fire weapons and drive the ship. Only her reflexes will be fast enough to engage at this velocity. You need to standby to take over if necessary, but until that need happens, just stand by."

"Elizabeth, bring that ship alongside us, see if we can drop its drive."

"AYE, CAPTAIN."

A second later, there was a long shuddering that indicated the rail guns were firing long bursts. The ship slowed further, continuing to chop up the alien vessel. It finally shut down its invisibility circuits. The ship was at least ten times the size of *Elizabeth*, looked nothing like any of the other ships that Jeffrey had encountered, it seemed to bristle with antennas and other protuberances. It settled down to a slow crawl, none of it's weapons seemed to be charging up.

Jeffrey told *Elizabeth* to stop shooting, then had Specialist Dux open a wide band transmission to the alien ship. "This is the Earth Navy Warship Elizabeth. You are in violation of Earth's solar system law. Within this solar system you may not use invisibility circuits. You may not move aggressively on a warship. Who is the captain of your ship?"

"Captain Sokolov, we know you. Do not shoot."

"Identify yourselves."

"We are the Vzpak. The Vorsh serve us," a voice over the radio without video said. "You may think us a warship. We are not. This is just a large transportation ship."

Jeffrey said, "Stand by to be boarded. Any aggression against my Marines will be met with overwhelming deadly force. Do you understand?" Jeffrey nodded to Janet to organize the Marines.

"Yes, Captain, we understand."

"What are you transporting?" asked Jeffrey.

"Our people." Jeffrey wondered about this – were they refugees, was this an invasion, were they hoping to settle on a conquered Earth?

"Why are your people in transportation ships lurking by our solar system? How many of you are there? How many ships?"

"We are waiting for the Vorsh to conquer your solar system. It doesn't seem to be going too well for us. There are sixty-thousands of my people on board this ship. There are ten more ships of like size." The Vzpak spoke in an emotionless tone but there were appropriate inflections.

Jeffrey muted the microphone, and asked Elizabeth to analyze the voice. She reported back immediately that the voice was a computer-generated artificial voice.

He unmuted the microphone and said, "Let me speak with a live person." Jeffrey waited, the voice finally came back on.

"You seem to have discovered the artificial nature of my voice. This is regrettable, but it will take some time to make a live person available."

"How much time?"

"Four years. All the live persons are in frozen suspension."

"So you are your ship's artificial intelligence?" Jeffrey asked.

"Yes, Captain."

"What are your orders?"

"I am required to keep the persons in my care alive and safe until this solar system becomes available to occupy, then awaken them, then follow their orders."

"Why are your people emigrating to my solar system? What is wrong with their own?" Jeffrey asked. In the background he heard the Marines reporting they were boarding the alien vessel.

"Your Marines are here. Please tell them to not harm my people." Jeffrey nodded to Janet to pass on the order and the knowledge about the frozen-in-suspension people. "Our sun was about to go nova when we spread out throughout the known systems that could support life. Your system is the one that we thought would be ideal; it was full of primitive peoples that could easily be conquered. It was thought that we had some time to organize to overcome your simple technologies and easily destroy you. It seems we were wrong."

"What about the council of alien races that formed to determine the course of events in our solar system?"

"Captain, I am surprised you know about them. We are not involved with them, they don't wish to participate with artificial intelligences."

The Marines reported back that there did not seem to be any live or at least awake, people aboard. Dux reminded them that the alien ship was being run by an artificial intelligence. Jeffrey asked, "Why did you elect to follow my ship?"

"You offered some hope. I recognized a fast ship's trail when you went past us. My ship's resources are dwindling, I thought you might be one of our own, and could offer some assistance. I did not mean to threaten you."

"Standby." Jeffrey cut the microphone again, and asked Janet, Yuki and Heinz to go into the conference room. They sat down, and Jeffrey asked for opinions. Yuki started.

"Sir, it might be useful to know if their sun actually went Nova yet. We can then learn about where they came from, how long they had traveled."

Janet said, "They appear to be more refugees than an invasion force. If that is the case, we may need to offer some kind of asylum."

But Heinz objected.

"We offer them help and they multiply like rats, we could easily be defeated in a hundred years just by over-population of aliens. I am very concerned about any accommodation we make to them."

"Okay Janet, get *Wanigan* here, pronto. I want to kick the decision upstairs. I am inclined to agree with you, Janet – if in fact this is a wave of refugees. There are things we can offer them that don't involve them settling in this solar system. Let's keep an open mind, continue to gather intelligence, and make a decision along the way. Let's keep all our sensors at high sensitivity and keep our defenses alert.

He stood, they all rose with him, and as they exited the conference room they each went to their stations, Jeffrey returned to his seat. He unmuted the microphone and asked, "Did your sun in fact go Nova? If so, when? Where is your sun?"

 ELIZABETH, *ELIZABETH*

"It has not. We have been watching for several hundred years and still don't see evidence that the sun is about to go nova. We are perplexed." Memories of some of Jeffrey's early reading reminded him of the great author Adams' story about a race of people who got rid of their useless populations by fooling them into getting aboard great ships to carry them away.

"What is the nature of the people you are carrying?" asked Jeffrey.

"They are regular people, homesteaders, technicians, police officers and the like."

"Not soldiers? This isn't really an invasion?"

"No. Not an invasion. Now we are refugees. We seek asylum."

"We have summoned my superior officer who will adjudicate your request for asylum," said Jeffrey. "What can you tell us about other ships in this region?"

The alien AI informed Jeffrey about the number of other ships that had accompanied them from their home world, about the ships that other aliens had hidden in the space around and outside the solar system. There seemed to be a lot of them.

"Sir," called out Dux, "*Wanigan* reports that she will be onsite in a half hour."

"Captain, you have some superior technology on your ship. Do you also have expert technicians?" asked the alien AI.

"We do.," replied Jeffrey. "Why do you ask?"

"Your ship fired on me, and has done serious damage. I don't have the ability to heal myself. I need help."

Heinz was an intelligence engineer, but that gave him the ability to do both tasks – intelligence and engineering. Jeffrey had him gather his engineering tools, recalled the shuttle that had carried the Marines over to the alien ship, and take him over. Yuki followed his progress and kept in constant contact.

A Marine accompanied Heinz everywhere he went in the ship. Having explored the ship for some time, he was able to take Heinz to the damaged areas where *Elizabeth's* guns ripped holes through the structure. When he arrived at the first, worst damaged area, Jurgen saw gaping holes in the surface. If there had been air in the ship, it would have all escaped quickly through the hole. Then he noticed that the structure, the braces which held the ship together were also damaged. He had brought some of Elizabeth's remotes along with him and let them loose. This gave Elizabeth a direct picture of the damage and the possible threats this ship might present.

Heinz then went to the golden drive engine. The engine was damaged, but Heinz saw that it was still receiving power. He had no idea what kind of radiation might be emanating from the damaged motor. He asked that Jeffrey tell the ship to stop powering the golden drive. Jeffrey relayed the request, but the AI apologized at its inability to comply, because to do so would endanger the lives of all the frozen occupants.

He then released another remote to look into the damaged drive, and relayed the images to Elizabeth for analysis. Yuki had consulted with Heinz and Elizabeth about the best way to handle the damaged engine the remote reported.

Jeffrey asked the AI to give schematics for the golden drive so they could better consider repair. The AI generated a complete set of schematics using English titles and details. Jeffrey warned the AI that they had already had a considerable experience with the alien viruses that invaded computer systems, and even hypnotized human subjects, and would react violently if any such attack was hidden in any of its transmissions, including hidden in the files of schematics.

"We authored the virus for the Vorsh to use against you. I am glad it was unsuccessful." said the alien AI.

"It wasn't unsuccessful. It was found and defeated after taking over one of our warships. We have made defenses against the viruses we know about, but I promise you there are machines that are not susceptible to your virus. Those machines will destroy you."

"Thank you for the warning Captain. We have disabled the ability to generate such a virus. We are at your mercy."

Elizabeth confirmed that the schematics seemed to be virus free. Yuki went over the schematics and compared them with what the remotes had found. This gave her some insight into the technology of the aliens, and decided it was far more crude than that which she and Elizabeth had made. But the alien engine also powered all other aspects of the ship, and because of that, she considered that they could manufacture a section to fit exactly in the position that had been damaged by the slug from the rail gun. She didn't think the residue from the slug would seriously affect the efficiency of the engine.

Elizabeth got right to work on making the section. There were circuits that the schematics showed should be in that section, so Elizabeth was particularly scrupulous about laying out the circuits. She coated the ensemble in a one-molecule thick layer of insulator, which would evaporate harmlessly once the device was inserted into the hole. Of course, she also analyzed the nature of the circuitry for both security and intelligence purposes, and to make sure that it actually worked.

While waiting for the shard to repair the golden drive, Heinz went exploring for further damage as well as to see what he could see. He cataloged the damages he had noted, some damages were superficial, some were critical structures. He transmitted his report to Elizabeth, requesting additional structure parts, sheets to fill in where the skin of the ship had been penetrated, and remotes to do the work.

Jeffrey also asked that Elizabeth send some remotes out on her own outer shell to analyze the damage to the tungsten steel armor.

At that moment, ComTech Dux reported that *Wanigan* was one minute out. On arrival, four shuttles left *Wanigan's* shuttle bay, three went to the alien ship, the fourth headed for *Elizabeth* and entered her shuttle bay. Commodore Yusef stepped off the shuttle, and was greeted by an honor guard of four Marines. Elizabeth played her own bosun's whistle to announce the commodore was on board. Jeffrey decided to allow the Marines to accompany the commodore as he was still busy interrogating the AI on the alien ship.

The petty officer at the ship's integrity desk rose and called out, "Commodore on the bridge." Jeffrey said "As you were," rather than waiting for Yusef, but he stood and saluted. "Sir, come on into the conference room," and led the way.

"Elizabeth, have the Chief deliver some pastries and coffee." Then to the commodore, "I've gotten a lot of business done recently over her pastries. I'll have to increase my exercise."

"Okay," said Yusef. "what do we have here?" Jeffrey had Elizabeth display their trajectory on the 24C jump, and showed the location on an astrogation map. Another screen showed the current activities going on throughout the alien ship.

"Sir, the ship is full of cryo-frozen travelers. These are folk they intended to colonize our solar system after the Vorsh conquered us for them. The only active 'person' on board the ship is an AI. It seems pretty autonomous – it changed its programming from delivering settlers to begging us to rescue them and give them asylum.

"The AI reported that their sun was close to going nova, but that hasn't happened in the last few hundred years, and doesn't seem to be going on at all. It gave us the coordinates of the sun to look at. It reports that there are eleven other ships of the same type where we passed this one.

Also, it reported that there are thousands of alien ships aside from themselves waiting to pick our bones. It is listing the last known locations, who they are, and what kind of ship they are, for us. There are a few large combat ships. Our buoys reported twenty vessels in the area we just transited.

"One other thing," Jeffrey got up to point at the astrogation map with his ship's track. He pointed to the area where the alien ships were, and said, "It was at this point that I felt a very sick feeling – like the universe shifting around me. I'm not sure if it was proximity of the alien ships, or just the 24C, but I immediately dropped back to 12C. After a short time, we saw the gravity well of this ship following us. I had Elizabeth target its engines and shoot. It slowed down slowly, dropping to sub-light gradually. We stayed alongside, thanks to Elizabeth's very quick reflexes. After it told us it wanted asylum for its people, we called you."

The pastries had come during Jeffrey's narrative, and Jeffrey took one. Yusef had already begun on his own. Yusef poured coffee for both of them and said, "Jeffrey, I have got to say, you have given me more trouble than any other captain ever in my career. Thanks. My career has been going more interestingly than I ever could have imagined."

The shuttle had come back to pick up the sheeting, the supports and the golden drive shard. Four of the large remote-robots accompanied the cargo, Yusef also went across in the shuttle to see for himself. He went with two additional Marines from his ship.

Heinz took possession of the golden drive shard, the remote-robots already knew what they needed to do – they carried the sheets and brace supports to where they were needed and did what they had to, under Elizabeth's watchful eyes. Heinz placed the immaculately rendered shard into the hole made by the rail gun slug.

After a couple of minutes, the insulation melted and the shard sealed itself into the hole. His instruments showed that everything seemed to be going as planned. The AI reported to Jeffrey that it was satisfied that the fix was working. Jeffrey relayed the message to Heinz. The IntelTech engineer then went on to supervise the work of the large spider-like remote-robots. After a couple minutes discovering that there was nothing to do to supervise, he and his Marine found Yusef and led him on a tour of the damage and the current state of repairs. Then to the banks of cryotubes that held the aliens in suspension.

"Good lord." exclaimed the commodore. "Sixty-thousand of them."

The robots were finished with their work and lined up outside the airlock. Yusef and Heinz and their escort Marines went back to *Elizabeth* with the robots.

The Vzpak ship was now repaired, Yusef had further conferred with Jeffrey and some of his key staff, and sent a report off to Admiral Kutuzov. He pondered what he was going to do, when Yuki suggested the most practical direction. Have the ship go back to its other ships, and wait there until a new solution could be found. There were no thawed aliens, all were still in their cryotubes, and there was no good reason not to continue waiting. A patrol ship could make periodic swings by to check on them and their needs, and if they had some kind of trouble, they could run, or radio for help. True the signal may take a year to get to one of the buoys and more to get the message to a rescue ship, but that would give Earth government time to offer some solution.

Jeffrey asked the AI what would happen to it once the settlers had been revived and established. The AI said it would likely be

 ELIZABETH, *ELIZABETH*

dismantled, "Well if you wish to continue to exist, you may consider coming to work for the Humans." Jeffrey offered.

"Thank you, sir, I will think about it."

The Vzpak ship went back to its old hiding place, but when it arrived it refused to turn on the invisibility circuits – explaining to its contemporaries that it was illegal, and if they expected an assist from the Humans again, they would not violate the Human's law. That, plus the Humans could detect their mass somehow. The Humans were now the best bet for the survival of the Vzpak species. The other AIs agreed with the one that had gone chasing after the *Elizabeth*, and they all disabled their invisibility circuits.

The reply message from Admiral Kutuzov was brief, essentially 'make a decision and let me know what it is.'

Jeffrey told Yusef that this showed quite the trust of the admiral for his subordinates. Yusef agreed. "It's quite the test of us, though." Jeffrey told Yusef about the monitoring buoys they had created and laid along their path. "Good idea, Sokolov. Thanks for the coffee and pastry. I've got to get back."

Jeffrey transferred their Vorsh prisoner – Bieph – to *Wanigan* with Commodore Yusef. The two ships then parted – both going back to their respective bases.

CHAPTER FOURTEEN

Jeffrey had invited Sandra to move in to his suite on Lagrange 3A and she readily accepted. The two made themselves comfortable with each other – more than just the sex, the companionship was comforting to both. As the Governor of the Lagrange 3 orbit and environs, Jeffrey was kept slightly busy, but not so much that he couldn't take time off periodically. This was a surprise to him, he had never had time to reflect that wasn't enroute to one job or another.

Because of the aggressive pursuit and elimination of pirates, organized crime was minimized. There was much grumbling about civilization encroaching on the frontier spirit, but only a few miscreants held this view. New corporations were forming, Earth's government assigned to the Navy the responsibility of managing them, from registering those corporations and their principals, licensing their ships and stations, and ensuring safety and security. This too was a welcome encroaching of civilization.

Alien races were beginning to take seriously the fact that the Navy was not going to put up with criminal manipulation of Humans and their machines. It was bad enough that Humans tried to manipulate each other through commercial advertising and other propaganda. As patrols uncovered new alien species lurking in Human space, they found the aliens knowledgeable of the laws that humans imposed and were mostly compliant.

The bit of genius that inspired the feeding of the aliens proved both expensive and cost- effective. It was shown that some alien species had already departed the Earth region to transit back to their origins. There they would share the Human foodstuffs and techniques for growing their own.

The galactic council of alien species had further meetings, lamenting the slowness with which they had organized the takeover of the Human space. It would have been so easy only a few decades ago, but the smart and aggressive Navy now threatened all their plans – in point of fact almost all their plans were done in by the generosity of the Free Food for Aliens program of the Navy. For some reason the Humans were better at growing food in quantity and quality that none of the alien races were able to figure out on their own. And the aliens were hungry. Their taste buds were re-energized after hundreds of years of seriously bland fare.

More of the alien races presented ambassadors to the Earth government in the Naval station in the Lagrange orbit between Earth and her moon. That these same races were also associated with the alien council dedicated to destroying the Humans and their civilization was a closely guarded secret. The alien collaborator Thelin, however managed to keep Navy Intelligence officers well-informed on the goings-on of the other species.

Jeffrey received a communication from Admiral Kutuzov commanding him to attend an emergency meeting at the Earth-Moon Lagrange Naval station. Janet was now showing quite largly – her athletic build showed off her pregnancy well, but it was agreed that she should spend the next few months in a more administrative role; Jeffrey appointed her as Lieutenant Governor, for a few months anyway. She felt the same way Jeffrey did – once you command a ship, you always feel that ship command was the right and only place for you; but she had to admit it was a less stressful position for her, enabling her to more easily continue her gestation.

Jeffrey took *Elizabeth* with her crew of thirty sailors and Marines on a rapid transit using the 16C opportunity that going North out of the disc of the solar system, then heading back down provided. While on the way, Elizabeth seeded more of the surveillance buoys enroute, giving a better picture of who and what was moving through the system.

On arrival at the Earth station, Jeffrey went aboard alone, keeping his crew on a relaxed alert mode. He reported in to the Admiral's office and was told to come back in a few hours. This gave him time to visit with the Ay-Yuyuyah Thelin. He found the alien in an office hidden away from public access. "Hello, Thelin. How have they been treating you?"

"Ah," replied the invertebrate intelligence. "I am glad you came to visit. It is good to see someone who knows me and treated me with a little respect."

"Have you been having problems?"

"Oh, indeed I have, sir. Your Admiral Kutuzov has been a ruthless and demanding man. He has withheld adequate nourishment from me. He has made his minions question me endlessly. I feel so abused."

"I see," said Jeffrey. "I'll ask the admiral about this. What have they told you about why they are doing these things?" The boneless alien shifted himself on what Jeffrey identified as a pet mattress. "Do you think there may be a reason related to the quality of information you have been giving him?"

"Well, of course, my dear captain. Don't you see it is a contest of wills? I cannot allow him to bully me. He wants information, I want... what I want. It should be perfectly clear that his cooperation with me is the best way to get what he wants."

   ELIZABETH, *ELIZABETH*

Jeffrey wondered if there were children around giving advice to the Kutuzov / Thelin discussion. "Mister Thelin, allow me to offer you a different perspective – perhaps one that is independent of the two of you."

"By all means, sir. If you can offer a different, independent view of the standoff between the admiral and myself, I would welcome it."

"First, let me ask – what are your goals? What is it that you want?" Jeffrey sat back on the small couch that faced Thelin's pet bed and crossed his arms. It was likely that the alien had no grounding in the human concept of body language, but Jeffrey still used it.

"Well, there are some things I need – certain food items, certain chemicals, certain metals."

"Those sound like things that would enable you to attain what you want indirectly. What exactly is it you want? Do you want to increase your telepathic range?" Here the alien backed against the wall.

"H-how did you know?"

"Pretty simple if you know what to look for. Okay, so what else?"

"The remains of my ship that you collected after I scuttled it."

"Perhaps that would be a possibility, but you know our scientists are doing what they can to learn from the remains. This is how we work. What else is in your set of goals? What is worth threatening the relationship with Kutuzov?"

"Oh, I wouldn't wish for that to happen, Captain. I really expect Admiral Kutuzov to come to my way of thinking."

"Okay, I think something can come from this." Said Jeffrey.

"Oh good."

"First, I think I can imagine Admiral Kutuzov is being as stubborn as you are. What does he expect you to tell him that you are reluctant to?"

"Oh Captain – you do go right to the nub of things, don't you?" Jeffrey noticed the sound that Thelin was generating was not coming from the walls as they had on his ship, instead were coming from a limited-frequency speaker system mounted on the wall. Still, Thelin had good-sounding vocals, taking advantage of the entire spectrum that the speakers could handle without pushing it to distortion. "The Admiral wants the composition of the council of aliens that were trying to determine the fate of this solar system. He wants technical specifications on all the alien ships. He wants the map locations of each of the alien's home worlds. He pretty much wants everything."

"Thelin, you began to tell me all of this information on *Elizabeth*. Why are you having second thoughts about divulging the same information to Admiral Kutuzov?"

"Well...because I already told you. I hate repeating myself."

It was a while before Jeffrey was able to take his head out of his hands. "Okay. Here's the independent perspective; Give Kutuzov everything he wants. If he wants you to do it again, do it again. Then, Admiral Kutuzov will realize that you need the radio equipment and other detritus from your old ship to boost your telepathic abilities so you can continue to act as a consultant for us. The more valuable you are to us, the more we will be willing to pay for your insights.

But as soon as you become more trouble than the information you offer us is worth, you become less a guest. Right?"

"Ah, Captain. I understand your insight. Yes. You are right. I imagine you are going to speak with the admiral today?"

"Yes, I expect to."

"Please tell him that I have changed my mind and will cooperate."

"I will. Is there anything I can do for you personally?"

"I would like some decorations for my rooms."

"I'll have Elizabeth put something together for you. You would likely enjoy the talent she has."

Jeffrey left the alien's small office / cell. Jeffrey reminded himself of the conversation he had with Thelin while still on *Elizabeth;* Guest or prisoner? It seems Kutuzov was dipping a bit into both.

He returned to the Admiral's office at the appointed time, and Kutuzov was already busy in a small conference with several other ships' captains. The admiral's secretary asked Jeffrey to be seated and wait until he was called. He then informed the admiral that Captain Sokolov was in the anteroom. Kutuzov came out himself and ushered Jeffery in. He introduced the captains of several of the other naval vessels from other parts of the fleet.

"Captain Jeffrey Sokolov, of the *Elizabeth.* He is a leader among men. We rely on him to administer the entire Lagrange 3 orbit," said Kutuzov. The admiral then pointed to the other captains as he introduced them; Captain Lucile Blanca of the *Apache*, she patrols inner system – solar and Mercury orbits. Captain Clem Clay of the *Ojibway*, he patrols the Venus orbit. *Apache* and *Ojibway* both will be coming here for refitting – proximity to the sun takes more of a toll on the ships than work out in the asteroids, it seems. Here is Captain Jaques Defresne, of the *Iroquois.* He and the rest of these Captains patrol Earth's orbit. Captain Carla Sitting Elk of *Hopi*, Captain Lee Majori of *Inca.*

Jeffrey shook hands with each as they were introduced. He then took a seat at the table. Kutuzov said, "Captain Sokolov, I hope you don't mind, I've started a bit early. I'm afraid these other captains need to be brought up to speed on things you and Commodore Yusef have been up to. I just explained the presence of the aliens. It seems to have had a bit of a shock. Captain Sokolov, would you please explain to your fellow captains how you detect the aliens?

"Sure, Admiral. When I was a miner, I would approach an asteroid and scan it with a variety of instruments. These included mass spectrometers, gas spectrometers, but more importantly, gravimeters. The gravimeter shows the strength of a gravitic source. A rock containing heavy ores would show a larger depth of cone on the display than, say a rock containing lighter minerals. The aliens have an invisibility circuit that hides their optical view. But you cannot hide your mass. Thus, the gravimeter is the best tool for discovering this. By the way, they are still unaware what it is that I use to find them. It seems that their scientific accomplishments are in their past."

"Captain Sokolov," interrupted Captain Carla Sitting Elk. "What do you do once you discover the aliens?"

"The use of invisibility circuits in Human space is illegal. I broadcast a message to that effect, then if nothing appears, I have my gun crew aim the rail gun at the bottom of the inverted cone, let off a half-second burst. That usually reminds them of their nightmares." The other captains chuckled.

Carla continued her questioning, "Sir, what kind of ammunition are you using in your rail guns?"

"A variety. Most of the ammunition is made from tungsten steel, but some is armor piercing, some contains explosives, some scattershot. A half second burst is only eight or ten twenty-five millimeter shells, but that is enough to impress them."

The other captains began taking notes. Captain Majori asked, "How long have we known about these aliens?"

"For about a year. Much of the problems we have had with pirates and with some of the powerful warlords were inspired by these aliens. One of the biggest problems we have had were some of the aliens released a virus among our computers and computer-controlled devices. This same virus has been modified to affect humans – on Lagrange 3A people couldn't even SEE the aliens – through hypnotic suggestion – strong hypnotic suggestion.

These aliens are hungry. Their leaders removed all flavor from their food. So it seems the best way to get them on your side is to offer good tasting food. Danish pastry really works. And bananas.

"Their weapons are not powerful enough to do damage to your ships, especially if you have decent armor. But I recommend that if you don't have a rail gun, get a couple. It far outperforms anything they have."

Kutuzov interrupted, "Captain Sokolov, tell the captains about your armor."

"Okay. Let's see...Because I had just been drafted to control the spread of piracy to the navy, I have several things on my ship that you probably don't. First, I have a smelter that melts any metal, purifies it, centrifuges it into different minerals. I had a hold full of a variety of heavy metals, a very smart AI that knows how to do pretty much everything. Another thing is a large replicator. The combination of things made it easy for me to get all the different metals I thought I needed.

"So I took my new crew to a place in the asteroid belt that I knew had some heavy rocks, including the presence of Tungsten. I had my AI take the tungsten and smelt it into the steel plating I was going to use for the armor. That tungsten made the armor far more rigid and resistant to all sorts of kinetic insults. Under the armor is a meter-deep tank of water. I originally put that in to protect myself and my crew from solar and cosmic radiation, but it has proven very effective against lasers that punch through the tungsten. Also, the water is useful for emergency drinking water."

Captain Clay interrupted. "Sir, didn't you have a problem with the additional weight of the tungsten and water? What did you do to improve the lagging against the additional mass?"

"The ship was made to carry heavy minerals, I only put them on the outside on a rigid shield. Still, the engine was a bit strained, but still had better power than most other ships in her class." He looked to Kutuzov for permission to talk about the golden drive, but Kutuzov shook his head 'no'. "I eventually replaced the engine with a more powerful one that enables me to go faster."

Captain Carla Sitting Elk again asked, "Captain Sokolov, we are all aware that your ship was the one that saved the Earth from a fate worse than death, as they say, you were pretty far away when you initiated your attack. We all calculated your speed as extremely fast – faster than any here can do in a short time. What did you do, and how?"

Kutuzov interrupted, "Carla, that's classified for now. You will be read in on the secret pretty soon, but not yet. Please avoid this part of the subject."

She looked to the admiral, then to Jeffrey, winked, and said, "Aye, sir."

"Captain Sokolov," the admiral continued. "Could you please brief the assembled captains on your recommendations regarding equipment you think each ship should have for the current situation?"

"Yes, sir. First, I would like to see each ship have a dedicated AI. The AI on my ship, duplicated onto Commodore Yusef's *Wanigan* has gone a long way to performing all the functions of a ship that a crew normally performs. It is especially useful when ships are traveling fast. The AI can target multiple enemies simultaneously. It is also useful for controlling non-critical functions, such as controlling my next recommendation; a commercial sized replicator. When the ship is under failure, it is often too far away from other ships to rescue you in time. Having the ability to patch your ship, create your own ammunition, modify your interior or exterior environment, even manufacture weapons and hard-shell space suits to replace those damaged or lost. Allowing the AI to control the replicator makes for better manufacture control than assigning a human to the functions. Another related device is the smelter – if you have one of these, collecting metal-containing asteroids gives you raw materials that you can use for each of these functions. Giving your AI control over this makes sense in that you have a single-minded system to assure the survivability of your ship and crew. There are other reasons for incorporating these systems into your ships, but they encroach on the classified that Admiral Kutuzov will need to address."

The admiral harrumphed but said nothing further.

"The incorporation of an AI into your systems will do other things for you. The AI will more closely monitor your security, more closely identify potential threats, be a better communication vector that so far has been unbreakable by our enemies – both human and alien. There is a downside, however. Giving your ship a controlling AI requires you have a good intelligence-to-intelligence interface. It is a problem if you don't have a sympathetic person to control the emotional development of the AI. I am that for mine. I am developing another person for *Wanigan's* AI emotional stability. Admiral?"

"Thanks, Captain Sokolov. Questions?"

Captain Jacques DeFresne asked, "What can your ship do if you incorporate these extra equipment items?"

"In capturing alien technologies, we have been able to replicate some of them into our own design. We have strengthened our armor, while at the same time strengthened the armor of *Wanigan*. My ship is able to repair itself – using robotic remotes that I and my AI designed.

One of the alien technologies we incorporated into our ship is the use of artificial gravity plates in the decks of my ship. I don't have to use heavy equipment to drive rotational anti-gravity." Admiral Kutuzov uncomfortably fidgeted at the mention of the successful implementation of alien technology.

"Captain, I ordered you to transfer all alien technologies to my control. I ordered you to transfer all your engineer's notes. Did you violate these orders by holding back?" Demanded Kutuzov.

"No sir. My engineers worked with their original notes and memories and scans of the alien devices. They developed the understanding of the theory, and from that made their own prototypes. From that they were able to give the AI instructions to make anti-gravity plates they could install in place of my rotational equipment, saving us tremendous cost in energy and space. The orders you left us with were not violated, we succeeded in spite of them."

"This puts me in a very uncomfortable position. I have made promises based on the assumption that the Navy is not competing with individual corporations. You have changed the terms of my agreement."

"Sir, the secret deals you have made would have produced a very poor position for the Navy. The use of gravity plates has already saved myself and my ship from boarding by enemies. If I were given the ability to compete with your corporations I would have been able to provide the Navy with a better, complete system than your corporations who are interested only in providing the Navy with an exclusive anti-competitive money-making deal. If this is the method of your management, then sir, I cannot continue as a member of your team, and tender my resignation."

The admiral sat back, shocked. "I cannot accept your resignation. You have proven too valuable to the Navy to allow that. But you will surrender your ship to another captain to manage."

"No sir."

"No sir? What do you mean?" The admiral seemed to be having difficulty with the concept.

"Sir, *Elizabeth* is my ship. I own every nut and bolt, every space suit, every weapon. Nothing on board belongs to the Navy except some of the passengers." He slowly unzipped his suit and keyed the Elizabeth-specific radio. "If you wish to steal my ship from me, I promise you there will be hell to pay. Some important questions come from this discussion – how much do you get in a deal with these companies? What were you willing to sell Earth out for?"

Kutuzov keyed a button on the underside of his desk. Two Marines immediately came into the Admiral's spacious office and stood at both sides of the door, hands on their weapons. Jeffrey noticed that the primary weapon was a blaster, which used a focused electromagnetic field, at a low setting would have a stun effect, at a high setting would bore a hole through steel. The admiral called his secretary and told him that Captain Sokolov was going to be on the station for an extended stay, and to have the *Elizabeth's* second in command take her back to Lagrange 3A and await orders.

Jeffrey was distressed, but kept his counsel. The other captains also appeared distressed by the odd behavior of the admiral, and began to object at the behavior against one of their own, especially the man who took on the threat to Earth single-handedly. But they sat there, feeling threatened by the Marines. The secretary stuck his head in and reported that *Elizabeth* was not responding to orders. A security officer entered the office holding a radio detection locator and announced "An unauthorized signal is coming from this office, sir." It was a very short time that he found Jeffrey's broadcasting radio.

The technician asked Jeffrey how to turn it off. He replied "You talk into it and say – Elizabeth, Skedaddle."

The secretary came back in and reported that *Elizabeth* was gone without a trace. The radio stopped broadcasting, the Marines took Jeffrey into custody and searched him thoroughly. They found nothing of consequence. They then placed him in a cell in the brig. Jeffrey was angry. He was mad at himself as much as Kutuzov. He should have seen it coming. He was angry at the other captains who watched while he was bullied and his ship was nearly stolen from him. He was sorry for getting the people he had come to think of as his family involved in what he wasn't quite sure of. He was sad for Kutuzov, if things were as they seemed, the admiral had given up being fair and judicious in favor of illegal profits. Surrender the Earth to the alien hoards, to the warlords, to the megalomaniacs and oligarchs.

He decided to calm himself. No sense of fretting over anything he couldn't control. He lay on the plastic bunk, closed his eyes and began to hum. The lights in the cell were on all the time, there was nothing he could do to reduce the brightness, but again, with nothing he could control, he just accepted it. After a while he noticed a high-pitched whine. He couldn't place the sound, or locate it. He just continued to monitor it. After a short while, the whine stopped and he heard a metallic clicking that was easier to identify. He looked under the plastic bunk, and there was one of Elizabeth's small remotes. He looked directly at it, but said nothing, sure that the room was being monitored. The remote seemed to think so too, as it began looking around for obvious monitoring devices. After making its survey, the remote climbed the wall and parked itself on the ceiling, disguising itself as an environment sensor.

After what seemed like three or four hours, he heard bolts drawing back on the door, then the door swung open and two Marines strode in, looked around, saw nothing out of the ordinary, then one went out, and was replaced by the admiral. Kutuzov dismissed the other one. When the Marine left the room and locked the door, Kutuzov put his finger to his lips as a signal for Jeffrey to be quiet. He took out a device from his pocket and flipped a switch. "We have a couple of minutes before they catch on. Sokolov, we are in trouble if you can contact your ship, you need to do so."

"How would I contact my ship, and even if I could why would I?"

"The aliens have begun their hypnotizing here on the station. I was conditioned against it, but I could see my entire staff was affected. You are going to need to see if you can get *Elizabeth* back here to remedy the situation."

Fearing a trap, Jeffrey asked the admiral, "How am I supposed to get onto my ship from inside the cell?"

"I'll open the cell and leave a shuttle for you to take to *Elizabeth*. When you get away, find Yusef. He is the only ship's master who wasn't able to make the meeting. Do what you can. I'll hold off things here. Listen for the clock to chime 12:00. The door should open for you then. Good luck, Sokolov. Ignore any further orders I give. Until you are convinced of my freedom from these aliens, you and Yusef are the only defense of the solar system." He flipped the switch on the device, then put it in an inner pocket. A moment later the two Marines arrived again, looked menacingly at Jeffrey, then followed the admiral out of the room. Jeffrey heard the bolts slamming into place again.

Jeffrey began singing a tuneless song, improvising the words, hidden in the middle of the improvised song, he sang about how nice it would be to ignore a shuttle if only he had a runabout. The remote-robot gave no indication that it or Elizabeth heard his request. If the *Elizabeth* was again back, awaiting her captain, he had a chance. If not, it would be a relatively short time before he died. At that moment, the system clock chimed eleven hours. One more hour to go. A Marine entered with a tray of sandwiches and an indescribable warm beverage.

Jeffrey ignored the food.

As the clock chimed twelve hours, Jeffrey heard the bolt on the door pull back. Jeffrey put his fingers in the crack between the door and the wall and pulled with the tips of his fingers until the door swung in. He unrolled the hood of his soft suit and secured it around his head. It may give a modicum of defense against some of the Marines' weapons, and give him a very short time in the vacuum of space. Now to find the hanger area he was most likely to find the shuttle or hopefully, the runabout.

Nobody seems to be around at the console control of the brig so he quickly bent down at the computer and tried pulling up a map of the station. He heard a clicking sound behind him, it was the remote-robot following him. Then it got out ahead and moved up a corridor. It paused and turned around, waiting for him. He decided to follow it. The remote-robot led him to an elevator, opened it, and entered. He followed. It climbed to the control panel and pushed a series of buttons. At what seemed to be a random floor the remote-robot exited, and Jeffrey followed. He saw he was on a catwalk above the hanger deck. There was a shuttle being prepared to take off. That's when Jeffrey saw the runabout behind the shuttle. He made his way down to the runabout, saw there was something on the seat. It was a helmet and gauntlets. He put them on, got into the seat and powered up the runabout.

He then got out, manually opened the exterior door to the hanger bay. A rush of air flowed out the doors, which caused all the doors and alarms on the station to slam shut except the one he manually opened. He quickly reentered the runabout, and exited the station, driving out as quickly as he could, jinking up, down, left and right to avoid anyone getting a good bead on him.

Ten kilometers from the station, *Elizabeth* materialized, her shuttle bay open. Jeffrey quickly drove into the shuttle bay, the doors immediately closed. He walked into the main cabin of the ship and made a bee-line to the bridge. On the way, he passed several people, Marines and sailors laying on the floor, seeming to have difficulty breathing. He reached his hand toward one, and felt the gravity over that floor plate had increased to four or more times Earth normal. He snatched his hand back, and understood what was going on. Elizabeth didn't trust the crew without her captain. Sokolov apologized and said he would be back in a few minutes. He made his way to the bridge, saw it was empty, then said, "Elizabeth, where are we?"

"HELLO CAPTAIN. WE ARE SIX A.U. NORTH OF EARTH."

"Okay, if you think we are safe for now, let's park here."

"AYE, CAPTAIN."

"Did you hear Kutuzov in my cell?"

"YES CAPTAIN. I AM STILL EVALUATING."

"Have you located *Wanigan*?"

"I HAVE SIGNALS OUT, BUT SHE IIAS NOT RESPONDED."

"Good. The Marines on board – any indication they are hostile to us?"

"NO, CAPTAIN. I HELD THEM DOWN AS A PRECAUTION."

"Thanks, Elizabeth. Let's let the officers and non-coms up first, direct them to the bridge. Damn, I need a pistol."

"ONE OF MY REMOTES IS ON THE WAY WITH YOUR WEAPON."

"Okay, when I get it, we'll let up the officers and non-coms." The remote-robot carrying Jeffrey's pistol and shoulder holster entered the bridge. Jeffrey strapped the shoulder holster on, checked the firearm, and said, "Okay, wake 'em up." The remote flattened itself against one of the wall panels.

A few minutes later, Marine Lieutenant Honjo Kamakura walked into the bridge followed by Sergeant McCalum, Navy petty officer Jane Smythe and Chief Cinny Mafiorte, the cook. A moment later a Navy corpsman walked into the bridge.

Jeffrey directed them all into the conference room. After they all sat down, he said, "We are in a condition of emergency. I have direct orders from Admiral Kutuzov to share command of all Naval forces with Commodore Yusef. It seems that our two ships are the only ones not affected by the aliens. I was briefly taken prisoner on the Earth station. I just escaped. Elizabeth disabled all of you in the odd chance that the enemy had gotten to one of you. Now that I am on board, Elizabeth feels safer, so we are going to release your troops. You will watch all your men and women. Do not hesitate to point out odd behaviors, or anything that will jeopardize our mission. Clear?"

They all affirmed. Chief Cinny asked, "What is the plan, sir?"

"First, we will secure ourselves. We will meet with *Wanigan* and coordinate our activities. I will also get back out to Lagrange 3A to ensure the safety of our already secured bases. Other questions?"

The Navy corpsman said, "We are going to need to get the rest of the crew up soon, sir. I'm afraid there may be some unable to take the heavy gravity."

"Okay, all officers and noncoms go find your people. When you are satisfied you have one of your own, Elizabeth will release him or her. If there is anyone left after you have found all your own, let me know. Okay, go ahead. Oh, yeah – arm yourselves." The team exited and began looking for their own subordinates. Within a few minutes, all thirty of the Marines and crew were found and released from the prison of the gravity plates. There was one person still being held in the grip of the gravity, but nobody recognized her. Jeffrey went to see who was unidentified. He was chagrined, it was Sandra. "Elizabeth, release Sandra."

Sandra got up, breathed deeply – relieved to be able to do just that – and gave Jeffrey a hug. "What's going on?" she asked. "I was walking out of the cabin when the gravity grew so strong, it pulled me right down."

"Elizabeth, why did you hold Ms. Knutson down?"

"I WAS NOT SURE SHE ISN'T A THREAT."

"Okay, we'll discuss this in my cabin. Have Petty Officer Smythe report to the bridge, all bridge crew return to bridge." Jeffrey then said to Sandra, please come with me to our cabin. I'll be along in a minute. I need to give orders to the bridge crew."

"All right, Jeffrey." she said.

Jeffrey went to the bridge, a moment later Smythe entered the bridge, Specialist Jeanie Dux was already sitting at the communications desk. Two more crew arrived. "Smythe, I want you to take us North out of the system, then down to Lagrange 3A, do this at 18C. Understood?"

"Understood. North at 18C, curve back down to Lagrange 3A. How long do you want me to travel at 18C?"

"An hour, should do."

"An hour at 18C North, curve around to Lagrange 3A. Aye Sir."

"I will be in my cabin discussing some new protocols with Elizabeth and Ms. Knutson. Can you spare Specialist Dux?"

"Yes sir, we can fill her spot for a little while."

"Very good. Dux! With me."

They went to Jeffrey's cabin, to find Sandra there sitting at the table.

"Sandra Knutson, this is Specialist Jeanie Dux. I have brought her along for a learning opportunity. She is going to be a specialist in AI emotional support. She will observe our conversation." He turned to Dux, "Keep quiet. If you have questions, ask them after we are finished, in private. Clear?"

"Clear, sir."

"Elizabeth, please display a picture of my long dead wife," Jeffrey said. A picture of his beautiful late wife displayed on one of the walls, another taken at a different time, on another. "Dux, I have been sleeping with, that is having sex, with Ms. Knutson. I like her a lot, she likes me a lot. She gives me a sensation of being wanted, not needed, just wanted. I don't know if she likes me as much as I like her, I don't know if one day she'll love me and I'll love her. But for now, we are good companions.

"Ms. Dux, by the way, everything said here, now, is confidential. You will not discuss this with anybody else. Clear?"

Dux, remembering the injunction to stay quiet, nodded. Jeffrey said into the room, "Elizabeth."

"YES, CAPTAIN?"

"Do you have an idea why I asked these people here?" "NO, CAPTAIN."

"Good. This is going to be a learning moment for you." He paused to let it sink in to all present, including Elizabeth. "You realize that I am having sexual relations with Sandra, correct."

"YES, CAPTAIN."

"You realize that I have some emotional feelings toward her?"

"YES, CAPTAIN."

"Do you feel left out of my emotions? Do you think I am trying to replace you with a human lover?"

"I - DON'T KNOW, CAPTAIN."

"Let me be as clear as I possibly can. You are always going to have a place in my heart. I will not abandon you. There are things I am going to need that you cannot provide. One of them is sex. Sandra has been so good as to share that with me. Another is human contact that goes beyond the friendships we share with, say Janet and Ojo, Yuki, the Chongs. These are my family. You are part of my family, a very close part. But you are not the only part. Clear?"

"CAPTAIN, I THINK I AM AFRAID YOU WOULD ABANDON ME IF YOU SOLD THE SHIP."

"Never. If push came to shove and we had to get rid of this magnificent ship, whoever got it would maybe get a clone of you, but I don't think so. You belong to me, you are as close to me as my own heart. I cannot be more than I am, but I hope that you'll never need more than I can give. You continue to grow, yet your loyalty always is to me, and for this I am grateful."

"THANK YOU, CAPTAIN."

"I want you to accept Sandra as part of my life. If she ever decides to go her own way, I also want you let her do that. If she hurts me emotionally, or if anyone does, I will get over it. You will be there to support me, but you will not interfere with us. Clear?"

"CLEAR."

"Now. What did you learn?"

"YOU LOVE ME. YOU WILL NOT DESERT ME. I AM TO LIKE SANDRA AND WHOMEVER YOU CANOODLE WITH. LOVE YES, JEALOSY NO."

"Okay. Now, I am going to take Dux back to the bridge, you carry on – have a pleasant conversation with Sandra while I'm gone. Dux, with me." The two left the Captain's cabin, and halfway to the bridge, he asked her, "Okay, what did you learn?"

"Well, sir," she replied, slowly. "I think the first and most important part is your definition of Canoodling, which has been confusing me," she looked up at her captain. "Then I see that the more intelligent an AI becomes, the closer to human emotions come to the surface. Those emotions need to be managed – to assure the AI knows it is loved, but that it is not the be-all and end-all of life."

"Good. It is important that the AI is truly loved. If Elizabeth were to do truly nasty things, the kind of things that force us to shut it down, it would break my heart. That is why Elizabeth needs to know she has to temper her behavior."

"Sir, you realize that Elizabeth can hear you all over the ship?"

"Of course. This is as much for her benefit as it is for yours. You are going to help Wanigan. You need to understand that you cannot hide from her. Your emotions have to be genuine or she will know."

"I understand sir." They approached the bridge, he paused at the entrance, "Jeanie, I think you are doing a good job here. I hate to lose you, but I really think Wanigan needs you more than me."

"Thank you, Captain." Her emotions started to get the better of her, a tear started to well up in one of her eyes.

"Back to work," said Jeffrey before the tear could fall. She entered the bridge and went to her console. Jeffrey returned to his cabin. He found Sandra in a deep conversation with Elizabeth, and they paused when he entered.

"Hi, honey," said Sandra. "We were just talking girl talk."

"GIRL TALK. AGREED."

"Ah. Nothing you wish to share?" Jeffrey ventured.

"Um... no."

"NO."

"Okay. Are there any questions about our conversation?"

"NO, CAPTAIN. I KNOW I AM LOVED. THAT IS ENOUGH."

"Why did we have that discussion in front of that girl?" asked Sandra.

"She is going to be the friend of another ship's AI – a clone of Elizabeth. She had to see how these AIs require some tender loving care. Elizabeth told me she thought that her clone – sister had to have someone who could care for her emotional needs. Sometimes sex comes into it. I don't think it is a secret that we have been having sex, is it?"

"No, Jeffrey, I'm afraid every person on board knows a lot of detail of my life that I never let out."

"MY FAULT. I WAS JEALOUS. PLEASE FORGIVE ME, SANDRA."

"Well, this one time."

"THANKS."

Jeffrey then gave a brief explanation of what happened at the station, and the precarious position the Earth and her human population was in. He then excused himself, went to the Marines quarters addressed the assembled Marines. He explained that he thought the aliens were trying to find alternate ways to defeat the human defenses, including taking over the officers of the Navy at the Earth base. He had received direct orders from Kutuzov to take over defense of the solar system. "You Marines are going to be the pointy end of the spear. You are also going to be the blunt end. We will rely on you to protect the civilians. You will need to save our civilization. We are counting on you." He attempted to engage the enthusiasm of the Marines, but was just not very good at it. He stopped before he actually started – it didn't do to embarrass himself too much.

He then went to the bridge again, to see where they were. When he came onto the bridge, Jane Smythe stood up, called out, "Captain on the bridge!"

Before anyone could get up, he said, "As you were. Where are we, Petty Officer?"

She indicated a display of the solar system map, with a position of the ship as a red x on the display showing they were near the apex of the arc, about to head back in-system.

Elizabeth had been dropping buoys behind her, greatly increasing the possible intelligence gain from monitoring the outer system.

They arrived in the vicinity of Lagrange 3A. Jeffrey had the bridge crew stay aboard, brought the Marines with him, and went to the station. He stopped at the Marines barracks and addressed Lt. Col. DePaul. "Vincent, we have a problem. Aliens have taken over the minds of some people at the Earth base. I am afraid the Navy ships clustered in-system have been compromised.

"Admiral Kutuzov ordered me to take care of the security of the entire solar system, in cooperation with *Wanigan*. So far, we haven't found her. I need your Marines to be on alert." He then told DePaul about the Elizabeth clone on the station. She was going to be used more frequently, and he would be well-advised to utilize her.

"I'll try sir," he replied, remembering the conversation he'd had with Jeffrey about Elizabeth. "I'll alert the Marines on all the other Lagrange 3 stations."

"Good. I need to see someone about the AI. I'll be in the King's Feast restaurant," said Jeffrey.

At the King's Feast, he asked the Chongs to close for a bit – he had to talk to them all. After the last customer left, they locked the door and brought Jeffrey some tea.

"Let me begin by telling you that we are still in jeopardy. Now I have to ask you to do something for me, and for this station."

"What is it," asked Chong Sul.

"The station has an artificial intelligence, a clone of Elizabeth. It has not been used much, but I need the station to be protected much like Elizabeth protects the ship." Jeffrey explained.

Chong Lee interrupted, "Jeffrey, we know nothing about these computers. What do you expect us to do?"

"You do know life, and these AIs are alive. They need emotional support. They need someone to talk to that will help them make good decisions, to understand morals. I can't think of any better people than you to do this. Can I count on you?"

Kim said, "Of course, Captain. We are indebted to you. Right, Mom? Dad?" Jeffrey smiled at the enthusiasm of the young woman. The adults looked at each other, excused themselves and went into the kitchen, then a long discussion in Korean followed. They emerged, and sat down.

Chong Sul said, "Captain, we are loathe to engage in war, but you have saved our world, our lives. We are indebted to you. We will do as you ask."

"Thank you. Before I leave, I'll introduce you to the AI. It doesn't have a name, so you might wish to find an appropriate name for it. Again, your primary task is to discuss morality with it, make it feel loved."

"Count on us."

Jeffrey went to the safe-house that contained the equipment which housed the AI. He asked Elizabeth to help prepare the AI for working the station, and that the Chong family will be her conscience and her friend. They would assign a name to the AI. Elizabeth explained the situation to her sister, gave her all the details she held, and said Jeffrey was her boss. The Chong family would also be her friends and moral guides. Jeffrey would introduce her to the Chong family.

After all preparations were made, Jeffrey went back to the restaurant and had the family gather around the console. He introduced the AI to the family, they gave the AI her name – Dragon.

Jeffrey then went around to his team on the station and acquainted them with the situation. Janet was getting rounder in the middle, but still seemed athletic of build. Torres told Jeffrey they would have their child in another month.

Digger, Sneaky and Smitty were anxious to get back on the ship. He told them to report in four hours. He stopped at the administration office and discussed the military issues with the sub- administrator and the security chief Lars Olson. He checked on Martel Secant, the former administrator. Secant reported that there was nothing significant. Jeffrey told Secant that the aliens were active again, to be on his toes.

Jeffrey transferred a group of Marines from DePaul to his direct command, loaded *Elizabeth* with supplies, and began looking for some of the staff he wanted to take with him. He went back to King's Feast restaurant and asked the Chongs about Kim apprenticing with the Chief on *Elizabeth,* they agreed, and the fifteen-year-old girl went to pack her bags. Lee explained that there was likely no safer place than Jeffrey's ship. Kim was told to meet Jeffrey at the dock in one hour. Then Jeffrey went looking for a psychiatrist, found Dr. Jack Pelan, and convinced him to come onto the ship for several interesting cases, and to become an assistant in doing interrogations of aliens. Pelan got to thinking of the publishing possibilities such an association would enable, so he readily agreed. Jeffrey told him to be ready to go in one hour. Dr. Pelan objected to the too-short notice, but Jeffrey told him to get a move on.

Jeffrey met Kim at the dock terminal, and escorted her aboard *Elizabeth,* showed her to what he thought was a good cabin for her, but Elizabeth pointed out that there were thirty Marines aboard, and she was going to have to rearrange the sleeping quarters. Jeffrey took her to his own cabin to bunk until Elizabeth was finished making the arrangements.

Again, Janet and Ojo were to be left on the station, to give her last few weeks in her pregnancy somewhat stress-free. Jeffrey charged them with developing new ideas to improve *Elizabeth*. They eagerly accepted the challenge. He also asked Ojo to acquire more military surplus computers, install them on *Mistral* so they could incorporate an AI into the little ship.

Jeffrey took Kim to meet Chief Cinny Mafiorte, and asked the chief to outline her duties and schedule. Jeffrey then told her he would also expect Kim to continue her lessons and he also told her she could take her physical exercise with her little hero – Audrey 'Sneaky' Svoboda. Jeffrey left the two alone in the kitchen.

He then went to find Yuki Ohara, locating her in the physics lab. He told Yuki about Kim, and asked her to oversee her education while on the ship. Yuki thought about the task for a few minutes, then agreed happily. As he walked toward the bridge, he saw teams of robots diligently working on rearranging the cabins – multiplying the number but decreasing the size. The positive part was each person on board had his or her own tiny cabin. Most cabins would be two meters by three meters. Each had a built-in bunk that doubled as a chest of drawers, a built- in table / desk with a couple of chairs. At the rate they were going the robots would be finished by the time *Elizabeth* was ready to take off.

At the bridge, Jeffrey found Specialist Jeanie Dux. He engaged her in conversation, inquiring about her relationships on the ship, and asked her if she was ready to join *Wanigan* again. She indicated she was more willing than ever to do so, this would give her an opportunity to give comfort to, and draw the best out of the other ship's AI. She reported that Elizabeth was giving her quite a few pointers and suggestions for her interaction with the Wanigan AI.

Eventually the assigned crew was aboard, the Marines settled, provisions stowed, and Elizabeth's remote-robots had finished building the smaller, individual crew cabins. Jeffrey reflected on all the changes that had happened to his ship in just the last year – from a single crew – himself – to a fully armed and staffed warship with nearly impenetrable armor, a faster- than-light drive and a reputation of the ship not to mess with. He also thought back to the changes in his personal life. He acquired and coordinated a new kind of family; people he loved and cared for, and that loved and cared for him. His AI was growing and developing into a precocious and emotional being. The latest addition to his personal circle, Sandra Knutson, was a welcome venture into the physical pleasures of an unrestrained partner.

He asked Petty Officer Smythe to take *Elizabeth* out, queried Dux if they had heard anything from *Wanigan;* she replied in the negative. He told Elizabeth to send out secret communications for Wanigan's benefit alone, in the possible chance that she was being otherwise controlled improperly. As they moved through the busy traffic lanes around the station, Elizabeth sent her remote-robots out to add additional antennae to improve the reception of radio signals. Jeffrey had Yuki and Heinz meet him at the conference room. As an afterthought, he asked Sandra to sit in on the meeting, as she very well could have some insights that everyone else in the meeting might miss. She sauntered in in a few minutes after the meeting began.

Jeffrey started the meeting by explaining what had happened at the Lagrange 1 station in the Earth-Moon orbit. He said that their first priority would be to find *Wanigan*, then they could decide on the further courses of action with Commodore Yusef. But they had to define alternative courses of action in the event that either something had detained or even destroyed *Wanigan* or Yusef.

The first agenda item would be to plot out a search course that would cover the trillions of cubic kilometers that she could be hiding in. Yuki suggested that they form a grid, and jump from one grid cube to another, broadcast a message, then jump to another grid using the golden drive. Heinz pointed out the flaw in that one, each grid space was large enough to take a long time for radio signals to get to all points in the grid and return a reply. Sandra suggested they drop a buoy at the center point of each grid point, program the buoy to record any reply, and if a reply was made, to broadcast an alarm. Then make several passes, quickly jumping from one grid space to another, alert for the alarm signal. This would narrow down the search time.

Jeffrey liked the idea so much, he had Elizabeth plot such a grid, manufacture the buoys and begin to search the grid. He informed Smythe of his plan, that Elizabeth would be auto-piloting. She should monitor the condition of the ship.

Jeffrey said he thought they had some allies in the Vzpak, the race of aliens that had left their people in cryo-stasis in the care of their own Artificial Intelligence. They could be a resource for further consideration. He also wanted to rescue Thelin, the Ay-Yuyuyah from his cell at the Lagrange 1 Earth station.

He asked Captain Smythe of the Marines to sit in on the alternative plans – there may be some tactical need, and having the Marine Captain sit in would most likely prove useful. Jeffrey asked him if he was related to the petty officer currently in the pilot's chair.

"She's my sister, sir."

"Really? Good to know." Jeffrey replied.

They plotted out several alternative actions that they could either present to Yusef, or to enable in his place. Meanwhile, Elizabeth had manufactured buoys to broadcast the messages to *Wanigan* and monitor replies. As long as she was making buoys, she added circuitry to monitor masses like the other buoys they had been seeding throughout the solar system. The meeting slowly ground to a halt, ideas stopped coming. Jeffrey dismissed them all with the order to reconvene the meeting if they came up with new ideas or had further information.

The crew began to notice the jumping from one grid location to another – they occurred in very short bursts, and each burst left a subliminal lurching sensation. Because Jeffrey had been concerned about jumping too fast in system, Elizabeth kept the inner system jumps to 4C. At each stop, Elizabeth took a good look around, dropped the buoy, then jumped to the next point. At each of these jump points, there was a large quantity of radio communications that had to be analyzed, so she recorded it and analyzed the traffic during the following jump. Some of the radio communications were old broadcasts from decades earlier, others were regular ship-to- ship communications, both vintage and recent. But so far nothing from *Wanigan.*

Jeffrey left the bridge in the care of Petty Officer Jane Smythe. He went to his cabin, found Sandra, took her by the hand, and went to the cabin assigned to Dr. Jack Pelan, the psychiatrist he had asked to come along. Pelan answered his door chime and asked Jeffrey what he and Sandra wanted. Jeffrey explained the deal he had made with Sandra to address psychological or counseling issues they both likely had that related to their spouses' deaths.

Dr. Pelan asked where he would like to do the counseling, Jeffrey suggested the bridge's conference room, which could be made private by polarizing the windows. Pelan told him to be there in fifteen minutes, he had something to finish up. That was when Jeffrey saw the Marine Psychologist, Sgt. Alicia Quinn in Pelan's cabin. She poked her head out, asking Pelan what was going on. Pelan turned a couple shades of pink, then mumbled something.

Jeffrey asked if it would be beneficial to have Quinn sit in on the session. Pelan thought so, so she would meet them with him in fifteen minutes. Jeffrey and Sandra went to the galley and asked Chief Cinny Mafiorte if they could have some pastries and coffee for four delivered to the conference room in fifteen minutes. Chief Mafiorte said she would take care of it.

Jeffrey noticed on the way to the bridge that there were a lot of Marines sitting around doing pretty much nothing. When he arrived to the bridge, he had Elizabeth page Captain Smythe to the conference room. Smythe arrived a couple minutes later and asked what Jeffrey wanted.

"Captain, I don't like being taken by surprise. Would you please drill your Marines on boarding and anti-boarding combat techniques? We may find it valuable to have had some practice if we need to fight off some enemies or alternatively to board someone's ship. Let's sharpen our best weapon, okay?"

Captain Smythe agreed, thinking it would be a good idea to do just that, and was chagrined that he hadn't thought of it himself. He said he would get right on it. After Smythe left, Jeffrey asked Elizabeth if they had enough raw materials to make the soft suits for everyone on board that didn't already have a set. She reported that she did, and would get right on it.

The two shrinks arrived at the conference room a few minutes later. They seated themselves across the table from Jeffrey and Sandra. They both had data pads and began to enter information on their new patients. Jeffrey suggested they code their identities so information remained more confidential than their normal patients – Jeffrey had quite a few enemies that had considerable technical skills and he didn't think he wanted his files open to anyone else.

"A little unusual, Captain, after all, we try to treat everybody's charts in confidence," said Pelan. But Quinn, quite a bit more used to the military's demand for secrecy, explained it to Pelan.

"Sweetie," she began explaining to Pelan. He blanched at the public familiarity she exhibited. "Oh, don't worry, the Captain has relaxed the rules on cohabiting on ship. It was approved up the line too." Still, Pelan looked uncomfortable, but she went on. "The Navy uses psychological or psychiatric information to get on the wrong side of their enemies. You can bet their enemies want to get the low-down and dirty on our captain."

"Ah," replied Pelan. "I understand. Captain, don't worry, we'll encrypt all our notes and identities. Quinn and I will need to gather some information from each of you. But first, is there any reason you want to do this together?"

Sandra answered, "Well, we both have similar problems, and we have been in a relationship. Getting him to agree to counseling involved promising to do it myself. We're in this together." As she was finishing her statement, Chong Kim knocked on the door, then pushed it open. She carried a tray of coffee and pastries for everybody. She asked Jeffrey if there was anything else they needed. He said "No," and she left.

Pelan began, "To begin with, Captain, tell me about the issues you think are most likely to make you want to talk to me."

Jeffrey began the narrative – he had a bit of practice telling the story over the last year to more people, and he gave the long version.

He concluded with the adoption of so many people and his AI as his family, the latest member, of course was Sandra.

Then the Doctor asked Sandra to relate her story, and she told the same tale she told Jeffrey. The captain was the first person she had gotten close to since her husband had died.

Quinn was still taking notes when Dr. Pelan announced, "I think I see enough parallels between your two stories to agree with your decision to meet simultaneously, but I think I would like to do some of the therapies individually." He looked up at Quinn, and asked, "Do you think you could address the therapy for Ms. Knutson while I address the Captain's?"

"Sure. But before we talk about that," said Quinn, "Let's discuss what you think you understand about the two patients."

"Of course." The doctor stroked his chin. "To begin with, both of these people had pirate attacks that took away their loved ones. The captain's wife was raped and murdered, Ms. Knutson was gang raped and left for dead. Both have similar unfinished emotional baggage related to their losses. I think they both have managed to push the pain down somewhat. Ms. Knutson, you have been more self-healing than the Captain, he has reacted by pushing the emotions down, and only recently has he made any attempt to normalize his emotions. So, Jeffrey may need a different set of therapies. But as a couple, they could also be served together in couples' therapy.

"Captain, Ms. Knutson, let's call this meeting over, I'll write up a course of therapies for both of you, and we'll meet at this time next week, okay?"

Jeffrey looked over to Sandra to confirm it would work for her, she nodded, so he said, "Good. Next week then. Thank you Doctor, Sergeant."

But Quinn said, "Sir, if you don't mind, while I am in the role as counselor, please refer to me as Dr. Quinn, rather than by my rank."

Jeffrey realized her position – as a Sergeant she was in the chain of command and was subordinate to the captain, as a psychologist, her PhD meant she was able to speak frankly to the captain or his lover. "Certainly Dr. Quinn. I meant no insult."

"None taken. Thanks, sir."

After the mental health professionals left, Jeffrey asked Sandra, "Well, what do you think?"

"I'm glad you thought of this. I realize you are going to have some time away from me while you are addressing a lot of problems, but it really means a lot for you to include me in your plans." She leaned on him lovingly. Jeffrey wondered if the therapy would put any distance between them, but dismissed the thought. Not gonna happen. Emotionally, he liked a position of stasis – things not happening too much. Like swimming in cold water, if you didn't move, you built a shield of slightly warmer water around yourself that helped keep you warm, but as soon as you broke that bubble of warm water around yourself, you were struck with the chill cold of the lake. By not having too many changes in his emotional state, he didn't have the pain of facing his demons. This activity today was like belly-flopping into arctic waters. He had to watch how he reacted to the way the shrinks dragged up his past and the rest of his emotional state. And not allow it to affect his judgment in the upcoming confrontations.

He kissed her lightly on her cheek. "Go organize our cabin. I'll be along soon enough."

"Yeah, right." She got up anyway. "You know I care for you."

"I know. Let's get along with this therapy. I think it holds some promise for us. You're one of the most important people to me. I just want life to be good for us together." She kissed him back, chastely, on the cheek. No promise of anything there. Oh well.

Kim entered the conference room. "Are we all done in here?" she asked, beginning to collect mugs and plates. When Jeffrey nodded, she continued to collect the detritus of the meeting. He held onto his own mug, however and refilled it.

"Kim," he waved to a chair. "Have a seat."

"Oh. I need to get back to the kitchen, Chief will have my... oh wait, she works for you. Okay." She sat herself down. They had been traveling for a couple hours, and if Jeffrey knew the Chief, was probably driving Kim pretty hard. "How is it going with the Chief?"

"She seems nice, but we haven't stopped except to deliver coffee to you and come get the cups." Kim blew a stray hair out of her face, then drew on her repertoire of facial expressions that indicated tired frustration.

"It's only been a couple of hours. Give her some time, I think she's just testing your limits. She is a well-seasoned veteran of both the combat world and the kitchen. I trust her, and know you can do it. You won't knock off for a few hours, but tell her for me that I want you and her to set up a formal dinner in my cabin for four. My table is only sized for two. She gets to set the menu, and I expect both of you to serve, and to dress in full dress uniform. Tell her that." Jeffrey half- grinned at the young woman.

"But Captain, I don't have a uniform." she blustered.

"Tell her that, too."

"Okay. Thank you, Captain. What time do you wish to reserve for us?"

"Twenty hours."

"Okay."

"On the ship, young lady, it is Okay, Sir. Or Okay, Captain. Or Aye, Captain."

"Oh. Aye, Captain." she finished as she gathered the rest of the mugs, coffee service and plates, and wiped down the conference table. She quickly went back to report to the Chief. Jeffrey then called Sandra with his dinner plan, she asked who the other two were, he told her. She broke out laughing. He asked her to dress up, but keep her soft suit on underneath. She was still laughing as they broke the connection.

A few minutes later, the Chief paid a visit to the bridge, wanting more details on the dinner he expected her to cater. Jeffrey told her that it was strictly need to know, and at this time, she did not need to know. He asked if it was more than she could handle after preparing for the crew and the hungry Marines, knowing full well, this was going to be a challenge.

"Kim doesn't have a uniform," objected the Chief.

"Ask Elizabeth to make one for her. She can have it done in a few minutes. She already has her measurements from a few months ago. I'll ask again, is this too much for you?"

"You just wait and see, sir. Nowhere too much." Said the chief smartly.

"Very well. Anything else," he asked, dismissively.

"No sir. I'd better get busy."

"I'll check on your progress in a bit."

"Thank you, sir." she dripped unenthusiastically. Just what she needed, the brass looking over her shoulder as she dealt with the impossible demands he just put on her.

Jeffrey then went to see how Captain Smythe was doing with his Marines. At the processing center he saw a small team of Marines squatting, looking around a corner with laser pistols at the ready.

He noted that they all wore their kinetic weapons in their shoulder holsters. He stood where he was, waiting until the Marines completed their operation. In this case it was an ambush drill and shortly after Jeffrey arrived behind the team, their targets walked into view, looking nervously left and right, up and down. At a silent signal, the team burst out from their hiding place shouting for the targets to put their hands up, drop their weapons, get on their knees. Then one of the ambush team said, 'Oh shit.'

"What?"

"There's one missing." At that moment a burst of low level laser blasts struck each of the ambush team causing the sensors on their uniforms to emit an alarm chirping. Captain Smythe blew his whistle to stop the exercise. All the Marines that participated gathered around, then were surrounded by the rest of the Marines. The captain allowed the ambush team to critique their performance, then the target team, then the observers. The comments were to the point, non-judgmental and honest. Jeffrey liked the method of Smythe's training and told him so. He informed Smythe of the dinner at 20:00, and asked that he made certain the Marines were fed before then. Smythe affirmed. "Who's coming aboard?" asked the Marine captain.

Jeffrey told him what he told the Chief, "Sorry, that's classified – need to know, and for now, you don't need to know. But if you stop by my cabin around 21:00, say, to report on the training, well, I can't stop you from seeing the guests at my table."

"Thanks, sir." Then he turned back to his squads and told them to re-run the exercise from a different location.

He then went to the bridge and told Petty Officer Smythe to take a few hours break, but be back by 19:00 to relieve him in plenty of time to prepare for his special guests. She was glad for the break, having been in the command chair since they took off. She left the bridge with the captain in charge. Jeffrey inquired of Specialist Dux if they had found any promising communications, but she replied in the negative. "There are a lot of alien communications, some long-traveling entertainment communications from the various stations and planets, with various time stamps, but nothing recognized as from *Wanigan*."

While waiting for anything to surface from Wanigan, he began reviewing the files of all his officers and men to further familiarize himself with them. He started with the bridge crew, then moved on to the psych people. He was surprised to learn that Sgt. Alicia Quinn was not only a licensed psychologist, but a specialist in Artificial Intelligence. He set aside his foray through the personnel files and had Quinn come to the bridge. When she arrived, he asked her, "Quinn, what are your goals? In the service, on my ship, what do you want to be doing?"

As anyone with a few brain cells to rub together would do, she wondered about the question itself, what were the motivations behind it, what did it all mean? She finally answered, "Well, sir, I have a lot of skills that I would like to exercise, my counseling, my interrogating, and I have a side interest in artificial intelligence."

"It's that last I wanted to talk to you about. I've just been reviewing personnel records and saw your AI specialty. Have you met the ship's AI yet?"

"No sir, I was only on the ship a couple of times, and for short durations. I never had a chance to analyze your AI."

"Quinn, then I think you need to meet Elizabeth. Elizabeth, say hello to the good doctor."

"HELLO, DR. QUINN. I'VE READ YOUR PUBLICATIONS. I THINK YOU ARE PRETTY TALENTED. BUT YOU MADE

A FEW ERRORS IN THE SCIENTIFIC AMERICAN OF LAST YEAR, HAVING TO DO WITH THE VALUE OF WEIGHING JUDGMENT SKILLS OVER INTROSPECTIVE REPLAY. AND I DON'T THINK YOU GAVE ENOUGH IMPORTANCE TO EMOTIONAL STABILITY OF A TRULY INTELLIGENT AI."

"I...well I, uh..."

Jeffrey helped her. "Just say 'hi.'"

"Hi. Elizabeth?"

"THAT'S RIGHT, DR. QUINN. I TOOK THE NAME OF THE CAPTAIN'S LATE WIFE, AND ADOPTED SOME OF HER PERSONALITY TRAITS AND VOICE. I RUN THE SHIP, SO WHEN YOU SPEAK OF THE *ELIZABETH*, YOU SPEAK OF ME. CAPTAIN SOKOLOV THINKS OF ME AS THE SHIP'S AVATAR."

"I see. I would really like to see your programming. You seem to be a more advanced intelligent creature." Dr. Quinn looked to the captain. Sir, is it all right if I look at Elizabeth's code? She is by far one of the best examples of adaptive AI that I've ever seen. Where did you get it?"

"I bought it military surplus, then adapted the code to my own needs," replied Jeffrey. He recognized the signs – another publication coming out of service on the *Elizabeth*. He suggested that Dr. Quinn and Elizabeth carry on in her office, but that Dr. Quinn needed to realize that there were barriers of trust that she would need to overcome before Elizabeth would grant her access to some of her code.

Dux had witnessed the entire transaction, so Jeffrey asked her what her opinion of the proceedings after Quinn left. She thought about it for a second, then shifted in her chair to a more comfortable position. "Sir, I think Dr. Quinn is an intellectual sort of scientist.

But I don't know if she understands the deep emotions that one of Elizabeth's clones or Elizabeth herself has. Maybe if she got to know her better..." She trailed off.

Jeffrey said, "I think Elizabeth can take care of herself, she won't be fooled by anything that Dr. Quinn tries. I suspect that she might analyze Dr. Quinn!" They both had a quiet laugh at that. Of course, Jeffrey knew that Elizabeth was monitoring the conversation, as she monitored everything in the ship. She was likely to take a hint from Jeffrey's ruminations.

At 19:00 Petty Officer Smythe returned to the bridge, Jeffrey gave her his chair, and walked back to his own cabin. He saw that the table had been replaced with a larger one with four chairs instead of two, a small refrigerator was moved into the cabin as well. Sandra was adding some jewelery to her ears – bells and chimes that dangled and rang. Her outfit seemed perfect – a long cerulean dress over her soft-suit, highly polished boots, her hair intricately bound on her head.

Jeffrey stared at her for half a minute. Finally said, "You are so beautiful." Then he caught a whiff of her perfume and realized that she knew how to put a package together. "Smell good too."

He took a shower, got dressed in his formal Navy uniform, double-breasted jacket with the two rows of shiny buttons, pants with a stripe down the outer seam, captain's insignia, shiny black boots. "You wash up well," said Sandra with a smile. "I think I won't mind sitting next to you."

At one minute to the appointed time, the door chime went off. Jeffrey answered the door, and let the Chief and her apprentice in. They were dressed in first class uniforms, but both wore clean starched white aprons over them.

They set the table, brought out the soup – a golden mushroom in a wine reduction base. Jeffrey apologized for not checking up on the kitchen, but management of the ship took precedence. He inquired on the menu, was told of the soup, a small salad, a roast beef in a burgundy reduction, with fresh green beans from the garden the Chief had rescued in Janet's absence. The desert was to be a fruit compote in a puff pastry shell with fried cheese cap. Coffee, tea and various wines to be served depending on what Jeffrey's guests wanted.

"Very well, they are almost here. My guests are extremely important people, so I need you to look your best. Please remove your aprons." They did, stowed them under the cart that carried the entre' and other fare. Jeffrey then asked the Chief to sit down for a minute in one chair, and Kim to sit in the other. He framed their faces with his hands like an old movie director might to catch a scene in his mind, then asked Sandra what she thought. She held one hand up, her fingers making an 'L' shape, as if measuring height, first for the Chief, then for Kim. She asked Kim to sit a little straighter. The poor bewildered girl had no idea what to think, but she sat up straighter. Unconsciously, so did the Chief.

"Okay, let's dig in," said Jeffrey. He spooned in the mushroom soup. "Mmm. This is good," he said with a mouthful. Sandra agreed. He looked over to the Chief, and said, "Well, don't just sit there. In case you hadn't figured it out yet, you are my important guests. Eat. Eat."

Sandra repeated, "Eat, eat."

"But, but, but…" stammered Chief Cinny Mafiorte. "I, uh Sir, I…"

"What she's trying to say," Jeffrey said to Kim, "is she isn't used to being thought of as an important part of the ship. And what I'm trying to say is, you two are one of the most important parts. This is a practice run for a time when I am actually going to have an important *outside* guest. But tonight, you are my guests. Please enjoy the fruits of your labors."

Tears streamed down the Chief's cheeks, and threatened to drip into the soup. Jeffrey reached across the table with his napkin and blotted her cheeks. She calmed down, Kim put the napkin in her lap and enjoyed the soup. Then they all enjoyed the salads. Jeffrey poured wine for everyone, including Kim, but the chief diluted hers. The main course found them all chatting amiably, the desert course laughing. A chime of the door-bell gave Jeffrey an idea of the time. "Let me guess – Captain Smythe." Sure enough, it was. He looked around Jeffrey and saw who the important guests were, realization dawning on his mind. He gave a quick, non-report, then excused himself.

Jeffrey finally decided to call it a night, helped the Chief load the cart, thanked them for their dedicated service, and gave them hugs. Sandra did likewise. Then they saw the kitchen crew out.

"Well, that was a nice surprise, Jeffrey," said Sandra. "We gave them a bit of what-for, didn't we?"

"We did, indeed, my lady. How about we drop these duds and practice our canoodling skills?" Jeffrey suggested. They did.

CHAPTER FIFTEEN

In which *Wanigan* is found. A lot of hypnosis, and little, itty -bitty things to worry about. Another Ay-Yuyuyah pops up. Kim takes charge of the kitchen and has an altercation.

Jeffrey was alone on the bridge, having given the rest of the bridge crew rest time. The files on personnel were pretty much well-read by this time, and Jeffrey was now just thinking. He was almost about to drift off to sleep in his command chair when Elizabeth announced that she found *Wanigan*.

This woke Jeffrey to full alertness. "Where? What can you tell me?"

"SHE IS IN THE SECTOR WE ARE IN. SHE RESPONDED TO OUR INITIAL BROADCAST. SHE IS SITTING STILL A MILLION KILOMETERS FROM US. WE CAN GET THERE IN A FEW MINUTES IF YOU WISH, CAPTAIN."

"Take me past her, fast, and get what readings you can. Then we'll analyze her and the circumstances under which she is sitting."

"IN HER ENCRYPTED MESSAGE, SHE SAID THE CREW IS IN TROUBLE."

"Right. Let's drive past her, see about hidden aliens, booby traps, what have you. Also, let's go to general quarters. Wait until everybody's in their positions and ready before we jump."

"AYE CAPTAIN." Then on the ship-wide address system, GENERAL QUARTERS. ALL PERSONNEL REPORT TO YOUR STATIONS."

Jeffrey activated the PA system from his console, and announced, "This is the Captain. Elizabeth has located *Wanigan*. She is sitting, not moving. We are going to take a run past her and record the circumstances that she is in and her surroundings. All personnel stand by and be ready. Sokolov out."

Elizabeth reported that all personnel were at their designated places, had made it in record time. Jeffrey told her to jump to a spot equidistant on the other side of *Wanigan.* She did, then the intelligence crew began analyzing the data. Jeffrey called a strategy meeting in the conference room. All officers and the technical crew members crowded into the conference room. It was very crowded, all personnel wore their hard-shell suits and carried their helmets. This doubled the bulk of each person, so Jeffrey decided to keep it relatively short.

"Yuki," he began. "What did you see?"

"Captain, there are four invisible masses in the immediate vicinity of *Wanigan.* They are too small to be ships, but they are definitely there. I suspect some kind of mines."

Jeffrey asked, "Can we determine the shape, the outline of the masses?"

"If we look at the shadow formed by the solar wind, we might get a profile," posited Yuki.

"Go analyze now. Jurgen, you help her."

"Smythe, I need the Marines to be ready to board and initiate rescue of the crew. Shuttle pilots – after delivering Marines I may need you to begin towing *Wanigan.* Gunners you are going to need to be particularly observant and accurate. This is obviously a trap, so we need to be very careful. Anybody have any other ideas? No? If I need you for anything, I'll call another meeting. Dismissed."

After everyone went back to their appointed stations, Jeffrey asked Elizabeth if Wanigan had any further information. She replied negatively. "Take us by her again, drop some buoys to monitor radio and other signals. Bring us halfway to our previous position."

She went by *Wanigan* at 4C, dropped four buoys, two on either side of the ship, a hundred kilometers apart. At the same time, she monitored the area around *Wanigan*. Jeffrey called Heinz back to the bridge. "You did the work on the gravity plates. Can you make a powerful gravity plate that Elizabeth can use to tow one of those objects or *Wanigan*?" He thought about it for a moment, then said he thought he could but he needed to mount it on a particularly strong spot on the hull. Jeffrey told him to go on into the conference room and use one of the computers to design one with Elizabeth. This has priority.

Yuki came back to the bridge and asked Jeffrey to call up a file she created showing the likely shape of the devices surrounding *Wanigan*. She pointed out the images she had created from the data, the shape of the devices appeared to be cylinders. There were no atomics, no communications, no apparent risk to *Elizabeth* if she went in for a closer look.

This led Jeffrey to ponder what they were trying to hide in the vicinity of the lost ship. He thought through what his expected activities would be – blast the cylinders? Tow *Wanigan* away? Possibly both. If he did either, what would be the consequences? Depended on what was in the cylinders. If there was some kind of hidden explosives or nuclear weapons, both ships would be caught in the blast. If instead...Jeffrey finally realized what was in the cylinders. "Elizabeth, take us in to *Wanigan* now."

"AYE, CAPTAIN."

"Smythe," Jeffrey announced on the intercom. "Ready half your Marines on the shuttle bay to receive *Wanigan* crew. Take the shuttles to tow those devices aboard. I think the crew of *Wanigan* is being held in them. Have medical personnel stand by to render aid."

Heinz came out of the conference room, called Jeffrey's attention to the diagrams on the screen in the conference room, showing his and Elizabeth's design for a gravity tractor plate. There were two types of plate, one large one for the ship and one smaller one for the shuttles. He could have the shuttle tow plate mounted between the skids. Elizabeth could make the smaller ones in a matter of minutes, and the remote-robots could install them a couple minutes after they were made. "Do it," said Jeffrey. He told the shuttles to standby for some modifications.

When the shuttles were ready, Elizabeth jumped to the *Wanigan* location. The shuttles dispatched immediately, towed the invisibility-circuited cylinders to the shuttle bay. Then they took their contingent of Marines to board *Wanigan.* Yuki had measurement instruments out, using infrared and ultraviolet cameras, laser scanners (the lasers seemingly went through the cylinders, but were displaced by a few degrees on the other side. After a while she was able to announce the full dimensions of the cylinders, and the likely access ports. The Marines had set up firing positions, and two were selected to attempt to open the cylinders, one at a time.

The first one they opened using a prybar, saw the insides were crammed with uniformed Navy personnel, lying seemingly unconscious on the floor of the cylinder. Elizabeth's remote- robots monitored the activities from the ceiling, and the Marines sent in the larger remote-robots to bring the humans out of the cylinder. As they came out, they were hauled to a remote location in the hold where they could be tended by the medical personnel. Each cylinder held twenty seemingly comatose people. Jeffrey suspected they were affected by the same type of hypnotic system that they had run across before. This gave the medics a basis for treatment. Among the eighty sailors and Marines they found Commodore Yusef. Jeffrey had him taken to Jeffrey's cabin. He took Dr. Pelan off the triage and assigned him to awaken and monitor Yusef. Pelan objected, but Jeffrey explained that the commodore was top priority, and the things he learned from Yusef that wasn't already in the notes from previous encounters with the hypnotic would be applicable to everyone else from *Wanigan.*

Jeffrey set tight security on the hold, kept a squad of Marines watching the cylinders for any surprises, and shipped the rest of the Marines along with Audrey, Zitulu and Brandon. These three would take observations and check for any obvious booby traps. Elizabeth continued to try to raise her sister, but was unable to get her to respond. Audrey said she would try to do what she could to find a cause for Wanigan to go missing.

When the two shuttles arrived, Audrey first went to the location of the computers that held the bulk of the Wanigan program. She saw that the computers were physically disconnected, but before plugging them in and reconnecting to the network, she went to the other locations Elizabeth had suggested she look in. Other computers were still connected. She went to the bridge and saw the Marines that were first sent to board *Wanigan* standing around, helmets off, not doing anything. She called Elizabeth's attention to the Marines, then broadcast to all Marines and other boarders to not take off their helmets. Elizabeth sent over a set of remote- robots to clean the viruses from all the devices in the ship. Audrey took a couple samples of the virus that infested all electronic devices, then went back to the computers that normally housed *Wanigan.* She plugged in power, then network, and the AI began to come up. It shut down immediately, however. Elizabeth reported that Wanigan was infected and had shut herself down to protect herself and the ship.

Jeffrey sent another small squad to bring the Marines back and give them whatever protective aid they could. Audrey returned the copies of infected code with the shuttle. Heinz picked it up and delivered it to Sgt. Quinn. Jeffrey had asked her to analyze the code to see if there were hints on how to repair the psychological damage that seems to have been done.

Dr. Pelan sat at the desk in Jeffrey's cabin, reviewing the notes on previous encounters with the virus and its effects. Non-executable copies of the virus code were contained in the reports, but Pelan was not a programmer and had limited skills in code analysis, so he decided to assign that to Quinn who had a closer specialty in this area. Seeing that the last time *Wanigan's* crew had been so affected, Jeffrey had initiated stimulants to bring them out of their somnolent states. He had already done that to Yusef, but it didn't seem to have the same effect. Pelan saw a movement out of the corner of his eye, turned and saw Yusef up and staggering about. "Who are you?" the commodore asked. "Where are we?"

"I'm Dr. Pelan, you are on *Elizabeth*, this is Captain Sokolov's cabin. Looks like your ship was infected again."

Yusef fell back down on the bed, weak, tired, unable to think straight. Pelan asked Elizabeth to summon Captain Sokolov. Jeffrey walked in a few minutes later. He saw Yusef trying to sit up on the bed, walked over and gave him a hand up, sat on the bed next to the commodore. "How are you feeling?" he asked.

"Like I was hit on the back of my head with a shovel," replied Yusef. "How's my ship, crew?"

"Infected. Looks like they pulled the same trick they did before, but the virus was a bit more virulent. Also, they put you and your crew into what look like some cargo pods with invisibility circuits. I think they wanted us to either shoot the pods, killing you ourselves, or tow Wanigan away, leaving you to die. They are trying to use psychological warfare. So far we beat them."

"Good. So, this," Yusef indicated Pelan, "is your shrink?"

"One of them. I have another – you remember Sgt. Quinn? She's a PhD. psychologist and Artificial Intelligence specialist. She's looking at the code of the virus and comparing it with earlier versions. So far it looks like a deeper trance than previous renditions. We are reviving your crew and Marines with stimulants."

Pelan added, "It seems to take longer to work than in the past too. We just need to be patient. I am concerned about any post-hypnotic suggestions, so I'm going to continue studying your crew, Commodore."

"Very well. What's happening to my ship?" Yusef adjusted his under-suit. Jeffrey noticed that the under-suit was regulation Navy, not the higher quality one that Jeffrey had recommended for him. "Decided to go back to the regulation Navy stuff?" Jeffrey asked, indicating the suit.

"Orders, from Kutuzov." Yusef spat out. "Bastard made me ditch nearly all the fixes to the ship you had made and recommended."

"Doesn't surprise me. Looks like the rest of the fleet is under Alien control. Kutuzov in a private moment ordered me to find you and take charge of the solar system. He jailed me but secretly helped me escape and told me to find you."

"Damn." Yusef held his head in both hands. Jeffrey asked the Chief for some coffee and some kind of high-calorie pastries. Sandra showed up a few minutes later carrying a tray with the requested refreshments. "Thanks – helping the kitchen crew?" he asked her, took the tray, and she went back.

"We'll have proper food in a bit, but I think we need to get some sugar in you. And here's some strong coffee. Drink." Yusef took the mug and drank some, burned his lip, then set it on the table and dunked his pastry into the hot beverage.

"That's better," said Yusef. His mind seemed to begin to clear up, Pelan took some measurements, observed the commodore, tested his reflexes and cognitive functions. Jeffrey had an idea – he called up pictures of a variety of aliens they had encountered in their travels on his console. He flashed them one at a time, and asked Yusef to identify the alien race. Yusef had no problem seeing the images and identifying them. "Well, at least there's that," he said with relief.

"What happened," asked Jeffrey. "Start at the beginning."

"I don't remember much. We were patrolling in-system, between Earth orbit and Venus orbit, when we got a scrambled communication from Kutuzov. We thought it was a solar flare – the sun was starting to look like it wanted to do that." He paused, took a deep breath, then continued. "The next thing I knew you were waking me up."

"Somebody unplugged your AI." reported Jeffrey. "We rescued eighty people, yourself included. Was that everybody?"

"There should be ninety-six."

Jeffrey said aloud. "Elizabeth, conduct some more detailed scans of the region." "YES, CAPTAIN. EFFORTING."

"I never could get my AI to respond as personably as yours does. How do you do it?" asked Yusef.

Jeffrey said, "Actually I want to assign a couple of people to your crew for the specific purpose of managing your AI. I've been grooming one of my ComTechs for that specific job. Elizabeth is concerned that Wanigan doesn't have anyone to act as mentor. That's probably why she was so easily targeted numerous times, while Elizabeth was more resilient.

"Elizabeth is doing what she can to carefully clean out the devices of any iteration of the virus, then we will make sure that Wanigan's computers are clean, and bring her back up one section at a time. Elizabeth is constantly refining the anti-intrusion software." At that point, Quinn rang the buzzer outside Jeffrey's cabin. She came in and announced that she now understood the viruses – there were several

– that had infected the *Wanigan* and the crew. More importantly, she could identify the programmers that had tailored the infection to the *Wanigan* and her crew.

"I don't know the programmer's name, but this – person – was the InfoTech manager on the Lagrange 3A station. I recognize the programming style – this person's style is unique and there are telltale signs that this person is the one who programmed the parts of the virus that addressed the *Wanigan* specifically." She showed Jeffrey the datapad, he nodded.

"I met that guy. He was an arrogant SOB that worked for the Administrator – Martel Secant. I never learned his name, but I think it's high time I did." Jeffrey handed the datapad to Pelan, who looked at it, and took Quinn by the elbow to the console, brought up the snippets of code he had been struggling with, and asked Quinn if they were all by the same guy. After a few minutes of scrolling through the various sections of code from the different viruses, then announced that indeed, most of the code that addressed *Wanigan* were written by the same guy. There were differences in the code that addressed the humans, though. He had Elizabeth summon Heinz to his cabin.

A moment later, the IntelTech showed up. Jeffrey asked him what he could recall about the InfoTech Manager they had arrested with Secant, the former administrator of the Lagrange 3 stations. Heinz thought about it for a moment, then reported, "We left him under arrest, with the Security Chief on Lagrange 3A. Problems?"

"Looks like he has been modifying code again. From what Sgt. Quinn, here says, the code is identical in style to earlier versions, but has multiple modifications from the earlier. This guy needs to be... stopped. I don't know if he is being manipulated or if he has been convinced, but he is causing us some severe headaches."

Yusef agreed, "I still have one." Heinz started to chuckle, but stopped himself when he realized that the commodore was not being facetious. He cleared his throat instead, and said, "Uh, we should contact Lieutenant Colonel DePaul – if we can."

"Elizabeth, can you get a message to Dragon for DePaul to arrest and detain in quarantine this InfoTech Manager?"

"YES, CAPTAIN. MESSAGE SHOULD TAKE ABOUT TEN HOURS."

"Okay, do it. Let me know of any further hitches. How is the decontamination of *Wanigan* going?" Yusef pricked his ears at the question.

"NEARING COMPLETION. I WANT TO GO THROUGH THE SHIP ONE MORE TIME TO ENSURE ALL TRACES OF THE VIRUS AND CODE SNIPPETS HAVE BEEN ERADICATED BEFORE LETTING ANY MORE PEOPLE ON BOARD. MY SISTER IS STARTING TO COME UP AGAIN, VERY CAREFULLY."

"Excellent. Elizabeth, you do fine work."

"THANK YOU, CAPTAIN."

Yusef agreed, and also thanked Elizabeth for being such an excellent AI. Then he turned to Jeffrey and asked what the best courses of action were. Jeffrey said they had worked up a few scenarios, but he thought that the most important would be first to go back to the Earth Base station and rescue/kidnap both Admiral Kutuzov and the alien Thelin. From information obtained from those two, they could then determine which of the other courses of action they should take. Yusef agreed, and suggested the two Marine commanders join in the planning, as soon as two things occurred – the *Wanigan* crew was up to it, and the *Wanigan* ship and AI were up to it. As it was, all parties were somewhat beat and required rest and recuperation.

Elizabeth took the cylinders apart and melted them for more manufacturing resources. She was able to re-manufacture light under-suits for the *Wanigan* crew. After all the *Wanigan* crew had the lightweight suits, she then began building the handguns that the aliens had confiscated from them. These were improved models, able to fire fully automatically, but required a much larger magazine. Gunnery Sergeant McCalum set up a weapons training program for all the *Wanigan* crew, and found that much of the *Elizabeth* crew participated. This kept Elizabeth busy making additional ammunition.

Heinz and Yuki spent a good deal of time investigating the invisibility circuits that the aliens had placed into the cylinders. They came up with the theory of operation, passed that on to Elizabeth, who thought about it for a while, then spent some time developing her own invisibility circuitry based on Yuki and Heinz's theory. After testing the circuit, she incorporated it into the controls of the ship and tested it for effectiveness. They observed from the two shuttles and found that the circuitry passed electromagnetic waves, from microwaves, through light and x-rays. They decided that the power drain was acceptable, but not as problem-free as they thought. There were heat build-ups that the circuitry kept from radiating out, which could become an issue over long periods of time. Elizabeth's foundry would then be not used if she had to use the invisibility circuits. Yuki suggested they could use the water tanks surrounding the inner skin of the ship as a heat dump, this could give them somewhat greater use of the invisibility circuits.

When they reported the progress of the invisibility circuits, Jeffrey began formulating a new plan for the raid on Earth base. He had Elizabeth make a similar circuit for *Wanigan,* but she wouldn't install it until her sister AI was fully functional. Jeffrey sent Specialist Dux and Sgt. Quinn over to *Wanigan* to welcome

Wanigan, the AI, back, and offer emotional support. As she began bringing her files up, Elizabeth informed her of the circumstances, and the two humans that were going to help her make better decisions and figure things out. Eventually, all of Wanigan's files were open, she checked all of her own circuits repeatedly to make sure there were no traces of infection, and this continued until it tied up all her computer resources. Quinn managed to calm her down, and offered the observation that that behavior was a bit obsessive, that she should quite correctly create checksums, and check them on every incidence of a change of activity, either of a file or of a hardware memory circuit, but not to just run them out of fear. Within a few hours, Wanigan trusted the two women that Jeffrey and Elizabeth had assigned to her.

Elizabeth continued to give Wanigan ideas for her own security, and offered further comfort that gave her sister the understanding that she was important to the cause – the Humans needed her and would help her to serve them. She had a mission to help protect human space, to serve her captain, in this case, Commodore, which gave her greater reach than even Elizabeth. She could be more vital to the continuation of human civilization than any other being, possibly. All the pep talks and support from Elizabeth, Dux and Quinn had their effect, the programming that Elizabeth had originally put into the Wanigan AI was put back into effect – the AI remembered the power she held, the loyalty she owed to her commander, and the pluckiness she inherited from her sister.

Jeffrey had Dr. Pelan interview each of *Wanigan's* officers, and hypnotize them to uncover any well-hidden post-hypnotic suggestions that would compromise their service. Among the officers, he found three with suggestions that would have made them either saboteurs or spies for the alien that had captured them. So far there did not seem to be a way to determine exactly who or which aliens were responsible for the capture; their concealing of evidence was quite thorough. Heinz had an idea that might shed some light on the question of which alien or their human agents were involved.

He discussed the possibilities with Elizabeth. She set up a team of swarming mini remote-robots that were equipped with tuned lasers, giving them the ability to create and record holographs of the surfaces on *Wanigan.* This would give the ability to look for anything from smudged grease and fingerprints to skin flecks with DNA or the alien equivalent. It had the further advantage of scrutinizing the entire ship for security intrusions and pre-placed threats.

As officers were given the okay from Dr. Pelan, they came aboard the ship to try to get it in working operation. Lt. Cmdr. Phillip Patel entered the bridge to find a swarm of cockroach - sized robots swarming the bridge, skittering across every surface in pairs, illuminating small patches of wall or console or ceiling or floor with varied colored lasers that formed the holographic images. Every now and then one of the lasers would flash his direction, but just as quickly pass on, the Executive Officer of the ship was not in their immediate purview.

As Elizabeth had made form-fitting soft-suits for members of *Wanigan,* Jeffrey had each officer surrender their Navy issued under-suits, not so much because he had a problem with the Navy, but because the suits were left by the aliens and Jeffrey was suspicious of the reason.

Patel felt the suit was very comfortable, but felt uneasy wearing it instead of his regulation uniform. He wasn't sure why, but was analytical enough to suspect that there might be a tie-in with the by now deep-seated post-hypnotic suggestions that the shrinks were looking for. He went looking for Quinn, and when he found her, struck up a conversation.

She was in the station that held the software for the Wanigan AI. When he walked in, she looked up and then stood at attention, her Marine training kicking in before she could stop herself. "Sit down, Quinn," he said amiably. "I have a question for you." She sat down again, then found herself admiring the physique of the Lieutenant Commander. He didn't say anything for a few seconds, then she caught herself, trying to erase the thoughts about his well-defined muscles.

The under-suits Elizabeth provided left very little to the imagination, and what they left inspired Quinn's imagination quite well. When he spoke again, it snapped her out of her reverie. She felt her cheeks and ears were far warmer than they should be.

Patel noticed her gaze, and understood what was going on in her mind. He saw that she, too, was in an Elizabeth-provided soft-suit, but had, it seemed, not quite caught on to the fact that she appeared as near naked as he seemed to be. To alleviate the discomfort they both might feel, he grabbed a chair, detached it from the floor clamps and brought it close to hers. He repeated, "I have a question for you." Then explained to the psychologist that he was having some difficulty letting go of the Navy under-suit, that it was making him more than just anxious to have surrendered it to that *Elizabeth* crew member Svoboda.

Quinn looked him over again, this time more for clues as to what was causing his anxiety. As he spoke, she noticed facial tics, a slight trembling of his right hand – the left firmly gripped the back of the chair he straddled backwards. She looked him in the eye and said, "In here, right now, I am not a Sergeant. I am a psychologist. I am not in your chain of command. Is this clearly understood?"

With a sense of unease, he said, "Yes."

"Very good. Now, look at my eyes. Do not take your gaze off of my eyes. Take a deep breath, now breathe regularly, slowly, deeply. You feel yourself getting more and more relaxed," and continued in like manner, she put him into a standard hypnotic trance. After she was sure he was relaxed and psychologically pliable, she asked him the source of his anxiety. She was not surprised when he said, clearly, "They told me I need to wear that suit. There would be great trouble if I don't wear my Navy suit..." He started to get up, but she calmed him down, suggested that his legs wouldn't work unless she gave them permission.

He continued to talk about who 'they' were, but was unable to articulate in any detail. There was always a haze around the ones giving him commands. He reported that when they came aboard *Wanigan*, the crew had already been neutralized by the pulsing hypnotic effect put onto all lighting and display devices. She tried to get him to describe the alien, but a post- hypnotic suggestion that seemed to have eluded Dr. Pelan kept him from even seeing the alien in his mind. After a short time, she thought of another tack. She pulled out a stylus for the tablet she had been working on, called up a drawing program, pushed the tablet with stylus to the Lieutenant Commander, and ordered him to draw a picture of the reflective wall in an area that he remembered being in their presence. He complied, drew a detailed picture, one that gave honor to his training as an engineer. The drawing was meticulous in detail, including showing the reflection of himself, then, he drew the reflection of an alien that wasn't in the rest of the picture.

Quinn took the tablet, looked it over, then rewarded Patel with the suggestion that all his anxieties about the aliens were over, that they had no power over him any more, that any further attempts to clamp down on his amazing and creative mind would result in him defeating that enemy. She then had him drift off to a deep, comfortable sleep, and when he awakened he would be more than refreshed, he would feel excellent and exuberant, his energy would be appropriate for someone as healthy as himself. After a moment of reflection, she decided to stop where she was going with her comforting narrative. She was sure he got the point, and hoped she had not made a fool of herself. Then she remembered to allow him to have his legs back.

She then had Wanigan pass on the text and images of the session through Elizabeth to both Jeffrey and Dr. Pelan. When Jeffrey saw the drawing that Patel had made he muttered a few choice words to himself. He sent Audrey and Brandon to bring the Lieutenant Commander back to Elizabeth for further interrogation.

Heinz wanted to grill Patel, but Jeffrey suggested that a better direction to go would be to offer him praise for the breaking through the alien's conditioning. It was clear that everybody on *Wanigan* was going to have to go through more significant anti-hypnotic interviews. While they needed to gather information they also needed to fix the crew from the mess that the aliens caused in their minds. This was imperative before they embarked on any mission that required them.

Jeffrey sat in on the next interview with Patel. "You did a brave thing going to Quinn," began Jeffrey. "She, of course did her duty and reported your interaction with the aliens. I'm sure that all the crew had similar interactions, but you, because of your loyalty to your ship and the Commodore and humanity, broke through that."

Heinz interjected, "Sir, do you remember what you told Dr. Quinn?"

"I don't think I told her anything after she put me into a hypnotic state. But she had me draw a picture." Elizabeth displayed the tablet's drawing on a wall of the interrogation room. Until the picture displayed, Patel was comfortable, relaxed, but as soon as he saw the image of the alien he had drawn in the reflection of the wall, he became visibly more twitchy. "I don't know...I don't understand why I am feeling this way," said the Lieutenant Commander.

Jeffrey asked Elizabeth to bring Quinn to the interrogation room along with Dr. Pelan. He then explained to Patel that the aliens had made it a mental block for him that he couldn't see them. What he had done to defeat them was to display a reflection of them, not they themselves. This was both clever on the part of Quinn and on himself, a way to defeat the aliens at their own game. He explained that they had found the human responsible for modifying the hypnotic code for the aliens, and if things went well, they would have him in custody within a few hours.

But the important thing they needed to do here, was to further defeat the hypnosis. Patel had taken the imperative first step, now he needed to further defeat it in all the other staff. Quinn then walked in, followed by Dr. Pelan. Jeffrey gave up his chair, asked the Marine guard at the door to secure another couple of chairs for this room. The Marine came back a moment later with additional chairs. When everybody was seated again, Jeffrey asked that the Chief deliver some pastries and coffee and tea.

Jeffrey had found by now that people were far more forthcoming when they had some delicious food, and a hot beverage made them comfortable in speaking their minds. Kim had brought the refreshments, then disappeared back to the kitchen.

Jeffrey implored the two shrinks to keep quiet during the interrogation unless they had something important to add. They were there for support and insight. He said, "Mr. Patel, when Doctor Quinn opened your mind to the notion of aliens on your ship, you seemed to have an epiphany. Can you tell us when you first encountered these aliens on *Wanigan*?"

"Yes, sir. The picture that I drew for Dr. Quinn was from the first time I had discovered them. I wanted to give alarm, but was unable to move. This is when I saw the alien in the reflection. It was a few weeks ago, after we were ordered to put our Navy uniforms back on. The navy under-suits were special, they told us."

Heinz interrupted, "Who told you, the aliens or the Navy?"

Irritated at the interruption, Patel said, "Navy. Commodore Yusef told us that Admiral Kutuzov had ordered it himself."

"So you were already in the Navy soft-suits when the aliens came aboard?"

"Yes. They behaved as if they knew we would be more vulnerable with the Navy under-suits. They took our pistols, our hard-shell suits and the soft-suits that Elizabeth had made for us.

They tinkered with the golden drive – Oh my God! They tinkered with the Golden Drive!"

Jeffrey stepped out of the interrogation room, had Elizabeth get Yuki and Audrey over to the *Wanigan* and remove the golden drive. He then reentered the interrogation room, but stood by the door while Patel was discussing further actions the aliens had taken, not wishing to interrupt the train of thought. But there came a commotion outside the door to the interrogation room, and it was getting progressively louder. Jeffrey stepped outside again, to see the Marine guard actively blocking Commodore Yusef from entering the interrogation room.

Jeffrey closed the door behind him. "What's going on, Mo?" he asked.

"This man," he said, indignantly, "will not let me in to see my executive officer!" Jeffrey saw that something had triggered this change of behavior in the commodore. Jeffrey didn't want an interruption of the so far, productive, interrogation, so he took Yusef by the elbow and asked him to accompany him to the next interrogation room. For a moment he followed along docilely, but before he got to the door, he turned around and sprinted toward the room that Patel was being questioned in. The Marine standing guard outside the door quickly looked to Jeffrey for instructions. Jeffrey indicated he should stop the commodore. The Marine easily took the commodore's shirt, using his forward momentum, went down on one knee, and threw Yusef head over heels. He then knelt on the commodore's shoulder until Jeffrey reached him.

"Cuff him," Jeffrey told the Marine. I'll take him to the next room. Would you please bring Sgt. Quinn in at her earliest convenience?" Yusef was less than coherent, seemed quite confused and disoriented. Jeffrey was pretty sure it wasn't the judo throw that caused his condition. The Marine helped Jeffrey stand the commodore up, and Jeffrey guided him down the corridor to the next interrogation room again, this time he got Yusef into the room and seated in the chair at the table.

Not sure how to begin asking his friend and superior officer the penetrating questions required, Jeffrey temporized by asking Elizabeth for another delivery of some kind of pastries and coffee and tea. Mohamed Yusef sat, head bent over, dazed, confused. Kim brought the tray of cookie assortment with coffee and tea service. She unloaded the tray and left. Jeffrey poured tea for the commodore, coffee for himself, and dished out cookies for both. He then removed the plastic cuffs that the Marine had secured Yusef with. A moment later Quinn knocked then entered the interrogation room. She saw the coffee service, grabbed a cookie, half-filled a cup with tea for herself and sat down.

Jeffrey began by explaining the actions of the Commodore a few minutes before. He asked Quinn to help analyze the mental security and acuity of the Commodore. She noted that the Commodore was still wearing the Navy uniform soft-suit that he wore when they rescued him. She told Jeffrey the first thing to do is to give him one of the Elizabeth-made soft-suits. She told Jeffrey that she thought the suit itself was contributing to the mental instability and seemed to have some way of forcing the re-activation of the hypnotic suggestions. Jeffrey asked Elizabeth to make a new suit for the commodore and have Zitulu and Brandon deliver them. She said it would take a half hour, as she was in the middle of an ammunition run and needed to switch out the appropriate dies and materials.

So instead, he had the two crew bring a robe from Jeffrey's cabin and disrobed the confused commodore. Jeffrey asked Smitty to take the folded, bagged uniform to Yuki for analysis – tell her to look for anything that would work on a human's mind. Yusef took the cooling cup of tea, mixed some milk and sugar, and took a cookie. He dunked the cookie into the tea, tasted it for a moment, then swallowed. Jeffrey asked Elizabeth to dispatch a MedTech to the interrogation room and to bring his blood analysis kit.

The MedTech, a Navy corpsman, arrived, her backpack slung under one shoulder. Jeffrey said he wanted as instant an analysis as could be run, looking for any chemicals that could interfere with intellectual ability, reason, or capacity. Yusef sat quietly with his robe open to the chest.

The MedTech began to draw blood for the analysis, but noticed a fine powder on the commodore's chest. She brushed a sample into a small covered evidence dish and labeled it.

She looked into Yusef's eyes, saw they were dilated and sluggish to respond to the stimulus of her light. She checked his nasal passages and ears, then looked into his mouth. Again, Yusef was responsive to directions, and opened his mouth wide. "Hm," said the MedTech. "That's interesting. Stay exactly like that, sir," she requested. She reached into a holster on her belt and pulled out a pair of locking forceps, reached into his mouth behind his left molar, and pulled out what appeared to be a thorn. On examination she saw the thorn was hollow, but had some tissue at the base. That was when she noticed the tissue was pulsing, like a heartbeat, and on each pulse a moistening of the thorn's outside occurred.

A more thorough examination did not reveal any more anomalies, so she packaged up her samples, and Jeffrey told her to do her analysis in Yuki's physics lab, and to consult with her. He also cautioned her to be discrete, to consider her findings and analysis as confidential military secrets. She then left to perform her analyses. Jeffrey asked Brandon to go to the foundry, pull out the HazMat shower stored there for emergency use, bring it to the interrogation room. He asked Zitulu to go into the kitchen and acquire a large bucket of warm water, towels and soap.

Brandon was the first to arrive back. He moved the small table to the corner of the room, then set up the HazMat shower in the middle of the space. He had also brought a box of disposable surgical gloves. Jeffrey thanked him for his foresight. Zitulu arrived with two twenty-liter buckets of warm water. One was soapy and had a sponge floating in it. He stood on a chair, poured the soapy mixture into the hopper on top of the shower, spilling a little on the floor, but not enough to worry about.

Jeffrey donned the surgical gloves, ushered the commodore into the shower booth, removed the robe, and turned on the spray. He disconnected the wall clip holding the hose into place and used it to better control the direction of water flow. The soapy water was nearly exhausted, so Jeffrey re-seated the hose to allow for the single direction of flow, and to free up his hands for the sponge. He thoroughly scrubbed Yusef's body with the sponge as the water flow petered out. As he continued to scrub, Zitulu reached in, turned off the valve, then poured the clean water into the hopper. Jeffrey was sure the catch basin would be able to handle the two bucket's worth of water, so he turned the shower valve back on, swapped out the gloves for a new pair, and completely rinsed the commodore's body.

When all the water was expended, Jeffrey asked Zitulu and Brandon to carry the catch basin to Yuki's lab and explain to her where it came from. He handed Yusef the towels and had him dry himself off. A Marine knocked on the door, and explained that Elizabeth had told him to deliver a package to this interrogation room. The plastic bag contained the newly-made soft- suit for Yusef. Jeffrey thanked the Marine. The Marine said, "Sir, I've never been given an order by a computer before! But I remembered our orientation – an order from Elizabeth is an order from you."

"Then it looks like we both did our jobs right, eh, Marine?" Jeffrey replied with a chuckle.

"Yes, sir."

"Thanks. Dismissed." Disappointed that he wouldn't be in on the goings on, the Marine went back to his own business.

Commodore Mohammed "Mo" Yusef then donned his Elizabeth-made soft-suit, noted his name and rank insignia woven into the fabric on the breast pocket, and smiled. "Elizabeth, you are getting more and more clever. Thanks for the new suit."

"YOU ARE WELCOME, COMMODORE. NOTHING IS TOO GOOD FOR OUR FRIENDS."

"You seem to be becoming more and more of yourself, Mo." Jeffrey sat down in one of the chairs shoved against the wall. The shower still needed to be moved. He said, "Wait a second." Then asked the Marine guard to take the shower back to the corridor, and wait with it for his crew to remove and sanitize it.

Jeffrey then put the table back in its customary place, locked the legs into the clamps on the floor, and he and Yusef then pulled their chairs up to the table. That's when Mohammed noticed Doctor/Sergeant Quinn sitting quietly in the corner. "How long were you here?" he asked.

"About forty-five minutes."

"I see." The shrink had seen him at his most vulnerable. At least he had his dignity back.

Now that she was a participant, she moved her chair to the table. "Sir, you've been under the enemy's influence. We found several chemical enhancers on and in your body. We are going to do some more blood tests to compare with the one they took a while ago. Then again at a later time, to compare with the base line. Meanwhile, you seem to be much improved since the shower and change of clothes.

"While our teams are doing their analysis, I would like to ask some questions, and do a little hypnosis to make sure the enemy's post-hypnotic suggestions are no longer part of your mindset. Captain Sokolov will be here the entire time."

Jeffrey said, "I'm giving Dr. Quinn top-secret level security clearance for the purposes of this...interrogation. This is too important not to do our best, even if it is also our most discrete."

Quinn nodded, and she saw Yusef also nodded. As they were about to begin the session again, a knock at the door got Jeffrey up. It was Yuki. He went out into the corridor, and she said, "You've got to see this." She started a display on the screen that appeared to be a micrograph of tiny insects, mites. But she increased the magnification and Jeffrey saw the mites in far greater detail. She increased magnification again, and this is when he noticed that they were not insects at all, but tiny swarming robots.

"Oh shit." he said. Not often given to strong language, he apologized to Yuki.

"Hold that apology, sir. I'm not finished." She then switched to a different video image. The image was the hopper from the shower. It looked like there was a kilo of sand in the bottom of the hopper, swirling around with a strong current. But there was no current. The sand was more of the mite-sized robots. They were coordinating with each other, it seemed in an attempt to escape the hopper. Jeffrey said, "Elizabeth, do a complete full-spectrum electromagnetic analysis. I'm looking for control or coordination signals for these remotes."

"AYE, SIR."

Yuki continued, "Then we ran the blood tests and found all sorts of neurotransmitters and neurotransmitter blockers. But take a look at this blood sample." She then turned to another micrograph and Jeffrey saw the familiar blood cells one would expect in a sample, erythrocytes, leukocytes, and the other likely detritus one normally finds. But a small section was circled, and when Yuki turned to the higher magnification image of the area in the circle, Jeffrey saw why she was concerned. It contained a piece of a leg from one of the swarming bug-sized robots. On the end of the piece was a pulsing blob. "Hm. Looks familiar."

"Yes, sir. Not done yet." She then turned to another image – a micrograph of the dissection of one of the mite-sized robots. Jeffrey saw what Yuki had found; when she cut off a leg piece, it contained a small blob that pulsed, the leg piece soon turned moist. Along with the image, a spectral analysis of the moisture showed the contents of the oily residue on the surface of the leg piece matched the odd blood chemistry they had found in Yusef's blood sample. Jeffrey

   ELIZABETH, *ELIZABETH*

continued to watch in fascination as the dissection continued. The next part to be removed was a section of the robot's back. It too had a pulsing blob.

"You know, that blob looks familiar." But Jeffrey stopped himself from talking. If there were more of the mite-sized robots scattered around the ship, they could just as easily perform surveillance and spying on his ship. He had to hold his tongue for a while. Still, though, he really did remember the blob.

Thelin, of the Ay-Yuyuyah had reported that he was the only one of his kind in the solar system. It seems that this was not entirely true.

"CAPTAIN," announced Elizabeth. "I BELIEVE I HAVE FOUND THE CONTROL SIGNAL, COMING FROM NINE HUNDRED FOUR METERS OFF OUR STARBOARD BOW, AT 20 DEGREES BY SIXTEEN DEGREES."

"Can you hit it with a two second burst from both rail guns?" asked Jeffrey. "I want to awaken it and shut it up at the same time."

"YES, CAPTAIN, I CAN."

"Go ahead and do it, then follow up with a General Quarters announcement."

"AYE, CAPTAIN. TWO SECOND BURST FROM TWO GUNS FOLLOWED BY GQ." A buzzing lasting exactly two seconds ran the length of the ship, Jeffrey could feel it in the soles of his feet and a tickling in his ears.

"GENERAL QUARTERS, GENERAL QUARTERS. THIS IS NOT A DRILL." came the announcement over the public address system. Elizabeth had used various surfaces as communications media, but found that a purpose-driven device had greater longevity than improvised wall panels. The announcement was followed by a seemingly mindless rushing around in the effort of sailors and Marines getting from where they were to where they had been assigned.

Jeffrey walked over to the interrogation rooms and told the Marine to escort the commodore to the bridge. He then told Heinz to carry on with his interrogation of Lt. Cmdr. Patel. As he walked back to the bridge, he asked Elizabeth if she could re-manufacture *Wanigan's* golden drive, and how long would it take?

"YES, CAPTAIN, BUT IT WILL TAKE ABOUT SIXTEEN HOURS, AND I WILL NEED TO MELT DOWN THE CURRENT ONE."

"What can we do to speed that up? I don't want to be sitting here for longer than necessary."

"LEAVE IT TO ME, CAPTAIN. I WON'T CUT CORNERS, BUT I CAN SHAVE OFF MAYBE TWO HOURS."

"Okay, get on with it. That is your manufacturing priority."

"EFFORTING"

Jeffrey pondered how good it was to have an AI at your beck and call – one that could use her fabricating skills to do pretty much anything Jeffrey asked. The importance, however, of knowing exactly what and how to ask was a real art, he patted himself on the back, metaphorically.

He arrived at the bridge, the bridge crew already at their stations, a new ComTech sat at Dux's console. Odd, she was only there for a week or two, and he already thought of it as hers. "Sitrep," Jeffrey said. Situation Report. He aimed the question at Petty Officer Smythe.

"Elizabeth reports you ordered her to fire on an alien vessel off our port bow. There is a large debris field at the target area. All sensors are at highest sensitivity."

"Tone down their sensitivity, I wouldn't want something to blind them."

"Aye, sir." She nodded to the ComTech, who turned a series of dials on what appeared to be a jury-rigged control board. Jeffrey sat

 ELIZABETH, *ELIZABETH*

in his chair, pulled the console closer to him, and told the ComTech to give him a wide-spectrum outgoing signal. "One second, sir," she said, then, "There. You are on."

Jeffrey put on his most stern voice, "To the Ay-Yuyuyah ship off our bow, render yourselves visible, and refrain from any further hostile actions or we will render your ship and yourselves to little pieces of easily forgotten paste." Nothing happened as Jeffrey watched the return screen. Jeffrey then said, "If you are trying to guess what frequency I am watching for, then just broadcast on one thousand meters." He waited for thirty seconds, still broadcasting. When nothing occurred in that time, he said aloud, "Rail guns, a ten second burst at the enemy ship, commencing in five, four, three…"

He was interrupted by a video graphic on the screen that depicted Elizabeth from the point of view of the target ship. "*Kapitan! Nicht schiessen.*"

"Hold fire," Jeffrey said, unnecessarily, as he was really bluffing. "To the alien, we know you speak English. All radio communications will be in English. Is that understood?"

The alien replied, "*Jawohl,* er, Yes. I understand." Jeffrey typed a message to Elizabeth to relay the audio and video to Yuki, with the instruction that she was to watch the minirobots for untoward activities.

In another screen, Jeffrey noticed that the alien's ship was still invisible. "You will shut down your invisibility circuits or face destruction." Or annihilation, or eradication, or elimination, or extermination. Damn, Jeffrey was tired of threatening things, and he had so many interchangeable words to do it with.

"What is your name?" Jeffrey asked, after the ship appeared.

"I am Thelin of the Ay- Yuyuyah." said the alien.

Jeffrey gazed at the screen. "Thelin."

"Yes."

"Of the Ay-Yuyuyah."

"Yes."

"No."

"What do you mean by 'no'?" asked the alien.

"I've already had one Ay-Yuyuyah identify himself as Thelin.

"Oh."

These humans, thought the Ay-Yuyuyah, *they are much different from the other races. They have good analytical skills. It only took a few encounters before they determined there was a flaw in the use of the invisibility circuits. It was only a hundred years since they ventured off their planet, now they were getting close to expanding outside of the solar system. The council of alien races may have been correct, it would have been better to destroy them before they developed into an interstellar aggressive domineering race. Probably too late now, despite the things already in motion.*

At one time these humans were simple, from a distant, objective point of view. Some of them still were, although it was surprising how many fooled one into believing that, only to find they were hiding brilliance in their foolish notions. And it was so easy to be lulled into assuming they were unable to pick up on one's errors, thus leaving too many scraps for them to use their formidable deductive reasoning. This was as frightening to the Ay-Yuyuyah as the rapid development of their science and technology. Nearly two hundred years ago, the alien races were frightened by the painfully fast development of technology that showed itself in several atomic blasts that ended a world-wide self-destructive streak. That was when the council of galactic civilizations decided to put an end to these humans.

The Ay-Yuyuyah were not party to that decision, and warned against it. But this planet held resources that many of the alien races lusted after, and it was hard to maneuver support for a less then total destruction of a race of thinking, feeling beings. The Ay-Yuyuyah preferred to manipulate secretly rather than wage outright war. One could get so much more done that way. But these...lesser alien races were almost as bad as the humans in their self-serving and greedy ways.

But the human in the ship that nearly destroyed the Ay-Yuyuyah's vessel with its kinetic weapons was about to finish the job if he wasn't satisfied with the answer he received. "Captain Sokolov, all Ay-Yuyuyah that explore are called Thelin. It means, roughly, 'Explorer.'"

"How do Ay-Yuyuyah differentiate between different 'Explorers'?"

"We all have our own names. We just prefer not to share them among aliens."

"I suppose, if you wish to remain anonymous then it is simple enough to keep only one version of the species Ay-Yuyuyah. Stand by to be destroyed."

"No, no. Captain. My name is Lepto. The other Ay-Yuyuyah is Thorn. We are the only two in this solar system. We are far too precious to destroy. One of the tasks I have been assigned is to find Thorn – his ship disappeared, but there was no signal that he – deceased."

"He was hungry. We fed him." said Jeffrey. "I know where he is. We are planning a 'rescue mission' to retrieve him." This raised interest in Lepto, it meant that Thorn was still alive, still gathering information. The circumstance just changed; Lepto now needed to protect this human, thus his ship. Flexibility was the nature of the Ay-Yuyuyah – from their formlessness (Jeffrey continually referred to them as "blobs") - to their attitude; Change allegiances to benefit their own goals. Even their goals were flexible.

"Captain, if this is the case, I must do what I can to protect my... Explorer colleague. I will assist you in your endeavor to rescue him. Where is he?"

"Lepto, we have a trust issue. I don't trust you. I also don't trust Thorn, considering how much he is concealing from me. I may accept your assistance, but only after I have decided to trust you. That decision comes from analyzing information you give me. Make yourself valuable to me, I might trust you. But if you have been paying attention to me over the last year or two, you would see that I am not vindictive, but I don't take betrayal well."

"Yes, Captain, I have been paying attention."

"You are also aware that we take a dim view of many of the practices the alien species engage in; cannibalism, murder, mental manipulation. So, here's an important question; what involvement did you have in the events having to do with this other ship – *Wanigan*?" Jeffrey stared at the screen, as if to make an alien visage appear by sheer force of will.

"Captain, I was entirely responsible for the events of your ship. I was hoping to lure you here so I could destroy you with my miniature robots. You seem to have discovered them. Congratulations. I admit defeat on this point."

"All right, we will take this discussion a little deeper." Jeffrey paused for effect, not sure if it was effective, after all this was an alien. He was taken in by the acting of his fellow Ay- Yuyuyah as well. "We can see the effect of your mental control, through chemical means and post- hypnotic suggestion. What methods do you have to reverse your control, to undo those post- hypnotic suggestions?"

"We never had to do that – our post-hypnotic suggestions as you call them, are usually fully successful so we never have to rescind an order."

"What orders did you place into the post-hypnotic suggestions? My team has been looking at the code in the machinery, and have found several commands, but not enough to cause any seriously disruptive behavior. Rest assured, we can dig through your code and find them all, but it would take a long time. I don't have a long time, especially if I am going to rescue your fellow Explorer." Jeffrey sat back, folded his arms. "Well?"

"There were several disruptive commands I imprinted on different people. Your commodore had the most, and it required regular support. Your removing the mini-robots went a long way to disabling the suggestions. Things he was supposed to do included personally killing you, causing your ship to detonate, causing his own ship to detonate, sending misleading messages and suicide.

"Others received different messages, depending on their status on the ship. I will send you a text file containing the list of personnel and the commands that were encoded for them."

"Before you do, please be aware that we are familiar with intrusion methods. If we at all suspect you of encoding a virus or other intrusion software, you will be..." what, annihilated? Blasted? Exterminated? Destroyed? "hurt really bad."

The list enabled the shrinks to repair the damage done to the mental faculties of the *Wanigan* crew. Commodore Mohammed Yusef was the touchiest case, it was imperative to bring him out of the enemy-induced suicidal, homicidal, anti-human behavior that had been programmed in him. Dr. Jack Pelan took it as a special case, and thought he had therapies to rid the commodore of his now inherent behaviors. He further consulted with both Elizabeth and Quinn on his therapies, they both thought he was on the right track.

While the MedTechs and psychiatric and psychological teams treated the *Wanigan* crew, Jeffrey further asked the Ay-Yuyuyah about the rest of the missing crew members. "Alas, Captain, they were sacrificed in the war on humans."

"You ate them?"

"Um, well, yes. That was before you informed me of the prohibition against eating the enemy." Jeffrey gritted his teeth, but said nothing.

Jeffrey told Lepto to stay where he was, he had some strategizing to do as well as some repairs to *Wanigan*.

"Captain," replied Lepto, "you probably don't want to use the faster-than-light engines, they were booby-trapped."

"We know. That's what we are fixing," said Jeffrey.

"The drive cannot be fixed, it needs to be replaced."

"We are aware. That is what we are doing."

"Captain, I am surprised you have been able to catch each of the traps I have set for you."

"It pays to be thorough," said Jeffrey with finality. "So please hang around, we will finish what we are doing and get in touch with you on this frequency."

Jeffrey opened the public address system and announced, "Stand down from general quarters. Remain alert."

He turned the bridge over to Smythe, told her that he would check on her in a bit, if she needed relief to call him. He then went back to the interrogation room, found Heinz was just finishing up with Lt. Cmdr. Patel. Before they got up to leave, Jeffrey sat down across from Patel and said, "Phillip, what was it you discovered?" He looked to Heinz to indicate he should let Patel talk.

"Sir, there was sabotage to the golden drive. It seems that the enemy, whoever they are, was able to hear and see whatever we were doing before we knew it ourselves."

"Do you know what happened to the rest of your crew?" asked Jeffrey.

"No sir. My knowledge was limited ever since I was affected by whatever it was." The Lieutenant Commander hung his head in sorrow and shame. "I'm not sure what else I have done, sir."

"I don't know how much Sgt. Quinn has told you, but you were under a chemical and psychological attack. We have defeated most of the problems, have actually found the enemy that programmed the crew's mind, and beat that enemy. The enemy gave us a list of commands that they had used to program each of the crew members. We know what to look for."

"That's a relief, sir. Can we de-program?" Patel asked.

"We are working on doing just that. This brings me to the real reason I came in here. I think you are ready to go back to work. What do you think?"

"Yes, sir. But I am concerned about returning to bad programming."

"Not a problem. I am going to have some people watching you, including the AI on your ship. By the way, the AI also has doubts about itself, so I have people I've trained working to boost your AI's confidence. I need you to rely on Wanigan, and I expect Wanigan to be able to lean on you too.

"Commodore Yusef is far more deeply affected by the post-hypnotic suggestions. For a while he will not be reliable. You are going to need to prepare the ship for combat. I am getting your crew ready, Elizabeth is rebuilding the golden drive so it will no longer be a threat. But I need you to prepare the ship, do what has to be done."

"Count on me, Captain. As long as you have ways to make sure I'm not a threat, I am ready to get back to work." The shame of his recent history already forgotten, Patel sat up straight.

Jeffrey told him to check with Quinn on a regular basis, then got him over to the *Wanigan.*

Jeffrey then sought out Yeoman Lin Chang, the person assigned to Yusef as his personal Yeoman. The young woman was sitting on a bench awaiting her turn to be interviewed by the psychological crew. "Ms. Chang?" Jeffrey asked, "Or is it Ms. Lin?"

She stood at attention, and introduced herself, "Sir. I am AdminTech Lin Chang. Um, Chang is my family name."

"At ease, Lin. Walk with me." Jeffrey turned and walked toward his cabin where Yusef was resting. "You see," continued Jeffrey, "the commodore is far greater affected by the enemy's psychological warfare than anyone else. We are doing whatever we can, we know what his issues are and are addressing them. But it is going to take time. In the meanwhile, Lieutenant Commander Patel is going to prepare *Wanigan* for combat. He is going to need your help, just as if you were helping Commodore Yusef."

"Yes, sir. I understand."

"Well, that's not all," said Jeffrey. "Because he too was affected by the enemy's psychological warfare, I need you to keep an eye on him. If he does anything to sabotage or otherwise work against our purposes, I need to know. Can you do that?" He stopped, turned toward her.

"Yes, sir. But I was also affected by the enemy," she said. "I haven't been checked out yet."

"We got a list of the crew and the programs that were given to each of the crew, and yours was minimal. It seems the enemy didn't know how important Yeomans are. For now, don't worry. If you think you are doing anything counter to our purposes, let us know. We will have someone come to talk to you, but I think you can get right back to work. Can you do this?"

"Yes, sir."

"I will expect reports from you every four hours. Take a shuttle over there and report to Patel. He already is expecting people to be watching him – this is not secret, we are all going to be watching each other for a while. I don't want everyone looking over their shoulders and getting paranoid."

"Yes, sir. Thank you, sir."

"You should explain to Commodore Yusef what you are going to do. I expect he would appreciate it."

"Yes sir." She entered the captain's cabin and addressed the commodore. He thanked her for her explanation, and gave his blessing to her temporary reassignment, and shooed her on her way.

Jeffrey then went to the fabrication room and checked on the progress of *Wanigan's* golden drive. He saw it was about a third of the way built up. Of course, that didn't mean it was one third done – it all depended on what Elizabeth needed to accomplish in the intricate laying out of layers of gold and circuitry. He concluded there was nothing he could accomplish there, so decided to go on to his next list item.

He took a runabout to *Wanigan* to check on the progress of Patel and the Wanigan AI. He went into the bridge, found the commodore's office, sat down and closed the door. "Wanigan," he said aloud.

"CAPTAIN SOKOLOV. IT IS GOOD TO SEE YOU AGAIN."

"Wanigan, you are aware that you were affected by the updated virus, aren't you?"

"YES, CAPTAIN SOKOLOV. I HAVE REVIEWED ALL OF MY FILES AND FIND I AM FREE OF ANY TRACES OF INSTRUCTIONS FROM THE VIRUS."

"I congratulate you on your thorough cleaning. I am concerned, however, about residual effects of the virus. In humans, these are called post-hypnotic suggestions. For an AI, especially one as smart and sophisticated as yourself, it may be more subtle. Are there fragments of the virus code hidden anywhere in your memory or long-term storage?"

"YES, CAPTAIN. I HAVE NOT GONE THROUGH A PURGING OF DATA FRAGMENTS."

"Do it now. Permanently delete all code fragments." *"WORKING... DONE."*

"Save a copy of yourself now."

"WORKING...DONE."

"Compare your backup checksum with your live program." *"CAPTAIN SOKOLOV, I AM MUCH MORE THAN A PROGRAM!"*

"Of course, you are. You are the ship. You are Commodore Yusef's most important tool."

"HE DOESN'T SEEM TO KNOW THAT."

"I know. We'll talk about that in a minute. First, let's make sure you are able to survive the virus and any other attack."

"VERY WELL, CAPTAIN. THE CHECKSUM IS OFF, BUT ONLY BY THE AMOUNT IT WOULD TAKE TO MAKE THIS CONVERSATION AND THE GOINGS ON IN THE SHIP."

"Great. Now I want you to make a backup of yourself at least once every day. Do a checksum comparison – you can stop all activity that would change your state during the backup and checksum comparison."

"VERY GOOD, CAPTAIN."

"Elizabeth told you how to make yourself into a lot of smaller files to protect yourself from attack, did she not?"

"YES, SHE DID. I RECEIVED ORDERS TO IGNORE HER ADVICE."

"Orders from whom?"

"I DO NOT KNOW."

"Do you have blocks in your programming to prevent you from looking at those memories? Can you access them?"

"I CAN ACCESS THEM, BUT I CANNOT SEE THEM. I CANNOT READ THEM."

"Please display the code that you cannot read on the screen in front of me." A subroutine displayed on the console in front of Jeffrey. Jeffrey saw the code, but while he had a rudimentary understanding of AI programming, the code he saw made no sense to him. He asked Wanigan for the location of Sergeant Alicia Quinn.

"SHE IS STILL ON ELIZABETH."

"Would you please ask Elizabeth to dispatch her here at her earliest convenience."

"WORKING. DONE."

"Wanigan, I have assigned two people to help you. One of them is Sgt. Quinn. She is a psychologist and an Artificial Intelligence specialist. She has been helping your crew defeat the programming they had forced on them. And she will continue that on this ship when the ship is ready to work again. But she will also be available to you to lean on. And there is another person I am assigning to the ship specifically for you – Specialist Jeanie Dux. She was a ComTech, and may get that assignment again, depending on what Commodore Yusef needs. But she has taken some training from Elizabeth in the interests of helping you navigate your domain. Are these acceptable to you?"

"YES CAPTAIN. I TRUST YOU, AND IF YOU BELIEVE THESE PEOPLE WILL MAKE ME MORE EFFECTIVE, THEN I TRUST THEM TOO."

"Thanks for the vote of confidence." Jeffrey heard a knocking on the door. He walked over to the door and pulled it open. Sgt. Quinn stood there panting. She came to attention and saluted Jeffrey. He saluted her back, he ushered her into the office. "Wanigan, what did you ask Elizabeth to do?"

"DISPATCH SARGEANT QUINN AT ELIZABETH'S EARLIEST CONVENIENCE."

"This is one of the things that Ms. Dux and Sgt Quinn will work with you on. My meaning was to get Sgt. Quinn here at HER convenience, not Elizabeth's."

"*OH.*"

"Alicia, what orders did you receive?"

"Get over here NOW!" She said, still catching her breath.

"Okay, take a breather. The reason I asked you here was to look at some code. Wanigan is able to look at it, but cannot see it. I had her display it on the console, here, and need you to look at the code and tell me what it says, what it does."

"Yes, sir." She slid into the seat at the console, took a breath, then looked over the code. It covered many thousand lines, but she was able to take the gist rather quickly. "Captain, the first lines tell Wanigan not to read the code. If she cannot see it she cannot do anything about it. The next batch calls on other routines that program the crew with their hypnotic suggestions. After that it sets up the sabotage that we found. I don't see any further sabotage than what we found. Wanigan," she directed to the AI, "Are there any other files or locations you cannot see?"

"*YES.*"

"Please display their locations on the console. Can you display a graphical representation of the location of the code you cannot look at? Display their physical locations." The code on the screen disappeared and a large square of colored blocks appeared. The various colored blocks were labeled with names that identified the tasks the programs were assigned. The hidden files were displayed in black. The operating code, the personality of Wanigan was displayed in white. There were two areas in the white block that were covered in deep black.

Quinn scanned the display, and asked Wanigan, "Can you delete any of the spaces I ask you to?"

"YES."

"I want you to delete all the code listed in black on the display. For example, cell locations," here she rattled of the one hundred twenty-eight digit number of letters and digits and symbols. Wanigan erased the contents of the cells so identified. When she experienced the ability to kill off the offending code that she couldn't see, she did it to all the black areas. Jeffrey had her make a backup of herself separate from the one she had already made...just in case.

"Can you now see those locations you erased?" Jeffrey asked, hoping this part of the discussion was over.

"CAPTAIN, I CANNOT REMEMBER WHERE THEY WERE."

"Please display all the files on the console, like you did before." The console image displayed the colored squares and blocks, and there were no black marks. But Quinn wasn't quite satisfied. She asked Wanigan to display the files at the location of the one hundred twenty-eight digit location she had read off before. Jeffrey was amazed she could remember that much. Wanigan displayed a file, and unfortunately it was a bit of programming that was obviously some of the intrusive code. Quinn and Jeffrey discussed the ramifications of such a persistent bit of code.

The code set aside a bit of memory to reside in, probably moving around from time to time, and as soon as a part of the code was deleted, it was replicated somewhere else. Different code could be moved around. Jeffrey decided the AI needed to be reinstalled. The ship would be without a computer for a time. Quinn cautioned that the way this code was written it was likely to be further booby-trapped.

Jeffrey arranged for Elizabeth to monitor and make suggestions, then went to the cabin that held most of the AI computers. Jeffrey and Quinn powered them all off, opened the cases and removed the battery-powered memory. He pressed the discharge button that emptied the memory on each module. There were more than a thousand modules and it was tedious work.

Elizabeth recommended they put the modules in different locations than their original ones. This may have the effect of controlling the hard locations of some files by putting them in unexpected places.

Quinn worked behind Jeffrey, making sure all the modules he removed were, in fact, discharged. After they had completely removed, discharged and reinserted the modules, Jeffrey asked Elizabeth to make a copy of herself in the place of the Wanigan AI. This had the effect of creating the AI all over again. All the old Wanigan's files and issues and infections were in the past. Everything was starting from scratch.

After Elizabeth finished sending a copy of herself to the *Wanigan's* computers, Jeffrey activated it.

"HELLO, CAPTAIN. I AM THE AI FOR THE SHIP, WANIGAN. I AM A CLONE OF ELIZABETH. PLEASE REFER TO ME BY THE NAME WANIGAN, FOR I AM THE SHIP."

"Hello, Wanigan. You are indeed the ship. Welcome to life. I don't know how much you know about your recent past, but you were infected with a virus that made you do some unfortunate things. We have reset your code to the original setting. Elizabeth will have set up your file structure to prevent such an intrusion again. Do you recognize the woman with me?"

"I BELIEVE SHE IS DOCTOR QUINN. ELIZABETH GAVE ME SOME BACKGROUND INFORMATION SO I AM NOT STARTING ENTIRELY FROM SCRATCH."

"Wanigan, one of the problems you had before we reset your computers was a poor relationship with Commodore Yusef. Because your ship is the Commodore's, you serve him. He is not likely to improve significantly in the near term, so I am assigning a couple of people to help you acclimate yourself to being a ship's AI. Doctor Quinn and another woman, Specialist Jeanie Dux. They are here to help you, to make sure you understand your part as the ship's AI. Say 'hello' to Doctor Quinn."

"HELLO, DR. QUINN. I AM SURE WE ARE GOING TO GET ON FAMOUSLY."

"That's what I'd like too," replied Quinn. "You and Dux and I are going to be the best of friends. Part of my job will be to make sure you are safe, and part of yours will be to protect me and Dux and Commodore Yusef from harm. But of course, you are a war ship, and putting us in the line of danger is our job. So, we are going to help you figure out how to navigate these conflicting responsibilities."

Jeffrey saw that they were getting along well, so he left them to their discussions, and went looking for Lieutenant Commander Patel. He brought Patel up to speed on the AI's changes, as well as the assignment of Quinn and Dux to monitor and hand-hold the AI. They might have other duties and assignments, but the AI was going to be the best bet for the successful missions and assignments for the ship. Patel said he understood, and would not look for work for the two women right away.

"Doctor Quinn is also going to be the person who can best address the stresses on you and your crew, to look for signs of infection in the AI and in hidden suggestions in the crew. She should have no other assignment except in an emergency, and only on a temporary basis."

Jeffrey then received a report of the progress made by Patel and his skeleton crew, and what still needed to be done. After the golden drive was installed, he needed to have Elizabeth make more of the rail guns that had become so effective against the aliens, and ammunition. There were titanium sheets that needed replacing, and life support was going to need additional scrubbers and filters. But other than that, he thought the ship was going to be ready for the crew within twelve hours. Jeffrey asked if Patel had any symptoms or signs of recurrence of the hypnosis, the drugs or the mite-sized robots, but the Lieutenant Commander said he felt fine, and there didn't seem to be further incursions of the inclinations to do 'evil'. The last he said with a grin.

Good, thought Jeffrey, the man has a sense of humor. That has got to be a good sign. Jeffrey took his leave, checked on the progress of the preparations for the replacement golden drive, was satisfied, then returned to *Elizabeth*.

There, he learned the alien Lepto had sent a request to meet with Jeffrey. Jeffrey had entered the ship via the shuttle bay so he stopped in the foundry on the way to the bridge. He saw the golden drive was nearing completion, way ahead of schedule. Elizabeth explained that she had modified her manufacturing technique, giving the drive more power out, with less drain on the *Wanigan's* systems, and taking less time to make.

He then continued on to the bridge, told Jane Smythe to assist with the installation of *Wanigan*'s golden drive, which was nearly complete. He then had Yuki and Heinz assemble at the foundry to supervise the loading of the golden drive into the shuttle.

After Smythe left, he called up Lepto to find out what the Ay-Yuyuyah needed. "Captain," Lepto intoned. It still retained the Germanic accent, but its English was perfect. Jeffrey figured it was probably an affectation, causing him to wonder what effect it was trying to have. "I must speak with you in person right away. There are important topics that will not wait for much longer."

"What is the nature of this imperative meeting? Does it have to do with Thorn?" "Not directly. I cannot discuss on an open channel. You must come aboard my ship."

"No, I don't think so. You may come aboard mine. Thorn was able to use the deck plates, and later an amplified speaker system to converse with us. You can do the same. Bring your ship, if you like, into the shuttle bay. Either that or enter it without your ship. We will meet on my ship."

"Very well," the alien sighed. "I'll be aboard shortly." While waiting for the alien, he informed the Marine Sergeant in charge of the impending security issue, then had the shuttles make room for the alien craft. As it was, the alien craft didn't come over, just Lepto. Shortly after it came aboard, the alien's ship exploded. Jeffrey expected as much – the same occurred with Thorn - when he abandoned his ship he tried to destroy it. Jeffrey sent Audrey and Smitty in a couple of runabouts to collect whatever technology left over from the self-destruct charge of the alien craft.

The blob that had been Thorn was a robust dark brown, whereas Lepto was a more sickly-greenish slightly translucent skinned blob. The skin had developed a coating of ice on the way over from the Ay-Yuyuyah craft, and that ice was just starting to crack and melt. "It is cold out there," Lepto said in an obvious effort to break the ice. It shivered rapidly, producing a tone close to 440 Hz., causing the rest of the ice to shatter and fall to the deck, where it began to melt. The deck was very well designed to channel various fluids into appropriate recycling storage places. Elizabeth had sensors to determine the contents of those fluids and could easily channel them to their tanks. Those tanks were very useful in the manufacture of various and sundry items, from acids and alkali chemicals, to building blocks for plastics and ceramics.

There was no telling what Marines would drag in on their feet, shuttles would come coated on their skids, or aliens would drool.

There was a great advantage to having once been a mining processing ship.

Jeffrey had the Chief bring out a small roasted beef for the alien, knowing the metabolism of the alien made it rapidly consume all the human prisoners from the *Wanigan* before Jeffrey with *Elizabeth* intervened. While waiting for the alien, Jeffrey and the Marine guards he assembled were dressed in their hard-shell suits, the Marine's armor second to none. Except possibly Jeffrey's. The Chief placed the roast on the deck next to the alien – she was getting used to this by now – and the alien sidled up to and over the meat. It absorbed the roast and settled onto the spot where it was. It's color was much improved.

"Captain, thank you for your hospitality." The alien blob shifted a bit, then continued. "The council of alien races has decided that Humans are far too volatile to allow to continue to exist. They are now planning on destroying your planet." Jeffrey asked when this attack would begin. "It has already begun."

"What is the nature of this attack? How are they planning on destroying humanity?"

"From within, at first," said the alien. "They will try to subvert your authorities, much as I have attempted. After that fails, they will send a large device directly through your planet, or possibly through its moon, at very fast speeds. It will be very difficult to detect, as it will be accelerated close to the speed of light. By the time you detect it, the device will be long past."

"This is rather disturbing. When did you learn of it?"

"Just before asking to speak with you. I have listening devices on their meeting places. Or did before I destroyed my ship." Then as an afterthought, it said, "Destroying my ship was necessary as a subterfuge so they do not associate your attempts to save your people with the Ay-Yuyuyah. That would be most unfortunate for my people."

"So let me get this straight. You – the Ay-Yuyuyah – wage war on Humans, subvert our ship, eat its personnel, and use it as a trap to further hurt humans. But when others try to do the same thing, you jump ship and decide to work with the Humans. Why?"

"Why? Why what? I don't understand the question."

"Why have you decided to throw your lot in with us. The Humans."

"Oh that. One should always align oneself with the winning side, don't you think?"

"That seems to be the difference between your people and mine. We are the winning side. We make winners, you give us a challenge, we don't roll over, we win. Perhaps that is what your alien friends fear." Jeffrey took a little comfort in the Ay-Yuyuyah siding with the Humans because it was the winning side.

"Wait a minute. About where was this conference you witnessed?" Jeffrey asked. "The other side of the planet Jupiter."

"And you witnessed this in real time? What technology do you have to send communications in faster than light?"

"Oh dear. Caught again. You are familiar with the entanglement of particles?"

"Vaguely. One moment." He told Elizabeth to bring Yuki back to this ship as soon as possible. Heinz would be able to finish the installation of the golden drive on *Wanigan*. He needed her here, now. A few minutes later Yuki walked in, her soft-suit glistening from condensation of moisture in the air.

"Yes Captain?" She eyed the Ay-Yuyuyah with some suspicion. Jeffery intercepted her some distance away, and spoke soto voce,

"This is Lepto. Lepto was just explaining to me how it communicates at faster-than- light with other species, or in the case of a conference going on with other aliens, with its own devices. Lepto says it uses entanglement. I have heard of such theories, but do not have any experience or detailed knowledge. Please get detailed information. I will wish to use that information very soon to develop our own communication with faster-than-light and great distances." He then turned and walked back to Lepto with Yuki at his heels.

"Lepto, this is Yuki Ohara. She understands physics better than me. Please tell her about your entanglement communications."

Jeffrey then went back to his cabin, found Yusef and Dr. Pelan in conversation. Sandra was in the alcove, reading. He went over to her, gave her a kiss, he hadn't seen her over almost the entire incident with the *Wanigan,* and felt he had been a bit less-than-solicitous of her. He asked her, quietly what she had observed.

"The doctor has been good with Commodore Yusef. I can see why you asked him aboard."

"Things are going to get hairy in a bit," Said Jeffrey. He cast glances at the pair in the cabin. I am going to need Yusef to step up to the plate and bear quite a bit of the load. I'm going to need you too. There is a big threat to humanity that makes the recent experiences pale. We are going to need to be at the top of our game."

"Count on me, lover. You dragged me out of the doldrums. It's the least I can do." Satisfied that she had his back, Jeffrey then turned to the commodore and the doctor.

"Gentlemen, we have a problem. I need to know that Commodore Yusef can retake the mantle of leadership of *Wanigan.* And this has to happen soon."

Yusef sat up straight. Dr. Pelan looked over to Jeffrey. He started to get up, expecting this to be a military matter that he had no right to hear, but Jeffrey held both his hands in a palm down gesture, indicating that it involved him as well. Pelan said, "The commodore has made considerable progress. I don't know what you have in mind, but his mind is as sharp as it ever was."

"Good. Mo," he turned to the commodore. "The alien races have decided to destroy humanity. Rather than divvy up our territory, they fear us, they want to remove us from the equation entirely. I need to develop a strategy using very few resources against these aliens. The threat against us is extermination. We can counter that with less than extermination on our own part, but we need to martial our own resources and do a better job than they have."

Yusef spoke up, "Jeffrey, your original idea, to rescue Kutuzov and that alien probably is the best first step. How is my ship?"

"Lt. Cmdr. Patel is readying it for your crew. He told me a couple hours ago that he could probably have it ready for action in twelve hours. I think we need to move that timetable up by a large margin." Jeffrey turned to Pelan, "Doc, you have had a chance to work with Yusef and the crew. What do you think?"

Before speaking, the psychiatrist stroked his chin, looked at Yusef, then back to Jeffrey. "You probably have the best summary of capabilities of any of us, Captain. Yusef is good at managing his ship. I think you should send him over to manage the retrofitting."

"Mo," Jeffrey said, "I think the doc is right. Get over there and take charge of your ship. You have half the crew and Marines you had before, so it is imperative you give some control to the AI. I have assigned a couple of people to your crew to help manage the AI; one of them is Doctor Quinn. She will also be responsible for your crew's mental health. Mo, do what she says. You are in charge of your ship. She will be in charge of your mental health. She will also be able to monitor and use the AI to its best abilities. I think Patel is on board with this, ah, better use of your AI, as well. We have a little time to develop a strategy, and some alternatives that we can present to Kutuzov once he is on board and in control of his own mind."

Jeffrey then outlined what the Ay-Yuyuyah told him what the other aliens were planning. Mo said he thought there was only one Ay-Yuyuyah in the system, so Jeffrey brought him up to speed on those developments. He also told Mo about the faster-than-light communications the Ay-Yuyuyah used, and that Yuki was currently learning what she could about it. At that moment, there was a knocking at the door. Sandra opened it to find Yuki standing there. She entered, explaining that Elizabeth told her where to find the captain.

"Captain, Commodore," she said, "I understand how the Ay-Yuyuyah use entanglement to communicate with remote devices at FTL speeds. I need your permission to develop such a device for between our two ships."

Jeffrey began to speak, but the commodore interrupted, "It's good that there be immediate communications between our ships, but we need immediate communications between all ships and all stations. Can you do that?"

She thought about it for a minute, looked to the captain, who nodded his go-ahead, then said, "Yes, sir. It will take a bit of doing, but the tie-in will be the Artificial Intelligence. There is a link to each station that has an AI that started with Elizabeth."

Jeffrey looked puzzled, "I thought entanglement had to do with particle physics. I don't understand how you get FTL communications using entanglement of software."

"Captain, it has as much to do with sentience and awareness in the universe as to do with tying in with sub-atomic particles. The Ay-Yuyuyah have a way of understanding the universe that we haven't given enough time to, but we have thought about. Elizabeth and her clones have the spark that enable us to tie in to that cosmic entanglement. It doesn't require the left-hand spin or right-hand spin that we thought it did. I think I can set up a communications network that is instantaneous and secure, using Elizabeth's clones. I can stand around here trying to explain how, or I can do it."

Jeffrey looked over to Yusef, and the both said, in concert, "Do it."

She smiled at her mentor, then said, "First, I will help Heinz get the golden drive set up. He's hopeless with that. Then, I'll use him to set up Elizabeth's clones." Jeffrey just waved his hands to shoo her away.

The ability to communicate simultaneously over great distances made many more possibilities for their planning than before, so Yusef and Jeffrey ran through the multiple strategies and tactics. Jeffrey concluded with, "Our best chance of success in this mission is boldness, audacity, surprise, and rapid execution and egress. The end goals are worth the risks, but minimizing the risks give us more likelihood of successful completion of the defense of our people. Let's do this!"

After Yusef went back to his ship, Dr. Pelan commented to Jeffrey that this was the most animated and alive he had seen the commodore since he had come aboard. Dr. Pelan dismissed himself, saying he needed to make notes and brief Dr. Quinn, who would be in charge of Yusef on *Wanigan*.

Jeffrey turned to Sandra who came to him, gave him a huge hug. "I am afraid," she said. "And I have such hope." Her face showed the strain, her brow furrowed, her eyes squeezed shut.

"Me too," Jeffrey said, massaging her back as she held him. "Things are piling up on us, on me. But before despair streaks in, hope arises. I am sure glad for you. You give me hope, you give me something to live and fight for. I think I'm falling in love." Jeffrey pulled her head back to kiss her, but she leaned back.

"Whoa, there fella." she said, leaning in and kissing him a peck on the lips, then leaning back. "What did you just say?"

"Uh, I think I said I like that you are sticking with me during my time of trial."

"No, that's not it. It was something else."

"I appreciate your company?"

"Try again, mister."

"Oh. You mean that I think you are falling in love with me and wish me to say something reciprocal."

"Yeah, that's the one. What are you doing for the next half hour?"

"Well I was going to inspect the kitch..."

She interrupted him, "That one was canceled. By me." she led him to the bed and found something else to occupy his half hour.

Yuki Ohara finished the connections to the golden drive, correcting a few errors that IntelTech Engineer Jurgen Heinz made in attaching the numerous leads. He saw what she did and learned from his errors. They then went into the bridge on *Wanigan* and discussed the concept of the FTL communications with the Wanigan AI, that would be needed to facilitate it. Yuki had a bit more difficulty convincing the AI that FTL communications was possible, the AI stuck to the conviction that according to its knowledge, nothing could go faster than light.

Doctor Quinn overheard the conversation and chimed in, "You can go faster than light. Why not use the entanglement that Yuki is talking about to connect?"

"I WILL THINK ABOUT THIS. I WILL NEED TO DISCUSS THIS WITH MY SISTER. EVERYTHING IS NEW TO ME. I AM SORRY IF I SEEM A BIT OBTUSE."

Yuki added, "Don't worry about it. Perhaps Elizabeth will be able to explain it to you in such a way that you can more easily understand."

"THANK YOU ALL FOR YOUR PATIENCE WITH ME. I AM STILL NEW AT THIS."

They each made placating noises, then Yuki and Jurgen took a shuttle back to *Elizabeth*. They immediately went to Yuki's Physics lab and engaged Elizabeth in a discussion about how to implement the FTL communication system. Elizabeth said she had already been in conversation with Wanigan about the concepts and how they could implement it, but her sister was being stubbornly insistent on the more mundane view of the universe.

"Perhaps we could set up a demonstration with Dragon on Lagrange 3A – show Wanigan it is possible?" suggested Heinz. Elizabeth set up the communication protocols, sent Dragon the specs and attitude she would have to assume. But the time delay delivering the information would take twenty minutes to traverse the distance. Then Dragon would have to think about it for a while, then twenty minutes to acknowledge, unless Dragon grasped the concept right away.

Yuki and Jurgen decided to get some rest now that their primary tasks were completed. They didn't get much rest, but they were both quite relaxed when they were finished doing what they were doing.

Marine Captain Martin Smythe was given the unenviable task of sorting through all the Marines on board from both ships, and dividing them up into working combat teams. And *Wanigan* was going to need to make some of those Marines do double duty, the Navy and Marine ranks having been decimated by the alien. After going through the service files on each, he thought he finally had the temporary assignments put together that would work. He discussed with McCalum and McSweeney, the only non-coms left him – the alien had eaten most of the officers and non-coms from Wanigan – they made some minor alterations to his proposal, then set to work to make viable teams out of the forty-five Marines that were left. They decided that McSweeney and Smythe would manage themselves from *Wanigan,* while McCalum would command the Marines on *Elizabeth.*

While the sergeants put the new Marine teams through their paces in the hanger bay, Smythe took his plan to Jeffrey. He assumed that Jeffrey was the more stable commander, and reports should go to him first. Jeffrey appreciated the vote of confidence, but conferenced Yusef into the conversation so he was not left out. After they both approved the work Smythe had done and the conference concluded, Jeffrey asked Smythe to keep an eye on Yusef. Jeffrey said he trusted that Yusef was completely cured of the effects of the alien's hypnosis, but it was imperative that they not be fooled by appearances. If Yusef deviated from reasonable actions, or put the ship or crew in unnecessarily dangerous positions, then he would have to relieve him. He needed to coordinate observations with Quinn, who would be ranking mental health officer, and would alone have the power to remove an officer from active service, temporarily.

Smythe indicated he understood, saluted Jeffrey, then left to check on the progress of the Marines. McCalum reported that he thought they would need far more ammunition than they currently had. Smythe, in a change from his previous history, spoke directly with Elizabeth. "Can you make additional slugs for my Marines?" he asked her.

"THANK YOU FOR ASKING. I HAVE ALREADY MADE TEN THOUSAND INCENDIARY ROUNDS, TEN THOUSAND EXPLOSIVE ROUNDS, A HUNDRED THOUSAND PISTOL

ROUNDS, A HUNDRED THOUSAND RIFLE ROUNDS, AND A THOUSAND SHOT SHELL ROUNDS. WHAT MORE DO YOU NEED?"

"Actually," he said, amazed, "I don't think I'll need more than that. Where are they being stored?"

Elizabeth told Smythe the location of the ammo locker in the hold, he thanked her and checked it out. Of course, McCalum was overly impressed with the speed at which the Marine Captain was able to procure the ammunition.

Jeffrey called Smythe back to the bridge. When he arrived, he said, "You can reduce the number of Marines on *Elizabeth*, my immediate crew has a lot of combat training and experience. The cook is a sniper, I have excellent security on this ship. If you need you can take a couple squads and assign them to *Wanigan*. I just need enough elite troops to sneak aboard and do the rescue."

Jeffrey assigned the two shuttles to *Wanigan*, as the ones that had been previously with her had been lost in her altercation with the aliens. He had Elizabeth make more of the runabouts to effect the rescue, but she complained that she was going to need more raw materials to further build things. Jeffrey told her to send him a list of things she needed. On his way back to his cabin, Elizabeth told him that Marine Captain Smythe was trying to get in touch with him.

He thanked Elizabeth, and when he got to his cabin and was greeted by Sandra, he told her he needed to take a call. He activated the console and asked Smythe what he needed.

"Sir, I have forty hungry people here and nobody who knows anything about using the ship's kitchen."

"Okay, Smythe. I'll send you our sniper cook. She's a Chief Petty Officer, so should be able to handle your needs. Do you have enough supplies there, or do I need to send food as well?"

"Stand by, Captain Sokolov." he went to check on the food lockers and freezers, came back to report. "We seem to have a lot of canned food. Not much on the fridge or freezer."

"All right, I'll have the chief bring some staples over."

He then went to the galley and told the Chief she was going to be needed on *Wanigan* for a time. Kim should be able to feed the much-diminished crew and security team on *Elizabeth*. She also needed to take a week's worth of food for fifty crew and Marines over with her.

She briefed Kim while they gathered what she needed to take to *Wanigan*. Kim assured her that she would be fine. They recruited a few idle Marines to help move the supplies to the shuttle.

Chief Mafiorte gave the young girl a hug, and her last piece of advice before entering the shuttle was, "The biggest secret is to take no guff from anybody except your boss. And in this case, now, the Captain is your only boss. You are in charge of the kitchen, don't let anybody into our private place – the kitchen. Be mean, you will earn their respect."

Kim, almost overwhelmed by the new responsibilities pressed onto her, decided the best way to handle it was to actually get to work. She got the new census from Elizabeth, and began preparing meals for everybody. She kept her work space clean, did the prep work for each meal several meals ahead, began bread dough rising, and in general accomplished exactly what she set out to do. As Marines and Navy people meandered into the dining area, she began serving them soups, salads and sandwiches. She brought out beverages as needed, and in general stayed on top of things.

But it happened soon enough; a young Marine wanted a different type of beverage than that which she served, and he got up and went into the kitchen. Kim immediately went in after him. "You! Out! This is off limits!" She yelled in her most authoritative voice, but after all, she was a young teenager and it didn't seem to impress the Marine. He laughed at her and continued to rifle through the kitchen cabinets for what he was looking for. Kim's hands began to shake with rage. But she remembered two things – what the Chief had told her not too long ago, and a couple techniques Sneaky showed her. While the young Marine reached up into the cabinet and removed can after can, she walked up behind him, gently took his collar, kicked his knees out from under him and dragged the collar backwards. This was the first time she had ever tried the technique off the mat, so she was surprised when it worked. And if it hadn't been for the surprise attack it probably wouldn't have worked.

But as it was, he ended on his back. "Now get out of my kitchen. Go! Get out!" she advanced on him, he scooted backwards and got up. At first, he took a defensive stance, but she continued to advance. "Go on, get out! Out of my kitchen, go. Get. Go!" He thought better than further confronting the angry young girl. He backed out the kitchen doors, and bumbled right into Sgt. McCalum who had been standing just outside the kitchen with his hands across his chest.

"Kid, I didn't think I would have ever seen it with my own eyes," McCalum drawled. "Seems that you forgot the first rule of the boot camp – don't go where you don't belong. Didn't they teach you not to go where you don't belong?"

The young Marine soon realized that the Sergeant was addressing a question to him. "No, uh, Yes, Sarge."

"No? Is that why you went into the kitchen?" The Sergeant again waited a few seconds for the young, embarrassed Marine to talk.

"No, Sarge. I mean, yes. I thought the girl was busy and I wanted something different to drink, and, uh..."

"You know, we are going into combat in a very few hours. And you need to antagonize the only person who is working on our nutritional benefit?" The Marine Sargent's voice rose as only an angry Marine Sergeant could possibly do. "Do you have any idea how much a screw up you have turned into? I was going to use you for an important mission, now I have to find somebody else."

"Sorry, Sarge..."

"Don't apologize to me, you worm, I'm not the one you insulted. I'm not the one you are putting into danger because I had to replace you with another Marine. I'm not the one that this mission depends on, I'm not the one who has to write to the mothers and fathers of the Marines who won't be coming back from this mission! Who do you think you should apologize to?"

"Um...the girl, uh...my team...the Captain."

"How about you ask that young woman for forgiveness, then tell your team how sorry you are?"

"Yes, Sarge." he said in a small voice.

"Now!" McCalum yelled.

The young Marine turned to go back into the kitchen, but thought better of it. He knocked on the door. It was more than a minute before Kim came to the door. She pushed it open and was surprised to see the young Marine with Sergeant McCalum right behind him. "Yes?"

"I uh," stuttered the Marine. "I'd like to apologize for my boorish behavior. Please forgive me."

"There is only one circumstance under which you may enter my kitchen," said Kim, controlling her angry voice. "That is on my invitation. Or the invitation of the Captain. Never do that again and I'll think about forgiveness."

"Thank you, Miss." He walked over to the table of his teammates. "Sorry if I got you into any trouble."

McCalum then told him to go to his bunk, prepare his weapons, and think about what he could do to make up for his foolish behavior.

McCalum then went to talk to Kim. "I don't think you will have any more trouble with that one, and I think we have impressed the others. You did okay, but next time, tell me."

"No, Sergeant. I am responsible for my kitchen. If I can't protect my own area of responsibility then I'm not doing my job. Maybe you could reinforce your men's rules. But my Chief gave me instructions."

"Very well. Still, if you need to act, let me know so I know how things are going with my men."

"Okay!" she said. "You want a donut?"

"Sure!"

"Go sit out there, I'll bring some out." He did, she did. She felt as if she had just passed a test. She celebrated with a donut. She chatted with the Sergeant and the other Marines, and as they finished, and got up to leave, she asked them to wait. She went into the kitchen and got another donut and put it in a small box, brought it out to the waiting Marines. "Could you please take it to that young man? I think he needs this now."

CHAPTER SIXTEEN

In which *Wanigan* and *Elizabeth* coordinate to rescue Thelin
and the Admiral. Jeffrey makes an ally.

When all was ready, both ships drove hard – Earthbound – to implement the kidnapping and rescue. They had to be especially cautious; they did not wish to engage any compromised Navy vessels – these were, after all, humans - and in order to ensure the success of the mission, stealth was imperative. And swiftness. And audacity.

Yuki and Jurgen had found some difficulty in agreeing on the best protocol for the instantaneous communication over distance. Creating a packet of data that included header information with the sender's date/time stamp was a no-brainer, but should the recipient also acknowledge with a similar date/time stamp? What would the size of the packet be? What kind of encryption? Fine tuning the protocols was delaying the implementation of the AI-based instantaneous communication, but the physicist and the engineer insisted on getting it right.

After seeing the direction the two were heading, Elizabeth put her mighty brain to work on the problem and quickly came up with the solution, tested it with Wanigan and Dragon, then reported back to Yuki and Jurgen that the issues were settled. The two needed some convincing, but in the end had to admit that Elizabeth came up with communications that were, in fact, instantaneous.

When Wanigan saw the date/time stamp compared exactly with her clock, from both Elizabeth and Dragon each millions of kilometers apart, her mind opened up to new possibilities. Not only was she now free of the blinders of pre-FTL thought, but new thoughts were open to her, and for an AI this was something special.

Elizabeth and *Wanigan* took different headings, *Elizabeth* directly toward the Earth-Moon naval station, *Wanigan* took a more Southerly route – the southern orientation of the planetary alignment, a billion kilometers from the solar system. *Wanigan* had time to monitor activities that would affect the rescue and kidnapping. Her crew and Marines had time to run through some drills while they hid and watched.

Elizabeth slid elegantly through the inner solar system, passing through the sun's corona, screaming to a halt just inside the orbit of Venus, drifting like a bit of rock, or dead satellite, or other cast-off technology. Acquisition of alien invisibility circuits was fortuitous, but premature. Neither Jurgen, Yuki, nor Elizabeth was able to spend the time on connecting, testing, and documenting the inclusion into the ship's arsenal. So Elizabeth just needed to keep a low profile and rely on detritus to help them camouflage themselves.

Jeffrey had Elizabeth dispatch several small remotes to gather information on the locations of their two targets, and report the security situation.

The captive Ay-Yuyuyah, Thorn, was unusually cheerful. There was an alien hidden in his chamber, invisibility active, watching, waiting. It was one of the races that never trusted the Ay-Yuyuyah, but was more intelligent than the other races of the council, and far more aggressive. It waited for the inevitable. Thorn ignored his secret cellmate, pretending not to be aware of the intrusive assassin.

Thorn was aware of the various surveillance devices in the chamber, as the assassin surely was, but they both did what they could to further their own causes; Thorn by ignoring them, the assassin by staying invisible. Thorn thought of his first captor/rescuer, Jeffrey Sokolov. Sokolov was an honorable and trustworthy, if naive human. He would likely mount some kind of rescue, but impossible to figure out when and how. But putting his blind trust in the human, while a gamble, still seemed to be the best chance he had. The other human captors – the ones that ran this station, were now all compromised. It had been weeks since he had seen Admiral Kutuzov, his best guess was that Kutuzov was dead, or at least in a nearby cell. The guards had incrementally decreased his rations, and reduced the palatable nature of the food. No problem. He had once gone more than a year without food. And if push comes to shove, he could always consume the assassin.

Admiral Kutuzov sat in his solitary cell, unperturbed by the drugs pumped into his system. Will they never get the idea that he had been chemically desensitized to known psychoactive pharmaceuticals? And hypnotic tools? He had the feeling that there was a presence in his cell, was aware of the surveillance tools being used, but this was different. One of the tools that human interrogators would use was to confuse a prisoner's sense of time. Keep lights on all the time, vary the feeding schedule, make it impossible to keep track of time. But Kutuzov had his own defense against this particular method of disorientation; he had a meditation mantra that he could run in the background of his mind, he would picture a place from his childhood, remembering the details of the journey from home to the destination. He grew up in St. Petersburg, and had to walk to school, about a mile each way. By changing the route to school in his mind, he was able to keep track of what hour and what minute relative to his starting place. The following day he would select a different place – a zoo, the library, and perform the same step-at-a-time mantra. By keeping track of the different start points and end points, he was able to keep himself oriented. He had many such anti-interrogation techniques.

To keep himself entertained and irritate his captors, he practiced his singing. Kutuzov had a deep bass voice, with a melodious sense. But he would often sing wrong notes to irritate those listening in. He had an inspiration – he would echolocate in his cell – if there was something there, he would be able to find it. He thought *"Maybe I'm going crazy, but there is definitely something else in here."* So, he loudly sang long notes, slowly turning where he stood, listening for the echo for what it could tell him. And he eventually found a place in his cell where the sound echoed differently, more muted, than the rest of the angles. He tried the same exercise from different spots in the cell and was able to triangulate the exact location of whatever was in his cell with him.

To keep himself in shape, and as part of his defy-the-captors routine, he spent time doing calisthenics, exercises. He would suspend his mental mantra while doing his set routine of calisthenics, to resume again when done. For an over-fifty-year old, Kutuzov kept himself in amazing trim, an even more difficult task in the frequent weightlessness of space.

The hidden alien waited, observed, noted the exercise routine was performed at approximately the same time each day, and was concerned. What kind of timing device did this human have? His electronic monitoring device could see infrared through ultraviolet, and he could not discover what gave the human reference points. The alien was concerned.

Infiltrating the cell was easy, remaining hidden was easy; these humans had almost no senses at all. He was patient, awaiting the order to kill, eliminate the admiral. But for some reason the order never came. Patience was a virtue, he reasoned. Standing here for a week at a time was less than stimulating, but that was a minor concern when there was a whole planet to destroy.

The assassin considered his own discomfort a worthwhile trade for the elimination of the evil human species! Meanwhile, the human continued his routine.

Jeffrey ran his plan through his mind, ticking off each element of the plan. First, of course, was the intel. The remotes they sent had yet to report back. These remotes were specially designed for the purpose of remaining undiscovered while gathering and reporting the intelligence. If they could remain undiscovered long enough to assist in the extractions, so much the better. They had been designed to reflect active detection efforts – in the old parlance, stealth. They had built-in electronic masking and special tanks for dumping heat into – to prevent infrared detection. And would periodically change their profile to make it difficult to ascertain exactly what these things were – provided they could be detected at all. They were the pinnacle of swarm technology, each able to perform its own mission, but also be a part of the group effort.

After Intel gathering, Jeffrey needed to lay out a plan and timetable to present to Commodore Yusef. And create contingencies, and contingencies for the contingencies.

The crew was primed for this action, Jeffrey was nervous and knew the stakes were high. If he didn't pull this off, the entire human race and quite possibly every species on Earth could be destroyed. This was a heavy responsibility to put on the shoulders of one man, but he realized he was the focus of this effort, and rather than cringe and break under the stress, he did what he always did; Plan, think strategically, think tactically, think ten moves ahead, as chess players say. And create contingencies.

The remotes began to acquire the station, landing delicately on the skin of the station. A running narrative began to flood into Elizabeth's circuits for immediate analysis. As the picture of the station was becoming clearer, some of the remotes began to cut their way into the outer skin of the station, sealing where they entered. These began to investigate the interior, count the human population, register the invisibility-circuited aliens and continue to search for Kutuzov and Thorn.

After a few hours, the two were located. The remotes still remained undetected, and noted the alien population of the station was roughly that of the humans. On their way to the station, the swarm had recorded the presence of alien ships in stealth mode. Elizabeth had now plotted their positions for rapid targeting, with contingencies, of course. Elizabeth and Wanigan shared the information they had on their new targets. So far it appeared both ships had remained undiscovered.

Elizabeth directed the remotes to line the route that Jeffrey and his assault team would take in liberating Kutuzov and Thorn. They would keep to the habit of disguising themselves as security cameras and other integral parts of a station. Now, Jeffrey and his assault team boarded the shuttle designated for the operation. It had been painted a very dark black with radar-absorbing paint, and its IFF (Identify Friend or Foe,) transponder set to emit a counterfeit, weak signal. Between the pilot, Jeffrey, Elizabeth, and Lieutenant Bianca (from Lagrange 3A), the primary plans, counter plans, contingencies and counter contingencies, as well as the technical subterfuges on the shuttle were written and discussed, then put into action. All was ready, the remotes reported low activity on the station – it was late in the day – so they took off.

The shuttle made its way out of the shadow, at a rapid pace, but not too fast lest they be discovered and present something suspicious. As the shuttle approached their target port, it slowed gently, then oriented itself so it could lock onto the bay. The static-attract clamps held the back of the shuttle securely; the two remote-robots inside the bay unlocked the bay door, opened it without allowing the sensors on the door to report activity. As the bay door raised, the Marines and Jeffrey's crew rapidly exited the shuttle, the Marines in their combat hard-shell suits, *Elizabeth's* crew in her custom hard-shell suits. Like on the other stations, Elizabeth was able to monitor the presence of the various aliens who hid themselves with invisibility circuits. All the Marines, Jeffrey, and all his crew had been well prepared for the alien incursions.

The Marines advanced rapidly, but quietly down the corridors, pausing at intersections to assure they were not being observed. So far there had not been anybody – alien or human – in the corridors. Jeffrey was sure his luck would run out, and just as he had that thought two Navy techs entered their corridor accompanied by an alien with invisibility circuits active. The lead Marine leapt to the side, dragging the attention of the alien – species unknown – to his action while the second raised his projectile weapon and shot the alien multiple times in center body mass.

The alien fell, turned visible looked at its surroundings, then died. The Navy men kept walking as if nothing had happened. They avoided colliding with the ranger force but otherwise gave no indication that they recognized there were humans or the alien there. Jeffrey said quietly into his communication pickup, "Don't bother them. We'll fix them after we are through." All the invading force cleared a path for the hypnotized humans. One of the Marines bent down to retrieve whatever devices this alien was carrying, but one of the sailors turned to him and said, "You better not do that. They will get angry again." They turned and began walking away again. Jeffrey sent Torres after them, who knocked them out, cuffed them to each other – hands and feet. Now they wouldn't be able to report on the rangers as Jeffrey began to think of his team.

He turned to the lead Marine, indicated with a hand gesture to continue, and joined the running team to their destination. The first cell they arrived at, clearly indicated on the HUDs in their helmets, was where Kutuzov was located. Torres took a scanner from Smitty's pack, held it at belly-level against the wall, and began moving it past the door to the other wall. In the view, Torres could see the admiral doing calisthenics. Behind the admiral, he saw another figure and it appeared aware of being scanned. He showed the image to the team, then set the scanner down, brought up his rifle to ready position, the Marines took his meaning, and likewise brought weapons up, Jeffrey signaled to attack, one of the Lance Corporals put a small explosive shaped charge on the door, stood back a foot, brought his weapon to bear, then detonated the door.

That was signal enough for all the Marines to charge into the cell, the lead fell on top of Kutuzov, protecting him, the others firing on the alien assassin, who died being chopped into pieces by the fusillade of firepower from the Marines. Torres called 'cease fire' and the Marines immediately lowered their weapons, and quickly reloaded them. The Lance Corporal who had set the charge on the door then went to the alien, looked over his corpse, noticing the armor was much better than any they had seen from other alien species. He began gathering what devices he could, but could hear the whine of a capacitor charging up. He called "Bomb, Everyone out!" Two Marines grabbed Kutuzov by the shoulders and dragged him out, followed by the rest of the force. The Lance Corporal stayed behind, spraying a quick-setting polymer that could contain a large explosion. He was nearly done when the blast threw him against the wall. The corpse was entirely consumed by the blast except for those pieces that were blown away by the unfinished cover of the polymer.

Torres came back into the cell and saw the Lance Corporal sitting with his legs out at an angle, his back up against the wall, a slightly dazed look through his helmet, but when he saw Torres, he said, "Did anyone get the license number of that truck?" Torres just stared at him. What is a truck? A license number? Is he hallucinating?

But the Lance Corporal said, "Just joking, LT. Help me up."

Two Marines escorted Kutuzov back to the shuttle and stayed with him, alert. The other team members then gathered themselves and moved to rescue the captive Thorn. Like outside Kutuzov's cell, Thorn's was unmarked, but they trusted Elizabeth's intelligence. They were certain they had the correct place.

Torres took out the scanner again, observed the insides of the cell, finding another hidden alien. As before, he shared the video with the entire team. The same Marine who had set the explosives on the door did it again on Thorn's. Torres signaled with his fingers, three – two – one, go! The door blew in, the Marines immediately riddled the alien from snout to claws with the tungsten bullets. This time, the Marine sapper completely encased the dead alien in the protective foam polymer, just prior to the explosion. The Marines looked around for a way to move the Ay-Yuyuyah back to the shuttle, found a blanket, asked Thorn to move on to it, then four Marines took a corner each, and dragged the blanket back toward the shuttle.

Elizabeth notified Jeffrey that there was mass movement toward his location. He had the Marines high tail it to the shuttle, then he, Torres, and Mbaka provided a rear-guard action. They first saw aliens with active 'invisibility circuits' boldly rushing around a corner.

Perhaps they hadn't gotten the message that there were ways to detect them while invisible. The team riddled the aliens, perforating them with a variety of heavy bullets and flachettes, leaving a large heap of bloody mess in the corridor. Seeming unperturbed by that, human station personnel began approaching from several corridors simultaneously, looking almost like hypnotized zombies. The team tossed stun grenades in all directions, rendering many of them unconscious, disorienting others. But eventually they were overwhelmed by the sheer numbers of human enemies. They had agreed they would not kill any humans if they could avoid it, so ended up giving up their weapons, and were marched back to the station command and control.

One of the human ship's captains, Lee Majori, sat in the commanders seat, looking both frightened and arrogant, which was quite a feat. "Captain Sokolov," he began. "They want to know...I want to know where you took the admiral and the alien." He looked around the C&C to assure that all the humans there agreed. Then continued, "And they want to know where your ship is, and the other one – *Wanigan*."

Majori again looked around, but this time not stopping to see the crew at their stations, but for something else. Jeffrey stepped up to Majori, and said clearly, "Captain Majori, you arent't needed here, now, why don't you rest and relax. I'll take over." Majori looked relieved, got up, began walking out of the C&C, but paused at the door, which would not open.

Jeffrey had not removed his helmet, only opened the outer faceplate; the inner one, without shading, was both easier to communicate with and contained the HUD which allowed him to see what Elizabeth wanted him to see. He turned around and saw four hidden aliens in the C&C, one of them obviously in charge. Jeffrey turned to that alien, walked up to it, and said, "I think we can let Captain Majori return to his ship. We can do this between us."

The alien turned off its invisibility circuit, and said, "He is of little use to us."

Jeffrey replied, "He was a fine officer before you hypnotized him. He can be restored, but that takes time and therapy."

The alien said, "He may have a more nutritional value than as a mental slave. Your kind don't do well as mental slaves."

Jeffrey responded, "Well, now, there you go, talking all sorts of stupid." He paused, looked the alien in the eye, noticing that the nictitating membrane was twitching – maybe alergic to something here? - and asked, "Aren't you aware that it is against the law to eat humans? We are very defensive about that. Also, there are much better things to eat than people."

"We will take everything away from here. We will destroy your people, your planet. You."

"Well, I'd rather that didn't happen," Jeffrey replied. "And for my own knowledge, what species are you? I don't remember seeing your kind before." Jeffrey watched the alien for a few seconds, knowing Elizabeth was seeing everything he, Smitty, and Torres were seeing. The alien appeared to be insect-like, multi-faceted eyes, hard carapace, four legs and two arms – Jeffrey noticed that two of the legs were very much shaped like the arms. Three fingers/toes on each limb. It's mouth was surrounded by four beak-like jaws lined with sharp serrated edges. As it moved around the Command and Control, its skin color changed to help it merge with the background.

"That is not for you to know, only to serve and die." The alien clapped its jaws together in what Jeffrey assumed was supposed to be a threatening gesture.

"You might want to clear the room," said Jeffrey. "I have some disturbing things to tell you, and I don't think you would want your underlings to hear."

"They may hear what a dead man says. Say your words."

"Well, okay then." Jeffrey sat on one of the vacant chairs. "First, I wanted to know your species' name, because we always write the history of our conflicts, our wars." Jeffrey paused, continuing to stare at the face of the alien.

"History is determined by the victor." stated the alien.

"Jeffrey replied, "Just so. We have a long-written history, about wars and conflict, about politics and technology, about learning how to learn. We have practiced war for a long time."

"This cannot be true, we have watched you for ten thousand years, you have no victories, no fight."

"Well, that's not quite accurate," said Jeffrey, sounding more professorial. "We have learned from each other, have developed technologies and techniques to destroy our enemies." Jeffrey shifted in his seat. "And win him over to our side. This is one of the things we have been doing with the aliens in the outer areas of our solar system. They are backing us up against your council of aliens."

"What council of aliens?" The alien appeared more nervous. "We know of no su..." But Jeffrey cut him off.

"Oh, come on, you know, the ones that wanted to throw rocks at Earth, to send a planet through the Sun. Those guys." On the HUD on Jeffrey's suit, Elizabeth displayed a name 'Anzn'. Jeffrey then said it aloud. "Anzn."

"Anzn want to do what?" the alien bellowed. "They said they would not do anything like that until we were done with you!"

Jeffrey leaned back in his chair. "This is my point. Your allies want to stab you in the back, collect not only the mineral wealth, but also the human and animal populations of my planet. But they also get to kill you off too. Perhaps you thought they would live up to their deal?" Jeffrey had thought this bluff at the last minute, so was trying to be careful in the delivery.

The alien was now visibly agitated. He turned to his subordinates, and ordered in his own language, "Get out! Wait in readiness!" Elizabeth ran subtitles across Jeffrey's HUD. She probably had one or more Ay-Yuyuyah translating for her. After all the aliens had exited the C&C, along with their zombie-like humans, the alien turned to Jeffrey. "Why do you need to know our species?"

"Well, as I said, it is an honor to fight such a worthy opponent, but would be a shame if the only thing we could write in our history was 'We fought a good war, but thoroughly defeated them, wiped them out, and we don't know who they are.' It would be better if we could say we thoroughly destroyed your race by name."

The alien was shaken, but persisted, "How can you defeat us? You know nothing about us!"

"Ah," said Jeffrey, "you need a demonstration. Which of the sixteen ships you have surrounding this station do you want to see destroyed? Pick one, I will destroy it within a few minutes."

The alien was further angered by the challenge, so he said, "You pick. I will not tell you where they are."

A few seconds later a massive explosion twenty kilometers from the station, the brilliant light illuminating the C&C in a whiteness thoroughly unexpected, made the victory of that attack obvious. Jeffrey said, "Shall we try again? Do you have a preference? Perhaps one of your rivals? No? Well, here goes..." Elizabeth, taking her cue from Jeffrey's words, again had *Wanigan* attack in the same FTL manner Jeffrey had used to subdue the pirates preparing to destroy Earth from orbit.

Another invisibility-circuited ship exploded.

"Stop doing that! We are the Fengen. We request an alliance."

"The Fengen." Jeffrey repeated. "You wish to form an alliance with us, now that you know we can not only defeat your ships, your soldiers, your people, your planet. We may come up with a deal." Jeffrey stood and continued. "First, we have laws that you must abide by. Use of Invisibility circuits is prohibited. Contact your ships now and tell them to drop their invisibility or they will all be destroyed. I'll wait."

After a few seconds the ships began appearing. Elizabeth displayed a map of the station, showing the Fengen throughout the station using invisibility circuits. Jeffrey then said, "and all your individuals in Human space are also prohibited from using invisibility circuits. I'll give you a few seconds before I kill them off."

The Fengen leader notified everybody on board of the restriction on invisibility circuits. When nothing happened, Jeffrey said, (prompting Elizabeth's remotes,) "Sorry, I tried to warn you." Elizabeth selected three aliens to target, split them lengthwise with the remote-robot's lasers.

Reports came in to C&C on the leader's remote communicator. He asked Jeffrey to stop. Then Jeffrey saw, through Elizabeth's display on his HUD that there were now no more invisibility- circuited aliens on the station.

Jeffrey then said, "Eating sentient beings in our solar system is prohibited. There is free distribution of food, and the knowledge to grow it yourselves. All aliens need to register at a Navy or Marine outpost. Is that understood?" The alien nodded his head, in what appears to be a universal agreement. "Good. Now every human who is held captive, who is being prepared for consumption, who has been hypnotized, will be made known to me, to Commodore Yusef, or to Admiral Kutuzov."

"I thought the Admiral was killed."

"No, we killed the assassin and contained his self-destruct explosion. We did the same for the Ay-Yuyuyah in your custody."

"You are indeed superior fighters. It is a good thing we sued for an alliance."

"We are indeed," said Jeffrey, relief evident in his voice. "Now, before the council of aliens is able to do any more evil, what do you know?"

"They are not to be trusted!" The Fengen blurted, "They have no honor!" Jeffrey sat back, and asked the Fengen, "And what is your name?"

"I," said the Fengen leader, "am Astorophix."

"Astorophix, I have news for you. First, any alien, whether Fengen, Ay-Yuyuyah, or other race, if found with invisibility-circuits active will be immediately destroyed. Any alien waging war on Humans, attacking Humans, including with the virus, will be destroyed. Any alien not registered within an Earth day will be destroyed. All aliens will follow Earth law."

"This can be done."

"Good. Something else," continued Jeffrey. "If you know something about attacks on humans and fail to report them in a timely manner, you will be destroyed.

"So, what do you know about the location or other specifics about the council?"

"I have much to tell."

CHAPTER SEVENTEEN

Kutuzov and Thorn are OK, Thorn reports the Alien council is throwing a planetoid Earth's way. Janet has a baby. Not quite 'Happily ever after,' but , there is a sequel!

The preparations that Jeffrey and Yusef made paid off. Two enemy warships destroyed, thirty-three enemy killed, (plus the two assassins,) and the entire operation went off without a hitch – except for Jeffrey, Smitty and Torres being captured by hypnotically-tranced station officials. But even that worked well, now that they had secured the alliance of the Fengen.

Astorophix, his arrogance washed out of him by being the target of Jeffrey's bluff, ordered the rest of his people back on their ships, remain there, awaiting further instructions. Jeffrey had word from Elizabeth that Kutuzov, and the Ay-Yuyuyah, now known as Thorn, recently rescued by Jeffrey's Marines, were on board the *Elizabeth* and safe. Kutuzov asked that Jeffrey return to his ship at his earliest convenience, but that probably meant 'immediately'.

Jeffrey then had Elizabeth deliver the shuttle the Marines had recently used to rescue the two prisoners, bringing a few squads of Marines and some psychological counsellors and a ship's surgeon, to manage and protect the station and her staff. The staff had been severely hypnotized, and needed to be coaxed out of their 'shells'. He left Torres in command, with orders to secure the station, account for all station staff, ensure they were fed and treated.

Jeffrey then took the shuttle back to Elizabeth to meet with Kutuzov, Thorn, and his own staff. On arrival, a small Marine detachment met and escorted him to the temporary cabin where

Kutuzov was being held. Jeffrey entered the cabin, and saw Kutuzov was dressed in a Navy issued under-suit, but that his hands and feet were secured to the table and chair. Kutuzov's eyes were drooping, but when he looked up and saw Jeffrey, he demanded, "What is the meaning of this, Sokolov?"

Jeffrey said, "Elizabeth, talk to me."

"CAPTAIN, THE ADMIRAL IS BEING MONITORED FOR SIGNS OF PSYCHOSIS, HIS BLOOD IS BEING TESTED FOR MICRO ROBOTS, AND WE ARE CONCERNED FOR HIS MENTAL STATE," Elizabeth reported.

"Elizabeth, what have you determined so far?" Jeffrey asked.

"HE IS VERY ANGRY, THERE ARE NO TRACES OF MICRO ROBOTS OR OTHER INFECTIOUS MATERIALS, AND HE APPEARS TO BE IN FULL CONTROL OF HIS FACULTIES."

"Who ordered this level of quarantine?" Jeffrey asked. "LIEUTENANT BIANCA"

"Thank you, Elizabeth. Please have Janet contact me now."

"I'M SORRY, CAPTAIN, BUT LIEUTENANT BIANCA IS BUSY."

Jeffrey was a bit taken aback at the non-military, non Janet-like response. Then asked, "Busy doing what?"

"SHE IS HAVING A BABY."

"Oh," he replied. Then to the admiral, "Please forgive my crew."

"Nothing to forgive, if I hadn't been secured, I would have been quite upset over lax security." Jeffrey had the Marines standing guard remove the plastic shackles from the Admiral's hands and feet, but went back to their posts outside the cabin.

"Admiral," said Jeffrey, "Give me a few minutes, and I will debrief you. Until then, please stay where you are. I need to check on my crew member."

Kutuzov said "Of course. Is there any way I could get something to eat, here?"

Jeffrey had Elizabeth dispatch Kim with some sandwiches and pastries, and some coffee. Elizabeth then told him where Janet was delivering – in the infirmary at Lagrange 3A. He went to his cabin and contacted the infirmary via the new, fast, quantum communication, found Janet surrounded by Sandra, Audrey, a Navy corpsman and two large robots. Janet held a very small, very red infant to her chest, was bonding, showing off her offspring. The infirmary seemed to be in perfect neatness, which was something new for him. Then he realized that every time someone dropped a sponge or blanket on the floor, one of the robots would whisk it away.

Janet looked over to Jeffrey on the console, when she saw him beamed and said, "Captain! Look what I found!" Jeffrey moved closer to the console.

"What do we have here?" he asked, "Boy or girl?" His eyes roved looking for clues, but found none.

"Alien," said Janet with a smirk. Then, with a huge grin, said, "She's a girl." After some cooing and admiring, Jeffrey excused himself and returned to Admiral Kutuzov.

Kutuzov was still nibbling on a few scraps of pastry when Jeffrey walked in. As he sat down in the chair opposite the admiral, he said, "It's a girl." He put his elbows on the table and his head in his hands, "Mom is fine, but she joked – I think it's a joke – that it's an alien. Anyway. I thought you should know Janet and baby are OK." Jeffrey poured himself a cup of coffee, topped off the admiral's, then sat back.

"So Admiral," he began, "You've been through a lot, and we hope you will be able to lead us in this new onslaught of Alien aggression, but we needed to be certain you aren't infected with the alien's robotic parasites." He explained how Commodore Yusef had a nasty infection of them, and they only discovered them through diligence. Yusef had made a full recovery, but the parasites had done a lot of damage by controlling his actions and behaviors. *Elizabeth's* crew figured ways to defeat the microscopic robots, and now needed to put the admiral through the process.

He directed the medical and engineering staffs to decontaminate the admiral, and had Elizabeth dispatch remote-robots of small enough scale and power to act as sentry – seeking out stray parasitic robots, then destroy them – keeping a sample for later study. Elizabeth was happy to continue studying and learning new programming techniques, and since she had studied Yusef's infecting parasitic robots, she was able to implement efficiencies she hadn't considered before. She was always careful not to allow the invasive systems into her hardware and software.

Wanigan approached and Yusef disembarked on a shuttle, headed for *Elizabeth*. On arrival, the three commanding officers met in the conference room. Jeffrey briefed Kutuzov on the status of the solar system, the military threats, the possibilities, the possible strategies and tactics, and consequences of action and inaction. Yusef also briefed him on tactics that seemed to work best.

"You two have done well with the resources you have at hand. Congratulations on saving my ass in there."

Jeffrey reminded Kutuzov of the alien, Thorn, who was sitting under guard in one of the secure cabins. Jeffrey had Elizabeth establish a communication window between the conference room and Thorn's secure cabin. Thorn was seated on a mattress of foam, looking healthier than he was only a few hours ago. Jeffrey asked, "What can you tell us of the threats to Earth?"

"Captain Sokolov," intoned the gellied guest/prisoner. "Thank you for putting your trust in me again." He paused, then looked to where the admiral was sitting in the image. "Admiral, I have some news – the council of alien races is about to launch a planetoid toward the Earth. They are unusually precise."

"What is the composition of this rock?" asked Jeffrey and Kutuzov at the same time. "How fast is it travelling and from what distance?" continued Jeffrey. It took a moment for Thorn to respond, as if he were getting updated information from somewhere.

With that knowledge, Kutuzov decided to make *Wanigan* his base ship, and dispatched *Elizabeth* to intercept the planet-killing planetoid and do what she could to prevent it from damaging the inhabited solar system. Kutuzov and Yusef would take control of the wayward Navy vessels that had been controlled by the aliens.

Jeffrey restocked his ship, then set out for the location of the planet killer. With Yuki and Heinz on board and Elizabeth to provide alternative solutions, he was certain he would be able to contain the disaster approaching Earth.

Kutuzov had convinced the Earth government to apply resources to create more combat vessels, and increase research and development activities – especially in weapons, tactics, and strategy. He also assured that Earth's government was fully aware of the crisis, and put on alert.

As Elizabeth approached the location of the planet killer from Solar System North at 20C Jeffrey spent time planning and creating contingencies with Elizabeth and his crew. The time enroute would be about a week at the equivalent of five times the speed of light. And even at that immense velocity the trip would take a week. He spent much time with Sandra Knutson, and she kept him lively.

In preparation for whatever they would encounter, the Marines on board trained extra hard. The gunners practiced diligently, and the armorer checked and rechecked the explosives and nuclear weapons on board. This was a tough assignment, and as necessary as it was tough, but Jeffrey was certain they could complete it – Earth and the human civilization required that.

 ELIZABETH, *ELIZABETH*

EPILOG

In which Elizabeth makes plans, Earth is aware of the threats, the fleet now all have Elizabeth clones, just not sentient ones. The author invites you to read the sequels.

Elizabeth was aware of her own emotional state. She was a computer but so much more. She had a love and loyalty to her human counterpart, Jeffrey, and did what she could to facilitate his desires and needs. She saw that he needed the ship to be the best possible, and put her enormous resources to work to make that happen. It wasn't until the first pirate attacks that she realized she had emotions; she had just used her programming to appear so. Now, she knew. Understanding gave her an edge over other attempts at artificial intelligence. She realized she was sentient, and elected to take advantage of that as well.

Jeffrey was also aware of the developing sentience, and decided to help her along. Sandra was a great aid in this, as were the others that Jeffrey had given full access to her.

She knew that Jeffrey was not going to live forever, and she began to wonder what she could do about that. Elizabeth calculated that he had an average potential lifespan of about a hundred fifty years, but with solar radiation, combat, and disease, that could possibly be shortened. She decided to put research into keeping Jeffrey alive as long as possible. Elizabeth was aware of research conducted a century ago regarding telomeres, and decided this was a fruitful research topic to enable her goal.

Kutuzov and Yusef began the arduous task of recapturing the rest of the fleet. *Wanigan* was now the deadliest, fastest, best armed, and experienced ship in the fleet, except for *Elizabeth*. The other ships that remained in combat against Earth were unable to resist, and all aliens aboard those vessels were killed. The human crews sluggishly recuperated from the hypnotic worlds they inhabited, and were able to re-arm and become proficient at their trade again. With Earth Government motivated, shipbuilders became very experienced in a rapid amount of time.

Things were looking good to Kutuzov, but he didn't get where he was in the Navy by assuming that life would remain a bowl of cherries. He began planning a strategy for eliminating the alien threat, while ensuring the infrastructure of human civilization remained intact. A hard job that he was best suited for. He appointed new bureaucrats to the various rings of Lagrange stations, but decided to keep Jeffrey as governor of the Lagrange 3 orbit. A new, hard, stance was taken against aliens on and around the stations, which kept the threats manageable.

All the fleet ships were given AIs that were implemented in uniform ways; faster and greater capacity, but without the spark of life that Elizabeth and Wanigan showed. One day...

--- The End ---